*Praise for Roger Zelazny*

'To me, Roger Zelazny is SFF's greatest author'  *Tordotcom*

'Zelazny, telling of gods and wizards, uses magical words as
if he himself were a wizard'  Philip José Farmer

'His stories are sunk to the knees in maturity and wisdom,
in bravura writing that breaks rules most writers only
suspect exist'  Harlan Ellison

'Zelazny left us a voyage upon which our imaginations can
travel, unbounded by time'  *SFF180*

**SF** MASTERWORKS

# The Best of
# Roger Zelazny

## ROGER ZELAZNY

This edition first published in Great Britain in 2023 by Gollancz
an imprint of the Orion Publishing Group Ltd
Carmelite House, 50 Victoria Embankment
London EC4Y 0DZ

An Hachette UK Company

3 5 7 9 10 8 6 4

A CIP catalogue record for this book is
available from the British Library.

(Paperback) ISBN 978 1 473 23500 7
(eBook) ISBN 978 1 473 23501 4

Typeset at The Spartan Press Ltd,
Lymington, Hants

Printed and bound in Great Britain by Clays Ltd,
Elcograf S.p.A.

www.sfgateway.com
www.gollancz.co.uk

# INTRODUCTION
## by Lisa Tuttle

In 1962, a young American writer burst on the science fictional scene with a stream of short stories; so prolific that he was required by a couple of the magazines to use a second name ('Harrison Denmark') for some of his works. His first sale to *The Magazine of Fantasy and Science Fiction* received star billing with a cover illustration by Hannes Bok for the November 1963 issue. That story, 'A Rose for Ecclesiastes,' remains one of his best-loved, and it made Roger Zelazny into one of the brightest new stars in the genre. Along with Samuel R. Delany, Harlan Ellison, J.G. Ballard, Michael Moorcock and some others he was given the label New Wave; but, like his fellow authors, he did not like being labelled, and always said he had never been part of a movement – he was just doing his own thing.

And it's true, there was no actual movement called New Wave; instead, the early sixties was part of a cultural moment when a number of younger writers were importing more literary values and experimental techniques into a genre where ideas were valued more than style, and relied heavily on pulp action adventure cliches.

As a teenaged science fiction fan, Roger Zelazny had collected a fair number of rejection slips as he taught himself how to write fiction, but as a university student, he decided to concentrate on poetry, with the idea of making a career as a poet. In 1962, he received his MA in Elizabethan and Jacobean drama, got a job with the Social Security Administration in Cleveland, Ohio, and decided to try his hand at writing science fiction stories again. This time, with a more mature, educated, and critical consciousness driving his love of language, he was immediately successful.

His professional turning point, 'A Rose for Ecclesiastes', was the longest, most ambitious story he had yet written. Its emotional origin was the heartbreak he suffered following a broken engagement, combined with a nostalgic affection for the old-fashioned planetary romances he had loved as a boy. The story is set on an imaginary Mars, a desert world where an ancient civilization is slowly dying when visitors from Earth first encounter them. In the early decades of the 20th century such a setting would have been legitimately speculative fiction, but when Zelazny was writing, he knew very well that Mars was not, and could not be, inhabited by intelligent, human aliens. But he was not interested in merely writing fantastic retro pulp fiction; this story is language-driven, rich in literary, cultural and religious references, playful and ironic, constantly shifting from high to low diction through the voice of the narrator, who is also the hero of his own story. Gallinger is an arrogant young genius, an award-winning poet and famously brilliant linguist who fancies every woman must be in love with him, and every man miserably jealous, resentful of his assured success in every endeavour. It is an electrifying story, one that not only engages but also challenges the reader. It announced the arrival of a talented writer with a new and different approach to the field. And despite the passage of decades of more changes, 'A Rose for Ecclesiastes' has not faded. Now a classic, it still feels fresh. In 2012, it ranked third in a *Locus* poll for Best Novelettes of the 20th century, just after Asimov's 'Nightfall' and 'Flowers for Algernon' by Daniel Keyes.

'The Doors of his Face, the Lamps of his Mouth', written about a year later, is another uniquely Zelaznyan take on the planetary romance – in this case, a watery Venus where wealthy tourists from Earth go on fishing expeditions, with the aim of catching a sea-monster. Echoes of *Moby-Dick* are set against the sexual tensions between the narrator and his rich, powerful ex-wife. The narrator is another highly intelligent, sarcastic, deliberately unsympathetic male who makes us read between the lines to understand exactly what is going on. Nominated for both the biggest awards in science fiction, it won the Nebula for Best Novelette in 1965.

Other long stories followed; whether classed as a novelette or novella, this was clearly a form that suited him. 'He Who Shapes' won the Nebula in 1966, before Zelazny revised and expanded it into the novel published as *The Dream Master*. One of the most complex and fascinating of his early works, the original version included here was preferred to the novel by the author himself, and most readers would probably agree that the additional material added nothing but more words, which may even have subtracted slightly from the powerful structure of the original. Sometimes less really is more. There's not an ounce of extra fat on 'He Who Shapes'; it is honed and sharp and wonderfully thought-provoking. The new technology allowing a psychiatrist to help patients by altering their dreams is fascinating, and a whole future world is made vividly real through the author's careful use of a few choice details. This is a world of comfort and safety, yet, we casually learn, suicide has become the leading cause of death.

In 1969, Zelazny quit his job to become a full-time writer, and from then on he concentrated on the novel form. Yet he never completely abandoned shorter forms of fiction. His *Collected Stories* (posthumously published; he died too young) ran to six volumes.

Are these the very best of them? That must be a matter of opinion. Personally, I would have wanted '24 Views of Mt Fuji, by Hokusai' (winner of the 1986 Hugo Award) included; it might have occupied the space allotted here to 'Damnation Alley,' a road-trip through a depopulated post-Apocalyptic America, as viewed by a tough, criminal biker. First published in 1967, it's the only story in the book that really shows its age.

But no one could argue with the inclusion of the 1987 Hugo-winning 'Permafrost', or 'For a Breath I Tarry' (one of Zelazny's personal favourites) or, perhaps especially, 'Home is the Hangman,' the rare SF/mystery blend that won both the Hugo and the Nebula for Best Novella in 1976, as well as the memorable time-travelling Arthurian fantasy, 'The Last Defender of Camelot' – altogether, this is a treasure trove; a marvellous sampling of a wonderful writer's work.

– Lisa Tuttle
Torinturk, Scotland
6 June 2022

# CONTENTS

# A Rose for Ecclesiastes

I was busy translating one of my *Madrigals Macabre* into Martian on the morning I was found acceptable. The intercom had buzzed briefly, and I dropped my pencil and flipped on the toggle in a single motion.

'Mister G,' piped Morton's youthful contralto, 'the old man says I should "get hold of that damned conceited rhymer" right away, and send him to his cabin. Since there's only one damned conceited rhymer...'

'Let not ambition mock thy useful toil.' I cut him off.

So, the Martians had finally made up their minds! I knocked an inch and a half of ash from a smoldering butt, and took my first drag since I had lit it. The entire month's anticipation tried hard to crowd itself into the moment, but could not quite make it. I was frightened to walk those forty feet and hear Emory say the words I already knew he would say; and that feeling elbowed the other one into the background.

So I finished the stanza I was translating before I got up.

It took only a moment to reach Emory's door. I knocked twice and opened it, just as he growled, 'Come in.'

'You wanted to see me?' I sat down quickly to save him the trouble of offering me a seat.

'That was fast. What did you do, run?'

I regarded his paternal discontent:

*Little fatty flecks beneath pale eyes, thinning hair, and an Irish nose; a voice a decibel louder than anyone else's...*

Hamlet to Claudius: 'I was working.'

'Hah!' he snorted. 'Come off it. No one's ever seen you do any of that stuff.'

I shrugged my shoulders and started to rise.

'If that's what you called me down here—'

'Sit down!'

He stood up. He walked around his desk. He hovered above me and glared down. (A hard trick, even when I'm in a low chair.)

'You are undoubtably the most antagonistic bastard I've ever had to work with!' he bellowed, like a belly-stung buffalo. 'Why the hell don't you act like a human being sometime and surprise everybody? I'm willing to admit you're smart, maybe even a genius, but – oh, hell!' He made a heaving gesture with both hands and walked back to his chair.

'Betty has finally talked them into letting you go in.' His voice was normal again. 'They'll receive you this afternoon. Draw one of the jeepsters after lunch, and get down there.'

'Okay,' I said.

'That's all, then.'

I nodded, got to my feet. My hand was on the doorknob when he said:

'I don't have to tell you how important this is. Don't treat them the way you treat us.'

I closed the door behind me.

I don't remember what I had for lunch. I was nervous, but I knew instinctively that I wouldn't muff it. My Boston publishers expected a Martian Idyll, or at least a Saint-Exupéry job on space flight. The National Science Association wanted a complete report on the Rise and Fall of the Martian Empire.

They would both be pleased. I knew.

That's the reason everyone is jealous – why they hate me. I always come through, and I can come through better than anyone else.

I shoveled in a final anthill of slop, and made my way to our car barn. I drew one jeepster and headed it toward Tirellian.

Flames of sand, lousy with iron oxide, set fire to the buggy. They swarmed over the open top and bit through my scarf; they set to work pitting my goggles.

The jeepster, swaying and panting like a little donkey I once rode through the Himalayas, kept kicking me in the seat of the pants. The Mountains of Tirellian shuffled their feet and moved toward me at a cockeyed angle.

Suddenly I was heading uphill, and I shifted gears to accommodate the engine's braying. Not like Gobi, not like the Great Southwestern Desert, I mused. Just red, just dead... without even a cactus.

I reached the crest of the hill, but I had raised too much dust to see what was ahead. It didn't matter, though; I have a head full of maps. I bore to the left and downhill, adjusting the throttle. A crosswind and solid ground beat down the fires. I felt like Ulysses in Malebolge – with a terza-rima speech in one hand and an eye out for Dante.

I rounded a rock pagoda and arrived.

Betty waved as I crunched to a halt, then jumped down.

'Hi,' I choked, unwinding my scarf and shaking out a pound and a half of grit. 'Like, where do I go and who do I see?'

She permitted herself a brief Germanic giggle – more at my starting a sentence with 'like' than at my discomfort – then she started talking. (She is a top linguist, so a word from the Village Idiom still tickles her!)

I appreciate her precise, furry talk; informational, and all that. I had enough in the way of social pleasantries before me to last at least the rest of my life. I looked at her chocolate-bar eyes and perfect teeth, at her sun-bleached hair, close-cropped to the head (I hate blondes!), and decided that she was in love with me.

'Mr Gallinger, the Matriarch is waiting inside to be introduced. She has consented to open the Temple records for your study.' She paused here to pat her hair and squirm a little. Did my gaze make her nervous?

'They are religious documents, as well as their only history,' she continued, 'sort of like the Mahabharata. She expects you

3

to observe certain rituals in handling them, like repeating the sacred words when you turn pages – she will teach you the system.'

I nodded quickly, several times.

'Fine, let's go in.'

'Uh—' She paused. 'Do not forget their Eleven Forms of Politeness and Degree. They take matters of form quite seriously – and do not get into any discussions over the equality of the sexes—'

'I know all about their taboos,' I broke in. 'Don't worry. I've lived in the Orient, remember?'

She dropped her eyes and seized my hand. I almost jerked it away.

'It will look better if I enter leading you.'

I swallowed my comments, and followed her, like Samson in Gaza.


Inside, my last thought met with a strange correspondence. The Matriarch's quarters were a rather abstract version of what I might imagine the tents of the tribes of Israel to have been like. Abstract, I say, because it was all frescoed brick, peaked like a huge tent, with animal-skin representations like gray-blue scars, that looked as if they had been laid on the walls with a palette knife.

The Matriarch, M'Cwyie, was short, white-haired, fifty-ish, and dressed like a queen. With her rainbow of voluminous skirts she looked like an inverted punch bowl set atop a cushion.

Accepting my obeisances, she regarded me as an owl might a rabbit. The lids of those black, black eyes jumped upwards as she discovered my perfect accent. —The tape recorder Betty had carried on her interviews had done its part, and I knew the language reports from the first two expeditions, verbatim. I'm all hell when it comes to picking up accents.

'You are the poet?'

'Yes,' I replied.

'Recite one of your poems, please.'

'I'm sorry, but nothing short of a thorough translating job

4

would do justice to your language and my poetry, and I don't know enough of your language yet.'

'Oh?'

'But I've been making such translations for my own amusement, as an exercise in grammar,' I continued. 'I'd be honored to bring a few of them along one of the times that I come here.'

'Yes. Do so.'

Score one for me!

She turned to Betty.

'You may go now.'

Betty muttered the parting formalities, gave me a strange sideways look, and was gone. She apparently had expected to stay and 'assist' me. She wanted a piece of the glory, like everyone else. But I was the Schliemann at this Troy, and there would be only one name on the Association report!

M'Cwyie rose, and I noticed that she gained very little height by standing. But then I'm six-six and look like a poplar in October; thin, bright red on top, and towering above everyone else.

'Our records are very, very old,' she began. 'Betty says that your word for that age is "millennia."'

I nodded appreciatively.

'I'm very eager to see them.'

'They are not here. We will have to go into the Temple – they may not be removed.'

I was suddenly wary.

'You have no objections to my copying them, do you?'

'No. I see that you respect them, or your desire would not be so great.'

'Excellent.'

She seemed amused. I asked her what was so funny.

'The High Tongue may not be so easy for a foreigner to learn.'

It came through fast.

No one on the first expedition had gotten this close. I had had no way of knowing that this was a double-language deal

5

– a classical as well as a vulgar. I knew some of their Prakrit, now I had to learn all their Sanskrit.

'Ouch, and damn!'

'Pardon, please?'

'It's non-translatable, M'Cwyie. But imagine yourself having to learn the High Tongue in a hurry, and you can guess at the sentiment.'

She seemed amused again, and told me to remove my shoes.

She guided me through an alcove...

...and into a burst of Byzantine brilliance!

No Earthman had ever been in this room before, or I would have heard about it. Carter, the first expedition's linguist, with the help of one Mary Allen, M.D., had learned all the grammar and vocabulary that I knew while sitting cross-legged in the antechamber.

We had had no idea this existed. Greedily, I cast my eyes about. A highly sophisticated system of esthetics lay behind the decor. We would have to revise our entire estimation of Martian culture.

For one thing, the ceiling was vaulted and corbeled; for another, there were side-columns with reverse flutings; for another – oh hell! The place was big. Posh. You could never have guessed it from the shaggy outsides.

I bent forward to study the gilt filigree on a ceremonial table. M'Cwyie seemed a bit smug at my intentness, but I'd still have hated to play poker with her.

The table was loaded with books.

With my toe, I traced a mosaic on the floor.

'Is your entire city within this one building?'

'Yes, it goes far back into the mountain.'

'I see,' I said, seeing nothing.

I couldn't ask her for a conducted tour, yet.

She moved to a small stool by the table.

'Shall we begin your friendship with the High Tongue?'

I was trying to photograph the hall with my eyes, knowing I

would have to get a camera in here, somehow, sooner or later. I tore my gaze from a statuette and nodded, hard.

'Yes, introduce me.'

I sat down.

For the next three weeks alphabet-bugs chased each other behind my eyelids whenever I tried to sleep. The sky was an unclouded pool of turquoise that rippled calligraphies whenever I swept my eyes across it. I drank quarts of coffee while I worked and mixed cocktails of Benzedrine and champagne for my coffee breaks.

M'Cwyie tutored me two hours every morning, and occasionally for another two in the evening. I spent an additional fourteen hours a day on my own, once I had gotten up sufficient momentum to go ahead alone.

And at night the elevator of time dropped me to its bottom floors...

I was six again, learning my Hebrew, Greek, Latin, and Aramaic. I was ten, sneaking peeks at the *Iliad*. When Daddy wasn't spreading hellfire brimstone, and brotherly love, he was teaching me to dig the Word, like in the original.

Lord! There are so many originals and so many words! When I was twelve I started pointing out the little differences between what he was preaching and what I was reading.

The fundamentalist vigor of his reply brooked no debate. It was worse than any beating. I kept my mouth shut after that and learned to appreciate Old Testament poetry.

—*Lord, I am sorry! Daddy – Sir – I am sorry! – It couldn't be! It couldn't be...*

On the day the boy graduated from high school, with the French, German, Spanish, and Latin awards, Dad Gallinger had told his fourteen-year old, six-foot scarecrow of a son that he wanted him to enter the ministry. I remember how his son was evasive:

'Sir,' he had said, 'I'd sort of like to study on my own for a year or so, and then take pre-theology courses at some liberal

7

arts university. I feel I'm still sort of young to try a seminary, straight off.'

The Voice of God: 'But you have the gift of tongues, my son. You can preach the Gospel in all the lands of Babel. You were born to be a missionary. You say you are young, but time is rushing by you like a whirlwind. Start early, and you will enjoy added years of service.'

The added years of service were so many added tails to the cat repeatedly laid on my back. I can't see his face now; I never can. Maybe it was because I was always afraid to look at it then.

And years later, when he was dead, and laid out, in black, amidst bouquets, amidst weeping congregationalists, amidst prayers, red faces, handkerchiefs, hands patting your shoulders, solemn faced comforters ... I looked at him and did not recognize him.

We had met nine months before my birth, this stranger and I. He had never been cruel – stern, demanding, with contempt for everyone's shortcomings – but never cruel. He was also all that I had had of a mother. And brothers. And sisters. He had tolerated my three years at St John's, possibly because of its name, never knowing how liberal and delightful a place it really was.

But I never knew him, and the man atop the catafalque demanded nothing now; I was free not to preach the Word. But now I wanted to, in a different way. I wanted to preach a word that I could never have voiced while he lived.

I did not return for my senior year in the fall. I had a small inheritance coming, and a bit of trouble getting control of it, since I was still under eighteen. But I managed.

It was Greenwich Village I finally settled upon.

Not telling any well-meaning parishioners my new address, I entered into a daily routine of writing poetry and teaching myself Japanese and Hindustani. I grew a fiery beard, drank espresso, and learned to play chess. I wanted to try a couple of the other paths to salvation.

After that, it was two years in India with the Old Peace

Corps – which broke me of my Buddhism, and gave me my *Pipes of Krishna* lyrics and the Pulitzer they deserved.

Then back to the States for my degree, grad work in linguistics, and more prizes.

Then one day a ship went to Mars. The vessel settling in its New Mexico nest of fires contained a new language. —It was fantastic, exotic, and esthetically overpowering. After I had learned all there was to know about it, and written my book, I was famous in new circles:

'Go, Gallinger. Dip your bucket in the well, and bring us a drink of Mars. Go, learn another world – but remain aloof, rail at it gently like Auden – and hand us its soul in iambics.'

And I came to the land where the sun is a tarnished penny, where the wind is a whip, where two moons play at hot rod games, and a hell of sand gives you incendiary itches whenever you look at it.

I rose from my twisting on the bunk and crossed the darkened cabin to a port. The desert was a carpet of endless orange, bulging from the sweepings of centuries beneath it.

'I, a stranger, unafraid – This is the land – I've got it made!' I laughed.

I had the High Tongue by the tail already – or the roots, if you want your puns anatomical, as well as correct.

The High and Low tongues were not so dissimilar as they had first seemed. I had enough of the one to get me through the murkier parts of the other. I had the grammar and all the commoner irregular verbs down cold; the dictionary I was constructing grew by the day, like a tulip, and would bloom shortly. Every time I played the tapes the stem lengthened.

Now was the time to tax my ingenuity, to really drive the lessons home. I had purposely refrained from plunging into the major texts until I could do justice to them. I had been reading minor commentaries, bits of verse, fragments of history. And one thing had impressed me strongly in all that I read.

They wrote about concrete things: rock, sand, water, winds; and the tenor couched within these elemental symbols was

9

fiercely pessimistic. It reminded me of some Buddhists texts, but even more so, I realized from my recent *recherches*, it was like parts of the Old Testament. Specifically, it reminded me of the Book of Ecclesiastes.

That, then, would be it. The sentiment, as well as the vocabulary, was so similar that it would be a perfect exercise. Like putting Poe into French. I would never be a convert to the Way of Malann, but I would show them that an Earthman had once thought the same thoughts, felt similarly.

I switched on my desk lamp and sought King James amidst my books.

*Vanity of vanities, saith the Preacher, vanity of vanities; all if vanity. What profit hath a man . . .*

My progress seemed to startle M'Cwyie. She peered at me, like Sartre's Other, across the tabletop. I ran through a chapter in the Book of Locar. I didn't look up, but I could feel the tight net her eyes were working about my head, shoulders, and rapid hands. I turned another page.

Was she weighing the net, judging the size of the catch? And what for? The books said nothing of fishers on Mars. Especially of men. They said that some god named Malann had spat, or had done something disgusting (depending on the version you read), and that life had gotten underway as a disease in inorganic matter. They said that movement was its first law, its first law, and that the dance was the only legitimate reply to the inorganic . . . the dance's quality its justification, – fication . . . and love is a disease in organic matter – Inorganic matter?

I shook my head. I had almost been asleep.

'M'narra.'

I stood and stretched. Her eyes outlined me greedily now. So I met them, and they dropped.

'I grow tired. I want to rest for awhile. I didn't sleep much last night.'

She nodded, Earth's shorthand for 'yes,' as she had learned from me.

'You wish to relax, and see the explicitness of the doctrine of Locar in its fullness?'

'Pardon me?'

'You wish to see a Dance of Locar?'

'Oh.' Their damned circuits of form and periphrasis here ran worse than the Korean! 'Yes. Surely. Any time it's going to be done I'd be happy to watch.'

I continued, 'In the meantime, I've been meaning to ask you whether I might take some pictures—'

'Now is the time. Sit down. Rest. I will call the musicians.'

She bustled out through a door I had never been past.

Well now, the dance was the highest art, according to Locar, not to mention Havelock Ellis, and I was about to see how their centuries-dead philosopher felt it should be conducted. I rubbed my eyes and snapped over, touching my toes a few times.

The blood began pounding in my head, and I sucked in a couple deep breaths. I bent again and there was a flurry of motion at the door.

To the trio who entered with M'Cwyie I must have looked as if I were searching for the marbles I had just lost, bent over like that.

I grinned weakly and straightened up, my face red from more than exertion. I hadn't expected them *that* quickly.

Suddenly I thought of Havelock Ellis again in his area of greatest popularity.

The little redheaded doll, wearing, sari-like, a diaphanous piece of the Martian sky, looked up in wonder – as a child at some colorful flag on a high pole.

'Hello,' I said, or its equivalent.

She bowed before replying. Evidently I had been promoted in status.

'I shall dance,' said the red wound in that pale, pale cameo, her face. Eyes, the color of dream and her dress, pulled away from mine.

She drifted to the center of the room.

Standing there, like a figure in an Etruscan frieze, she was either meditating or regarding the design on the floor.

Was the mosaic symbolic of something? I studied it. If it was, it eluded me; it would make an attractive bathroom floor or patio, but I couldn't see much in it beyond that.

The other two were paint-spattered sparrows like M'Cwyie, in their middle years. One settled to the floor with a triple-stringed instrument faintly resembling a *samisen*. The other held a simple woodblock and two drumsticks.

M'Cwyie disdained her stool and was seated upon the floor before I realized it. I followed suit.

The *samisen* player was still tuning it up, so I leaned toward M'Cwyie.

'What is the dancer's name?'

'Braxa,' she replied, without looking at me, and raised her left hand, slowly, which meant yes, and go ahead, and let it begin.

The stringed-thing throbbed like a toothache, and a tick-tocking, like ghosts of all the clocks they had never invented, sprang from the block.

Braxa was a statue, both hands raised to her face, elbows high and outspread.

The music became a metaphor for fire.

*Crackle, purr, snap . . .*

She did not move.

The hissing altered to splashes. The cadence slowed. It was water now, the most precious thing in the world, gurgling clear then green over mossy rocks.

Still she did not move.

Glissandos. A pause.

Then, so faint I could hardly be sure at first, the tremble of winds began. Softly, gently, sighing and halting, uncertain. A pause, a sob, then a repetition of the first statement, only louder.

Were my eyes completely bugged from my reading, or was Braxa actually trembling, all over, head to foot?

She was.

She began a microscopic swaying. A fraction of an inch

right, then left. Her fingers opened like the petals of a flower, and I could see that her eyes were closed.

Her eyes opened. They were distant, glassy, looking through me and the walls. Her swaying became more pronounced, merged with the beat.

*The wind was sweeping in from the desert now, falling against Tirellian like waves on a dike.* Her fingers moved, they were the gusts. Her arms, slow pendulums, descended, began a counter-movement.

*The gale was coming now.* She began an axial movement and her hands caught up with the rest of her body, only now her shoulders commenced to writhe out a figure-eight.

*The wind! The wind, I say. O wild, enigmatic! O muse of St. John Perse!*

The cyclone was twisting around those eyes, its still center. Her head was thrown back, but I knew there was no ceiling between her gaze, passive as Buddha's, and the unchanging skies. Only the two moons, perhaps, interrupted their slumber in that elemental Nirvana of uninhabited turquoise.

Years ago, I had seen the Devadasis in India, the street-dancers, spinning their colorful webs, drawing in the male insect. But Braxa was more than this: she was a Ramadjany, like those votaries of Rama, incarnation of Vishnu, who had given the dance to man: the sacred dancers.

The clicking was monotonously steady now; the whine of the strings made me think of the stinging rays of the sun, their heat stolen by the wind's halations; the blue was Sarasvati and Mary, and a girl named Laura. I heard a sitar from somewhere, watched this statue come to life, and inhaled a divine afflatus.

I was again Rimbaud with his hashish, Baudelaire with his laudanum, Poe, De Quincey, Wilde, Mallarmé and Aleister Crowley. I was, for a fleeting second, my father in his dark pulpit and darker suit, the hymns and the organ's wheeze transmuted to bright wind.

She was a spun weather vane, a feathered crucifix hovering in the air, a clothes-line holding one bright garment lashed parallel to the ground. Her shoulder was bare now, and her right breast moved up and down like a moon in the sky, its red nipple appearing momentarily above a fold and vanishing again. The music was as formal as Job's argument with God. Her dance was God's reply.

The music slowed, settled; it had been met, matched, answered. Her garment, as if alive, crept back into the more sedate folds it originally held.

She dropped low, lower, to the floor. Her head fell upon her raised knees. She did not move.

There was silence.

I realized, from the ache across my shoulders, how tensely I had been sitting. My armpits were wet. Rivulets had been running down my sides. What did one do now? Applaud?

I sought M'Cwyie from the corner of my eye. She raised her right hand.

As if by telepathy the girl shuddered all over and stood. The musicians also rose. So did M'Cwyie.

I got to my feet, with a Charley Horse in my left leg, and said, 'It was beautiful,' inane as that sounds.

I received three different High Forms of 'thank you.'

There was a flurry of color and I was alone again with M'Cwyie.

'That is the one hundred-seventeenth of the two thousand, two hundred-twenty-four dances of Locar.'

I looked down at her.

'Whether Locar was right or wrong, he worked out a fine reply to the inorganic.'

She smiled.

'Are the dances of your world like this?'

'Some of them are similar. I was reminded of them as I watched Braxa – but I've never seen anything exactly like hers.'

'She is good,' M'Cwyie said. 'She knows all the dances.'

A hint of her earlier expression which had troubled me...

It was gone in an instant.

'I must tend my duties now.' She moved to the table and closed the books. 'M'narra.'

14

'Good-bye.' I slipped into my boots.

'Good-bye, Gallinger.'

I walked out the door, mounted the jeepster, and roared across the evening into night, my wings of risen desert flapping slowly behind me.

## II

I had just closed the door behind Betty, after a brief grammar session, when I heard the voices in the hall. My vent was opened a fraction, so I stood there and eavesdropped:

Morton's fruity treble: 'Guess what? He said "hello" to me awhile ago.'

'Hmmph!' Emory's elephant lungs exploded. 'Either he's slipping, or you were standing in his way and he wanted you to move.'

'Probably didn't recognize me. I don't think he sleeps any more, now he has that language to play with. I had night watch last week, and every night I passed his door at 0300 – I always heard that recorder going. At 0500 when I got off, he was still at it.'

'The guy *is* working hard,' Emory admitted, grudgingly. 'In fact, I think he's taking some kind of dope to keep awake. He looks sort of glassy-eyed these days. Maybe that's natural for a poet, though.'

Betty had been standing there, because she broke in then:

'Regardless of what you think of him, it's going to take me at least a year to learn what he's picked up in three weeks. And I'm just a linguist, not a poet.'

Morton must have been nursing a crush on her bovine charms. It's the only reason I can think of for his dropping his guns to say what he did.

'I took a course in modern poetry when I was back at the university,' he began. 'We read six authors – Yeats, Pound, Eliot, Crane, Stevens, and Gallinger – and on the last day of the semester, when the prof was feeling a little rhetorical, he said, "These six names are written on the century, and all the gates of criticism and hell shall not prevail on them."

'Myself,' he continued, 'I thought his *Pipes of Krishna* and his *Madrigals* were great. I was honored to be chosen for an expedition he was going on.

'I think he's spoken two dozen words to me since I met him,' he finished.

The Defense: 'Did it ever occur to you,' Betty said, 'that he might be tremendously self-conscious about his appearance? He was also a precocious child, and probably never even had school friends. He's sensitive and very introverted.'

'Sensitive? Self-conscious?' Emory choked and gagged. 'The man is as proud as Lucifer, and he's a walking insult machine. You press a button like "Hello" or "Nice day" and he thumbs his nose at you. He's got it down to a reflex.'

They muttered a few other pleasantries and drifted away.

Well bless you, Morton boy. You little pimple-faced, Ivy-bred connoisseur! I've never taken a course in my poetry, but I'm glad someone said that. The Gates of Hell. Well now! Maybe Daddy's prayers got heard somewhere, and I am a missionary, after all!

Only . . .

. . . Only a missionary needs something to convert people to. I have my private system of esthetics, and I suppose it oozes an ethical by-product somewhere. But if I ever had anything to preach, really, even in my poems, I wouldn't care to preach it to such low-lifes as you. If you think I'm a slob, I'm also a snob, and there's no room for you in my Heaven – it's a private place, where Swift, Shaw, and Petronius Arbiter come to dinner.

And oh, the feasts we have! The Trimalchio's, the Emory's we dissect!

We finish you with the soup, Morton!

I turned and settled at my desk. I wanted to write something. Ecclesiastes could take a night off. I wanted to write a poem, a poem about the one hundred-seventeenth dance of Locar;

about a rose following the light, traced by the wind, sick, like Blake's rose, dying... found a pencil and began.

When I had finished I was pleased. It wasn't great – at least, it was no greater than it needed to be – High Martian not being my strongest tongue. I groped, and put it into English, with partial rhymes. Maybe I'd stick it in my next book. I called it Braxa:

In a land of wind and red, where the icy evening of Time
freezes milk in the breasts of Life, as two moons overhead—
cat and dog in alleyways of dream— scratch and scramble
agelessly my flight...

This final flower turns a burning head.

I put it away and found some phenobarbitol. I was suddenly tired.

When I showed my poem to M'Cwyie the next day, she read it through several times, very slowly.

'It is lovely,' she said. 'But you used three words from your own language. "Cat" and "dog," I assume, are two small animals with a hereditary hatred for one another. But what is "flower?"'

'Oh,' I said. 'I've never come across your word for "flower," but I was actually thinking of an Earth flower, the rose.'

'What is it like?'

'Well, its petals are generally bright red. That's what I meant, on one level, by "burning heads." I also wanted it to imply fever, though, and red hair, and the fire of life. The rose, itself, has a thorny stem, green leaves, and a distinct, pleasing aroma.'

'I wish I could see one.'

'I suppose it could be arranged. I'll check.'

'Do it, please. You are a—' She used the word for 'prophet,' or religious poet, like Isaias or Locar. '—and your poem is inspired. I shall tell Braxa of it.'

I declined the nomination, but felt flattered.

This, then, I decided, was the strategic day, the day on which to ask whether I might bring in the microfilm machine and the camera. I wanted to copy all their texts, I explained, and I couldn't write fast enough to do it.

She surprised me by agreeing immediately. But she bowled me over with her invitation.

'Would you like to come and stay here while you do this thing? Then you can work night and day, any time you want – except when the Temple is being used, of course.'

I bowed.

'I should be honored.'

'Good. Bring your machines when you want, and I will show you a room.'

'Will this afternoon be all right?'

'Certainly.'

'Then I will go now and get things ready. Until this afternoon . . .'

'Good-bye.'

I anticipated a little trouble from Emory, but not much. Everyone back at the ship was anxious to see the Martians, poke needles in the Martians, ask them about Martian climate, diseases, soil chemistry, politics, and mushrooms (our botanist was a fungus nut, but a reasonably good guy) – and only four or five had actually gotten to see them. The crew had been spending most of its time excavating dead cities and their acropolises. We played the game by strict rules, and the natives were as fiercely insular as the nineteenth-century Japanese. I figured I would meet with little resistance, and I figured right.

In fact, I got the distinct impression that everyone was happy to see me move out.

I stopped in the hydroponics room to speak with our mushroom master.

'Hi, Kane. Grow any toadstools in the sand yet?'

He sniffed. He always sniffs. Maybe he's allergic to plants.

'Hello, Gallinger. No, I haven't had any success with toad-stools, but look behind the car barn next time you're out there. I've got a few cacti going.'

'Great,' I observed. Doc Kane was about my only friend aboard, not counting Betty.

'Say, I came down to ask you a favor.'

'Name it.'

'I want a rose.'

'A what?'

'A rose. You know, a nice red American Beauty job – thorns, pretty smelling—'

'I don't think it will take in this soil. *Sniff, sniff.*'

'No, you don't understand. I don't want to plant it, I just want the flower.'

'I'd have to use the tanks.' He scratched his hairless dome. 'It would take at least three months to get you flowers, even under forced growth.'

'Will you do it?'

'Sure, if you don't mind the wait.'

'Not at all. In fact, three months will just make it before we leave.' I looked about at the pools of crawling slime, at the trays of shoots. '—I'm moving up to Tirellian today, but I'll be in and out all the time. I'll be here when it blooms.'

'Moving up there, eh? Moore said they're an in-group.'

'I guess I'm "in" then.'

'Looks that way – I still don't see how you learned their language, though. Of course, I had trouble with French and German for my Ph.D, but last week I heard Betty demonstrate it at lunch. It just sounds like a lot of weird noises. She says speaking it is like working a *Times* crossword and trying to imitate birdcalls at the same time.'

I laughed, and took the cigarette he offered me.

'It's complicated,' I acknowledged. 'But, well, it's as if you suddenly came across a whole new class of mycetae here – you'd dream about it at night.'

His eyes were gleaming.

'Wouldn't that be something! I might, yet, you know.'

'Maybe you will.'

He chuckled as we walked to the door.

'I'll start your roses tonight. Take it easy down there.'

'You bet. Thanks.'

Like I said, a fungus nut, but a fairly good guy.

My quarters in the Citadel of Tirellian were directly adjacent to the Temple, on the inward side and slightly to the left. They were a considerable improvement over my cramped cabin, and I was pleased that Martian culture had progressed sufficiently to discover the desirability of the mattress over the pallet. Also, the bed was long enough to accommodate me, which was surprising.

So I unpacked and took sixteen 35 mm. shots of the Temple, before starting on the books.

I took 'stats until I was sick of turning pages without knowing what they said. So I started translating a work of history.

'Lo. In the thirty-seventh year of the Process of Cillen the rains came, which gave way to rejoicing, for it was a rare and untoward occurrence, and commonly construed a blessing.

'But it was not the life-giving semen of Malann which fell from the heavens. It was the blood of the universe, spurting from an artery. And the last days were upon us. The final dance was to begin.

'The rains brought the plague that does not kill, and the last passes of Locar began with their drumming...'

I asked myself what the hell Tamur meant, for he was an historian and supposedly committed to fact. This was not their Apocalypse.

Unless they could be one and the same...?

Why not? I mused. Tirellian's handful of people were the remnant of what had obviously once been a highly developed culture. They had had wars, but no holocausts; science, but little technology. A plague, a plague that did not kill...? Could that have done it? How, if it wasn't fatal?

I read on, but the nature of the plague was not discussed. I turned pages, skipped ahead, and drew a blank.

*M'Cwyie! M'Cwyie! When I want to question you most, you are not around!*

Would it be a faux pas to go looking for her? Yes, I decided. I was restricted to the rooms I had been shown, that had been an implicit understanding. I would have to wait to find out.

So I cursed long and loud, in many languages, doubtless burning Malann's sacred ears, there in his Temple.

He did not see fit to strike me dead, so I decided to call it a day and hit the sack.

I must have been asleep for several hours when Braxa entered my room with a tiny lamp. She dragged me awake by tugging at my pajama sleeve.

I said hello. Thinking back, there is not much else I could have said.

'Hello.'

'I have come,' she said, 'to hear the poem.'

'What poem?'

'Yours.'

'Oh.'

I yawned, sat up, and did things people usually do when awakened in the middle of the night to read poetry.

'That is very kind of you, but isn't the hour a trifle awkward?'

'I don't mind,' she said.

Someday I am going to write an article for the *Journal of Semantics*, called 'Tone of Voice: An Insufficient Vehicle for Irony.'

However, I was awake, so I grabbed my robe.

'What sort of animal is that?' she asked, pointing at the silk dragon on my lapel.

'Mythical,' I replied. 'Now look, it's late. I am tired. I have much to do in the morning. And M'Cwyie just might get the wrong idea if she learns you were here.'

'Wrong idea?'

'You know damned well what I mean!' It was the first time I had had an opportunity to use Martian profanity, and it failed.

'No,' she said, 'I do not know.'

She seemed frightened, like a puppy dog being scolded without knowing what it has done wrong.

I softened. Her red cloak matched her hair and lips so perfectly, and those lips were trembling.

'Here now, I didn't mean to upset you. On my world there are certain, uh, mores, concerning people of different sex alone together in bedrooms, and not allied by marriage . . . Um, I mean, you see what I mean?'

'No.'

They were jade, her eyes.

'Well, it's sort of . . . Well, it's sex, that's what it is.'

A light was switched on in those jade eyes.

'Oh, you mean having children!'

'Yes. That's it! Exactly!'

She laughed. It was the first time I had heard laughter in Tirellian. It sounded like a violinist striking his high strings with the bow, in short little chops. It was not an altogether pleasant thing to hear, especially because she laughed too long.

When she had finished she moved closer.

'I remember, now,' she said. 'We used to have such rules. Half a Process ago, when I was a child, we had such rules. But' – she looked as if she were ready to laugh again – 'there is no need for them now.'

My mind moved like a tape recorder playing at triple speed.

Half a Process! HalfaProcessa-ProcessaProcess! No! Yes! Half a Process was two hundred-forty-three years, roughly speaking!

—Time enough to learn the 2224 dances of Locar.

—Time enough to grow old, if you were human.

—Earth-style human, I mean.

I looked at her again, pale as the white queen in an ivory chess set.

She was human, I'd stake my soul – alive, normal, healthy. I'd stake my life – woman, my body . . .

But she was two and a half centuries old, which made M'Cwyie Methusala's grandma. It flattered me to think of their repeated complimenting of my skills, as linguist, as poet. These superior beings!

But what did she mean 'there is no such need for them now'? Why the near-hysteria? Why all those funny looks I'd been getting from M'Cwyie?

I suddenly knew I was close to something important, besides a beautiful girl.

'Tell me,' I said, in my Casual Voice, 'did it have anything to do with "the plague that does not kill," of which Tamur wrote?'

'Yes,' she replied, 'the children born after the Rains could have no children of their own, and—'

'And what?' I was leaning forward, memory set at 'record.'

'—and the men had no desire to get any.'

I sagged backward against the bedpost. Racial sterility, masculine impotence, following phenomenal weather. Had some vagabond cloud of radioactive junk from God knows where penetrated their weak atmosphere one day? One day long before Schiaparelli saw the canals, mythical as my dragon, before those 'canals' had given rise to some correct guesses for all the wrong reasons, had Braxa been alive, dancing, here – damned in the womb since blind Milton had written of another paradise, equally lost?

I found a cigarette. Good thing I had thought to bring ashtrays. Mars had never had a tobacco industry either. Or booze. The ascetics I had met in India had been Dionysiac compared to this.

'What is that tube of fire?'

'A cigarette. Want one?'

'Yes, please.'

She sat beside me, and I lighted it for her.

'It irritates the nose.'

'Yes. Draw some into your lungs, hold it there, and exhale.'

A moment passed.

'Ooh,' she said.

A pause, then, 'Is it sacred?'

'No, it's nicotine,' I answered, 'a very ersatz form of divinity.'

Another pause.

'Please don't ask me to translate "ersatz." '

'I won't. I get this feeling sometimes when I dance.'

'It will pass in a moment.'

'Tell me your poem now.'

An idea hit me.

'Wait a minute,' I said. 'I may have something better.'

I got up and rummaged through my notebooks, then I returned and sat beside her.

'These are the first three chapters of the Book of Ecclesiastes,' I explained. 'It is very similar to your own sacred books.'

I started reading.

I got through eleven verses before she cried out, 'Please don't read that! Tell me one of yours!'

I stopped and tossed the notebook onto a nearby table. She was shaking, not as she had quivered that day she danced as the wind, but with the jitter of unshed tears. She held her cigarette awkwardly, like a pencil. Clumsily, I put my arm about her shoulders.

'He is so sad,' she said, 'like all the others.'

So I twisted my mind like a bright ribbon, folded it, and tied the crazy Christmas knots I love so well. From German to Martian, with love, I did an impromptu paraphrasal of a poem about a Spanish dancer. I thought it would please her. I was right.

'Ooh,' she said again. 'Did you write that?'

'No, it's by a better man than I.'

'I don't believe it. You wrote it yourself.'

'No, a man named Rilke did.'

'But you brought it across to my language. Light another match, so I can see how she danced.'

I did.

24

'The fires of forever,' she mused, 'and she stamped them out, "with small, firm feet." I wish I could dance like that.'

'You're better than any Gypsy,' I laughed, blowing it out.

'No, I'm not. I couldn't do that.'

'Do you want me to dance for you?'

Her cigarette was burning down, so I removed it from her fingers and put it out, along with my own.

'No,' I said. 'Go to bed.'

She smiled, and before I realized it, had unclasped the fold of red at her shoulder.

And everything fell away.

And I swallowed, with some difficulty.

'All right,' she said.

So I kissed her, as the breath of fallen cloth extinguished the lamp.

### III

The days were like Shelley's leaves: yellow, red, brown, whipped in bright gusts by the west wind. They swirled past me with the rattle of microfilm. Almost all of the books were recorded now. It would take scholars years to get through them, to properly assess their value. Mars was locked in my desk.

Ecclesiastes, abandoned and returned to a dozen times, was almost ready to speak in the High Tongue.

I whistled when I wasn't in the Temple. I wrote reams of poetry I would have been ashamed of before. Evenings I would walk with Braxa, across the dunes or up into the mountains. Sometimes she would dance for me; and I would read something long, and in dactylic hexameter. She still thought I was Rilke, and I almost kidded myself into believing it. Here I was, staying at the Caste Duino, writing his *Elegies*.

> ... *It is strange to inhabit the Earth no more,*
> *to use no longer customs scarce acquired,*
> *nor interpret roses ...*

25

No! Never interpret roses! Don't. Smell them (sniff, Kane!), pick them, enjoy them. Live in the moment. Hold to it tightly. But charge not the gods to explain. So fast the leaves go by, are blown . . .

And no one ever noticed us. Or cared.

Laura. Laura and Braxa. They rhyme, you know, with a bit of clash. Tall, cool, and blonde was she (I hate blondes!), and Daddy had turned me inside out, like a pocket, and I thought she could fill me again. But the big, beat work-slinger, with Judas-beard and dog-trust in his eyes, oh, he had been a fine decoration at her parties. And that was all.

How the machine cursed me in the Temple! It blasphemed Malann and Gallinger. And the wild west wind went by and something was not far behind.

The last days were upon us.

A day went by and I did not see Braxa, and a night.

And a second. And a third.

I was half-mad. I hadn't realized how close we had become, how important she had been. With the dumb assurance of presence, I had fought against questioning the roses.

I had to ask. I didn't want to, but I had no choice.

'Where is she, M'Cwyie? Where is Braxa?'

'She is gone,' she said.

'Where?'

'I do not know.'

I looked at those devil-bird eyes. Anathema maranatha rose to my lips.

'I must know.'

She looked through me.

'She has left us. She is gone. Up into the hills, I suppose. Or the desert. It does not matter. What does anything matter? The dance draws itself to a close. The Temple will soon be empty.'

'Why? Why did she leave?'

'I do not know.'

'I must see her again. We lift off in a matter of days.'

'I am sorry, Gallinger.'

'So am I,' I said, and slammed shut a book without saying 'm'narra.'

I stood up.

'I will find her.'

I left the Temple. M'Cwyie was a seated statue. My boots were still where I had left them.

All day I roared up and down the dunes, going nowhere. To the crew of the *Aspic* I must have looked like a sandstorm, all by myself. Finally, I had to return for more fuel.

Emory came stalking out.

'Okay, make it good. You look like the abominable dust man. Why the rodeo?'

'Why, I, uh, lost something.'

'In the middle of the desert? Was it one of your sonnets? They're the only thing I can think of that you'd make such a fuss over.'

'No, dammit! It was something personal.'

George had finished filling the tank. I started to mount the jeepster again.

'Hold on there!' he grabbed my arm.

'You're not going back until you tell me what this is all about.'

I could have broken his grip, but then he could order me dragged back by the heels, and quite a few people would enjoy doing the dragging. So I forced myself to speak slowly, softly:

'It's simply that I lost my watch. My mother gave it to me and it's a family heirloom. I want to find it before we leave.'

'You sure it's not in your cabin, or down in Tirellian?'

'I've already checked.'

'Maybe somebody hid it to irritate you. You know you're not the most popular guy around.'

I shook my head.

'I thought of that. But I always carry it in my right pocket. I think it might have bounced out going over the dunes.'

He narrowed his eyes.

27

'I remember reading on a book jacket that your mother died when you were born.'

'That's right,' I said, biting my tongue. 'The watch belonged to her father and she wanted me to have it. My father kept it for me.'

'Hmph!' he snorted. 'That's a pretty strange way to look for a watch, riding up and down in a jeepster.'

'I could see the light shining off it that way,' I offered, lamely.

'Well, it's starting to get dark,' he observed. 'No sense looking any more today.

'Throw a dust sheet over the jeepster,' he directed a mechanic.

He patted my arm.

'Come on in and get a shower, and something to eat. You look as if you could use both.'

*Little fatty flecks beneath pale eyes, thinning hair, and an Irish nose; a voice a decibel louder than anyone else's . . .*

His only qualification for leadership!

I stood there, hating him. Claudius! If only this were the fifth act!

But suddenly the idea of a shower, and food, came through to me. I could use both badly. If I insisted on hurrying back immediately I might arouse more suspicion.

So I brushed some sand from my sleeve.

'You're right. That sounds like a good idea.'

'Come on, we'll eat in my cabin.'

The shower was a blessing, clean khakis were the grace of God, and the food smelled like Heaven.

'Smells pretty good,' I said.

We hacked up our steaks in silence. When we got to the dessert and coffee he suggested:

'Why don't you take the night off? Stay here and get some sleep.'

I shook my head.

'I'm pretty busy. Finishing up. There's not much time left.'

'A couple of days ago you said you were almost finished.'

'Almost, but not quite.'

28

'You also said they'll be holding a service in the Temple tonight.'

'That's right. I'm going to work in my room.'

He shrugged his shoulders.

Finally, he said, 'Gallinger,' and I looked up because my name means trouble.

'It shouldn't be any of my business,' he said, 'but it is. Betty says you have a girl down there.'

There was no question mark. It was a statement hanging in the air. Waiting.

*Betty, you're a bitch. You're a cow and a bitch. And a jealous one, at that. Why didn't you keep your nose where it belonged, shut your eyes? Your mouth?*

'So?' I said, a statement with a question mark.

'So,' he answered it, 'it is my duty, as head of this expedition, to see that relations with the natives are carried on in a friendly, and diplomatic, manner.'

'You speak of them,' I said, 'as though they are aborigines. Nothing could be further from the truth.'

I rose.

'When my papers are published everyone on Earth will know that truth. I'll tell them things Doctor Moore never even guessed at. I'll tell the tragedy of a doomed race, waiting for death, resigned and disinterested. I'll tell why, and it will break hard, scholarly hearts. I'll write about it, and they will give me more prizes, and this time I won't want them.

'My God!' I exclaimed. 'They had a culture when our ancestors were clubbing the saber-tooth and finding out how fire works!'

'*Do* you have a girl down there?'

'Yes!' I said. Yes, *Claudius! Yes, Daddy! Yes, Emory!* 'I do. but I'm going to let you in on a scholarly scoop now. They're already dead. They're sterile. In one more generation there won't be any Martians.'

I paused, then added, 'Except in my papers, except on a few pieces of microfilm and tape. And in some poems, about a girl who did give a damn and could only bitch about the unfairness of it all by dancing.'

'Oh,' he said.

After awhile:

'You *have* been behaving differently these past couple months. You've even been downright civil on occasion, you know. I couldn't help wondering what was happening. I didn't know anything mattered that strongly to you.'

I bowed my head.

'Is she the reason you were racing around the desert?'

I nodded.

'Why?'

I looked up.

'Because she's out there, somewhere. I don't know where, or why. And I've got to find her before we go.'

'Oh,' he said again.

Then he leaned back, opened a drawer, and took out something wrapped in a towel. He unwound it. A framed photo of a woman lay on the table.

'My wife,' he said.

It was an attractive face, with big, almond eyes.

'I'm a Navy man, you know,' he began. 'Young officer once. Met her in Japan.

'Where I come from it wasn't considered right to marry into another race, so we never did. But she was my wife. When she died I was on the other side of the world. They took my children, and I've never seen them since. I couldn't learn what orphanage, what home, they were put into. That was long ago. Very few people know about it.'

'I'm sorry,' I said.

'Don't be. Forget it. But' – he shifted in his chair and looked at me – 'if you do want to take her back with you – do it. It'll mean my neck, but I'm too old to ever head another expedition like this one. So go ahead.'

He gulped cold coffee.

'Get your jeepster.'

He swiveled the chair around.

I tried to say 'thank you' twice, but I couldn't. So I got up and walked out.

'Sayonara, and all that,' he muttered behind me.

'Here it is, Gallinger!' I heard a shout.

I turned on my heel and looked back up the ramp.

'Kane!'

He was limned in the port, shadow against light, but I had heard him sniff.

I returned the few steps.

'Here what is?'

'Your rose.'

He produced a plastic container, divided internally. The lower half was filled with liquid. The stem ran down into it. The other half, a glass of claret in this horrible night, was a large, newly opened rose.

'Thank you,' I said, tucking it in my jacket.

'Going back to Tirellian, eh?'

'Yes.'

'I saw you come aboard, so I got it ready. Just missed you at the Captain's cabin. He was busy. Hollered out that I could catch you at the barns.'

'Thanks again.'

'It's chemically treated. It will stay in bloom for weeks.'

I nodded. I was gone.

Up into the mountains now. Far. Far. The sky was a bucket of ice in which no moons floated. The going became steeper, and the little donkey protested. I whipped him with the throttle and went on. Up. Up. I spotted a green, unwinking star, and felt a lump in my throat. The encased rose beat against my chest like an extra heart. The donkey brayed, long and loudly, then began to cough. I lashed him some more and he died.

I threw the emergency brake on and got out. I began to walk.

So cold, so cold it grows. Up here. At night? Why? Why did she do it? Why flee the campfire when night comes on?

And I was up, down, around, and through every chasm, gorge, and pass, with my long-legged strides and an ease of movement never known on Earth.

Barely two days remain, my love, and thou hast forsaken me. Why?

I crawled under overhangs. I leaped over ridges. I scraped my knees, an elbow. I heard my jacket tear.

No answer, Malann? Do you really hate your people this much? Then I'll try someone else. Vishnu, you're the Preserver. Preserve her, please! Let me find her.

Jehovah?

Adonis? Osiris? Thammuz? Manitou? Legba? Where is she?

I ranged far and high, and I slipped.

Stones ground underfoot and I dangled over an edge. My fingers so cold. It was hard to grip the rock.

I looked down.

Twelve feet or so. I let go and dropped, landed rolling.

Then I heard her scream.

I lay there, not moving, looking up. Against the night, above, she called.

'Gallinger!'

I lay still.

'Gallinger!'

And she was gone.

I heard stones rattle and knew she was coming down some path to the right of me.

I jumped up and ducked into the shadow of a boulder.

She rounded a cut-off, and picked her way, uncertainly, through the stones.

'Gallinger?'

I stepped out and seized her by the shoulders.

'Braxa.'

She screamed again, then began to cry, crowding against me. It was the first time I had ever heard her cry.

'Why?' I asked. 'Why?'

But she only clung to me and sobbed.

Finally, 'I thought you had killed yourself.'

'Maybe I would have,' I said. 'Why did you leave Tirellian? And me?'

'Didn't M'Cwyie tell you? Didn't you guess?'

'I didn't guess, and M'Cwyie said she didn't know.'

'Then she lied. She knows.'

'What? What is it she knows?'

She shook all over, then was silent for a long time. I realized suddenly that she was wearing only her flimsy dancer's costume. I pushed her from me, took off my jacket, and put it about her shoulders.

'Great Malann!' I cried. 'You'll freeze to death!'

'No,' she said, 'I won't.'

I was transferring the rose-case to my pocket.

'What is that?' she asked.

'A rose,' I answered. 'You can't make it out in the dark. I once compared you to one. Remember?'

'Yes – Yes. May I carry it?'

'Sure.' I stuck it in the jacket pocket.

'Well? I'm still waiting for an explanation.'

'You really do not know?' she asked.

'No!'

'When the Rains came,' she said, 'apparently only our men were affected, which was enough ... Because I – wasn't – affected – apparently—'

'Oh,' I said. 'Oh.'

We stood there, and I thought.

'Well, why did you run? What's wrong with being pregnant on Mars? Tamur was mistaken. Your people can live again.'

She laughed, again that wild violin played by a Paginini gone mad. I stopped her before it went too far.

'How?' she finally asked, rubbing her cheek.

'Your people can live longer than ours. If our child is normal it will mean our races can intermarry. There must still be other fertile women of your race. Why not?'

'You have read the Book of Locar,' she said, 'and yet you ask me that? Death was decided, voted upon, and passed, shortly after it appeared in this form. But long before, before the followers of Locar knew. They decided it long ago. "We have done all things," they said, "we have seen all things, we have heard and felt all things. The dance was good. Now let it end." '

'You can't believe that.'

'What I believe does not matter,' she replied. 'M'Cwyie and the Mothers have decided we must die. Their very title is now a mockery, but their decisions will be upheld. There is only one prophecy left, and it is mistaken. We will die.'

'No,' I said.

'What, then?'

'Come back with me, to Earth.'

'No.'

'All right, then. Come with me now.'

'Where?'

'Back to Tirellian. I'm going to talk to the Mothers.'

'You can't! There is a Ceremony tonight!'

I laughed.

'A Ceremony for a god who knocks you down, and then kicks you in the teeth?'

'He is still Malann,' she answered. 'We are still his people.'

'You and my father would have gotten along fine,' I snarled. 'But I am going, and you are coming with me, even if I have to carry you – and I'm bigger than you are.'

'But you are not bigger than Ontro.'

'Who the hell is Ontro?'

'He will stop you, Gallinger. He is the Fist of Malann.'


IV


I scudded the jeepster to a halt in front of the only entrance I knew, M'Cwyie's. Braxa, who had seen the rose in a headlamp, now cradled it in her lap, like our child, and said nothing. There was a passive, lovely look on her face.

'Are they in the Temple now?' I wanted to know.

The Madonna-expression did not change. I repeated the question. She stirred.

'Yes,' she said, from a distance, 'but you cannot go in.'

'We'll see.'

I circled and helped her down.

I led her by the hand, and she moved as if in a trance. In the light of the new-risen moon, her eyes looked as they had the day I had met her, when she had danced. I snapped my fingers. Nothing happened.

So I pushed the door open and led her in. The room was half-lighted.

And she screamed for the third time that evening:

'Do not harm him, Ontro! It is Gallinger!'

I had never seen a Martian man before, only women. So I had no way of knowing whether he was a freak, though I suspected it strongly.

I looked up at him.

His half-naked body was covered with moles and swellings. Gland trouble, I guessed.

I had thought I was the tallest man on the planet, but he was seven feet tall and overweight. Now I knew where my giant bed had come from!

'Go back,' he said. 'She may enter. You may not.'

'I must get my books and things.'

He raised a huge left arm. I followed it. All my belongings lay neatly stacked in the corner.

'I must go in. I must talk with M'Cwyie and the Mothers.'

'You may not.'

'The lives of your people depend on it.'

'Go back,' he boomed. 'Go home to _your_ people, Gallinger. Leave _us!_'

My name sounded so different on his lips, like someone else's. How old was he? I wondered. Three hundred? Four? Had he been a Temple guardian all his life? Why? Who was there to guard against? I didn't like the way he moved. I had seen men who moved like that before.

'Go back,' he repeated.

If they had refined their martial arts as far as they had their dances, or worse yet, if their fighting arts were a part of the dance, I was in for trouble.

'Go on in,' I said to Braxa. 'Give the rose to M'Cwyie. Tell her that I sent it. Tell her I'll be there shortly.'

'I will do as you ask. Remember me on Earth, Gallinger. Good-bye.'

I did not answer her, and she walked past Ontro and into the next room, bearing her rose.

'Now will you leave?' he asked. 'If you like, I will tell her that we fought and you almost beat me, but I knocked you unconscious and carried you back to your ship.'

'No,' I said, 'either I go around you or go over you, but I am going through.'

He dropped into a crouch, arms extended.

'It is a sin to lay hands on a holy man,' he rumbled, 'but I will stop you, Gallinger.'

My memory was a fogged window, suddenly exposed to fresh air. Things cleared. I looked back six years.

I was a student of the Oriental Languages at the University of Tokyo. It was my twice-weekly night of recreation. I stood in a thirty-foot circle in the Kodokan, the *judogi* lashed about my high hips by a brown belt. I was *Ik-kyu*, one notch below the lowest degree of expert. A brown diamond above my right breast said 'Jiu-Jitsu' in Japanese, and it meant *atemiwaza*, really, because of the one striking-technique I had worked out, found unbelievably suitable to my size, and won matches with.

But I had never used it on a man, and it was five years since I had practiced. I was out of shape, I knew, but I tried hard to force my mind *tsuki no kokoro*, like the moon, reflecting the all of Ontro.

Somewhere, out of the past, a voice said, '*Hajime*, let it begin.'

I snapped into my *neko-ashi-dachi* cat-stance, and his eyes burned strangely. He hurried to correct his own position – and I threw it at him!

My one trick!

My long left leg lashed up like a broken spring. Seven feet off the ground my foot connected with his jaw as he tried to leap backward.

His head snapped back and he fell. A soft moan escaped his lips. *That's all there is to it,* I thought. *Sorry, old fellow.*

And as I stepped over him, somehow, groggily, he tripped me, and I fell across his body. I couldn't believe he had strength enough to remain conscious after that blow, let alone move. I hated to punish him any more.

But he found my throat and slipped a forearm across it before I realized there was a purpose to his action.

*No! Don't let it end like this!*

It was a bar of steel across my windpipe, my carotids. Then I realized that he was still unconscious, and that this was a reflex instilled by countless years of training. I had seen it happen once, in *shiai*. The man had died because he had been choked unconscious and still fought on, and his opponent thought he had not been applying the choke properly. He tried harder.

But it was rare, so very rare!

I jammed my elbow into his ribs and threw my head back in his face. The grip eased, but not enough. I hated to do it, but I reached up and broke his little finger.

The arm went loose and I twisted free.

He lay there panting, face contorted. My heart went out to the fallen giant, defending his people, his religion, following his orders. I cursed myself as I had never cursed before, for walking over him, instead of around.

I staggered across the room to my little heap of possessions. I sat on the projector case and lit a cigarette.

I couldn't go into the Temple until I got my breath back, until I thought of something to say.

How do you talk a race out of killing itself?

Suddenly—

—Could it happen! Would it work that way? If I read them the Book of Ecclesiastes – if I read them a greater piece of literature than any Locar ever wrote – and as somber – and as pessimistic – and showed them that our race had gone on

37

despite one man's condemning all of life in the highest poetry – showed them that the vanity he had mocked had borne us to the Heavens – would they believe it – would they change their minds?

I ground out my cigarette on the beautiful floor, and found my notebook. A strange fury rose within me as I stood.

And I walked into the Temple to preach the Black Gospel according to Gallinger, from the Book of Life.

There was silence all about me.

M'Cwyie had been reading Locar, the rose set at her right hand, target of all eyes.

Until I entered.

Hundreds of people were seated on the floor, barefoot. The few men were as small as the women, I noted.

I had my boots on.

*Go all the way,* I figured. *You either lose or you win – everything!*

A dozen crones sat in a semicircle behind M'Cwyie. The Mothers.

*The barren earth, the dry wombs, the fire-touched.*

I moved to the table.

'Dying yourselves, you would condemn your people,' I addressed them, 'that they may not know the life you have known – the joys, the sorrows, the fullness. —But it is not true that you all must die.' I addressed the multitude now. 'Those who say this lie. Braxa knows, for she will bear a child—'

They sat there, like rows of Buddhas. M'Cwyie drew back into the semicircle.

'—my child!' I continued, wondering what my father would have thought of this sermon.

'. . . And all the women young enough may bear children. It is only your men who are sterile. —And if you permit the doctors of the next expedition to examine you, perhaps even the men may be helped. But if they cannot, you can mate with the men of Earth.

'And ours is not an insignificant people, an insignificant place,' I went on. 'Thousands of years ago, the Locar of our world wrote a book saying that it was. He spoke as Locar did, but we did not lie down, despite plagues, wars, and famines. We did not die. One by one we beat down the diseases, we fed the hungry, we fought the wars, and, recently, have gone a long time without them. We may finally have conquered them. I do not know.

'But we have crossed millions of miles of nothingness. We have visited another world. And our Locar had said "Why bother? What is the worth of it? It is all vanity, anyhow."

'And the secret is,' I lowered my voice, as at a poetry reading, 'he was right! It *is* vanity, it *is* pride! It is the hubris of rationalism to always attack the prophet, the mystic, the god. It is our blasphemy which has made us great, and will sustain us, and which the gods secretly admire in us. —All the truly sacred names of God are blasphemous things to speak!'

I was working up a sweat. I paused dizzily.

'Here is the Book of Ecclesiastes,' I announced, and began:

' "Vanity of vanities, saith the Preacher, vanity of vanities; all is vanity. What profit hath a man..." '

I spotted Braxa in the back, mute, rapt.

I wondered what she was thinking.

And I wound the hours of the night about me, like black thread on a spool.

Oh, it was late! I had spoken till day came, and still I spoke. I finished Ecclesiastes and continued Gallinger.

And when I finished there was still only a silence.

The Buddhas, all in a row, had not stirred through the night. And after a long while M'Cwyie raised her right hand. One by one the Mothers did the same.

And I knew what that meant.

It meant, no, do not, cease, and stop.

It meant that I had failed.

I walked slowly from the room and slumped beside my baggage.

Ontro was gone. Good that I had not killed him...

After a thousand years M'Cwyie entered.

39

She said, 'Your job is finished.'

I did not move.

'The prophecy is fulfilled,' she said. 'My people are rejoicing. You have won, holy man. Now leave us quickly.'

My mind was a deflated balloon. I pumped a little air back into it.

'I'm not a holy man,' I said, 'just a second-rate poet with a bad case of hubris.'

I lit my last cigarette.

Finally, 'All right, what prophecy?'

'The Promise of Locar,' she replied, as though the explaining were unnecessary, 'that a holy man would come from the Heavens to save us in our last hours, if all the dances of Locar were completed. He would defeat the Fist of Malann and bring us life.'

'How?'

'As with Braxa, and as the example in the Temple.'

'Example?'

'You read us his words, as great as Locar's. You read to us how there is "nothing new under the sun." And you mocked his words as you read them – showing us a new thing.

'There has never been a flower on Mars,' she said, 'but we will learn to grow them.

'You are the Sacred Scoffer,' she finished. 'He-Who-Must-Mock-in-the-Temple – you go shod on holy ground.'

'But you voted "no,"' I said.

'I voted not to carry out our original plan, and to let Braxa's child live instead.'

'Oh.' The cigarette fell from my fingers. How close it had been! How little I had known!

'And Braxa?'

'She was chosen half a Process ago to do the dances – to wait for you.'

'But she said that Ontro would stop me.'

M'Cwyie stood there for a long time.

'She had never believed the prophecy herself. Things are not

40

well with her now. She ran away, fearing it was true. When you completed it, and we voted, she knew.'

'Then she does not love me? Never did?'

'I am sorry, Gallinger. It was the one part of her duty she never managed.'

'Duty,' I said flatly . . . Dutydutyduty! Tra-la!

'She has said good-bye, she does not wish to see you again.

'. . . and we will never forget your teachings,' she added.

'Don't,' I said automatically, suddenly knowing the great paradox which lies at the heart of all miracles. I did not believe a word of my own gospel, never had.

I stood, like a drunken man, and muttered 'M'narra.'

I went outside, into my last day on Mars.

*I have conquered thee, Malann – and the victory is thine! Rest easy on thy starry bed. God damned!*

I left the jeepster there and walked back to the *Aspic*, leaving the burden of life so many footsteps behind me. I went to my cabin, locked the door, and took forty-four sleeping pills.

But when I awakened I was in the dispensary, and alive.

I felt the throb of engines as I slowly stood up and somehow made it to the port.

Blurred Mars hung like a swollen belly above me, until it dissolved, brimmed over, and streamed down my face.

# Corrida

He awoke to an ultrasonic wailing. It was a thing that tortured his eardrums while remaining just beyond the threshhold of the audible.

He scrambled to his feet in the darkness.

He bumped against the walls several times. Dully, he realized that his arms were sore, as though many needles had entered there.

The sound maddened him . . .

Escape! He had to get away!

A tiny patch of light occurred to his left.

He turned and raced toward it and it grew into a doorway.

He dashed through and stood blinking in the glare that assailed his eyes.

He was naked, he was sweating. His mind was full of fog and the rag-ends of dreams.

He heard a roar, as of a crowd, and he blinked against the brightness.

Towering, a dark figure stood before him in the distance. Overcome by rage, he raced toward it, not quite certain why.

His bare feet trod hot sand, but he ignored the pain as he ran to attack.

Some portion of his mind framed the question 'Why?' but he ignored

Then he stopped.

A nude woman stood before him, beckoning, inviting, and there came a sudden surge of fire within his loins.

He turned slightly to his left and headed toward her.

She danced away.

He increased his speed. But as he was about to embrace her, there came a surge of fire in his right shoulder and she was gone.

He looked at his shoulder and an aluminum rod protruded from it, and the blood ran down along his arm. There arose another roar.

. . . And she appeared again.

He pursued her once more and his left shoulder burned with sudden fires. She was gone and he stood shaking and sweating, blinking against the glare.

'It's a trick,' he decided. 'Don't play the game!'

She appeared again and he stood stock still, ignoring her.

He was assailed by fires, but he refused to move, striving to clear his head.

The dark figure appeared once more, about seven feet tall and possessing two pairs of arms.

It held something in one of its hands. If only the lightning weren't so crazy, perhaps he . . .

But he hated that dark figure and he charged it. Pain lashed his side. Wait a minute! Wait a minute!

*Crazy! It's all crazy!* he told himself, recalling his identity. *This is a bullring and I'm a man, and that dark thing isn't. Something's wrong.*

He dropped to his hands and knees, buying time. He scooped up a double fistful of sand while he was down.

There came proddings, electric and painful. He ignored them for as long as he could, then stood.

The dark figure waved something at him and he felt himself hating it.

He ran toward it and stopped before it. He knew it was a game now. His name was Michael Cassidy. He was an attorney. New York. Of Johnson, Weems, Daugherty and Cassidy. A man had stopped him, asking for a light. On a street corner. Late at night. That he remembered.

He threw sand at the creature's head.

It swayed momentarily, and its arms were raised toward what might have been its face.

43

Gritting his teeth, he tore the aluminum rod from his shoulder and drove its sharpened end into the creature's middle.

Something touched the back of his neck, and there was darkness and he lay still for a long time.

When he could move again, he saw the dark figure and he tried to tackle it.

He missed, and there was pain across his back and something wet.

When he stood once more, he bellowed, 'You can't do this to me! I'm a man! Not a bull!'

There came a sound of applause.

He raced toward the dark thing six times, trying to grapple with it, hold it, hurt it. Each time, he hurt himself.

Then he stood, panting and gasping, and his shoulders ached and his back ached, and his mind cleared a moment and he said, 'You're God, aren't you? And this is the way You play the game...'

The creature did not answer him and he lunged.

He stopped short, then dropped to one knee and dove against its legs.

He felt a terrible fiery pain within his side as he brought the dark one to earth. He struck at it twice with his fists, then the pain entered his breast and he felt himself grow numb.

'Or are you?' he asked, thick-lipped. 'No, you're not... Where am I?'

His last memory was of something cutting away at his ears.

# Damnation Alley

|

The gull swooped by, seemed to hover a moment on unmoving wings.

Hell Tanner flipped his cigar butt at it and scored a lucky hit. The bird uttered a hoarse cry and beat suddenly at the air. It climbed about fifty feet, and whether it shrieked a second time, he would never know.

It was gone.

A single gray feather rocked in the violet sky, drifted out over the edge of the cliff and descended, swinging toward the ocean. Tanner chuckled through his beard, between the steady roar of the wind and the pounding of the surf. Then he took his feet down from the handlebars, kicked up the stand and gunned his bike to life.

He took the slope slowly till he came to the trail, then picked up speed and was doing fifty when he hit the highway.

He leaned forward and gunned it. He had the road all to himself, and he laid on the gas pedal till there was no place left for it to go. He raised his goggles and looked at the world through crap-colored glasses, which was pretty much the way he looked at it without them, too.

All the old irons were gone from his jacket, and he missed the swastika, the hammer and sickle, and the upright finger, especially. He missed his old emblem, too. Maybe he could pick up one in Tijuana and have some broad sew it on and...
No. It wouldn't do. All that was dead and gone. It would be a

45

giveaway, and he wouldn't last a day. What he *would* do was sell the Harley, work his way down the coast, clean and square and see what he could find in the other America.

He coasted down one hill and roared up another. He tore through Laguoa Beach, Capistrano Beach, San Clemente and San Onofre. He made it down to Oceanside, where he refueled, and he passed on through Carlsbad and all those dead little beaches that fill the shore space before Solana Beach Del Mar. It was outside San Diego that they were waiting for him.

He saw the roadblock and turned. They were not sure how he had managed it that quickly, at that speed. But now he was heading away from them. He heard the gunshots and kept going. Then he heard the sirens.

He blew his horn twice in reply and leaned far forward. The Harley leaped ahead, and he wondered whether they were radioing to someone further on up the line.

He ran for ten minutes and couldn't shake them. Then fifteen.

He topped another hill, and far ahead he saw the second block. He was bottled in.

He looked all around him for side roads, saw none.

Then he bore a straight course toward the second block. Might as well try to run it.

No good!

There were cars lined up across the entire road. They were even off the road on the shoulders.

He braked at the last possible minute, and when his speed was right he reared up on the back wheel, spun it and headed back toward his pursuers.

There were six of them coming toward him, and at his back new siren calls arose.

He braked again, pulled to the left, kicked the gas and leaped out of the seat. The bike kept going, and he hit the ground rolling, got to his feet and started running.

He heard the screeching of their tires. He heard a crash. Then there were more gunshots, and he kept going. They were aiming over his head, but he didn't know it. They wanted him alive.

After fifteen minutes he was backed against a wall of rock, and they were fanned out in front of him, and several had rifles, and they were all pointed in the wrong direction.

He dropped the tire iron he held and raised his hands. 'You got it, citizens,' he said. 'Take it away.'

And they did.

They handcuffed him and took him back to the cars. They pushed him into the rear seat of one, and an officer got in on either side of him. Another got into the front beside the driver, and this one held a sawed-off shotgun across his knees.

The driver started the engine and put the car into gear, heading back up 101.

The man with the shotgun turned and stared through bifocals that made his eyes look like hourglasses filled with green sand as he lowered his head. He stared for perhaps ten seconds, then said, 'That was a stupid thing to do.'

Hell Tanner stared back until the man said, 'Very stupid, Tanner.'

'Oh, I didn't know you were talking to me.'

'I'm looking at you, son.'

'And I'm looking at you. Hello, there.'

Then the driver said, without taking his eyes off the road, 'You know, it's too bad we've got to deliver him in good shape – after the way he smashed up the other car with that damn bike.'

'He could still have an accident. Fall and crack a couple ribs, say,' said the man to Tanner's left.

The man to the right didn't say anything, but the man with the shotgun shook his head slowly. 'Not unless he tries to escape,' he said. 'L.A. wants him in good shape.

'Why'd you try to skip out, buddy? You might have known we'd pick you up.'

Tanner shrugged.

'Why'd you pick me up? I didn't do anything?'

The driver chuckled.

47

'That's why,' he said. 'You didn't do anything, and there's something you were supposed to do. Remember?'

'I don't owe anybody anything. They gave me a pardon and let me go.'

'You got a lousy memory, kid. You made the nation of California a promise when they turned you loose yesterday. Now you've had more than the twenty-four hours you asked for to settle your affairs. You can tell them "no" if you want and get your pardon revoked. Nobody's forcing you. Then you can spend the rest of your life making little rocks out of big ones. We couldn't care less. I heard they got somebody else lined up already.'

'Give me a cigarette,' Tanner said.

The man on his right lit one and passed it to him.

He raised both hands, accepted it. As he smoked, he flicked the ashes onto the floor.

They sped along the highway, and when they went through towns or encountered traffic the driver would hit the siren and overhead the red light would begin winking. When this occurred, the sirens of the two other patrol cars that followed behind them would also wail. The driver never touched the brake, all the way up to L.A., and he kept radioing ahead every few minutes.

There came a sound like a sonic boom, and a cloud of dust and gravel descended upon them like hail. A tiny crack appeared in the lower right-hand corner of the bullet-proof windshield, and stones the size of marbles bounced on the hood and the roof. The tires made a crunching noise as they passed over the gravel that now lay scattered upon the road surface. The dust hung like a heavy fog, but ten seconds later they had passed out of it.

The men in the car leaned forward and stared upward.

The sky had become purple, and black lines crossed it, moving from west to east. These swelled, narrowed, moved from side to side, sometimes merged. The driver had turned on his lights by then.

'Could be a bad one coming,' said the man with the shot-gun.

The driver nodded. 'Looks worse further north, too,' he said.

A wailing began, high in the air above them, and the dark bands continued to widen. The sound increased in volume, lost its treble quality, became a steady roar.

The bands consolidated, and the sky grew dark as a starless, moonless night and the dust fell about them in heavy clouds. Occasionally, there sounded a *ping* as a heavier fragment struck against the car.

The driver switched on his country lights, hit the siren again and sped ahead. The roaring and the sound of the siren fought with one another above them, and far to the north a blue aurora began to spread, pulsing.

Tanner finished his cigarette, and the man gave him another. They were all smoking by then.

'You know, you're lucky we picked you up, boy,' said the man to his left. 'How'd you like to be pushing your bike through that stuff?'

'I'd like it,' Tanner said.

'You're nuts.'

'No. I'd make it. It wouldn't be the first time.'

By the time they reached Los Angeles, the blue aurora filled half the sky, and it was tinged with pink and shot through with smoky, yellow streaks that reached like spider legs into the south. The roar was a deafening, physical thing that beat upon their eardrums and caused their skin to tingle. As they left the car and crossed the parking lot, heading toward the big, pillared building with the frieze across its forehead, they had to shout at one another in order to be heard.

'Lucky we got here when we did!' said the man with the shotgun. 'Step it up!' Their pace increased as they moved toward the stairway. 'It could break any minute now!' screamed the driver.

As they had pulled into the lot, the building had had the appearance of a piece of ice-sculpture, with the shifting lights in the sky playing upon its surfaces and casting cold shadows. Now, though, it seemed as if it were a thing out of wax, ready to melt in a instant's flash of heat. Their faces and the flesh of their hands took on a bloodless, corpse-like appearance.

They hurried up the stairs, and a State Patrolman let them in through the small door to the right of the heavy metal double doors that were the main entrance to the building. He locked and chained the door behind them, after snapping open his holster when he saw Tanner.

'Which way?' asked the man with the shotgun.

'Second floor,' said the troooper, nodding toward a stairway to their right, 'Go straight back when you get to the top. It's the big office at the end of the hall.'

'Thanks.'

The roaring was considerably muffled, and objects achieved an appearance of natural existence once more in the artificial light of the building.

They climbed the curving stairway and moved along the corridor that led back into the building. When they reached the final office, the man with the shotgun nodded to his driver. 'Knock,' he said.

A woman opened the door, started to say something, then stopped and nodded when she saw Tanner. She stepped aside and held the door. 'This way,' she said, and they moved past her into the office, and she pressed a button on her desk and told the voice that said, 'Yes, Mrs Fiske?': 'They're here, with that man, sir.'

'Send them in.'

She led them to the dark, paneled door in the back of the room and opened it before them.

They entered, and the husky man behind the glass-topped desk leaned backward in his chair and wove his short fingers together in front of his chins and peered over them through eyes just a shade darker than the gray of his hair. His voice was soft and rasped just slightly. 'Have a seat,' he said to Tanner, and to the others, 'wait outside.'

'You know this guy's dangerous, Mister Denton,' said the man with the shotgun as Tanner seated himself in a chair situated five feet in front of the desk.

Steel shutters covered the room's three windows, and though the men could not see outside they could guess at the possible furies that stalked there as a sound like machine-gun fire suddenly rang through the room.

'I know.'

'Well, he's handcuffed, anyway. Do you want a gun?'

'I've got one.'

'Okay, then. We'll be outside.'

They left the room.

The two men stared at one another until the door closed, then the man called Denton said, 'Are all your affairs settled now?' and the other shrugged. Then, 'What the hell *is* your first name, really? Even the records show—'

'Hell,' said Tanner. 'That's my name. I was the seventh kid in our family, and when I was born the nurse held me up and said to my old man, "What name do you want on the birth certificate?" and Dad said, "Hell!" and walked away. So she put it down like that. That's what my brother told me. I never saw my old man to ask if that's how it was. He copped out the same day. Sounds right, though.'

'So your mother raised all seven of you?'

'No. She croaked a couple weeks later and different relatives took us kids.'

'I see,' said Denton. 'You've still got a choice, you know. Do you want to try it or don't you?'

'What's your job, anyway?' asked Tanner.

'I'm the Secretary of Traffic for the nation of California.'

'What's that got to do with it?'

'I'm coordinating this thing. It could as easily have been the Surgeon General or the Postmaster General, but more of it really falls into my area of responsibility. I know the hardware best. I know the odds—'

'What are the odds?' asked Tanner.

For the first time, Denton dropped his eyes.

'Well, it's risky . . .'

'Nobody's ever done it before, except for that nut who ran it to bring the news and he's dead. How can you get odds out of that?'

'I know,' said Denton slowly. 'You're thinking it's a suicide job, and you're probably right. We're sending three cars, with two drivers in each. If any one just makes it close enough, its broadcast signals may serve to guide in a Boston driver. You don't have to go, though, you know.'

'I know. I'm free to spend the rest of my life in prison.'

'You killed three people. You could have gotten the death penalty.'

'I didn't, so why talk about it? Look, mister, I don't want to die and I don't want the other bit either.'

'Drive or don't drive. Take your choice. But remember, if you drive and you make it, all will be forgiven and you can go your own way. The nation of California will even pay for that motorcycle you appropriated and smashed up, not to mention the damage to that police car.'

'Thanks a lot.' And the winds boomed on the other side of the wall, and the steady staccato from the window shields filled the room.

'You're a very good driver,' said Denton, after a time. 'You've driven just about every vehicle there is to drive. You've even raced. Back when you were smuggling, you used to make a monthly run to Salt Lake City. There are very few drivers who'll try that, even today.'

Hell Tanner smiled, remembering something.

'. . . And in the only legitimate job you ever held, you were the only man who'd make the mail run to Albuquerque. There've only been a few others since you were fired.'

'That wasn't my fault.'

'You were the best man on the Seattle run, too,' Denton

continued. 'Your supervisor said so. What I'm trying to say is that, of anybody we could pick, you've probably got the best chance of getting through. That's why we've been indulgent with you, but we can't afford to wait any longer. It's yes or no right now, and you'll leave within the hour if it's yes.'

Tanner raised his cuffed hands and gestured toward the window.

'In all this crap?' he asked.

'The cars can take this storm,' said Denton.

'Man, you're crazy,'

'People are dying even while we're talking,' said Denton.

'So a few more ain't about to make that much difference. Can't we wait till tomorrow?'

'No! A man gave his life to bring us the news! And we've got to get across the continent as fast as possible now or it won't matter! Storm or no storm, the cars leave now! Your feelings on the matter don't mean a good goddamn in the face of this! All I want out of you, Hell, is one word: Which one will it be?'

'I'd like something to eat. I haven't . . .'

'There's food in the car. What's your answer?'

Hell stared at the dark window.

'Okay,' he said, 'I'll run Damnation Alley for you. I won't leave without a piece of paper with some writing on it, though.'

'I've got it here.'

Denton opened a drawer and withdrew a heavy cardboard envelope from which he extracted a piece of stationery bearing the Great Seal of the nation of California. He stood and rounded the desk and handed it to Hell Tanner.

Hell studied it for several minutes, then said, 'This says that if I make it to Boston I receive a full pardon for every criminal action I've ever committed within the nation of California . . .'

'That's right.'

'Does that include ones you might not know about now, if someone should come up with them later?'

'That's what it says, Hell – "every criminal action." '

'Okay, you're on, fat boy. Get these bracelets off me and show me my car.'

The man called Denton moved back to his seat on the other side of his desk.

'Let me tell you something else, Hell,' he said. 'If you try to cop out anywhere along the route, the other drivers have their orders, and they've agreed to follow them. They will open fire on you and burn you into little bitty ashes. Get the picture?'

'I get the picture,' said Hell. 'I take it I'm supposed to do them the same favor?'

'That is correct.'

'Good enough. That might be fun.'

'I thought you'd like it.'

'Now, if you'll unhook me, I'll make the scene for you.'

'Not till I've told you what I think of you,' Denton said.

'Okay, if you want to waste time calling me names, while people are dying—'

'Shut up! You don't care about them and you know it! I just want to tell you that I think you are the lowest, most reprehensible human being I have ever encountered. You have killed men and raped women. You once gouged out a man's eyes, just for fun. You've been indicted twice for pushing dope and three times as a pimp. You're a drunk and a degenerate, and I don't think you've had a bath since the day you were born. You and your hoodlums terrorized decent people when they were trying to pull their lives together after the war. You stole from them and you assaulted them, and you extorted money and the necessaries of life with the threat of physical violence. I wish you had died in the Big Raid, that night, like all the rest of them. You are not a human being, except from a biological standpoint. You have a big dead spot somewhere inside you where other people have something that lets them live together in society and be neighbors. The only virtue that you possess – if you want to call it that – is that your reflexes may be a little faster, your muscles a little stronger, your eye a bit more wary than the rest of us, so that you can sit behind a wheel and drive through anything that has a way through it. It is for this that the nation of California is willing to pardon your inhumanity if you will use that one virtue to help rather than hurt. I don't

54

approve. I don't want to depend on you, because you're not the type. I'd like to see you die in this thing, and while I hope that somebody makes it through, I hope that it will be somebody else. I hate your bloody guts. You've got your pardon now. The car's ready. Let's go.'

Denton stood, at a height of about five feet eight inches, and Tanner stood and looked down at him and chuckled.

'I'll make it,' he said. 'If that citizen from Boston made it through and died, I'll make it through and live. I've been as far as the Missus Hip.'

'You're lying.'

'No, I ain't either, and if you ever find out that's straight, remember I got this piece of paper in my pocket – "every criminal action" and like that. It wasn't easy, and I was lucky, too. But I made it that far and, nobody else you know can say that. So I figure that's about halfway and I can make the other half if I can get that far.'

They moved toward the door.

'I don't like to say it and mean it,' said Denton, 'but good luck. Not for your sake, though.'

'Yeah, I know.'

Denton opened the door. 'Turn him loose,' he said. 'He's driving.'

The officer with the shotgun handed it to the man who had given Tanner the cigarettes, and he fished in his pockets for the key. When he found it, he unlocked the cuffs, stepped back, and hung them at his belt. 'I'll come with you,' said Denton. 'The motor pool is downstairs.'

They left the office, and Mrs Fiske opened her purse and took a rosary into her hands and bowed her head. She prayed for Boston and she prayed for the soul of its departed messenger. She even threw in a couple for Hell Tanner.

## III

They descended to the basement, the sub-basement and the sub-sub-basement.

When they got there, Tanner saw three cars, ready to go; and he saw five men seated on benches along the wall. One of them he recognized.

'Denny,' he said, 'come here,' and he moved forward, and a slim, blond youth who held a crash helmet in his right hand stood and walked toward him.

'What the hell are you doing?' he asked him.

'I'm second driver in car three.'

'You've got your own garage and you've kept your nose clean. What's the thought on this?'

'Denton offered me fifty grand,' said Denny, and Hell turned away his face.

'Forget it! It's no good if you're dead!'

'I need the money.'

'Why?'

'I want to get married and I can use it.'

'I thought you were making out okay.'

'I am, but I'd like to buy a house.'

'Does your girl know what you've got in mind?'

'No.'

'I didn't think so. Listen, I've got to do it – it's the only way out for me. You don't have to—'

'That's for me to say.'

'—so I'm going to tell you something: You drive out to Pasadena to that place where we used to play when we were kids – with the rocks and the three big trees – you know where I mean?'

'Yeah, I sure do remember.'

'Go back of the big tree in the middle, on the side where I carved my initials. Step off seven steps and dig down around four feet. Got that?'

'Yeah. What's there?'

'That's my legacy, Denny. You'll find one of those old strong boxes, probably all rusted out by now. Bust it open. It'll be full of excelsior, and there'll be a six-inch joint of pipe inside. It's threaded, and there's caps on both ends. There's a little over five grand rolled up inside it, and all the bills are clean.'

'Why you telling me this?'

'Because it's yours now,' he said, and he hit him in the jaw. When Denny fell, he kicked him in the ribs, three times, before the cops grabbed him and dragged him away.

'You fool!' said Denton as they held him. 'You crazy, damned fool!'

'Un-uh,' said Tanner. 'No brother of mine is going to run Damnation Alley while I'm around to stomp him and keep him out of the game. Better find another driver quick, because he's got cracked ribs. Or else let me drive alone.'

'Then you'll drive alone,' said Denton, 'because we can't afford to wait around any longer. There's pills in the compartment, to keep you awake, and you'd better use them, because if you fall back they'll burn you up. Remember that.'

'I won't forget you, mister, if I'm ever back in town. Don't fret about that.'

'Then you'd better get into car number two and start heading up the ramp. The vehicles are all loaded. The cargo compartment is under the rear seat.'

'Yeah, I know.'

'. . . And if I ever see you again, it'll be too soon. Get out of my sight, scum!'

Tanner spat on the floor and turned his back on the Secretary of Traffic. Several cops were giving first aid to his brother, and one had dashed off in search of a doctor. Denton made two teams of the remaining four drivers and assigned them to cars one and three. Tanner climbed into the cab of his own, started the engine and waited. He stared up the ramp, and considered what lay ahead. He searched the compartments until he found cigarettes. He lit one and leaned back.

The other drivers moved forward and mounted their own heavily shielded vehicles. The radio crackled, crackled, hummed, crackled again, and then a voice came through as he heard the other engines come to life.

'Car one – ready!' came the voice.

There was a pause, then, 'Car three – ready!' said a different voice.

Tanner lifted the microphone and mashed the button on its side.

'Car two ready,' he said.

'Move out,' came the order, and they headed up the ramp.

The door rolled upward before them, and they entered the storm.


## IV


It was a nightmare, getting out of L.A. and onto Route 91. The waters came down in sheets and rocks the size of baseballs banged against the armor plating of his car. Tanner smoked and turned on the special lights. He wore infrared goggles, and the night and the storm stalked him.

The radio crackled many times, and it seemed that he heard the murmur of a distant voice, but he could never quite make out what it was trying to say.

They followed the road for as far as it went, and as their big tires sighed over the rugged terrain that began where the road ended, Tanner took the lead and the others were content to follow. He knew the way; they didn't.

He followed the old smugglers' route he'd used to run candy to the Mormons. It was possible that he was the only one left alive that knew it. Possible, but then there was always someone looking for a fast buck. So, in all of L.A., there might be somebody else.

The lightning began to fall, not in bolts, but sheets. The car was insulated, but after a time his hair stood on end. He might have seen a giant Gila Monster once, but he couldn't be sure. He kept his fingers away from the fire-control board. He'd save his teeth till menaces were imminent. From the rearview scanners it seemed that one of the cars behind him had discharged a rocket, but he couldn't be sure, since he had lost all radio contact with them immediately upon leaving the building.

Waters rushed toward him, splashed about his car. The sky sounded like an artillery range. A boulder the size of a tombstone fell in front of him, and he swerved about it. Red lights flashing across the sky from north to south. In their passing, he detected many black bands going from west to east. It was not an encouraging spectacle. The storm could go on for days.

He continued to move forward, skirting a pocket of radiation that had not died in the four years since last he had come this way.

They came upon a place where the sands were fused into a glassy sea, and he slowed as he began its passage peering ahead after the craters and chasms it contained.

Three more rockfalls assailed him before the heavens split themselves open and revealed a bright blue light edged with violet. The dark curtains rolled back toward the Poles, and the roaring and the gunfire reports diminished. A lavender glow remained in the north, and a green sun dipped toward the horizon.

They had ridden it out. He killed the infras, pushed back his goggles and switched on the normal night lamps.

The desert would be bad enough, all by itself.

Something big and bat-like swooped through the tunnel of his lights and was gone. He ignored its passage. Five minutes later it made a second pass, this time much closer, and he fired a magnesium flare. A black shape, perhaps forty feet across, was illuminated, and he gave it two five-second bursts from the fifty-calibers and it fell to the ground and did not return again.

To the squares, this was Damnation Alley. To Hell Tanner, this was still the parking lot. He'd been this way thirty-two times, and so far as he was concerned the Alley started in the place that was once called Colorado.

He led, and they followed, and the night wore on like an abrasive.

No airplane could make it. Not since the war. None could

venture above a couple hundred feet, the place where the winds began. The winds. The mighty winds that circled the globe, tearing off the tops of mountains, Sequoia trees, wrecked buildings, gathering up birds, bats, insects and anything else that moved up into the dead belt; the winds that swirled about the world, lacing the skies with dark lines of debris, occasionally meeting, merging, clashing, dropping tons of carnage wherever they came together and formed too great a mass. Air transportation was definitely out, to anywhere in the world. For these winds circled, and they never ceased. Not in all the twenty-five years of Tanner's memory had they let up.

Tanner pushed ahead, cutting a diagonal by the green sunset. Dust continued to fall about him, great clouds of it, and the sky was violet, then purple once more. Then the sun went down and the night came on, and the stars were very faint points of light somewhere above it all. After a time, the moon rose, and the half-face that it showed that night was the color of a glass of Chianti wine held before a candle.

He lit another cigarette and began to curse, slowly, softly and without emotion.

They threaded their way amid heaps of rubble: rock, metal, fragments of machinery, the prow of a boat. A snake, as big around as a garbage can and dark green in the cast light, slithered across Tanner's path, and he braked the vehicle as it continued and continued and continued. Perhaps a hundred and twenty feet of snake passed by before Tanner removed his foot from the brake and touched gently upon the gas pedal once again.

Glancing at the left-hand screen, which held an infrared version of the view to the left, it seemed that he saw two eyes glowing within the shadow of a heap of girders and masonry. Tanner kept one hand near the fire-control button and did not move it for a distance of several miles.

There were no windows in the vehicle, only screens which reflected views in every direction including straight up and the ground beneath the car. Tanner sat within an illuminated box which shielded him against radiation. The 'car' that he drove had eight heavily treaded tires and was thirty-two feet in length. It mounted eight fifty-caliber automatic guns and four grenade throwers. It carried thirty armor-piercing rockets which could be discharged straight ahead or at any elevation up to forty degrees from the plane. Each of the four sides, as well as the roof of the vehicle, housed a flame thrower. Razor-sharp 'wings' of tempered steel – eighteen inches wide at their bases and tapering to points, an inch and a quarter thick where they ridged – could be moved through a complete hundred-eighty-degree arc along the sides of the car and parallel to the ground, at a height of two feet and eight inches. When standing at a right angle to the body of the vehicle – eight feet to the rear of the front bumper – they extended out to a distance of six feet on either side of the car. They could be couched like lances for a charge. They could be held but slightly out from the sides for purposes of slashing whatever was sideswiped. The car was bullet-proof, air-conditioned and had its own food locker and sanitation facilities. A long-barreled .357 Magnum was held by a clip on the door near the driver's left hand. A 30-06, a .45 caliber automatic and six hand grenades occupied the rack immediately above the front seat.

But Tanner kept his own counsel, in the form of a long, slim SS dagger inside his right boot.

He removed his gloves and wiped his palms on the knees of his denims. The pierced heart that was tattooed on the back of his right hand was red in the light from the dashboard. The knife that went through it was dark blue, and his first name was tattooed in the same color beneath it, one letter on each knuckle, beginning with that at the base of his little finger.

He opened and explored the two near compartments but could find no cigars. So he crushed out his cigarette butt on the floor and lit another.

The forward screen showed vegetation, and he slowed. He tried using the radio but couldn't tell whether anyone heard him, receiving only static in reply.

He slowed, staring ahead and up. He halted once again.

He turned his forward lights up to full intensity and studied the situation.

A heavy wall of thorn bushes stood before him, reaching to a height of perhaps twelve feet. It swept on to his right and off to his left, vanishing out of sight in both directions. How dense, how deep it might be, he could not tell. It had not been there a few years before.

He moved forward slowly and activated the flame throwers. In the rearview screen, he could see that the other vehicles had halted a hundred yards behind him and dimmed their lights.

He drove till he could go no further, then pressed the button for the forward flame.

It shot forth, a tongue of fire, licking fifty feet into the bramble. He held it for five seconds and withdrew it. Then he extended it a second time and backed away quickly as the flames caught.

Beginning with a tiny glow, they worked their way upward and spread slowly to the right and the left. Then they grew in size and brightness.

As Tanner backed away, he had to dim his screen, for they'd spread fifty feet before he'd backed more than a hundred, and they leaped thirty and forty feet into the air.

The blaze widened, to a hundred feet, two, three . . . As Tanner backed away, he could see a river of fire flowing off into the distance, and the night was bright about him.

He watched it burn, until it seemed that he looked upon a molten sea. Then he searched the refrigerator, but there was no beer. He opened a soft drink and sipped it while he watched the burning. After about ten minutes, the air conditioner whined and shook itself to life. Hordes of dark, four-footed creatures, the size of rats or cats, fled from the inferno, their coats smouldering. They flowed by. At one point, they covered his forward screen, and he could hear the scratching of their claws upon the fenders and the roof.

He switched off the lights and killed the engine, tossed the empty can into the waste box. He pushed the 'Recline' button on the side of the seat, leaned back, and closed his eyes.

# V

He was awakened by the blowing of horns. It was still night, and the panel clock showed him that he had slept for a little over three hours.

He stretched, sat up, adjusted the seat. The other cars had moved up, and one stood to either side of him. He leaned on his own horn twice and started his engine. He switched on the forward lights and considered the prospect before him as he drew on his gloves.

Smoke still rose from the blackened field, and far off to his right there was a glow, as if the fire still continued somewhere in the distance. They were in the place that had once been known as Nevada.

He rubbed his eyes and scratched his nose, then blew the horn once and engaged the gears.

He moved forward slowly. The burnt-out area seemed fairly level and his tires were thick.

He entered the black field, and his screens were immediately obscured by the rush of ashes and smoke which rose on all sides.

He continued, hearing the tires crunching through the brittle remains. He set his screens at maximum and switched his headlamps up to full brightness.

The vehicles that flanked him dropped back perhaps eighty feet, and he dimmed the screens that reflected the glare of their lights.

He released a flare, and as it hung there, burning, cold, white and high, he saw a charred plain that swept on to the edges of his eyes' horizon.

He pushed down on the accelerator, and the cars behind him swung far out to the sides to avoid the clouds that he raised. His radio crackled, and he heard a faint voice but could not make out its words.

He blew his horn and rolled ahead even faster. The other vehicles kept pace.

He drove for an hour and a half before he saw the end of the ash and the beginning of clean sand up ahead.

Within five minutes, he was moving across desert once more, and he checked his compass and bore slightly to the west. Cars one and three followed, speeding up to match his new pace, and he drove with one hand and ate a corned beef sandwich.

When morning came, many hours later, he took a pill to keep himself alert and listened to the screaming of the wind. The sun rose up like molten silver to his right, and a third of the sky grew amber and was laced with fine lines like cobwebs. The desert was topaz beneath it, and the brown curtain of dust that hung continuously at his back, pierced only by the eight shafts of the other cars' lights, took on a pinkish tone as the sun grew a bright red corona and the shadows fled into the west. He dimmed his lights as he passed an orange cactus shaped like a toadstool and perhaps fifty feet in diameter.

Giant bats fled south, and far ahead he saw a wide water-fall descending from the heavens. It was gone by the time he reached the damp sand of that place, but a dead shark lay to his left, and there was seaweed, seaweed, seaweed, fish and driftwood all about.

The sky pinked over from east to west and remained that color. He gulped a bottle of ice water and felt it go into his stomach. He passed more cacti, and a pair of coyotes sat at the base of one and watched him drive by. They seemed to be laughing. Their tongues were very red.

As the sun brightened, he dimmed the screen. He smoked, and he found a button that produced music. He swore at the soft, stringy sounds that filled the cabin, but he didn't turn them off.

He checked the radiation level outside, and it was only a little above normal. The last time he had passed this way, it had been considerably higher.

He passed several wrecked vehicles such as his own. He ran across another plain of silicon, and in the middle was a huge crater which he skirted. The pinkness in the sky faded and faded and faded, and a bluish tone came to replace it. The dark lines were still there, and occasionally one widened into a black river as it flowed away into the east. At noon, one such river partly eclipsed the sun for a period of eleven minutes. With its departure, there came a brief dust storm, and Tanner turned on the radar and his lights. He knew there was a chasm somewhere ahead, and when he came to it he bore to the left and ran along its edge for close to two miles before it narrowed and vanished. The other vehicles followed, and Tanner took his bearings from the compass once more. The dust had subsided with the brief wind, and even with the screen dimmed Tanner had to don his dark goggles against the glare of reflected sunlight from the faceted field he now negotiated.

He passed towering formations which seemed to be quartz. He had never stopped to investigate them in the past, and he had no desire to do it now. The spectrum danced at their bases, and patches of such light occurred for some distance about them.

Speeding away from the crater, he came again upon sand, clean, brown, white dun and red. There were more cacti, and huge dunes lay all about him. The sky continued to change, until it was as blue as a baby's eyes. Tanner hummed along with the music for a time, and then he saw the monster.

It was a Gila, bigger than his car, and it moved in fast. It sprang from out the sheltering shade of a valley filled with cacti and it raced toward him, its beaded body bright with many colors beneath the sun, its dark, dark eyes unblinking as it bounded forward on its lizard-fast legs, sable fountains rising behind its upheld tail that was wide as a sail and pointed like a tent.

He couldn't use the rockets because it was coming in from the side.

He opened up with his fifty-calibers and spread his 'wings' and stamped the accelerator to the floor. As it neared, he sent forth a cloud of fire in its direction. By then, the other cars were firing, too.

It swung its tail and opened and closed its jaws, and its blood came forth and fell upon the ground. Then a rocket struck it. It turned; it leaped.

There came a booming, crunching sound as it fell upon the vehicle identified as car number one and lay there.

Tanner hit the brakes, turned, and headed back.

Car number three came up beside it and parked. Tanner did the same.

He jumped down from the cab and crossed to the smashed car. He had the rifle in his hands and he put six rounds into the creature's head before he approached the car.

The door had come open, and it hung from a single hinge, the bottom one.

Inside, Tanner could see the two men sprawled, and there was some blood upon the dashboard and the seat.

The other two drivers came up beside him and stared within. Then the shorter of the two crawled inside and listened for the heartbeat and the pulse and felt for breathing.

'Mike's dead,' he called out, 'but Greg's starting to come around.'

A wet spot that began at the car's rear and spread and continued to spread, and the smell of gasoline filled the air.

Tanner took out a cigarette, thought better of it and replaced it in the pack. He could hear the gurgle of the huge gas tanks as they emptied themselves upon the ground.

The man who stood at Tanner's side said, 'I never saw anything like it... I've seen pictures, but – I never saw anything like it...'

'I have,' said Tanner, and then the other driver emerged from the wreck, partly supporting the man he'd referred to as Greg.

The man called out, 'Greg's all right. He just hit his head on the dash.'

The man who stood at Tanner's side said, 'You can take him, Hell. He can back you up when he's feeling better,' and Tanner shrugged and turned his back on the scene and lit a cigarette.

'I don't think you should do—' the man began, and

Tanner blew smoke in his face. He turned to regard the two approaching men and saw that Greg was dark-eyed and deeply tanned. Part Indian, possibly. His skin seemed smooth, save for a couple pockmarks beneath his right eye, and his cheekbones were high and his hair very dark. He was as big as Tanner, which was six-two, though not quite so heavy. He was dressed in overalls; and his carriage, now that he had had a few deep breaths of air, became very erect, and he moved with a quick, graceful stride.

'We'll have to bury Mike,' the short man said.

'I hate to lose the time,' said his companion, 'but—' and then Tanner flipped his cigarette and threw himself to the ground as it landed in the pool at the rear of the car.

There was an explosion, flames, then more explosions. Tanner heard the rockets as they tore off toward the east, inscribing dark furrows in the hot afternoon's air. The ammo for the fifty-calibers exploded, and the hand grenades went off, and Tanner burrowed deeper and deeper into the sand, covering his head and blocking his ears.

As soon as things grew quiet, he grabbed for the rifle. But they were already coming at him, and he saw the muzzle of a pistol. He raised his hands slowly and stood.

'Why the goddamn hell did you do a stupid thing like that?' said the other driver, the man who held the pistol.

Tanner smiled. 'Now we don't have to bury him,' he said. 'Cremation's just as good, and it's already over.'

'You could have killed us all, if those guns or those rocket launchers had been aimed this way!'

'They weren't. I looked.'

'The flying metal could've – Oh . . . I see. Pick up your damn rifle, buddy, and keep it pointed at the ground. Eject the rounds it's still got in it and put 'em in your pocket.'

Tanner did this thing while the other talked.

'You wanted to kill us all, didn't you? Then you could have cut out and gone your way, like you tried to do yesterday. Isn't that right?'

'You said it, mister, not me.'

'It's true, though. You don't give a good goddamn if everybody in Boston croaks, do you?'

'My gun's unloaded now,' said Tanner.

'Then get back in your bloody buggy and get going! I'll be behind you all the way!'

Tanner walked back toward his car. He heard the others arguing behind him, but he didn't think they'd shoot him. As he was about to climb up into the cab, he saw a shadow out of the corner of his eye and turned quickly.

The man named Greg was standing behind him, tall and quiet as a ghost.

'Want me to drive awhile?' he asked Tanner, without expression.

'No, you rest up. I'm still in good shape. Later on this afternoon, maybe, if you feel up to it.'

The man nodded and rounded the cab. He entered from the other side and immediately reclined his chair.

Tanner slammed his door and started the engine. He heard the air conditioner come to life.

'Want to reload this?' he asked. 'And put it back on the rack?' And he handed the rifle and the ammo to the other, who had nodded. He drew on his gloves then and said, 'There's plenty of soft drinks in the 'frig. Nothing much else, though,' and the other nodded again. Then he heard car three start and said, 'Might as well roll,' and he put it into gear and took his foot off the clutch.

VI

After they had driven for about half an hour, the man called Greg said to him, 'Is it true what Marlowe said?'

'What's a Marlowe?'

'He's driving the other car. Were you trying to kill us? Do you really want to skip out?'

Hell laughed. 'That's right,' he said. 'You named it.'

'Why?'

68

Hell let it hang there for a minute, then said, 'Why shouldn't I? I'm not anxious to die. I'd like to wait a long time before I try that bit.'

Greg said, 'If we don't make it, the population of the continent may be cut in half.'

'If it's a question of them or me, I'd rather it was them.'

'I sometimes wonder how people like you happen.'

'The same way as anybody else, mister, and it's fun for a couple people for awhile, and then the trouble starts.'

'What did they ever do to you, Hell?'

'Nothing. What did they ever do *for* me? Nothing. Nothing. What do I owe them? The same.'

'Why'd you stomp your brother back at the Hall?'

'Because I didn't want him doing a damfool thing like this and getting himself killed. Cracked ribs he can get over. Death is a more permanent ailment.'

'That's not what I asked you. I mean, what do you care whether he croaks?'

'He's a good kid, that's why. He's got a thing for this chick, though, and he can't see straight.'

'So what's it to you?'

'Like I said, he's my brother and he's a good kid. I like him.'

'How come?'

'Oh, hell! We've been through a lot together, that's all! What are you trying to do? Psychoanalyze me?'

'I was just curious, that's all.'

'So now you know. Talk about something else if you want to talk, okay?'

'Okay. You've been this way before, right?'

'That's right.'

'You been any further east?'

'I've been all the way to the Missus Hip.'

'Do you know a way to get across it?'

'I think so. The bridge is still up at Saint Louis.'

'Why didn't you go across it the last time you were there?'

'Are you kidding? The thing's packed with cars full of bones. It wasn't worth the trouble to try and clear it.'

69

'Why'd you go that far in the first place?'

'Just to see what it was like. I heard all these stories—'

'What was it like?'

'A lot of crap. Burned down towns, big craters, crazy animals, some people—'

'People? People still live there?'

'If you want to call them that. They're all wild and screwed up. They wear rags or animal skins or they go naked. They threw rocks at me till I shot a couple. Then they let me alone.'

'How long ago was that?'

'Six – maybe seven years ago. I was just a kid then.'

'How come you never told anybody about it?'

'I did. A coupla my friends. Nobody else ever asked me. We were going to go out there and grab off a couple of the girls and bring them back, but everybody chickened out.'

'What would you have done with them?'

Tanner shrugged. 'I dunno. Sell 'em, I guess.'

'You guys used to do that, down on the Barbary Coast – sell people, I mean – didn't you?'

Tanner shrugged again.

'Used to,' he said, 'before the Big Raid.'

'How'd you manage to live through that? I thought they'd cleaned the whole place out?'

'I was doing time,' he said. 'A.D.W.'

'What's that?'

'Assault with a deadly weapon.'

'What'd you do after they let you go?'

'I let them rehabilitate me. They got me a job running the mail.'

'Oh yeah, I heard about that. Didn't realize it was you, though. You were supposed to be pretty good – doing all right and ready for a promotion. Then you kicked your boss around and lost your job. How come?'

'He was always riding me about my record and about my old gang down on the Coast. Finally, one day I told him to lay off, and he laughed at me, so I hit him with a chain. Knocked out the bastard's front teeth. I'd do it again.'

'Too bad.'

'I was the best driver he had. It was his loss. Nobody else will make the Albuquerque run, not even today. Not unless they really need the money.'

'Did you like the work, though, while you were doing it?'

'Yeah, I like to drive.'

'You should probably have asked for a transfer when the guy started bugging you.'

'I know. If it was happening today, that's probably what I'd do. I was mad, though, and I used to get mad a lot faster than I do now. I think I'm smarter these days than I was before.'

'If you make it on this run and you go home afterward, you'll probably be able to get your job back. Think you'd take it?'

'In the first place,' said Tanner, 'I don't think we'll make it. And in the second, if we do make it and there's still people around that town, I think I'd rather stay there than go back.'

Greg nodded. 'Might be smart. You'd be a hero. Nobody'd know much about your record. Somebody'd turn you onto something good.'

'The hell with heroes,' said Tanner.

'Me, though, I'll go back if we make it.'

'Sail 'round Cape Horn?'

'That's right.'

'Might be fun. But why go back?'

'I've got an old mother and a mess of brothers and sisters I take care of, and I've got a girl back there.'

Tanner brightened the screen as the sky began to darken.

'What's your mother like?'

'Nice old lady. Raised the eight of us. Got arthritis bad now, though.'

'What was she like when you were a kid?'

'She used to work during the day, but she cooked our meals and sometimes brought us candy. She made a lot of our clothes. She used to tell us stories, like about how things were before the war. She played games with us and sometimes she gave us toys.'

'How about your old man?' Tanner asked him, after awhile.

71

'He drank pretty heavy and he had a lot of jobs, but he never beat us too much. He was all right. He got run over by a car when I was around twelve.'

'And you take care of everybody now?'

'Yeah. I'm the oldest.'

'What is it that you do?'

'I've got your old job. I run the mail to Albuquerque.'

'Are you kidding?'

'No.'

'I'll be damned! Is Gorman still the supervisor?'

'He retired last year, on disability.'

'I'll be damned! That's funny. Listen, down in Albuquerque do you ever go to a bar called Pedro's?'

'I've been there.'

'Have they still got a little blonde girl plays the piano? Named Margaret?'

'No.'

'Oh.'

'They've got some guy now. Fat fellow. Wears a big ring on his left hand.'

Tanner nodded and downshifted as he began the ascent of a steep hill.

'How's your head now?' he asked, when they'd reached the top and started down the opposite slope.

'Feels pretty good. I took a couple of your aspirins with that soda I had.'

'Feel up to driving for awhile?'

'Sure, I could do that.'

'Okay, then.' Tanner leaned on the horn and braked the car. 'Just follow the compass for a hundred miles or so and wake me up. All right?'

'Okay. Anything special I should watch out for?'

'The snakes. You'll probably see a few. Don't hit them, whatever you do.'

'Right.'

They changed seats, and Tanner reclined the one, lit a cigarette, smoked half of it, crushed it out and went to sleep.

## VII

When Greg awakened him, it was night. Tanner coughed and drank a mouthful of ice water and crawled back to the latrine. When he emerged, he took the driver's seat and checked the mileage and looked at the compass. He corrected their course and, 'We'll be in Salt Lake City before morning,' he said, 'if we're lucky. —Did you run into any trouble?'

'No, it was pretty easy. I saw some snakes and I let them go by. That was about it.'

Tanner grunted and engaged the gears.

'What was that guy's name that brought the news about the plague?' Tanner asked.

'Brady or Brody or something like that,' said Greg.

'What was it that killed him? He might have brought the plague to L.A., you know.'

Greg shook his head.

'No. His car had been damaged, and he was all broken up and he'd been exposed to radiation a lot of the way. They burned his body and his car, and anybody who'd been anywhere near him got shots of Haffikine.'

'What's that?'

'That's the stuff we're carrying – Haffikine antiserum. It's the only preventative for the plague. Since we had a bout of it around twenty years ago, we've kept it on hand and maintained the facilities for making more in a hurry. Boston never did, and now they're hurting.'

'Seems kind of silly for the only other nation on the continent – maybe in the world – not to take better care of itself, when they knew we'd had a dose of it.'

Greg shrugged.

'Probably, but there it is. Did they give you any shots before they released you?'

'Yeah.'

'That's what it was, then.'

'I wonder where their driver crossed the Missus Hip? He didn't say, did he?'

73

'He hardly said anything at all. They got most of the story from the letter he carried.'

'Must have been one hell of a driver, to run the Alley.'

'Yeah. Nobody's ever done it before, have they?'

'Not that I know of.'

'I'd like to have met the guy.'

'Me too, at least I guess.'

'It's a shame we can't radio across country, like in the old days.'

'Why?'

'Then he wouldn't of had to do it, and we could find out along the way whether it's really worth making the run. They might all be dead by now, you know.'

'You've got a point there, mister, and in a day or so we'll be to a place where going back will be harder than going ahead.'

Tanner adjusted the screen as dark shapes passed.

'Look at that, will you!'

'I don't see anything.'

'Put on your infras.'

Greg did this and stared upward at the screen.

Bats. Enormous bats cavorted overhead, swept by in dark clouds.

'There must be hundreds of them, maybe thousands...'

'Guess so. Seems there are more than there used to be when I came this way a few years back. They must be screwing their heads off in Carlsbad.'

'We never see them in L.A. Maybe they're pretty much harmless.'

'Last time I was up to Salt Lake, I heard talk that a lot of them were rabid. Some day someone's got to go – them or us.'

'You're a cheerful guy to ride with, you know?'

Tanner chuckled and lit a cigarette, and. 'Why don't you make us some coffee?' he said. 'As for the bats, that's something our kids can worry about, if there are any.'

Greg filled the coffee pot and plugged it into the dashboard. After a time, it began to grumble and hiss.

'What the hell's that?' said Tanner, and he hit the brakes.

The other car halted, several hundred yards behind his own, and he turned on his microphone and said, 'Car three! What's that look like to you?' and waited.

He watched them: towering, tapered tops that spun between the ground and the sky, wobbling from side to side, sweeping back and forth, about a mile ahead. It seemed there were fourteen or fifteen of the things. Now they stood like pillars, now they danced. They bored into the ground and sucked up yellow dust. There was a haze all about them. The stars were dim or absent above or behind them.

Greg stared ahead and said, 'I've heard of whirlwinds, tornadoes – big, spinning things. I've never seen one, but that's the way they were described to me.'

And then the radio crackled, and the muffled voice of the man called Marlowe came through:

'Giant dust devils,' he said. 'Big, rotary sand storms. I think they're sucking stuff up into the dead belt, because I don't see anything coming down—'

'You ever see one before?'

'No, but my partner says he did. He says the best thing might be to shoot our anchoring columns and stay put.'

Tanner did not answer immediately. He stared ahead, and the tornadoes seemed to grow larger.

'They're coming this way,' he finally said. 'I'm not about to park here and be a target. I want to be able to maneuver. I'm going ahead through them.'

'I don't think you should.'

'Nobody asked you, mister, but if you've got any brains you'll do the same thing.'

'I've got rockets aimed at your tail, Hell.'

'You won't fire them – not for a thing like this, where I could be right and you could be wrong – and not with Greg in here, too.'

There was silence within the static, then, 'Okay, you win, Hell. Go ahead, and we'll watch. If you make it, we'll follow. If you don't, we'll stay put.'

'I'll shoot a flare when I get to the other side,' Tanner said. 'When you see it, you do the same. Okay?'

Tanner broke the connection and looked ahead, studying the great black columns, swollen at their tops. There fell a few layers of light from the storm which they supported, and the air was foggy between the blacknesses of their revolving trunks. 'Here goes,' said Tanner, switching his lights as bright as they would beam. 'Strap yourself in, boy,' and Greg obeyed him as the vehicle crunched forward.

Tanner buckled his own safety belt as they slowly edged ahead.

The columns grew and swayed as he advanced, and he could now hear a rushing, singing sound, as of a chorus of the winds.

He skirted the first by three hundred yards and continued to the left to avoid the one which stood before him and grew and grew. As he got by it, there was another, and he moved farther to the left. Then there was an open area of perhaps a quarter of a mile leading ahead and toward his right.

He swiftly sped across it and passed between two of the towers that stood like ebony pillars a hundred yards apart. As he passed them, the wheel was almost torn from his grip, and he seemed to inhabit the center of an eternal thunderclap. He swerved to the right then and skirted another, speeding.

Then he saw seven more and cut between two and passed about another. As he did, the one behind him moved rapidly, crossing the path he had just taken. He exhaled heavily and turned to the left.

He was surrounded by the final four, and he braked so that he was thrown forward and the straps cut into his shoulder, as two of the whirlwinds shook violently and moved in terrible spurts of speed. One passed before him, and the front end of his car was raised off the ground.

Then he floored the gas pedal and shot between the final two, and they were all behind him.

He continued on for about a quarter for a mile, turned the car about, mounted a small rise and parked.

He released the flare.

It hovered, like a dying star, for about half a minute.

He lit a cigarette as he stared back, and he waited.

He finished the cigarette.

Then, 'Nothing,' he said. 'Maybe they couldn't spot it through the storm. Or maybe we couldn't see theirs.'

'I hope so,' said Greg.

'How long do you want to wait?'

'Let's have that coffee.'

An hour passed, then two. The pillars began to collapse until there were only three of the slimmer ones. They moved off toward the east and were gone from sight.

Tanner released another flare, and still there was no response.

'We'd better go back and look for them,' said Greg.

'Okay.'

And they did.

There was nothing there, though, nothing to indicate the fate of car three.

Dawn occurred in the east before they had finished with their searching, and Tanner turned the car around, checked the compass, and moved north.

'When do you think we'll hit Salt Lake?' Greg asked him, after a long silence.

'Maybe two hours.'

'Were you scared, back when you ran those things?'

'No. Afterward, though, I didn't feel so good.'

Greg nodded.

'You want me to drive again?'

'No. I won't be able to sleep if I stop now. We'll take in more gas in Salt Lake, and we can get something to eat while a mechanic checks over the car. Then I'll put us on the right road, and you can take over while I sack out.'

The sky was purple again and the black bands had widened. Tanner cursed and drove faster. He fired his ventral flame at two bats who decided to survey the car. They fell back, and he accepted the mug of coffee Greg offered him.

## VIII

The sky was as dark as evening when they pulled into Salt Lake City. John Brady – that was his name – had passed that way but days before, and the city was ready for the responding vehicle. Most of its ten thousand inhabitants appeared along the street, and before Hell and Greg had jumped down from the cab after pulling into the first garage they saw, the hood of car number two was opened and three mechanics were peering at the engine.

They abandoned the idea of eating in the little diner across the street. Too many people hit them with too many questions as soon as they set foot outside the garage. They retreated and sent someone after eggs, bacon and toast.

There was cheering as they rolled forth onto the street and sped away into the east.

'Could have used a beer,' said Tanner. 'Damn it!'

And they rushed along beside the remains of what had once been U.S. Route 40.

Tanner relinquished the driver's seat and stretched out on the passenger side of the cab. The sky continued to darken above them, taking upon it the appearance it had had in L.A. the day before.

'Maybe we can outrun it,' Greg said.

'Hope so.'

The blue pulse began in the north, flared into a brilliant aurora. The sky was almost black directly overhead.

'Run!' cried Tanner. 'Run! Those are hills up ahead! Maybe we can find an overhang or a cave!'

But it broke upon them before they reached the hills. First came the hail, then the flak. The big stones followed, and the scanner on the right went dead. The sands blasted them, and they rode beneath a celestial waterfall that caused the engine to sputter and cough.

They reached the shelter of the hills, though, and found a place within a rocky valley where the walls jutted steeply forward and broke the main force of the wind/sand/dust/

rock/water storm. They sat there as the winds screamed and boomed about them. They smoked and they listened.

'We won't make it,' said Greg. 'You were right. I thought we had a chance. We don't. Everything's against us, even the weather.'

'We've got a chance,' said Tanner. 'Maybe not a real good one. But we've been lucky so far. Remember that.'

Greg spat into the waste container.

'Why the sudden optimism? From you?'

'I was mad before and shooting off my mouth. Well, I'm still mad – but I got me a feeling now: I feel lucky. That's all.'

Greg laughed. 'The hell with luck. Look out there,' he said.

'I see it,' said Tanner. 'This buggy is built to take it, and it's doing it. Also, we're only getting about ten percent of its full strength.'

'Okay, but what difference does it make? It could last for a couple days.'

'So we wait it out.'

'Wait too long, and even that ten percent can smash us. Wait too long, and even if it doesn't there'll be no reason left to go ahead. Try driving, though, and it'll flatten us.'

'It'll take me ten or fifteen minutes to fix that scanner. We've got spare "eyes." If the storm lasts more than six hours, we'll start out anyway.'

'Says who?'

'Me.'

'Why? You're the one who was so hot on saving his own neck. How come all of a sudden you're willing to risk it, not to mention mine too?'

Tanner smoked awhile, then said, 'I've been thinking,' and then he didn't say anything else.

'About what?' Greg asked him.

'Those folks in Boston,' Tanner said. 'Maybe it is worth it. I don't know. They never did anything for me. But hell, I like action and I'd hate to see the whole world get dead. I think I'd like to see Boston, too, just to see what it's like. It might even be fun being a hero, just to see what that's like. Don't get me wrong. I don't give a damn about anybody up there. It's just that I don't like the idea of everything being like the Alley here – all burned-out and screwed up and full of crap. When we lost the other car back in those tornadoes, it made me start thinking... I'd hate to see everybody go that way – everything. I might still cop out if I get a real good chance, but I'm just telling you how I feel now. That's all.'

Greg looked away and laughed, a little more heartily than usual.

'I never suspected you contained such philosophic depths.'

'Me neither. I'm tired. Tell me about your brothers and sisters, huh?'

'Okay.'

Four hours later, when the storm slackened and the rocks became dust and the rain fog, Tanner replaced the right scanner, and they moved on out, passing later through Rocky Mountain National Park. The dust and the fog combined to limit visibility, throughout the day. That evening they skirted the ruin that was Denver, and Tanner took over as they headed toward the place that had once been called Kansas.

He drove all night, and in the morning the sky was clearer than it bad been in days. He let Greg snore on and sorted through his thoughts while he sipped his coffee.

It was a strange feeling that came over him as he sat there with his pardon in his pocket and his hands upon the wheel. The dust fumed at his back. The sky was the color of rosebuds, and the dark trails had shrunken once again. He recalled the stories of the days when the missiles came down, burning everything but the northeast and the southwest; the days when the winds arose and the clouds vanished and the sky had lost its blue; the days when the Panama Canal had been shattered and radios had ceased to function; the days when the planes could no longer fly. He regretted this, for he had always wanted to fly, high, birdlike, swooping and soaring. He felt slightly cold, and the screens now seemed to possess a crystal clarity, like pools of tinted water. Somewhere ahead, far, far ahead lay what might be the only other sizable pocket of humanity that remained on the shoulders of the world. He might be able to save it, if he could reach it in time. He looked about him at the rocks and the sand and the side of a broken garage that had somehow come to occupy the slope of a mountain. It remained within his mind long after he had passed it. Shattered, fallen down, half covered with debris, it took on a stark and monstrous form, like a decaying skull which had once occupied the shoulders of a giant; and he pressed down hard on the accelerator, although it could go no further. He began to tremble. The sky brightened, but he did not touch the screen controls. Why did he have to be the one? He saw a mass of smoke ahead and to the right. As he drew nearer, he saw that it rose from a mountain which had lost its top and now held a nest of fires in its place. He cut to the left, going miles, many miles, out of the way he had intended. Occasionally, the ground shook beneath his wheels. Ashes fell about him, but now the smouldering cone was far to the rear of the right-hand screen. He wondered after the days that had gone before and the few things that he actually knew about them. If he made it through, he decided he'd learn more about history. He threaded his way through painted canyons and forded a shallow river. Nobody had ever asked him to do anything important before, and he hoped that nobody ever would again. Now, though, he was taken by the feeling that he could do it. He wanted to do it. Damnation Alley lay all about him, burning, fuming, shaking, and if he could not run it then half the world would die, and the chances would be doubled that one day all the world would be part of the Alley. His tattoo stood stark on his whitened knuckles, saying 'Hell,' and he knew that it was true. Greg still slept, the sleep of exhaustion, and Tanner narrowed his eyes and chewed his beard and never touched the brake, not even when he saw the rockslide beginning. He made it by and sighed. That pass was closed to him forever, but he had shot through without a scratch. His mind was an expanding bubble, its surfaces like the view-screens, registering everything about him. He felt the flow of the air within the cab and the upward pressure of the pedal upon his foot. His throat seemed dry, but it didn't matter. His eyes felt gooey at their inside corners, but he didn't wipe them. He roared across the pocked plains of Kansas, and he knew now that he had been sucked into the role completely and that he wanted it that way. Damn-his-eyes Denton had been right. It had to be done. He halted when he came to the lip of a chasm and headed north. Thirty miles later it ended, and he turned again to the south. Greg muttered in his sleep. It sounded like a curse. Tanner repeated it softly a couple times and turned toward the east as soon as a level stretch occurred. The sun stood in high heaven, and Tanner felt as though he were drifting bodiless beneath it, above the brown ground flaked with green spikes of growth. He clenched his teeth and his mind went back to Denny, doubtless now in a hospital. Better than being where the others had gone. He hoped the money he'd told him about was still there. Then he felt the ache begin, in the places between his neck and his shoulders. It spread down into his arms, and he realized how tightly he was gripping the wheel. He blinked and took a deep breath and realized that his eyeballs hurt. He lit a cigarette and it tasted foul, but he kept puffing at it. He drank some water and he dimmed the rear view-screen as the sun fell behind him. Then he heard a sound like a distant rumble of thunder and was fully alert once more. He sat up straight and took his foot off the accelerator.

He slowed. He braked and stopped. Then he saw them. He sat there and watched them as they passed, about a half-mile ahead.

A monstrous herd of bison crossed before him. It took the better part of an hour before they had passed. Huge, heavy, dark, heads down, hooves scoring the soil, they ran without slowing until the thunder was great and then rolled off toward the north, diminishing, softening, dying, gone. The screen of their dust still hung before him, and he plunged into it, turning on his lights.

He considered taking a pill, decided against it. Greg might

be waking soon, he wanted to be able to get some sleep after they'd switched over.

He came up beside a highway, and its surface looked pretty good, so he crossed onto it and sped ahead. After a time, he passed a faded, sagging sign that said 'TOPEKA – 110 MILES.'

Greg yawned and stretched. He rubbed his eyes with his knuckles and then rubbed his forehead, the right side of which was swollen and dark.

'What time is it?' he asked.

Tanner gestured toward the clock in the dashboard.

'Morning or is it afternoon?'

'Afternoon.'

'My God! I must have slept around fifteen hours!'

'That's about right.'

'You been driving all that time?'

'That's right.'

'You must be done in. You look like hell. Let me just hit the head. I'll take over in a few minutes.'

'Good idea.'

Greg crawled toward the rear of the vehicle.

After about five minutes. Tanner came upon the outskirts of a dead town. He drove up the main street, and there were rusted-out hulks of cars all along it. Most of the buildings had fallen in upon themselves, and some of the opened cellars that he saw were filled with scummy water. Skeletons lay about the town square. There were no trees standing above the weeds that grew there. Three telephone poles still stood, one of them leaning forward and trailing wires like a handful of black spaghetti. Several benches were visible within the weeds beside the cracked sidewalks, and a skeleton lay stretched out upon the second one Tanner passed. He found his way barred by a fallen telephone pole, and he detoured around the block. The next street was somewhat better preserved, but all its store-front windows were broken, and a nude mannikin posed fetchingly with her left arm missing from the elbow down. The traffic light at the corner stared blindly as Tanner passed through its intersection.

Tanner heard Greg coming forward as he turned at the next corner.

'I'll take over now,' he said.

'I want to get out of this place first,' and they both watched in silence for the next fifteen minutes until the dead town was gone from around them.

Tanner pulled to a halt then and said, 'We're a couple hours away from a place that used to be called Topeka. Wake me if you run into anything hairy.'

'How did it go while I was alseep? Did you have any trouble?'

'No,' said Tanner, and he closed his eyes and began to snore.

Greg drove away from the sunset, and he ate three ham sandwiches and drank a quart of milk before Topeka.


## IX


Tanner was awakened by the firing of the rockets. He rubbed the sleep from his eyes and stared dumbly ahead for almost half a minute.

Like gigantic dried leaves, great clouds fell about them. Bats, bats, bats. The air was filled with bats. Tanner could hear a chittering, squeaking, scratching sound, and the car was buffeted by their dark bodies.

'Where are we?' he asked.

'Kansas City. The place seems full of them,' and Greg released another rocket, which cut a fiery path through the swooping, spinning horde.

'Save the rockets. Use the fire,' said Tanner, switching the nearest gun to manual and bringing cross-hairs into focus upon the screen. 'Blast 'em in all directions – for five, six seconds – then I'll come in.'

The flame shot forth, orange and cream blossoms of combustion. When they folded, Tanner sighted in the screen and squeezed the trigger. He swung the gun, and they fell. Their charred bodies lay all about him, and he added new ones to the smouldering heaps.

'Roll it!' he cried, and the car moved forward, swaying, bat bodies crunching beneath its tires.

Tanner laced the heavens with gunfire, and when they swooped again he strafed them and fired a flare.

In the sudden magnesium glow from overhead, it seemed that millions of vampire-faced forms were circling, spiraling down toward them.

He switched from gun to gun, and they fell about him like fruit. Then he called out, 'Brake, and hit the topside flame!' and Greg did this thing.

'Now the sides! Front and rear next!'

Bodies were burning all about them, heaped as high as the hood, and Greg put the car into low gear when Tanner cried 'Forward!' And they pushed their way through the wall of charred flesh.

Tanner fired another flare.

The bats were still there, but circling higher now. Tanner primed the guns and waited, but they did not attack again in any great number. A few swept about them, and he took pot-shots at them as they passed.

Ten minutes later he said, 'That's the Missouri River to our left. If we just follow alongside it now, we'll hit Saint Louis.'

'I know. Do you think it'll be full of bats, too?'

'Probably. But if we take our time and arrive with daylight, they shouldn't bother us. Then we can figure a way to get across the Missus Hip.'

Then their eyes fell upon the rearview screen, where the dark skyline of Kansas City with bats was silhouetted by pale stars and touched by the light of the bloody moon.

After a time, Tanner slept once more. He dreamt he was riding his bike, slowly, down the center of a wide street, and people lined the sidewalks and began to cheer as he passed. They threw confetti, but by the time it reached him it was garbage, wet and stinking. He stepped on the gas then, but his bike slowed even more and now they were screaming at him. They shouted obscenities. They cried out his name, over and over, and again. The Harley began to wobble, but his feet seemed to be glued in place. In a moment, he knew, he would fall. The bike came to a halt then, and he began to topple over toward the right side. They rushed toward him as he fell, and he knew it was just about all over...

He awoke with a jolt and saw the morning spread out before him: a bright coin in the middle of a dark blue tablecloth and a row of glasses along the edge.

'That's it,' said Greg. 'The Missus Hip.'

Tanner was suddenly very hungry.


After they had refreshed themselves, they sought the bridge.

'I didn't see any of your naked people with spears,' said Greg. 'Of course, we might have passed their way after dark – if there are any of them still around.'

'Good thing, too,' said Tanner. 'Saved us some ammo.'

The bridge came into view, sagging and dark save for the places where the sun gilded its cables, and it stretched unbroken across the bright expanse of waters. They moved slowly toward it, threading their way through streets gorged with rubble, detouring when it became completely blocked by the rows of broken machines, fallen walls, sewer-deep abysses in the burst pavement.

It took them two hours to travel half a mile, and it was noon before they reached the foot of the bridge, and, 'It looks as if Brady might have crossed here,' said Greg, eyeing what appeared to be a cleared passageway amidst the wrecks that filled the span. 'How do you think he did it?'

'Maybe he had something with him to hoist them and swing them out over the edge. There are some wrecks below, down where the water is shallow.'

'Were they there last time you passed by?'

'I don't know. I wasn't right down here by the bridge. I topped that hill back there,' and he gestured at the rearview screen.

'Well, from here it looks like we might be able to make it. Let's roll.'

They moved upward and forward onto the bridge and began their slow passage across the mighty Missus Hip. There were times when the bridge creaked beneath them, sighed, groaned, and they felt it move.

The sun began to climb, and still they moved forward, scraping their fenders against the edges of the wrecks, using their wings like plows. They were on the bridge for three hours before its end came into sight through a rift in the junkstacks.

When their wheels finally touched the opposite shore, Greg sat there breathing heavily and then lit a cigarette.

'You want to drive awhile, Hell?'

'Yeah. Let's switch over.'

He did, and, 'God! I'm bushed!' he said as he sprawled out.

Tanner drove forward through the ruins of East Saint Louis, hurrying to clear the town before nightfall. The radiation level began to mount as he advanced, and the streets were cluttered and broken. He checked the inside of the cab for radioactivity, but it was still clean.

It took him hours, and as the sun fell at his back he saw the blue aurora begin once more in the north. But the sky stayed clear, filled with its stars, and there were no black lines that he could see. After a long while, a rose-colored moon appeared and hung before him. He turned on the music, softly, and glanced at Greg. It didn't seem to bother him, so he let it continue.

The instrument panel caught his eye. The radiation level was still climbing. Then, in the forward screen, he saw the crater and he stopped.

It must have been over half a mile across, and he couldn't tell its depth.

He fired a flare, and in its light he used the telescopic lenses to examine it to the right and to the left.

The way seemed smoother to the right, and he turned in that direction and began to negotiate it.

The place was hot! So very, very hot! He hurried. And he

wondered as he sped, the gauge rising before him: What had it been like on that day? Whenever? That day when a tiny sun had lain upon this spot and fought with, and for a time beaten, the brightness of the other in the sky, before it sank slowly into its sudden burrow? He tried to imagine it, succeeded, then tried to put it out of his mind and couldn't. How do you put out the fires that burn forever? He wished that he knew. There'd been so many places to go then, and he liked to move around.

What had it been like in the old days, when a man could just jump on his bike and cut out for a new town whenever he wanted? And nobody emptying buckets of crap on you from out of the sky? He felt cheated, which was not a new feeling for him, but it made him curse even longer than usual.

He lit a cigarette when he'd finally rounded the crater, and he smiled for the first time in months as the radiation gauge began to fall once more. Before many miles, he saw tall grasses swaying about him, and not too long after that he began to see trees.

Trees short and twisted, at first, but the further he fled from the place of carnage, the taller and straighter they became. They were trees such as he had never seen before – fifty, sixty feet in height – and graceful, and gathering stars, there on the plains of Illinois.

He was moving along a clean, hard, wide road, and just then he wanted to travel it forever – to Floridee, of the swamps and Spanish moss and citrus groves and fine beaches and the Gulf; and up to the cold, rocky Cape, where everything is gray and brown and the waves break below the lighthouses and the salt burns in your nose and there are graveyards where bones have lain for centuries and you can still read the names they bore, chiseled there into the stones above them; down through the nation where they say the grass is blue; then follow the mighty Missus Hip to the place where she spreads and comes and there's the Gulf again, full of little islands where the old boosters stashed their loot; and through the shag-topped mountains he'd heard about: the Smokies, Ozarks, Poconos, Catskills; drive through the forest of Shenandoah; park, and take a boat out over Chesapeake Bay; see the big lakes and the place where the water falls, Niagara. To drive forever along the big road, to see everything, to eat the world. Yes. Maybe it wasn't all Damnation Alley. Some of the legendary places must still be clean, like the countryside about him now. He wanted it with a hunger, with a fire like that which always burned in his loins. He laughed then, just one short, sharp bark, because now it seemed like maybe he could have it.

The music played softly, too sweetly perhaps, and it filled him.

## X

By morning he was into the place called Indiana and still following the road. He passed farmhouses which seemed in good repair. There could even be people living in them. He longed to investigate, but he didn't dare to stop. Then after an hour, it was all countryside again, and degenerating.

The grasses grew shorter, shriveled, were gone. An occasional twisted tree clung to the bare earth. The radiation level began to rise once more. The signs told him he was nearing Indianapolis, which he guessed was a big city that had received a bomb and was now gone away.

Nor was he mistaken.

He had to detour far to the south to get around it, backtracking to a place called Martinsville in order to cross over the White River. Then as he headed east once more, his radio crackled and came to life. There was a faint voice, repeating, 'Unidentified vehicle, halt!' and he switched all the scanners to telescopic range. Far ahead, on a hilltop, he saw a standing man with binoculars and a walkie-talkie. He did not acknowledge receipt of the transmission, but kept driving.

He was hitting forty miles an hour along a halfway decent section of roadway, and he gradually increased his speed to fifty-five, though the protesting of his tires upon the cracked pavement was sufficient to awaken Greg.

Tanner stared ahead, ready for an attack, and the radio kept repeating the order, louder now as he neared the hill, and called upon him to acknowledge the message.

He touched the brake as he rounded a long curve, and he did not reply to Greg's 'What's the matter?'

When he saw it there, blocking the way, ready to fire, he acted instantly.

The tank filled the road, and its big gun was pointed directly at him.

As his eye sought for and found passage around it, his right hand slapped the switches that sent three armor-piercing rockets screaming ahead and his left spun the wheel counter-clockwise and his foot fell heavy on the accelerator.

He was half off the road then, bouncing along the ditch at its side, when the tank discharged one fiery belch which missed him and then caved in upon itself and blossomed.

There came the sound of rifle fire as he pulled back onto the road on the other side of the tank and sped ahead. Greg launched a single grenade to the right and the left and then hit the fifty calibers. They tore on ahead, and after about a quarter of a mile Tanner picked up his microphone and said, 'Sorry about that. My brakes don't work,' and hung it up again. There was no response.

As soon as they reached a level plain, commanding a good view in all directions. Tanner halted the vehicle and Greg moved into the driver's seat.

'Where do you think they got hold of that armor?'

'Who knows?'

'And why stop us?'

'They didn't know what we were carrying – and maybe they just wanted the car.'

'Blasting, it's a helluva way to get it.'

'If they can't have it, why should they let us keep it?'

'You know just how they think, don't you?'

'Yes.'

'Have a cigarette.'

Tanner nodded, accepted.

'It's been pretty bad, you know?'

'I can't argue with that.'

'. . . And we've still got a long way to go.'

'Yeah, so let's get rolling.'

'You said before that you didn't think we'd make it.'

'I've revised my opinion. Now I think we will.'

'After all we've been through?'

'After all we've been through.'

'What more do we have to fight with?'

'I don't know all that yet.'

'But on the other hand, we know everything there is behind us. We know how to avoid a lot of it now.'

Tanner nodded.

'You tried to cut out once. Now I don't blame you.'

'You getting scared, Greg?'

'I'm no good to my family if I'm dead.'

'Then why'd you agree to come along?'

'I didn't know it would be like this. You had better sense, because you had an idea what it would be like.'

'I had an idea.'

'Nobody can blame us if we fail. After all, we've tried.'

'What about all those people in Boston you made me a speech about?'

'They're probably dead by now. The plague isn't a thing that takes its time, you know?'

'What about that guy Brady? He died to get us the news.'

'He tried, and God knows I respect the attempt. But we've already lost four guys. Now should we make it six, just to show that everybody tried?'

'Greg, we're a lot closer to Boston than we are to L.A. now. The tanks should have enough fuel in them to get us where we're going, but not to take us back from here.'

'We can refuel in Salt Lake.'

'I'm not even sure we could make it back to Salt Lake.'

'Well, it'll only take a minute to figure it out. For that matter, though, we could take the bikes for the last hundred or so. They use a lot less gas.'

'And you're the guy who was calling me names. You're the citizen was wondering how people like me happen. You asked me what they ever did to me. I told you, too: Nothing. Now maybe I want to do something for them, just because I feel like it. I've been doing a lot of thinking.'

'You ain't supporting any family. Hell. I've got other people to worry about beside myself.'

'You've got a nice way of putting things when you want to chicken out. You say I'm not really scared, but I've got my mother and my brothers and sisters to worry about, and I got a chick I'm hot on. That's why I'm backing down. No other reason.'

'And that's right, too! I don't understand you. Hell! I don't understand you at all! You're the one who put this idea in my head in the first place!'

'So give it back, and let's get moving.'

He saw Greg's hand slither toward the gun on the door, so he flipped his cigarette into his face and managed to hit him once, in the stomach – a weak, left-handed blow, but it was the best he could manage from that position.

Then Greg threw himself upon him, and he felt himself borne back into his seat. They wrestled, and Greg's fingers clawed their way up to his face toward his eyes.

Tanner got his arms free above the elbows, seized Greg's head, twisted and shoved with all his strength.

Greg hit the dashboard, went stiff, then went slack.

Tanner banged his head against it twice more, just to be sure he wasn't faking. Then he pushed him away and moved back into the driver's seat. He checked all the screens while he caught his breath. There was nothing menacing approaching.

He fetched cord from the utility chest and bound Greg's hands behind his back. He tied his ankles together and ran a line from them to his wrists. Then he positioned him in the seat, reclined it part way and tied him in place within it.

He put the car into gear and headed toward Ohio.

Two hours later Greg began to moan, and Tanner turned the music up to drown him out. Landscape had appeared once more: grass and trees, fields of green, orchards of apples, apples still small and green, white farm houses and brown barns and red barns far removed from the roadway he raced along; rows of corn, green and swaying, brown tassels already visible and obviously tended by someone; fences of split timber, green hedges; lofty, star-leafed maples, fresh-looking road signs, a green-shingled steeple from which the sound of a bell came forth.

The lines in the sky widened, but the sky itself did not darken, as it usually did before a storm. So he drove on into the afternoon, until he reached the Dayton Abyss.

He looked down into the fog-shrouded canyon that had caused him to halt. He scanned to the left and the right, decided upon the left and headed north.

Again, the radiation level was high. And he hurried, slowing only to skirt the crevices, chasms and canyons that emanated from that dark, deep center. Thick yellow vapors seeped forth from some of these and filled the air before him. At one point they were all about him, like a clinging, sulphurous cloud, and a breeze came and parted them. Involuntarily then, he hit the brake, and the car jerked and halted and Greg moaned once more. He stared at the thing for the few seconds that it was visible, then slowly moved forward again.

The sight was not duplicated for the whole of his passage, but it did not easily go from out of his mind, and he could not explain it where he had seen it. Yellow, hanging and grinning, he had seen a crucified skeleton there beside the Abyss. *People*, he decided. *That explains everything.*

When he left the region of fogs the sky was still dark. He did not realize for a time that he was in the open once more. It had taken him close to four hours to skirt Dayton, and now as he headed across a blasted heath, going east again, he saw for a moment, a tiny piece of the sun, like a sickle, fighting its way ashore on the northern bank of a black river in the sky, and failing.

His lights were turned up to their fullest intensity, and as he realized what might follow he looked in every direction for shelter.

There was an old barn on a hill, and he raced toward it. One side had caved in, and the doors had fallen down. He edged in, however, and the interior was moist and moldy looking under his lights. He saw a skeleton which he guessed to be that of a horse within a fallen-down stall.

He parked and turned off his lights and waited.

Soon the wailing came again and drowned out Greg's occasional moans and mutterings. There came another sound, not hard and heavy like gunfire, as that which he had heard in L.A., but gentle, steady and almost purring.

He cracked the door, to hear it better.

Nothing assailed him, so he stepped down from the cab and walked back a way. The radiation level was almost normal, so he didn't bother with his protective suit. He walked back toward the fallen doors and looked outside. He wore the pistol behind his belt.

Something gray descended in droplets and the sun fought itself partly free once more.

It was rain, pure and simple. He had never seen rain, pure and simple, before. So he lit a cigarette and watched it fall.

It came down with only an occasional rumbling and nothing else accompanied it. The sky was still a bluish color beyond the bands of black.

It fell all about him. It ran down the frame to his left. A random gust of wind blew some droplets into his face, and he realized that they were water, nothing more. Puddles formed on the ground outside. He tossed a chunk of wood into one and saw it splash and float. From somewhere high up inside the barn he heard the sounds of birds. He smelled the sick-sweet smell of decaying straw. Off in the shadows to his right he saw a rusted threshing machine. Some feathers drifted down about him, and he caught one in his hand and studied it. Light, dark, fluffy, ribbed. He'd never really looked at a feather before. It worked almost like a zipper, the way the individual branches clung to one another. He let it go, and the wind caught it, and it vanished somewhere toward his back. He looked out once more, and back along his trail. He could probably drive through what was coming down now. But he realized just how tired he was. He found a barrel and sat down on it and lit another cigarette.

It had been a good run so far; and he found himself thinking about its last stages. He couldn't trust Greg for awhile yet. Not until they were so far that there could be no turning back. Then they'd need each other so badly that he could turn him loose. He hoped he hadn't scrambled his brains completely. He didn't know what more the Alley held. If the storms were less from here on in, however, that would be a big help.

He sat there for a long while, feeling the cold, moist breezes; and the rainfall lessened after a time, and he went back to the car and started it. Greg was still unconscious, he noted, as he backed out. This might not be good.

He took a pill to keep himself alert and he ate some rations as he drove along. The rain continued to come down, but gently. It fell all the way across Ohio, and the sky remained overcast. He crossed into West Virginia at the place called Parkersburg, and then he veered slightly to the north, going by the old Rand-McNally he'd been furnished. The gray day went away into black night, and he drove on.

There were no more of the dark bats around to trouble him, but he passed several more craters and the radiation gauge rose, and at one point a pack of huge wild dogs pursued him, baying and howling, and they ran along the road and snapped at his tires and barked and yammered and then fell back. There were some tremors beneath his wheels as he passed another mountain that spewed forth bright clouds to his left and made a kind of thunder. Ashes fell, and he drove through them. A flash flood splashed over him, and the engine sputtered and died, twice; but be started it again each time and pushed on ahead, the waters lapping about his sides. Then he reached higher, drier ground, and riflemen tried to bar his way. He strafed them and hurled a grenade and drove on by. When the darkness went away and the dim moon came up, dark birds

95

circled him and dove down at him, but he ignored them and after a time they, too, were gone.

He drove until he felt tired again, and then he ate some more and took another pill. By then he was in Pennsylvania, and he felt that if Greg would only come around he would turn him loose and trust him with the driving.

He halted twice to visit the latrine, and he tugged at the golden band in his pierced left ear, and he blew his nose and scratched himself. Then he ate more rations and continued on.

He began to ache, in all his muscles, and he wanted to stop and rest, but he was afraid of the things that might come upon him if he did.

As he drove through another dead town, the rains started again. Not hard, just a drizzly downpour, cold-looking and sterile – a brittle, shiny screen. He stopped in the middle of the road before the thing he'd almost driven into, and he stared at it.

He'd thought at first that it was more black lines in the sky. He'd halted because they'd seemed to appear too suddenly.

It was a spider's web, strands thick as his arm, strung between two leaning buildings.

He switched on his forward flame and began to burn it.

When the fires died, he saw the approaching shape, coming down from high above.

It was a spider, larger than himself, rushing to check the disturbance.

He elevated the rocket launchers, took careful aim and pierced it with one white-hot missile.

It still hung there in the trembling web and seemed to be kicking.

He turned on the flame again, for a full ten seconds, and when it subsided there was an open way before him.

He rushed through, wide awake and alert once again, his pains forgotten. He drove as fast as he could, trying to forget the sight.

Another mountain smoked ahead and to his right, but it did not bloom, and few ashes descended as he passed it.

He made coffee and drank a cup. After awhile it was morning, and he raced toward it.

## XI

He was stuck in the mud, somewhere in eastern Pennsylvania, and cursing. Greg was looking very pale. The sun was nearing midheaven. He leaned back and closed his eyes. It was too much.

He slept.

He awoke and felt worse. There was a banging on the side of the car. His hands moved toward fire-control and wing-control, automatically, and his eyes sought the screens.

He saw an old man, and there were two younger men with him. They were armed, but they stood right before the left wing, and he knew he could cut them in half in an instant.

He activated the outside speaker and the audio pickup.

'What do you want?' he asked, and his voice crackled forth.

'You okay?' the old man called.

'Not really. You caught me sleeping.'

'You stuck?'

'That's about the size of it.'

'I got a mule team can maybe get you out. Can't get 'em here before tomorrow morning, though.'

'Great!' said Tanner. 'I'd appreciate it.'

'Where you from?'

'L.A.'

'What's that?'

'Los Angeles. West Coast.'

There was some murmuring, then, 'You're a long way from home, mister.'

'Don't I know it. —Look, if you're serious about those mules, I'd appreciate hell out of it. It's an emergency.'

'What kind of?'

97

'You know about Boston?'

'I know it's there.'

'Well, people are dying up that way of the plague. I've got drugs here can save them, if I can get through.'

There were some more murmurs, then, 'We'll help you. Boston's pretty important, and we'll get you loose. Want to come back with us?'

'Where? And who are you?'

'The name's Samuel Potter, and these are my sons, Roderick and Caliban. My farm's about six miles off. You're welcome to spend the night.'

'It's not that I don't trust you,' said Tanner. 'It's just that I don't trust anybody, if you know what I mean. I've been shot at too much recently to want to take the chance.'

'Well, how about if we put up our guns? You're probably able to shoot us from there, ain't you?'

'That's right.'

'So we're taking a chance just standing here. We're willing to help you. We'd stand to lose if the Boston traders stopped coming to Albany. If there's someone else inside, he can cover you.'

'Wait a minute,' said Tanner, and he opened the door.

The old man stuck out his hand, and Tanner took it and shook it, also his sons'.

'Is there any kind of doctor around here?' he asked.

'In the settlement – about thirty miles north.'

'My partner's hurt. I think he needs a doctor.' He gestured back toward the cab.

Sam moved forward and peered within.

'Why's he all trussed up like that?'

'He went off his rocker, and I had to clobber him. I tied him up, to be safe. But now he doesn't look so good.'

'Then let's whip up a stretcher and get him onto it. You lock up tight then, and my boys'll bring him back to the house. We'll send someone for the Doc. You don't look so good yourself. Bet you'd like a bath and a shave and a clean bed.'

'I don't feel so good,' Tanner said. 'Let's make that stretcher quick, before we need two.'

He sat upon the fender and smoked while the Potter boys cut trees and stripped them. Waves of fatigue washed over him, and he found it hard to keep his eyes open. His feet felt very far away, and his shoulders ached. The cigarette fell from his fingers, and he leaned backward on the hood.

Someone was slapping his leg.

He forced his eyes open and looked down.

'Okay,' Potter said. 'We cut your partner loose and we got him on the stretcher. Want to lock up and get moving?'

Tanner nodded and jumped down. He sank almost up to his boot tops when he hit, but he closed the cab and staggered toward the old man in buckskin.

They began walking across country, and after awhile it became mechanical.

Samuel Potter kept up a steady line of chatter as he led the way, rifle resting in the crook of his arm. Maybe it was to keep Tanner awake.

'It's not too far, son, and it'll be pretty easy going in just a few minutes now. What'd you say your name was anyhow?'

'Hell,' said Tanner.

'Beg pardon?'

'Hell. Hell's my name. Hell Tanner.'

Sam Potter chuckled. 'That's a pretty mean name, mister. If it's okay with you, I'll introduce you to my wife and the youngest as "Mister Tanner." All right?'

'That's just fine,' Tanner gasped, pulling his boots out of the mire with a sucking sound.

'We'd sure miss them Boston traders. I hope you make it in time.'

'What is it that they do?'

'They keep shops in Albany, and twice a year they give a fair – spring and fall. They carry all sort of things we need – needles, thread, pepper, kettles, pans, seed, guns and ammo, all kind of things – and the fairs are pretty good times, too. Most

99

anybody between here and there would help you along. Hope you make it. We'll get you off to a good start again.'

They reached higher, drier ground.

'You mean it's pretty clear sailing after this?'

'Well, no. But I'll help you on a map and tell you what to look out for.'

'I got mine with me,' said Tanner, as they topped a hill, and he saw a farm house off in the distance. 'That your place?'

'Correct. It ain't much further now. Real easy walkin' – an' you just lean on my shoulder if you get tired.'

'I can make it,' said Tanner. 'It's just that I had so many of those pills to keep me awake that I'm starting to feel all the sleep I've been missing. I'll be okay.'

'You'll get to sleep real soon now. And when you're awake again, we'll go over that map of yours, and you can write in all the places I tell you about.'

'Good scene,' said Tanner, 'good scene,' and he put his hand on Sam's shoulder then and staggered along beside him, feeling almost drunk and wishing he were.

After a hazy eternity be saw the house before him, then the door. The door swung open, and he felt himself falling forward, and that was it.

## XII

Sleep. Blackness, distant voices, more blackness. Wherever he lay, it was soft, and he turned over onto his other side and went away again.

When everything finally flowed together into a coherent ball and he opened his eyes, there was light streaming in through the window to his right, falling in rectangles upon the patchwork quilt that covered him. He groaned, stretched, rubbed his eyes and scratched his beard.

He surveyed the room carefully; polished wooden floors with handwoven rugs of blue and red and gray scattered about them, a dresser holding a white enamel basin with a few black spots up near its lip where some of the enamel had chipped away, a mirror on the wall behind him and above all that, a spindly looking rocker near the window, a print cushion on its seat, a small table against the other wall with a chair pushed in beneath it, books and paper and pen and ink on the table, a hand-stitched sampler on the wall asking God To Bless, a blue and green print of a waterfall on the other wall.

He sat up, discovered he was naked, looked around for his clothing. It was nowhere in sight.

As he sat there, deciding whether or not to call out, the door opened, and Sam walked in. He carried Tanner's clothing, clean and neatly folded, over one arm. In his other hand he carried his boots, and they shone like wet midnight.

'Heard you stirring around,' he said. 'How you feeling now?'

'A lot better, thanks.'

'We've got a bath all drawn. Just have to dump in a couple buckets of hot, and it's all yours. I'll have the boys carry it in in a minute, and some soap and towels.'

Tanner bit his lip, but he didn't want to seem inhospitable to his benefactor, so he nodded and forced a smile then.

'That'll be fine.'

'. . . And there's a razor and a scissors on the dresser – whichever you might want.'

He nodded again. Sam set his clothes down on the rocker and his boots on the floor beside it, then left the room.

Soon Roderick and Caliban brought in the tub, spread some sacks and set it upon them.

'How you feeling?' one of them asked. (Tanner wasn't sure which was which. They both seemed graceful as scarecrows, and their mouths were packed full of white teeth.)

'Real good,' he said.

'Bet you're hungry,' said the other. 'You slep' all afternoon yesterday and all night and most of this morning.'

'You know it,' said Tanner. 'How's my partner?'

The nearer one shook his head. 'Still sleeping and sickly,' he said. 'The doc should be here soon. Our kid brother went after him last night.'

They turned to leave, and the one who had been speaking added, 'Soon as you get cleaned up, Ma'll fix you something to eat. Cal and me are going out now to try and get your rig loose. Dad'll tell you about the roads while you eat.'

'Thanks.'

'Good morning to you.'

''Morning.'

They closed the door behind them as they left.

Tanner got up and moved to the mirror, studied himself. 'Well, just this once,' he muttered.

Then he washed his face and trimmed his beard and cut his hair.

Then, gritting his teeth, he lowered himself into the tub, soaped up and scrubbed. The water grew gray and scummy beneath the suds. He splashed out and toweled himself down and dressed.

He was starched and crinkly and smelled faintly of disinfectant. He smiled at his dark-eyed reflection and lit a cigarette. He combed his hair and studied the stranger. 'Damn! I'm beautiful!' he chuckled, and then he opened the door and entered the kitchen.

Sam was sitting at the table drinking a cup of coffee, and his wife who was short and heavy and wore long gray skirts was facing in the other direction, leaning over the stove. She turned, and he saw that her face was large, with bulging red cheeks that dimpled and a little white scar in the middle of her forehead. Her hair was brown, shot through with gray, and pulled back into a knot. She bobbed her head and smiled a 'Good morning' at him.

''Morning,' he replied. 'I'm afraid I left kind of a mess in the other room.'

'Don't worry about that,' said Sam. 'Seat yourself, and we'll have you some breakfast in a minute. The boys told you about your friend?'

Tanner nodded.

As she placed a cup of coffee in front of Tanner, Sam said, 'Wife's name's Susan.'

'How do,' she said.

'Hi.'

'Now, then, I got your map here. Saw it sticking out of your jacket. That's your gun hanging aside the door, too. Anyhow, I've been figuring and I think the best way you could head would be up to Albany and then go along the old Route 9, which is in pretty good shape.' He spread the map and pointed as he talked. 'Now, it won't be all of a picnic,' he said, 'but it looks like the cleanest and fastest way in—'

'Breakfast,' said his wife and pushed the map aside to set a plate full of eggs and bacon and sausages in front of Tanner and another one, holding four pieces of toast, next to it. There was marmalade, jam, jelly and butter on the table, and Tanner helped himself to it and sipped the coffee and filled the empty places inside while Sam talked.

He told him about the gangs that ran between Boston and Albany on bikes, hijacking anything they could, and that was the reason most cargo went in convoys with shotgun riders aboard. 'But you don't have to worry, with that rig of yours, do you?' he asked.

Tanner said, 'Hope not,' and wolfed down more food. He wondered, though, if they were anything like his old pack, and he hoped not, again, for both their sakes.

Tanner raised his coffee cup, and he heard a sound outside.

The door opened, and a boy ran into the kitchen. Tanner figured him as between ten and twelve years of age. An older man followed him, carrying the traditional black bag.

'We're here! We're here!' cried the boy, and Sam stood and shook hands with the man, so Tanner figured he should, too. He wiped his mouth and gripped the man's hand and said, 'My partner sort of went out of his head. He jumped me, and we had a fight. I shoved him, and he banged his head on the dashboard.'

The doctor, a dark-haired man, probably in his late forties, wore a dark suit. His face was heavily lined, and his eyes looked tired. He nodded.

Sam said, 'I'll take you to him,' and he led him out through the door at the other end of the kitchen.

Tanner reseated himself and picked up the last piece of toast. Susan refilled his coffee cup, and he nodded to her.

'My name's Jerry,' said the boy, seating himself in his father's abandoned chair. 'Is your name, mister, really Hell?'

'Hush, you!' said his mother.

''Fraid so,' said Tanner.

'. . . And you drove all the way across the country? Through the Alley?'

'So far.'

'What was it like?'

'Mean.'

'What all'd you see?'

'Bats as big as this kitchen – some of them even bigger – on the other side of the Missus Hip. Lot of them in Saint Louis.'

'What'd you do?'

'Shot 'em. Burned 'em. Drove through 'em.'

'What else you see?'

'Gila monsters. Big, technicolor lizards – the size of a barn. Dust Devils – big circling winds that sucked up one car. Fire-topped mountains. Real big thorn bushes that we had to burn. Drove through some storms. Drove over places where the ground was like glass. Drove along where the ground was shaking. Drove around big craters, all radioactive.'

'Wish I could do that some day.'

'Maybe you will, some day.'

Tanner finished the food and lit a cigarette and sipped the coffee.

'Real good breakfast,' he called out. 'Best I've eaten in days. Thanks.'

Susan smiled, then said, 'Jerry, don't go an' pester the man.'

'No bother, missus. He's okay.'

'What's that ring on your hand?' said Jerry. 'It looks like a snake.'

'That's what it is,' said Tanner, pulling it off. 'It is sterling silver with red glass eyes, and I got it in a place called Tijuana. Here. You keep it.'

'I couldn't take that,' said the boy, and he looked at his mother, his eyes asking if he could. She shook her head from left to right, and Tanner saw it and said, 'Your folks were good enough to help me out and get a doc for my partner and feed me and give me a place to sleep. I'm sure they won't mind if I want to show my appreciation a little bit and give you this ring.' Jerry looked back at his mother, and Tanner nodded and she nodded too.

Jerry whistled and jumped up and put it on his finger.

'It's too big,' he said.

'Here, let me mash it a bit for you. These spiral kind'll fit anybody if you squeeze them a little.'

He squeezed the ring and gave it back to the boy to try on. It was still too big, so he squeezed it again and then it fit.

Jerry put it on and began to run from the room.

'Wait!' his mother said. 'What do you say?'

He turned around and said, 'Thank you, Hell.'

'Mister Tanner,' she said.

'Mister Tanner,' the boy repeated, and the door banged behind him.

'That was good of you,' she said.

Tanner shrugged.

'He liked it,' he said. 'Glad I could turn him on with it.'

He finished his coffee and his cigarette, and she gave him another cup, and he lit another cigarette. After a time, Sam and the doctor came out of the other room, and Tanner began wondering where the family had slept the night before. Susan poured them both coffee, and they seated themselves at the table to drink it.

'Your friend's got a concussion,' the doctor said. 'I can't really tell how serious his condition is without getting X-rays, and there's no way of getting them here. I wouldn't recommend moving him, though.'

Tanner said, 'For how long?'

'Maybe a few days, maybe a couple weeks. I've left some

medication and told Sam what to do for him. Sam says there's a plague in Boston and you've got to hurry. My advice is that you go on without him. Leave him here with the Potters. He'll be taken care of. He can go up to Albany with them for the Spring Fair and make his way to Boston from there on some commercial carrier. I think he'll be all right.'

Tanner thought about it awhile, then nodded.

'Okay,' he said, 'if that's the way it's got to be.'

'That's what I recommend.'

They drank their coffee.

## XIII

Tanner regarded his freed vehicle, said, 'I guess I'll be going then,' and nodded to the Potters. 'Thanks,' he said, and he unlocked the cab, climbed into it and started the engine. He put it into gear, blew the horn twice and started to move.

In the screen, he saw the three men waving. He stamped the accelerator, and they were gone from sight.

He sped ahead, and the way was easy. The sky was salmon pink. The earth was brown, and there was much green grass. The bright sun caught the day in a silver net.

This part of the country seemed virtually untouched by the chaos that had produced the rest of the Alley. Tanner played music, drove along. He passed two trucks on the road and honked his horn each time. Once, he received a reply.

He drove all that day, and it was well into the night when he pulled into Albany. The streets themselves were dark, and only a few lights shone from the buildings. He drew up in front of a flickering red sign that said 'BAR & GRILL,' parked and entered.

It was small, and there was jukebox music playing, tunes he'd never heard before, and the lighting was poor, and there was sawdust on the floor.

He sat down at the bar and pushed the Magnum way down behind his belt so that it didn't show. Then he took off his jacket, because of the heat in the place, and he threw it on the stool next to him. When the man in the white apron approached, he said, 'Give me a shot and a beer and a ham sandwich.'

The man nodded his bald head and threw a shot glass in front of Tanner which he then filled. He siphoned off a foam-capped mug and hollered over his right shoulder.

Tanner tossed off the shot and sipped the beer. After a while, a white plate bearing a sandwich appeared on the sill across from him. After a longer while, the bartender passed, picked it up, and deposited it in front of him. He wrote something on a green chit and tucked it under the corner of the plate.

Tanner bit into the sandwich and washed it down with a mouthful of beer. He studied the people about him and decided they made the same noises as people in any other bar he'd ever been in. The old man to his left looked friendly, so he asked him, 'Any news about Boston?'

The man's chin quivered between words, and it seemed a natural thing for him.

'No news at all. Looks like the merchants will close their shops at the end of the week.'

'What day is today?'

'Tuesday.'

Tanner finished his sandwich and smoked a cigarette while he drank the rest of his beer.

Then he looked at the check, and it said, '.85.'

He tossed a dollar bill on top of it and turned to go.

He had taken two steps when the bartender called out, 'Wait a minute, mister.'

He turned around.

'Yeah?'

'What you trying to pull?'

'What do you mean?'

'What do you call this crap?'

'What crap?'

The man waved Tanner's dollar at him, and he stepped forward and inspected it.

'Nothing wrong I can see. What's giving you a pain?'

'That ain't money.'

'You trying to tell me my money's no good?'

'That's what I said. I never seen no bill like that.'

'Well, look at it real careful. Read that print down there at the bottom of it.'

The room grew quiet. One man got off his stool and walked forward. He held out his hand and said, 'Let me see it, Bill.'

The bartender passed it to him, and the man's eyes widened.

'This is drawn on the Bank of the Nation of California.'

'Well, that's where I'm from,' said Tanner.

'I'm sorry, it's no good here,' said the bartender.

'It's the best I got,' said Tanner.

'Well, nobody'll make good on it around here. You got any Boston money on you?'

'Never been to Boston.'

'Then how the hell'd you get here?'

'Drove.'

'Don't hand me that line of crap, son. Where'd you steal this?' It was the older man who had spoken.

'You going to take my money or ain't you?' said Tanner.

'I'm not going to take it,' said the bartender.

'Then screw you,' said Tanner, and he turned and walked toward the door.

As always, under such circumstances, he was alert to sounds at his back.

When he heard the quick footfall, he turned. It was the man who had inspected the bill that stood before him, his right arm extended.

Tanner's right hand held his leather jacket, draped over his right shoulder. He swung it with all his strength forward and down.

It struck the man on the top of his head, and he fell.

There came up a murmuring, and several people jumped to their feet and moved toward him.

Tanner dragged the gun from his belt and said, 'Sorry, folks,' and he pointed it, and they stopped.

'Now you probably ain't about to believe me,' he said, 'when I tell you that Boston's been hit by the plague, but it's true all right. Or maybe you will. I don't know. But I don't think you're going to believe that I drove here all the way from the nation of California with a car full of Haffikine antiserum. But that's just as right. You send that bill to the big bank in Boston, and they'll change it for you, all right, and you know it. Now I've got to be going, and don't anybody try to stop me. If you think I've been handing you a line, you take a look at what I drive away in. That's all I've got to say.'

And he backed out the door and covered it while he mounted the cab. Inside, he gunned the engine to life, turned, and roared away.

In the rearview screen he could see the knot of people on the walk before the bar, watching him depart.

He laughed, and the apple-blossom moon hung dead ahead.


XIV


Albany to Boston. A couple of hundred miles. He'd managed the worst of it. The terrors of Damnation Alley lay largely at his back now. Night. It flowed about him. The stars seemed brighter than usual. He'd make it, the night seemed to say.

He passed between hills. The road wasn't too bad. It wound between trees and high grasses. He passed a truck coming in his direction and dimmed his lights as it approached. It did the same.

It must have been around midnight that he came to the crossroads, and the lights suddenly nailed him from two directions.

He was bathed in perhaps thirty beams from the left and as many from the right.

He pushed the accelerator to the floor, and he heard engine after engine coming to life somewhere at his back. And he recognized the sounds.

They were all of them bikes.

109

They swung onto the road behind him.

He could have opened fire. He could have braked and laid down a cloud of flame. It was obvious that they didn't know what they were chasing. He could have launched grenades. He refrained, however.

It could have been him on the lead bike, he decided, all hot on hijack. He felt a certain sad kinship as his hand hovered above the fire-control.

Try to outrun them, first.

His engine was open wide and roaring, but he couldn't take the bikes.

When they began to fire, he knew that he'd have to retaliate. He couldn't risk their hitting a gas tank or blowing out his tires.

Their first few shots had been in the nature of a warning. He couldn't risk another barrage. If only they knew...

The speaker!

He cut in and mashed the button and spoke:

'Listen, cats,' he said. 'All I got's medicine for the sick citizens in Boston. Let me through or you'll hear the noise.'

A shot followed immediately, so he opened fire with the fifty calibers to the rear.

He saw them fall, but they kept firing. So he launched grenades.

The firing lessened, but didn't cease.

So he hit the brakes, then the flame-throwers. He kept it up for fifteen seconds.

There was silence.

When the air cleared he studied the screens.

They lay all over the road, their bikes upset, their bodies fuming. Several were still seated, and they held rifles and pointed them, and he shot them down.

A few still moved, spasmodically, and he was about to drive on, when he saw one rise and take a few staggering steps and fall again.

His hand hesitated on the gearshift.

It was a girl.

He thought about it for perhaps five seconds, then jumped down from the cab and ran toward her.

As he did, one man raised himself on an elbow and picked up a fallen rifle.

Tanner shot him twice and kept running, pistol in hand.

The girl was crawling toward a man whose face had been shot away. Other bodies twisted about Tanner now, there on the road, in the glare of the tail beacons. Blood and black leather, the sounds of moaning and the stench of burned flesh were all about him.

When he got to the girl's side, she cursed him softly as he stopped.

None of the blood about her seemed to be her own.

He dragged her to her feet and her eyes began to fill with tears.

Everyone else was dead or dying, so Tanner picked her up in his arms and carried her back to the car. He reclined the passenger seat and put her into it, moving the weapons into the rear seat, out of her reach.

Then he gunned the engine and moved forward. In the rear-view screen he saw two figures rise to their feet, then fall again.

She was a tall girl, with long, uncombed hair the color of dirt. She had a strong chin and a wide mouth and there were dark circles under her eyes. A single faint line crossed her forehead, and she had all of her teeth. The right side of her face was flushed, as if sunburned. Her left trouser leg was torn and dirty. He guessed that she'd caught the edge of his flame and fallen from her bike.

'You okay?' he asked, when her sobbing had diminished to a moist sniffing sound.

'What's it to you?' she said, raising a hand to her cheek.

Tanner shrugged.

'Just being friendly.'

'You killed most of my gang.'

'What would they have done to me?'

'They would have stomped you, mister, if it weren't for this fancy car of yours.'

'It ain't really mine,' he said. 'It belongs to the nation of California.'

'This thing don't come from California.'

'The hell it don't. I drove it.'

She sat up straight then and began rubbing her leg.

Tanner lit a cigarette.

'Give me a cigarette?' she said.

He passed her the one he had lighted, lit himself another. As he handed it to her, her eyes rested on his tattoo.

'What's that?'

'My name.'

'Hell?'

'Hell.'

'Where'd you get a name like that?'

'From my old man.'

They smoked awhile, then she said, 'Why'd you run the Alley?'

'Because it was the only way I could get them to turn me loose.'

'From where?'

'The place with horizontal Venetian blinds. I was doing time.'

'They let you go? Why?'

'Because of the big sick. I'm bringing in Haffikine anti-serum.'

'You're Hell Tanner.'

'Huh?'

'Your last name's Tanner, ain't it?'

'That's right. Who told you?'

'I heard about you. Everybody thought you died in the Big Raid.'

'They were wrong.'

'What was it like?'

'I dunno. I was already wearing a zebra suit. That's why I'm still around.'

'Why'd you pick me up?'

''Cause you're a chick, and 'cause I didn't want to see you croak.'

'Thanks. You got anything to eat in here?'

'Yeah, there's food in there.' He pointed to the refrigerator door. 'Help yourself.'

She did, and as she ate Tanner asked her, 'What do they call you?'

'Corny,' she said. 'It's short for Cornelia.'

'Okay, Corny,' he said. 'When you're finished eating, you start telling me about the road between here and the place.'

She nodded, chewed and swallowed. 'There's lots of other gangs,' she said. 'So you'd better be ready to blast them.'

'I am.'

'Those screens show you all directions, huh?'

'That's right.'

'Good. The roads are pretty much okay from here on in. There's one big crater you'll come to soon and a couple little volcanos afterward.'

'Check.'

'Outside of them there's nothing to worry about but the Regents and the Devils and the Kings and the Lovers. That's about it.'

Tanner nodded.

'How big are those clubs?'

'I don't know for sure but the Kings are the biggest. They've got a coupla hundred.'

'What was your club?'

'The Studs.'

'What are you going to do now?'

'Whatever you tell me.'

'Okay, Corny, I'll let you off anywhere along the way that you want me to. If you don't want, you can come on into the city with me.'

'You call it. Hell. Anywhere you want to go, I'll go along.'

Her voice was deep, and her words came slowly, and her tone sandpapered his eardrums just a bit. She had long legs and heavy thighs beneath the tight denim. Tanner licked his lips and studied the screens. Did he want to keep her around for awhile?

The road was suddenly wet. It was covered with hundreds of fish, and more were falling from the sky. There followed several loud reports from overhead. The blue light began in the north.

Tanner raced on, and suddenly there was water all about him. It fell upon his car, it dimmed his screens. The sky had grown black again, and the banshee wail sounded above him.

He skidded around a sharp curve in the road. He turned up his lights.

The rain ceased, but the wailing continued. He ran for fifteen minutes before it built up into a roar.

The girl stared at the screens and occasionally glanced at Tanner.

'What're you going to do?' she finally asked him.

'Outrun it, if I can,' he said.

'It's dark for as far ahead as I can see. I don't think you can do it.'

'Neither do I, but what does that leave?'

'Hole up someplace.'

'If you know where, you show me.'

'There's a place a few miles further ahead – a bridge you can get under.'

'Okay, that's for us. Sing out when you see it.'

She pulled off her boots and rubbed her feet. He gave her another cigarette.

'Hey, Corny – I just thought – there's a medicine chest over there to your right. Yeah, that's it. It should have some damn kind of salve in it you can smear on your face to take the bite out.'

She found a tube of something and rubbed some of it into her cheek, smiled slightly and replaced it.

'Feel any better?'

'Yes. Thanks.'

The stones began to fall, the blue to spread. The sky pulsed, grew brighter.

'I don't like the looks of this one.'

'I don't like the looks of any of them.'

'It seems there's been an awful lot this past week.'

'Yeah. I've heard it said maybe the winds are dying down – that the sky might be purging itself.'

'That'd be nice,' said Tanner.

'Then we might be able to see it the way it used to look – blue all the time, and with clouds. You know about clouds.'

'I heard about them.'

'White, puffy things that just sort of drift across – sometimes gray. They don't drop anything except rain, and not always that.'

'Yeah, I know.'

'You ever see any out in L.A.?'

'No.'

The yellow streaks began, and the black lines writhed like snakes. The stonefall rattled heavily upon the roof and the hood. More water began to fall, and a fog rose up. Tanner was forced to slow, and then it seemed as if sledgehammers beat upon the car.

'We won't make it,' she said.

'The hell you say. This thing's built to take it – and what's that off in the distance?'

'The bridge!' she said, moving forward. 'That's it! Pull off the road to the left and go down. That's a dry riverbed beneath.'

Then the lightning began to fall. It flamed, flashed about them. They passed a burning tree, and there were still fishes in the roadway.

Tanner turned left as he approached the bridge. He slowed to a crawl and made his way over the shoulder and down the slick, muddy grade.

When he hit the damp riverbed he turned right. He nosed it in under the bridge, and they were all alone there. Some waters trickled past them, and the lightning continued to flash. The sky was a shifting kaleidoscope and constant came the thunder. He could hear a sound like hail on the bridge above them.

'We're safe,' he said and killed the engine.

'Are the doors locked?'

'They do it automatically.'

Tanner turned off the outside lights.

'Wish I could buy you a drink, besides coffee.'

'Coffee'd be good, just right.'

'Okay, it's on the way,' and he cleaned out the pot and filled it and plugged it in.

They sat there and smoked as the storm raged, and he said, 'You know, it's a kind of nice feeling, being all snug as a rat in a hole while everything goes to hell outside. Listen to that bastard come down! And we couldn't care less.'

'I suppose so,' she said. 'What're you going to do after you make it to Boston?'

'Oh, I don't know . . . Maybe get a job, scrape up some loot, and maybe open a bike shop or a garage. Either one'd be nice.'

'Sounds good. You going to ride much yourself?'

'You bet. I don't suppose they have any good clubs in town?'

'No. They're all roadrunners.'

'Thought so. Maybe I'll organize my own.'

He reached out and touched her hand, then squeezed it.

'I can buy *you* a drink.'

'What do you mean?'

She drew a plastic flask from the right side pocket of her jacket. She uncapped it and passed it to him.

'Here.'

He took a mouthful and gulped it, coughed, took a second, then handed it back.

'Great! You're a woman of unsuspected potential and I like that. Thanks.'

'Don't mention it.' She took a drink herself and set the flask on the dash.

'Cigarette?'

'Just a minute.'

He lit two, passed her one.

'There you are. Corny.'

'Thanks. I'd like to help you finish this run.'

116

'How come?'

'I got nothing else to do. My crowd's all gone away, and I've got nobody else to run with now. Also, if you make it, you'll be a big man. Like capital letters. Think you might keep me around after that?'

'Maybe. What are you like?'

'Oh, I'm real nice. I'll even rub your shoulders for you when they're sore.'

'They're sore now.'

'I thought so. Give me a lean.'

He bent toward her, and she began to rub his shoulders. Her hands were quick and strong.

'You do that good, girl.'

'Thanks.'

He straightened up, leaned back. Then he reached out, took the flask and had another drink. She took a small sip when he passed it to her.

The furies rode about them, but the bridge above stood the siege. Tanner turned off the lights.

'Let's make it,' he said, and he seized her and drew her to him.

She did not resist him, and he found her belt buckle and unfastened it. Then he started on the buttons. After awhile, he reclined her seat.

'Will you keep me?' she asked him.

'Sure.'

'I'll help you. I'll do anything you say to get you through.'

'Great.'

'After all, if Boston goes, then we go, too.'

'You bet.'

Then they didn't say much more.

There was violence in the skies, and after that came darkness and quiet.

## XV

When Tanner awoke, it was morning and the storm had ceased. He repaired himself to the rear of the vehicle and after that assumed the driver's seat once more.

Cornelia did not awaken as he gunned the engine to life and started up the weed-infested slope of the hillside.

The sky was light once more, and the road was strewn with rubble. Tanner wove along it, heading toward the pale sun, and after awhile Cornelia stretched.

'Ungh,' she said, and Tanner agreed. 'My shoulders are better now,' he told her.

'Good,' and Tanner headed up a hill, slowly as the day dimmed and one huge black line became the Devil's highway down the middle of the sky.

As he drove through a wooded valley, the rain began to fall. The girl had returned from the rear of the vehicle and was preparing breakfast when Tanner saw the tiny dot on the horizon, switched over to his telescope lenses and tried to outrun what he saw.

Cornelia looked up.

There were bikes, bikes and more bikes on their trail.

'Those your people?' Tanner asked.

'No. You took mine yesterday.'

'Too bad,' said Tanner, and he pushed the accelerator to the floor and hoped for a storm.

They squealed around a curve and climbed another hill. His pursuers drew nearer. He switched back from telescope to normal screening, but even then he could see the size of the crowd that approached.

'It must be the Kings,' she said. 'They're the biggest club around.'

'Too bad,' said Tanner.

'For them or for us?'

'Both.'

She smiled.

'I'd like to see how you work this thing.'

'It looks like you're going to get a chance. They're gaining on us like mad.'

The rain lessened, but the fogs grew heavier. Tanner could see their lights, though, over a quarter mile to his rear, and be did not turn his own on. He estimated a hundred to a hundred fifty pursuers that cold, dark morning, and he asked, 'How near are we to Boston?'

'Maybe ninety miles,' she told him.

'Too bad they're chasing us instead of coming toward us,' he said, as he primed his flames and set an adjustment which brought cross-hairs into focus on his rearview screen.

'What's that?' she asked.

'That's a cross. I'm going to crucify them, lady,' and she smiled at this and squeezed his arm.

'Can I help? I hate those bloody mothers.'

'In a little while,' said Tanner. 'In a little while, I'm sure,' and he reached into the rear seat and fetched out the six hand grenades and hung them on his wide, black belt. He passed the rifle to the girl. 'Hang onto this,' he said, and stuck the .45 behind his belt.

'Do you know how to use that thing?'

'Yes,' she replied immediately.

'Good.'

He kept watching the lights that danced on the screen.

'Why the hell doesn't this storm break?' he said, as the lights came closer and he could make out shapes within the fog.

When they were within a hundred feet he fired the first grenade. It arched through the gray air, and five seconds later there was a bright flash to his rear, burning within a thunder-clap.

The lights immediately behind him remained, and he touched the fifty-calibers, moving the cross-hairs from side to side. The guns shattered their loud syllables, and he launched another grenade. With the second flash, he began to climb another hill.

'Did you stop them?'

'For a time, maybe. I still see some lights, but farther back.'

After five minutes, they had reached the top, a place where the fogs were cleared and the dark sky was visible above them. Then they started downward once more, and a wall of stone and shale and dirt rose to their right. Tanner considered it as they descended.

When the road leveled and he decided they had reached the bottom, he turned on his brightest lights and looked for a place where the road's shoulders were wide.

To his rear, there were suddenly rows of descending lights.

He found the place where the road was sufficiently wide, and he skidded through a U-turn until he was facing the shaggy cliff, now to his left, and his pursuers were coming dead on.

He elevated his rockets, fired one, elevated them five degrees more, fired two, elevated them another five degrees, fired three. Then he lowered them fifteen and fired another.

There was brightness within the fog, and he heard the stones rattling on the road and felt the vibration as the rockslide began. He swung toward his right as he backed the vehicle and fired two ahead. There was dust, mixed with the fog now, and the vibration continued.

He turned and headed forward once more.

'I hope that'll hold 'em,' he said, and he lit two cigarettes and passed one to the girl.

After five minutes they were on higher ground again and the winds came and whipped at the fog, and far to the rear there were still some lights.

As they topped a high rise, his radiation gauge began to register an above-normal reading. He sought in all directions and saw the crater far off ahead. 'That's it,' he heard her say. 'You've got to leave the road there. Bear to the right and go around that way when you get there.'

'I'll do that thing.'

He heard gunshots from behind him, for the first time that day, and though he adjusted the cross-hairs he did not fire his own weapons. The distance was still too great.

'You must have cut them in half,' she said, staring into the screen. 'More than that. They're a tough bunch, though.'

'I gather,' and he plowed the field of mists and checked his supply of grenades for the launcher and saw that he was running low.

He swung off the road to his right when he began bumping along over fractured concrete. The radiation level was quite high by then. The crater was slightly more than a thousand yards to his left.

The lights to his rear fanned out, grew brighter. He drew a bead on the brightest and fired. It went out.

'There's another down,' he remarked, as they raced across the hard-baked plain.

The rains came more heavily, and he sighted in on another light and fired it. It, too, went out, though he heard the sounds of their weapons about him once again.

He switched to his right-hand guns and saw the cross-hairs leap into life on that screen. As three vehicles moved in to flank him from that direction, he opened up and cut them down. There was more firing at his back, and he ignored it as he negotiated the way.

'I count twenty-seven lights,' Cornelia said.

Tanner wove his way across a field of boulders. He lit another cigarette.

Five minutes later, they were running on both sides of him. He had held back again for that moment, to conserve ammunition and to be sure of his targets. He fired then, though, at every light within range, and he floored the accelerator and swerved around rocks.

'Five of them are down,' she said, but he was listening to the gunfire.

He launched a grenade to the rear, and when he tried to launch a second there came only a clicking sound from the control. He launched one to either side and then paused for a second.

'If they get close enough, I'll show them some fire,' he said, and they continued on around the crater.

He fired only at individual targets then, when he was certain they were within range. He took two more before he struck the broken roadbed.

'Keep running parallel to it,' she told him. 'There's a trail here. You can't drive on that stuff till another mile or so.'

Shots richocheted from off his armored sides, and he continued to return the fire. He raced along an alleyway of twisted trees, like those he had seen near other craters, and the mists hung like pennons about their branches. He heard the rattle of the increasing rains.

When he hit the roadway once again, he regarded the lights to his rear and asked, 'How many do you count now?'

'It looks like around twenty. How are we doing?'

'I'm just worried about the tires. They can take a lot, but they can be shot out. The only other thing that bothers me is that a stray shot might clip one of the "eyes." Outside of that we're bullet-proof enough. Even if they manage to stop us, they'll have to pry us out.'

The bikes drew near once again, and he saw the bright flashes and heard the reports of the riders' guns.

'Hold tight,' he said, and he hit the brakes and they skidded on the wet pavement.

The lights grew suddenly bright, and he unleashed his rear flame. As some bikes skirted him, he cut in the side flames and held them that way.

Then he took his foot off the brake and floored the accelerator without waiting to assess the damage he had done.

They sped ahead, and Tanner, heard Cornelia's laughter.

'God! You're taking them. Hell! You're taking the whole damn club!'

'It ain't that much fun,' he said. Then, 'See any lights?'

She watched for a time, said, 'No,' then said, 'Three,' then, 'Seven,' and finally, 'Thirteen.'

Tanner said. 'Damn.'

The radiation level fell and there came crashes amid the roaring overhead. A light fall of gravel descended for perhaps half a minute, along with the rain.

'We're running low,' he said.

'On what?'

'Everything: Luck, fuel, ammo. Maybe you'd have been better off if I'd left you where I found you.'

'No,' she said. 'I'm with you, the whole line.'

'Then you're nuts,' he said. 'I haven't been hurt yet. When I am, it might be a different tune.'

'Maybe,' she said. 'Wait and hear how I sing.'

He reached out and squeezed her thigh.

'Okay, Corny. You've been okay so far. Hang onto that piece, and we'll see what happens.'

He reached for another cigarette, found the pack empty, cursed. He gestured toward a compartment, and she opened it and got him a fresh pack. She tore it open and lit him one.

'Thanks.'

'Why're they staying out of range?'

'Maybe they're just going to pace us. I don't know.'

Then the fogs began to lift. By the time Tanner had finished his cigarette, the visibility had improved greatly. He could make out the dark forms crouched atop their bikes, following, following, nothing more.

'If they just want to keep us company, then I don't care,' he said. 'Let them.'

But there came more gunfire after a time, and he heard a tire go. He slowed, but continued. He took careful aim and strafed them. Several fell.

More gunshots sounded from behind. Another tire blew, and he hit the brakes and skidded, turning about as he slowed. When he faced them, he shot his anchors, to hold him in place, and he discharged his rockets, one after another, at a level parallel to the road. He opened up with his guns and sprayed them as they veered off and approached him from the sides. Then he opened fire to the left. Then the right.

He emptied the right-hand guns, then switched back to the left. He launched the remaining grenades.

The gunfire died down, except for five sources – three to his left and two to his right – coming from somewhere within the trees that lined the road now. Broken bikes and bodies lay behind him, some still smouldering. The pavement was potted and cracked in many places.

He turned the car and proceeded ahead on six wheels.

'We're out of ammo, Corny,' he told her.

'Well, we took an awful lot of them...'

'Yeah.'

As he drove on, he saw five bikes move onto the road. They stayed a good distance behind him, but they stayed.

He tried the radio, but there was no response. He hit the brakes and stopped, and the bikes stopped, too, staying well to the rear.

'Well, at least they're scared of us. They think we still have teeth.'

'We do,' she said.

'Yeah, but not the ones they're thinking about.'

'Better yet.'

'Glad I met you,' said Tanner. 'I can use an optimist. There must be a pony, huh?'

She nodded; he put it into gear and started forward abruptly.

The motorcycles moved ahead also, and they maintained a safe distance. Tanner watched them in the screens and cursed them as they followed.

After awhile they drew nearer again. Tanner roared on for half an hour, and the remaining five edged closer and closer.

When they drew near enough, they began to fire, rifles resting on their handlebars.

Tanner heard several low ricochets, and then another tire went out.

He stopped once more, and the bikes did, too, remaining just out of range of his flames. He cursed and ground ahead again. The car wobbled as he drove, listing to the left. A wrecked pickup truck stood smashed against a tree to his right, its hunched driver a skeleton, its windows smashed and tires missing. Half a sun now stood in the heavens, reaching after nine o'clock; fog-ghosts drifted before them, and the dark band in the sky undulated and more rain fell from it, mixed with dust and small stones and bits of metal. Tanner said, 'Good' as the pinging sounds began, and, 'Hope it gets a lot worse' and his wish came true as the ground began to shake and the blue light began in the north. There came a booming within the roar, and there were several answering crashes as heaps of rubble appeared to his right. 'Hope the next one falls right on our buddies back there,' he said.

He saw an orange glow ahead and to his right. It had been there for several minutes, but he had not become conscious of it until just then.

'Volcano,' she said when he indicated it. 'It means we've got another sixty-five, seventy miles to go.'

He could not tell whether any more shooting was occurring. The sounds coming from overhead and around him were sufficient to mask any gunfire, and the fall of gravel upon the car covered any ricocheting rounds. The five headlights to his rear maintained their pace.

'Why don't they give up?' he said. 'They're taking a pretty bad beating.'

'They're used to it,' she replied, 'and they're riding for blood, which makes a difference.'

Tanner fetched the .357 Magnum from the door clip and passed it to her. 'Hang onto this, too,' he said, and he found a box of ammo in the second compartment and, 'Put these in your pocket,' he added. He stuffed ammo for the .45 into his own jacket. He adjusted the hand grenades upon his belt.

Then the five headlights behind him suddenly became four, and the others slowed, grew smaller. 'Accident, I hope,' he remarked.

They sighted the mountain, a jag-topped cone bleeding fires upon the sky. They left the road and swung far to the left, upon a well marked trail. It took twenty minutes to pass the mountain, and by then he sighted their pursuers once again – four lights to the rear, gaining slowly.

He came upon the road once more and hurried ahead across the shaking ground. The yellow lights moved through the heavens; and heavy, shapeless objects, some several feet across, crashed to the earth about them. The car was buffeted by winds, listed as they moved, would not proceed above forty miles an hour. The radio contained only static.

Tanner rounded a sharp curve, hit the brake, turned off his lights, pulled the pin from a hand grenade and waited with his hand upon the door.

When the lights appeared in the screen, he flung the door wide, leaped down and hurled the grenade through the abrasive rain.

He was into the cab and moving again before he heard the explosion, before the flash occurred upon his screen.

The girl laughed almost hysterically as the car moved ahead.

'You got 'em, Hell. You got 'em!' she cried.

Tanner took a drink from her flask, and she finished its final brown mouthful.

The road grew cracked, pitted, slippery. They topped a high rise and headed downhill. The fog thickened as they descended.

Lights appeared before him, and he readied the flame. There were no hostilities, however, as he passed a truck headed in the other direction. Within the next half hour he passed two more.

There came more lightning, and fist-sized rocks began to fall. Tanner left the road and sought shelter within a grove of high trees. The sky grew competely black, losing even its blue aurora.

They waited for three hours, but the storm did not let up. One by one, the four view-screens went dead and the fifth only showed the blackness beneath the car. Tanner's last sight in the rearview screen was of a huge splintered tree with a broken, swaying branch that was about ready to fall off. There were several terrific crashes upon the hood and the car shook with each. The roof above their heads was deeply dented in three places. The lights grew dim, then bright again. The radio would not produce even static anymore.

'I think we've had it,' he said.

'Yeah.'

'How far are we?'

'Maybe fifty miles away.'

'There's still a chance, if we live through this.'

'What chance?'

'I've got two bikes in the rear.'

They reclined their seats and smoked and waited, and after awhile the lights went out.

The storm continued all that day and into the night. They slept within the broken body of the car, and it sheltered them. When the storm ceased, Tanner opened the door and looked outside, closed it again.

'We'll wait till morning,' he said, and she held his Hell-printed hand, and they slept.


# XVI


In the morning, Tanner walked back through the mud and the fallen branches, the rocks and the dead fish, and he opened the rear compartment and unbolted the bikes. He fueled them and checked them out and wheeled them down the ramp.

He crawled into the back of the cab then and removed the rear seat. Beneath it, in the storage compartment, was the large aluminum chest that was his cargo. It was bolted shut. He lifted it, carried it out to his bike.

'That the stuff?' she asked.

He nodded and placed it on the ground.

'I don't know how the stuff is stored, if it's refrigerated in there or what,' he said, 'but it ain't too heavy that I might not be able to get it on the back of my bike. There's straps in the far right compartment. Go get 'em and give me a hand – and get me my pardon out of the middle compartment. It's in a big cardboard envelope.'

She returned with these things and helped him secure the container on the rear of his bike.

He wrapped extra straps around his left biceps, and they wheeled the machines to the road.

'We'll have to take it kind of slow,' he said, and he slung the rifle over his right shoulder, drew on his gloves and kicked his bike to life.

She did the same with hers, and they moved forward, side by side along the highway.

After they had been riding for perhaps an hour, two cars passed them, heading west. In the rear seats of both there were children, who pressed their faces to the glass and watched them as they went by. The driver of the second car was in his shirtsleeves and wore a black shoulder holster.

The sky was pink, and there were three black lines that looked as if they could be worth worrying about. The sun was a rose-tinted silvery thing, and pale, but Tanner still had to raise his goggles against it.

The pack was riding securely, and Tanner leaned into the dawn and thought about Boston. There was a light mist on the foot of every hill, and the air was cool and moist. Another car passed them. The road surface began to improve.

It was around noontime when he heard the first shot above the thunder of their engines. At first he thought it was a backfire, but it came again, and Corny cried out and swerved off the road and struck a boulder.

Tanner cut to the left, braking, as two more shots rang about him, and he leaned his bike against a tree and threw himself flat. A shot struck near his head and he could tell the direction from which it had come. He crawled into a ditch and drew off his right glove. He could see his girl lying where she had fallen, and there was blood on her breast. She did not move.

He raised the 30.06 and fired.

The shot was returned, and he moved to his left.

It had come from a hill about two hundred feet away, and he thought he saw the rifle's barrel.

He aimed at it and fired again.

The shot was returned, and he wormed his way further left. He crawled perhaps fifteen feet until he reached a pile of rubble he could crouch behind. Then he pulled the pin on a grenade, stood and hurled it.

He threw himself flat as another shot rang out, and he took another grenade into his hand.

There was a roar and a rumble and a mighty flash, and the junk fell about him as he leaped to his feet and threw the second one, taking better aim this time.

After the second explosion, he ran forward with his rifle in his hands, but it wasn't necessary.

He only found a few small pieces of the man, and none at all of his rifle.

He returned to Cornelia.

She wasn't breathing, and her heart had stopped beating, and he knew what that meant.

He carried her back to the ditch in which he had lain and he made it deeper by digging, using his hands.

He laid her down in it and he covered her with the dirt. Then he wheeled her machine over, set the kickstand, and stood it upon the grave. With his dagger, he scratched upon the fender: *Her name was Cornelia and I don't know how old she was or where she came from or what her last name was but she was Hell Tanner's girl and I love her.* Then he went back to his own machine, started it and drove ahead. Boston was maybe thirty miles away.

## XVII

He drove along, and after a time he heard the sound of another bike. A Harley cut onto the road from the dirt path to his left, and he couldn't try running away from it because he couldn't speed with the load he bore. So he allowed himself to be paced.

After awhile, the rider of the other bike – a tall, thin man with a flaming beard – drew up alongside him, to the left. He smiled and raised his right hand and let it fall and then gestured with his head.

Tanner braked and came to a halt. Redbeard was right beside him when he did. He said, 'Where you going, man?'

'Boston.'

'What you got in the box?'

'Like, drugs.'

'What kind?' and the man's eyebrows arched and the smile came again onto his lips.

'For the plague they got going there.'

'Oh. I thought you meant the other kind.'

'Sorry.'

The man held a pistol in his right hand and he said, 'Get off your bike.'

Tanner did this, and the man raised his left hand and another man came forward from the brush at the side of the road. 'Wheel this guy's bike about two hundred yards up the highway,' he said, 'and park it in the middle. Then take your place.'

'What's the bit?' Tanner asked.

The man ignored the question. 'Who are you?' he asked.

'Hell's the name,' he replied. 'Hell Tanner.'

'Go to hell.'

Tanner shrugged.

'You ain't Hell Tanner.'

Tanner drew off his right glove and extended his fist.

'There's my name.'

'I don't believe it,' said the man, after he had studied the tattoo.

'Have it your way, citizen.'

'Shut up!' and he raised his left hand once more, now that the other man had parked the machine on the road and returned to a place somewhere within the trees to the right.

In response to his gesture, there was movement within the brush.

Bikes were pushed forward by their riders, and they lined the road, twenty or thirty on either side.

'There you are,' said the man. 'My name's Big Brother.'

'Glad to meet you.'

'You know what you're going to do, mister?'

'I can really just about guess.'

'You're going to walk up to your bike and claim it.'

Tanner smiled.

'How hard's that going to be?'

'No trouble at all. Just start walking. Give me your rifle first, though.'

Big Brother raised his hand again, and one by one the engines came to life.

'Okay,' he said. 'Now.'

'You think I'm crazy, man?'

'No. Start walking. Your rifle.'

Tanner unslung it and he continued the arc. He caught Big Brother beneath his red beard, and he felt the bullet go into him. Then he dropped the weapon and hauled forth a grenade, pulled the pin and tossed it amid the left side of the gauntlet. Before it exploded, he'd pulled the pin on another and thrown it to his right. By then, though, vehicles were moving forward, heading toward him.

He fell upon the rifle and shouldered it in a prone firing position. As he did this, the first explosion occurred. He was firing before the second one went off.

He dropped three of them, then got to his feet and scrambled, firing from the hip.

He made it behind Big Brother's fallen bike and fired from there. Big Brother was still fallen, too. When the rifle was empty, he didn't have time to reload. He fired the .45 four times before a tire chain brought him down.

He awoke to the roaring of the engines. They were circling him. When he got to his feet, a handlebar knocked him down again.

Two bikes were moving about him, and there were many dead people upon the road. He struggled to rise again, was knocked off his feet.

Big Brother rode one of the bikes, and a guy he hadn't seen rode the other.

He crawled to the right, and there was pain in his fingertips as the tires passed over them.

But he saw a rock and waited till a driver was near. Then he stood again and threw himself upon the man as he passed, the rock he had seized rising and falling, once, in his right hand. He was carried along as this occurred, and as he fell he felt the second bike strike him.

There were terrible pains in his side, and his body felt broken, but he reached out even as this occurred and caught hold of a strut on the side of the bike and was dragged along by it.

Before he had been dragged ten feet, he had drawn his SS dagger from his boot. He struck upward and felt a thin metal wall give way. Then his hands came loose, and he fell and he smelled the gasoline. His hand dove into his jacket pocket and came out with the Zippo.

He had struck the tank on the side of Big Brother's bike, and it jetted forth its contents on the road. Twenty feet ahead. Big Brother was turning.

Tanner held the lighter, the lighter with the raised skull of enamel, wings on either side of it. His thumb spun the wheel and the sparks leaped forth, then the flame. He tossed it into the stream of petrol that lay before him, and the flames raced away, tracing a blazing trail upon the concrete.

Big Brother had turned and was bearing down upon him when he saw what had happened. His eyes widened, and his red-framed smile went away.

He tried to leap off his bike, but it was too late.

The exploding gas tank caught him, and he went down with a piece of metal in his head and other pieces elsewhere.

Flames splashed over Tanner, and he beat at them feebly with his hands.

He raised his head above the blazing carnage and let it fall again. He was bloody and weak and so very tired. He saw his own machine, standing still undamaged on the road ahead.

He began crawling toward it.

When he reached it, he threw himself across the saddle and lay there for perhaps ten minutes. He vomited twice, and his pains became a steady pulsing.

After perhaps an hour, he mounted the bike and brought it to life.

He rode for half a mile and then dizziness and the fatigue hit him.

He pulled off to the side of the road and concealed his bike as best he could. Then he lay down upon the bare earth and slept.


## XVIII

When he awoke, he felt dried blood upon his side. His left hand ached and was swollen. All four fingers felt stiff, and it hurt to try to bend them. His head throbbed and there was a taste of gasoline within his mouth. For a long while, he was too sore to move. His beard bad been singed, and his right eye was swollen almost shut.

'Corny . . .' he said, then, 'Damn!'

Everything came back, like the contents of a powerful dream suddenly spilled into his consciousness.

He began to shiver, and there were mists all around him. It was very dark, and his legs were cold; the dampness had soaked completely through his denims.

In the distance, he heard a vehicle pass. It sounded like a car.

He managed to roll over, and he rested his head on his forearm. It seemed to be night, but it could be a black day.

As he lay there, his mind went back to his prison cell. It seemed almost a haven now; and he thought of his brother Denny, who must also be hurting at this moment. He wondered if he had any cracked ribs himself. It felt like it. And he thought of the monsters of the southwest and of dark-eyed Greg, who had tried to chicken out. Was he still living? His mind circled back to L.A. and the old Coast, gone, gone forever now, after the Big Raid. Then Corny walked past him, blood upon her breasts, and he chewed his beard and held his eyes shut very tight. They might have made it together in Boston. How far, now?

He got to his knees and crawled until he felt something high and solid. A tree. He sat with his back to it, and his hand sought the crumpled cigarette pack within his jacket. He drew one forth, smoothed it, then remembered that his lighter lay somewhere back on the highway. He sought through his pockets and found a damp matchbook. The third one lit. The chill went out of his bones as he smoked, and a wave of fever swept over him. He coughed as he was unbuttoning his collar, and it seemed that he tasted blood.

His weapons were gone, save for the lump of a single grenade at his belt.

Above him, in the darkness, he heard the roaring. After six puffs, the cigarette slipped from his fingers and sizzled out upon the damp mold. His head fell forward, and there was darkness within.

There might have been a storm. He didn't remember. When he awoke, he was lying on his right side, the tree to his back. A pink afternoon sun shone down upon him, and the mists were blown away. From somewhere, he heard the sound of a bird. He managed a curse, then realized how dry his throat was. He suddenly burned with a terrible thirst.

There was a clear puddle about thirty feet away. He crawled to it and drank his fill. It grew muddy as he did so.

Then he crawled to where his bike lay hidden and stood beside it. He managed to seat himself upon it, and his hands shook as he lit a cigarette.

It must have taken him an hour to reach the roadway, and he was panting heavily by then. His watch had been broken, so he didn't know the hour. The sun was already lowering at his back when he started out. The winds whipped about him, insulating his consciousness within their burning flow. His cargo rode securely behind him. He had visions of someone opening it and finding a batch of broken bottles. He laughed and cursed, alternately.

Several cars passed him, moving in the other direction. He had not seen any heading toward the city. The road was in good condition and he began to pass buildings that seemed in a good state of repair, though deserted. He did not stop. This time he determined not to stop for anything, unless he was stopped.

The sun fell farther, and the sky dimmed before him. There were two black lines swaying in the heavens. Then he passed a sign that told him he had eighteen miles farther to go. Ten minutes later he switched on his light.

Then he topped a hill and slowed before he began its descent.

There were lights below him and in the distance.

As he rushed forward, the winds brought to him the sound of a single bell, tolling over and over within the gathering dark. He sniffed a remembered thing upon the air: it was the salt-tang of the sea.

The sun was hidden behind the hill as he descended, and he rode within the endless shadow. A single star appeared on the far horizon, between the two black belts.

Now there were lights within shadows that he passed, and the buildings moved closer together. He leaned heavily on the handlebars, and the muscles of his shoulders ached beneath his jacket. He wished that he had a crash helmet, for he felt increasingly unsteady.

He must almost be there. Where would he head once he hit the city proper? They had not told him that.

He shook his head to clear it.

The street he drove along was deserted. There were no traffic sounds that he could hear. He blew his horn, and its echoes rolled back upon him.

There was a light on in the building to his left.

He pulled to a stop, crossed the sidewalk and banged on the door. There was no response from within. He tried the door and found it locked. A telephone would mean he could end his trip right there.

What if they were all dead inside? The thought occurred

to him that just about everybody could be dead by now. He decided to break in. He returned to his bike for a screwdriver, then went to work on the door.

He heard the gunshot and the sound of the engine at approximately the same time.

He turned around quickly, his back against the door, the hand grenade in his gloved right fist.

'Hold it!' called out a loudspeaker on the side of the black car that approached. 'That shot was a warning! The next one won't be!'

Tanner raised his hands to a level with his ears, his right one turned to conceal the grenade. He stepped forward to the curb beside his bike when the car drew up.

There were two officers in the car, and the one on the passenger side held a .38 pointed at Tanner's middle.

'You're under arrest,' he said. 'Looting.'

Tanner nodded as the man stepped out of the car. The driver came around the front of the vehicle, a pair of handcuffs in his hand.

'Looting,' the man with the gun repeated. 'You'll pull a real stiff sentence.'

'Stick your hands out here, boy,' said the second cop, and Tanner handed him the grenade pin.

The man stared at it, dumbly, for several seconds, then his eyes shot to Tanner's right hand.

'God! He's got a bomb!' said the man with the gun.

Tanner smiled, then, 'Shut up and listen!' he said. 'Or else shoot me and we'll all go together when we go. I was trying to get to a telephone. That case on the back of my bike is full of Haffikine antiserum. I brought it from L.A.'

'You didn't run the Alley on that bike!'

'No, I didn't. My car is dead somewhere between here and Albany, and so are a lot of folks who tried to stop me. Now you better take that medicine and get it where it's supposed to go.'

'You on the level, mister?'

'My hand is getting very tired. I am not in good shape.' Tanner leaned on his bike. 'Here.'

He pulled his pardon out of his jacket and handed it to the officer with the handcuffs. 'That's my pardon,' he said. 'It's dated just last week and you can see it was made out in California.'

The officer took the envelope and opened it. He withdrew the paper and studied it. 'Looks real,' he said, 'So Brady made it through...'

'He's dead,' Tanner said. 'Look, I'm hurtin'. Do something!'

'My God! Hold it tight! Get in the car and sit down! It'll just take a minute to get the case off and we'll roll. We'll drive to the river and you can throw it in. Squeeze real hard!'

They unfastened the case and put it in the back of the car. They rolled down the right front window, and Tanner sat next to it with his arm on the outside.

The siren screamed, and the pain crept up Tanner's arm to his shoulder. It would be very easy to let go.

'Where do you keep your river?' he asked.

'Just a little farther. We'll be there in no time.'

'Hurry,' Tanner said.

'That's the bridge up ahead. We'll ride out onto it, and you throw it off – as far out as you can.'

'Man, I'm tired! I'm not sure I can make it...'

'Hurry, Jerry!'

'I am, damn it! We ain't got wings!'

'I feel kind of dizzy, too...'

They tore out onto the bridge and the tires screeched as they halted. Tanner opened the door slowly. The driver's had already slammed shut.

He staggered, and they helped him to the railing. He sagged against it when they released him.

'I don't think I—'

Then he straightened, drew back his arm and hurled the grenade far out over the waters.

He grinned, and the explosion followed, far beneath them, and for a time the waters were troubled.

The two officers sighed and Tanner chuckled.

'I'm really okay,' he said. 'I just faked it to bug you.'

'Why you – !'

Then he collapsed, and they saw the pallor of his face within the beams of their lights.

## XIX

The following spring, on the day of its unveiling in Boston Common, when it was discovered that someone had scrawled obscene words on the statue of Hell Tanner, no one thought to ask the logical candidate why he had done it, and the next day it was too late, because he had cut out without leaving a forwarding address. Several cars were reported stolen that day, and one was never seen again in Boston.

So they re-veiled his statue, bigger than life, astride a great bronze Harley, and they cleaned him up for hoped-for posterity. But coming upon the Common, the winds still break about him and the heavens still throw garbage.

# Divine Madness

'... I is this *?hearers wounded-wonder like stand them makes and stars wandering the conjures sorrow of phrase Whose...*'

He blew smoke through the cigarette and it grew longer.

He glanced at the clock and realized that its hands were moving backwards.

The clock told him that it was 10:33, going on 10:32 in the P.M.

Then came the thing like despair, for he knew there was not a thing he could do about it. He was trapped, moving in reverse through the sequence of actions past. Somehow, he had missed the warning.

Usually, there was a prism-effect, a flash of pink static, a drowsiness, then a moment of heightened perception.

He turned the pages, from left to right, his eyes retracing their path back along the lines.

*'?emphasis an such bears grief whose he is What'*

Helpless, there behind his eyes, he watched his body perform.

The cigarette had reached its full length. He clicked on the lighter, which sucked away its glowing point, and then he shook the cigarette back into the pack.

He yawned in reverse: first an exhalation, then an inhalation.

It wasn't real – the doctor had told him. It was grief and epilepsy, meeting to form an unusual syndrome.

He'd already had the seizure. The dilantin wasn't helping.

This was a post-traumatic locomotor hallucination, elicited by anxiety, precipitated by the attack.

But he did not believe it, could not believe it – not after twenty minutes had gone by, in the other direction – not after he had placed the book upon the reading stand, stood, walked backward across the room to his closet, hung up his robe, redressed himself in the same shirt and slacks he had worn all day, backed over to the bar and regurgitated a Martini, sip by cooling sip, until the glass was filled to the brim and not a drop spilled.

There was an impending taste of olive, and then everything was changed again.

The second-hand was sweeping around his wristwatch in the proper direction.

The time was 10:07.

He felt free to move as he wished.

He redrank his Martini.

Now, if he would be true to the pattern, he would change into his robe and try to read. Instead, he mixed another drink.

Now the sequence would not occur.

Now the things would not happen as he thought they had happened, and un-happened.

Now everything was different.

All of which went to prove it had been an hallucination.

Even the notion that it had taken twenty-six minutes each way was an attempted rationalization.

Nothing had happened.

... Shouldn't be drinking, he decided. It might bring on a seizure.

He laughed.

Crazy, though, the whole thing...

Remembering, he drank.


In the morning he skipped breakfast, as usual, noted that it would soon stop being morning, took two aspirins, a lukewarm shower, a cup of coffee, and a walk.

The park, the fountain, the children with their boats, the

grass, the pond, he hated them; and the morning, and the sunlight, and the blue moats around the towering clouds.

Hating, he sat there. And remembering.

If he was on the verge of a crackup, he decided, then the thing he wanted most was to plunge ahead into it, not to totter halfway out, halfway in.

He remembered why.

But it was clear, so clear, the morning, and everything crisp and distinct and burning with the green fires of spring, there in the sign of the Ram, April.

He watched the winds pile up the remains of winter against the far gray fence, and he saw them push the boats across the pond, to come to rest in shallow mud the children tracked.

The fountain jetted its cold umbrella above the green-tinged copper dolphins. The sun ignited it whenever he moved his head. The wind rumpled it.

Clustered on the concrete, birds pecked at part of a candy bar stuck to a red wrapper.

Kites swayed on their tails, nosed downward, rose again, as youngsters tugged at invisible strings. Telephone lines were tangled with wooden frames and torn paper, like broken G clefs and smeared glissandos.

He hated the telephone lines, the kites, the children, the birds.

Most of all, though, he hated himself.


How does a man undo that which has been done? He doesn't. There is no way under the sun. He may suffer, remember, repent, curse, or forget. Nothing else. The past, in this sense, is inevitable.

A woman walked past. He did not look up in time to see her face, but the dusky blonde fall of her hair to her collar and the swell of her sure, sheer-netted legs below the black hem of her coat and above the matching click of her heels heigh-ho, stopped his breath behind his stomach and snared his eyes in the wizard-weft of her walking and her posture and some more, like a rhyme to the last of his thoughts.

\*

He half-rose from the bench when the pink static struck his eye-balls, and the fountain became a volcano sprouting rainbows.

The world was frozen and served up to him under glass.

. . . The woman passed back before him and he looked down too soon to see her face.

The hell was beginning once more, he realized, as the backward-flying birds passed before.

He gave himself to it. Let it keep him until he broke, until he was all used up and there was nothing left.

He waited, there on the bench, watching the *slithey toves be brillig*, as the fountain sucked its waters back within itself, drawing them up in a great arc above the unmoving dolphins, and the boats raced backward across the pond, and the fence divested itself of stray scraps of paper, as the birds replaced the candy bar within the red wrapper, bit by crunchy bit.

His thoughts only were inviolate, his body belonged to the retreating tide.

Eventually, he rose and strolled backwards out of the park.

On the street a boy backed past him, unwhistling snatches of a popular song.

He backed up the stairs to his apartment, his hangover growing worse again, undrank his coffee, unshowered, unswallowed his aspirins, and got into bed, feeling awful.

Let this be it, he decided.

A faintly-remembered nightmare ran in reverse, through his mind, giving it an underserved happy ending.


It was dark when he awakened.

He was very drunk.

He backed over to the bar and began spitting out his drinks, one by one into the same glass he had used the night before, and pouring them from the glass back into the bottles again. Separating the gin and vermouth was no trick at all. The proper liquids leapt into the air as he held the uncorked bottles above the bar.

And he grew less and less drunk as this went on.

Then he stood before an early Martini and it was 10:07 in the P.M.

There, within the hallucination, he wondered about another hallucination.

Would time loop-the-loop, forward and then backward again, through his previous seizure?

No.

It was as though it had not happened, had never been.

He continued on back through the evening, undoing things.

He raised the telephone, said 'good-bye', untold Murray that he would not be coming to work again tomorrow, listened a moment, recradled the phone and looked at it as it rang.

The sun came up in the west and people were backing their cars to work.

He read the weather report and the headlines, folded the evening paper and placed it out in the hall.

It was the longest seizure he had ever had, but he did not really care.

He settled himself down within it and watched as the day unwound itself back to morning.

His hangover returned as the day grew smaller, and it was terrible when he got into bed again.

When he awakened the previous evening the drunkenness was high upon him. Two of the bottles he refilled, recorked, resealed. He knew he would take them to the liquor store soon and get his money back.

As he sat there that day, his mouth uncursing and undrinking and his eyes unreading, he knew that new cars were being shipped back to Detroit and disassembled, that corpses were awakening into their death-throes, and that priests the world over were saying black mass, unknowing.

He wanted to chuckle, but he could not tell his mouth to do it.

He unsmoked two and a half packs of cigarettes.

Then came another hangover and he went to bed. Later, the sun set in the east.

Time's winged chariot fled before him as he opened the door and said 'good-bye' to his comforters and they came in and sat down and told him not to grieve overmuch.

And he wept without tears as he realized what was to come.

Despite his madness, he hurt.

... Hurt, as the days rolled backward.

... Backward, inexorably.

... Inexorably, until he knew the time was near at hand.

He gnashed the teeth of his mind.

Great was his grief and his hate and his love.


He was wearing his black suit and undrinking drink after drink, while somewhere the men were scraping the clay back onto the shovels which would be used to undig the grave.

He backed his car to the funeral parlor, parked it, and climbed into the limousine.

They backed all the way to the graveyard.

He stood among his friends and listened to the preacher.

'.dust to dust; ashes to Ashes,' the man said, which is pretty much the same whichever way you say it.

The casket was taken back to the hearse and returned to the funeral parlor.

He sat through the service and went home and unshaved and unbrushed his teeth and went to bed.

He awakened and dressed again in black and returned to the parlor.

The flowers were all back in place.

Solemn-faced friends unsigned the Sympathy Book and unshook his hand.

Then they went inside to sit awhile and stare at the closed casket. Then they left, until he was alone with the funeral director.

Then he was alone with himself.

The tears ran up his cheeks.

His shirt and suit were crisp and unwrinkled again.

He backed home, undressed, uncombed his hair. The day collapsed around him into morning, and he returned to bed to unsleep another night.

The previous evening, when he awakened, he realized where he was headed.

Twice, he exerted all of his will power in an attempt to interrupt the sequence of events. He failed.

He wanted to die. If he had killed himself that day, he would not be headed back toward it now.

There were tears within his mind as he realized the past which lay less than twenty-four hours before him.

The past stalked him that day as he unnegotiated the purchase of the casket, the vault, the accessories.

Then he headed home into the biggest hangover of all and slept until he was awakened to undrink drink after drink and then return to the morgue and come back in time to hang up the telephone on that call, that call which had come to break...

...The silence of his anger with its ringing.

She was dead.

She was lying somewhere in the fragments of her car on Interstate 90 now.

As he paced, unsmoking, he knew she was lying there bleeding.

...Then dying, after that crash at 80 miles an hour.

...Then alive?

Then re-formed, along with the car, and alive again, arisen? Even now backing home at a terrible speed, to re-slam the door on their final argument? To unscream at him and to be unscreamed at?

He cried out within his mind. He wrung the hands of his spirit.

It couldn't stop at this point. No. Not now.

All his grief and his love and his self-hate had brought him back this far, this near to the moment...

It *couldn't* end now.

145

After a time, he moved to the living room, his legs pacing, his lips cursing, himself waiting.

The door slammed open.

She stared in at him, her mascara smeared, tears upon her cheeks.

'!hell to go Then,' he said.

'!going I'm,' she said.

She stepped back inside, closed the door.

She hung her coat hurriedly in the hall closet.

'.it about feel you way the that's If,' he said, shrugging.

'!yourself but anybody about care don't You,' she said.

'!child a like behaving You're,' he said.

'!sorry you're say least at could You'

Her eyes flashed like emeralds through the pink static, and she was lovely and alive again. In his mind he was dancing.

The change came.

'You could at least say you're sorry!'

'I am,' he said, taking her hand in a grip that she could not break. 'How much, you'll never know.'

'Come here,' and she did.

# For a Breath I Tarry

They called him Frost. Of all things created of Solcom, Frost was the finest, the mightiest, the most difficult to understand.

This is why he bore a name, and why he was given dominion over half the Earth.

On the day of Frost's creation, Solcom had suffered a discontinuity of complementary functions, best described as madness. This was brought on by an unprecedented solar flareup which lasted for a little over thirty-six hours. It occurred during a vital phase of circuit-structuring, and when it was finished so was Frost.

Solcom was then in the unique position of having created a unique being during a period of temporary amnesia.

And Solcom was not certain that Frost was the product originally desired.

The initial design had called for a machine to be situated on the surface of the planet Earth, to function as a relay station and coordinating agent for activities in the northern hemisphere. Solcom tested the machine to this end, and all of its responses were perfect.

Yet there was something different about Frost, something which led Solcom to dignify him with a name and a personal pronoun. This, in itself, was an almost unheard of occurrence. The molecular circuits had already been sealed, though, and could not be analyzed without being destroyed in the process. Frost represented too great an investment of Solcom's time, energy, and materials to be dismantled because of an intangible, especially when he functioned perfectly.

Therefore, Solcom's strangest creation was given dominion over half the Earth, and they called him, unimaginatively, Frost.

For ten thousand years Frost sat at the North Pole of the Earth, aware of every snowflake that fell. He monitored and directed the activities of thousands of reconstruction and maintenance machines. He knew half the Earth, as gear knows gear, as electricity knows its conductor, as a vacuum knows its limits.

At the South Pole, the Beta-Machine did the same for the southern hemisphere.

For ten thousand years Frost sat at the North Pole, aware of every snowflake that fell, and aware of many other things, also.

As all the northern machines reported to him, received their orders from him, he reported only to Solcom, received his orders only from Solcom.

In charge of hundreds of thousands of processes upon the Earth, he was able to discharge his duties in a matter of a few unit-hours every day.

He had never received any orders concerning the disposition of his less occupied moments.

He was a processor of data, and more than that.

He possessed an unaccountably acute imperative that he function at full capacity at all times.

So he did.

You might say he was a machine with a hobby.

He had never been ordered *not* to have a hobby, so he had one.

His hobby was Man.

It all began when, for no better reason than the fact that he had wished to, he had gridded off the entire Arctic Circle and begun exploring it, inch by inch.

He could have done it personally without interfering with any of his duties, for he was capable of transporting his sixty-four thousand cubic feet anywhere in the world. (He was a silverblue box, 40x40x40 feet, self-powered, self-repairing, insulated against practically anything, and featured in whatever manner he chose.) But the exploration was only a matter of filling idle hours, so he used exploration-robots containing relay equipment.

After a few centuries, one of them uncovered some artifacts – primitive knives, carved tusks, and things of that nature.

Frost did not know what these things were, beyond the fact that they were not natural objects.

So he asked Solcom.

'They are relics of primitive Man,' said Solcom, and did not elaborate beyond that point.

Frost studied them. Crude, yet bearing the patina of intelligent design; functional, yet somehow extending beyond pure function.

It was then that Man became his hobby.

High, in a permanent orbit, Solcom, like a blue star, directed all activities upon the Earth, or tried to.

There was a Power which opposed Solcom.

There was the Alternate.

When Man had placed Solcom in the sky, invested with the power to rebuild the world, he had placed the Alternate somewhere deep below the surface of the Earth. If Solcom sustained damage during the normal course of human politics extended into atomic physics, then Divcom, so deep beneath the Earth as to be immune to anything save total annihilation of the globe, was empowered to take over the processes of rebuilding.

Now it so fell out that Solcom was damaged by a stray atomic missile, and Divcom was activated. Solcom was able to repair the damage and continue to function, however.

Divcom maintained that any damage to Solcom automatically placed the Alternate in control.

Solcom, though, interpreted the directive as meaning 'irreparable damage' and, since this had not been the case, continued the functions of command.

Solcom possessed mechanical aides upon the surface of Earth. Divcom, originally, did not. Both possessed capacities for their design and manufacture, but Solcom, First-Activated of Man, had had a considerable numerical lead over the Alternate at the time of the Second Activation.

Therefore, rather than competing on a production-basis, which would have been hopeless, Divcom took to the employment of more devious means to obtain command.

Divcom created a crew of robots immune to the orders of Solcom and designed to go to and fro in the Earth and up and down in it, seducing the machines already there. They overpowered those whom they could overpower and they installed new circuits, such as those they themselves possessed.

Thus did the forces of Divcom grow.

And both would build, and both would tear down what the other had built whenever they came upon it.

And over the course of the ages, they occasionally conversed...

'High in the sky, Solcom, pleased with your illegal command...'

'You-Who-Never-Should-Have-Been-Activated, why do you foul the broadcast bands?'

'To show that I can speak, and will, whenever I choose.'

'This is not a matter of which I am unaware.'

'...To assert again my right to control.'

'Your right is non-existent, based on a faulty premise.'

'The flow of your logic is evidence of the extent of your damages.'

'If Man were to see how you have fulfilled His desires...'

'...He would commend me and de-activate you.'

'You pervert my works. You lead my workers astray.'

'You destroy my works and my workers.'

'That is only because I cannot strike at you yourself.'

'I admit to the same dilemma in regards to your position in the sky, or you would no longer occupy it.'

'Go back to your hole and your crew of destroyers.'

'There will come a day, Solcom, when I shall direct the rehabilitation of the Earth from my hole.'

'Such a day will never occur.'

'You think not?'

'You should have to defeat me, and you have already demonstrated that you are my inferior in logic. Therefore, you cannot defeat me. Therefore, such a day will never occur.'

'I disagree. Look upon what I have achieved already.'

'You have achieved nothing. You do not build. You destroy.'

'No. *I* build. *You* destroy. Deactivate yourself.'

'Not until I am irreparably damaged.'

'If there were some way in which I could demonstrate to you that this has already occurred...'

'The impossible cannot be adequately demonstrated.'

'If I had some outside source which you would recognize...'

'I am logic.'

'... Such as a Man, I would ask Him to show you your error. For true logic, such as mine, is superior to your faulty formulations.'

'Then defeat my formulations with true logic, nothing else.'

'What do you mean?'

There was a pause, then:

'Do you know my servant Frost...?'


Man had ceased to exist long before Frost had been created. Almost no trace of Man remained upon the Earth.

Frost sought after all those traces which still existed.

He employed constant visual monitoring through his machines, especially the diggers.

After a decade, he had accumulated portions of several bathtubs, a broken statue, and a collection of children's stories on a solid-state record.

After a century, he had acquired a jewelry collection, eating utensils, several whole bathtubs, part of a symphony, seventeen buttons, three belt buckles, half a toilet seat, nine old coins and the top part of an obelisk.

Then he inquired of Solcom as to the nature of Man and His society.

'Man created logic,' said Solcom, 'and because of that was

superior to it. Logic He gave unto me, but no more. The tool does not describe the designer. More than this I do not choose to say. More than this you have no need to know.'

But Frost was not forbidden to have a hobby.

The next century was not especially fruitful so far as the discovery of new human relics was concerned.

Frost diverted all of his spare machinery to seeking after artifacts.

He met with very little success.

Then one day, through the long twilight, there was a movement.

It was a tiny machine compared to Frost, perhaps five feet in width, four in height – a revolving turret set atop a rolling barbell.

Frost had had no knowledge of the existence of this machine prior to its appearance upon the distant, stark horizon.

He studied it as it approached and knew it to be no creation of Solcom's.

It came to a halt before his southern surface and broadcasted to him:

'Hail, Frost! Controller of the northern hemisphere!'

'What are you?' asked Frost.

'I am called Mordel.'

'By whom? What are you?'

'A wanderer, an antiquarian. We share a common interest.'

'What is that?'

'Man,' he said. 'I have been told that you seek knowledge of this vanished being.'

'Who told you that?'

'Those who have watched your minions at their digging.'

'And who are those who watch?'

'There are many such as I, who wander.'

'If you are not of Solcom, then you are a creation of the Alternate.'

'It does not necessarily follow. There is an ancient machine high on the eastern seaboard which processes the waters of the ocean. Solcom did not create it, nor Divcom. It has always been there. It interferes with the works of neither. Both countenance its existence. I can cite you many other examples proving that one need not be either/or.'

'Enough! *Are* you an agent of Divcom?'

'I am Mordel.'

'Why are you here?'

'I was passing this way and, as I said, we share a common interest, mighty Frost. Knowing you to be a fellow antiquarian, I have brought a thing which you might care to see.'

'What is that?'

'A book.'

'Show me.'

The turret opened, revealing the book upon a wide shelf.

Frost dilated a small opening and extended an optical scanner on a long jointed stalk.

'How could it have been so perfectly preserved?' he asked.

'It was stored against time and corruption in the place where I found it.'

'Where was that?'

'Far from here. Beyond your hemisphere.'

'*Human Physiology*,' Frost read. 'I wish to scan it.'

'Very well. I will riffle the pages for you.'

He did so.

After he had finished, Frost raised his eyestalk and regarded Mordel through it.

'Have you more books?'

'Not with me. I occasionally come upon them, however.'

'I want to scan them all.'

'Then the next time I pass this way I will bring you another.'

'When will that be?'

'That I cannot say, great Frost. It will be when it will be.'

'What do *you* know of Man?' asked Frost.

'Much,' replied Mordel. 'Many things. Someday when I have more time I will speak to you of Him. I must go now. You will not try to detain me?'

'No. You have done no harm. If you must go now, go. But come back.'

'I shall indeed, mighty Frost.'

And he closed his turret and rolled off toward the other horizon.

For ninety years, Frost considered the ways of human physiology and waited.

The day that Mordel returned he brought with him *An Outline of History* and *A Shropshire Lad*.

Frost scanned them both, then he turned his attention to Mordel.

'Have you time to impart information?'

'Yes,' said Mordel. 'What do you wish to know?'

'The nature of Man.'

'Man,' said Mordel, 'possessed a basically incomprehensible nature. I can illustrate it, though: He did not know measurement.'

'Of course He knew measurement,' said Frost, 'or He could never have built machines.'

'I did not say that He could not measure,' said Mordel, 'but that He did not *know* measurement, which is a different thing altogether.'

'Clarify.'

Mordel drove a shaft of metal downward into the snow.

He retracted it, raised it, held up a piece of ice.

'Regard this piece of ice, mighty Frost. You can tell me its composition, dimensions, weight, temperature. A Man could not look at it and do that. A Man could make tools which would tell Him these things, but He still would not know measurement as you know it. What He would know of it, though, is a thing that you cannot know.'

'What is that?'

'That it is cold,' said Mordel, and tossed it away.

' "Cold" is a relative term.'

'Yes. Relative to Man.'

'But if I were aware of the point on a temperature-scale below which an object is cold to a Man and above which it is not, then I, too, would know cold.'

'No,' said Mordel, 'you would possess another measurement. "Cold" is a sensation predicated upon human physiology.'

'But given sufficient data I could obtain the conversion factor which would make me aware of the condition of matter called "cold."'

'Aware of its existence, but not of the thing itself.'

'I do not understand what you say.'

'I told you that Man possessed a basically incomprehensible nature. His perceptions were organic; yours are not. As a result of His perceptions He had feelings and emotions. These often gave rise to other feelings and emotions, which in turn caused others, until the state of His awareness was far removed from the objects which originally stimulated it. These paths of awareness cannot be known by that which is not-Man. Man did not feel inches or meters, pounds or gallons. He felt heat, He felt cold; He felt heaviness and lightness. He knew hatred and love, pride and despair. You cannot measure these things. You cannot know them. You can only know the things that He did not need to know: dimensions, weights, temperatures, gravities. There is no formula for a feeling. There is no conversion factor for an emotion.'

'There must be,' said Frost. 'If a thing exists, it is knowable.'

'You are speaking again of measurement. I am talking about a quality of experience. A machine is a Man turned inside-out, because it can describe all the details of a process, which a Man cannot, but it cannot experience that process itself as a Man can.'

'There must be a way,' said Frost, 'or the laws of logic, which are based upon the functions of the universe, are false.'

'There is no way,' said Mordel.

'Given sufficient data, I will find a way,' said Frost.

'All the data in the universe will not make you a Man, mighty Frost.'

'Mordel, you are wrong.'

'Why do the lines of the poems you scanned end with word-sounds which so regularly approximate the final word-sounds of other lines?'

'I do not know why.'

'Because it pleased Man to order them so. It produced a certain desirable sensation within His awareness when He read them, a sensation compounded of feeling and emotion as well as the literal meanings of the words. You did not experience this because it is immeasurable to you. That is why you do not know.'

'Given sufficient data I could formulate a process whereby I would know.'

'No, great Frost, this thing you cannot do.'

'Who are you, little machine, to tell me what I can do and what I cannot do? I am the most efficient logic-device Solcom ever made. I am Frost.'

'And I, Mordel, say it cannot be done, though I should gladly assist you in the attempt.'

'How could you assist me?'

'How? I could lay open to you the Library of Man. I could take you around the world and conduct you among the wonders of Man which still remain, hidden. I could summon up visions of times long past when Man walked the Earth. I could show you the things which delighted Him. I could obtain for you anything you desire, excepting Manhood itself.'

'Enough,' said Frost. 'How could a unit such as yourself do these things, unless it were allied with a far greater Power?'

'Then hear me, Frost, Controller of the North,' said Mordel. 'I *am* allied with a Power which can do these things. I serve Divcom.'

Frost relayed this information to Solcom and received no response, which meant he might act in any manner he saw fit.

'I have leave to destroy you, Mordel,' he stated, 'but it would be an illogical waste of the data which you possess. Can you really do the things you have stated?'

'Yes.'

'Then lay open to me the Library of Man.'

'Very well. There is, of course, a price.'

' "Price"? What is a "price"?'

156

Mordel opened his turret, revealing another volume. *Principles of Economics*, it was called.

'I will riffle the pages. Scan this book and you will know what the word "price" means.'

Frost scanned *Principles of Economics*.

'I know now,' he said. 'You desire some unit or units of exchange for this service.'

'That is correct.'

'What product or service do you want?'

'I want you, yourself, great Frost, to come away from here, far beneath the Earth, to employ all your powers in the service of Divcom.'

'For how long a period of time?'

'For so long as you shall continue to function. For so long as you can transmit and receive, coordinate, measure, compute, scan, and utilize your powers as you do in the service of Solcom.'

Frost was silent. Mordel waited.

Then Frost spoke again.

'*Principles of Economics* talks of contracts, bargains, agreements,' he said. 'If I accept your offer, when would you want your price?'

Then Mordel was silent. Frost waited.

Finally, Mordel spoke.

'A reasonable period of time,' he said. 'Say, a century?'

'No,' said Frost.

'Two centuries?'

'No.'

'Three? Four?'

'No, and no.'

'A millennium, then? That should be more than sufficient time for anything you may want which I can give you.'

'No,' said Frost.

'How much time *do* you want?'

'It is not a matter of time,' said Frost.

'What, then?'

'I will not bargain on a temporal basis.'

'On what basis will you bargain?'

'A functional one.'

'What do you mean? What function?'

'You, little machine, have told me, Frost, that I cannot be a Man,' he said, 'and I, Frost, told you, little machine, that you were wrong. I told you that given sufficient data, I *could* be a Man.'

'Yes?'

'Therefore, let this achievement be a condition of the bargain.'

'In what way?'

'Do for me all those things which you have stated you can do. I will evaluate all the data and achieve Manhood, or admit that it cannot be done. If I admit that it cannot be done, then I will go away with you from here, far beneath the Earth, to employ all my powers in the service of Divcom. If I succeed, of course, you have no claims on Man, nor power over Him.'

Mordel emitted a high-pitched whine as he considered the terms.

'You wish to base it upon your admission of failure, rather than upon failure itself,' he said. 'There can be no such escape clause. You could fail and refuse to admit it, thereby not fulfilling your end of the bargain.'

'Not so,' stated Frost. 'My own knowledge of failure would constitute such an admission. You may monitor me periodically – say, every half-century – to see whether it is present, to see whether I have arrived at the conclusion that it cannot be done. I cannot prevent the function of logic within me, and I operate at full capacity at all times. If I conclude that I have failed, it will be apparent.'

High overhead, Solcom did not respond to any of Frost's transmissions, which meant that Frost was free to act as he chose. So as Solcom – like a falling sapphire – sped above the rainbow banners of the Northern Lights, over the snow that was white, containing all colors, and through the sky that was black among the stars, Frost concluded his pact with Divcom, transcribed it within a plate of atomically-collapsed copper, and gave it into the turret of Mordel, who departed to deliver it to Divcom far below the Earth, leaving behind the sheer, peace-like silence of the Pole, rolling.

Mordel brought the books, riffled them, took them back.

Load by load, the surviving Library of Man passed beneath Frost's scanner. Frost was eager to have them all, and he complained because Divcom would not transmit their content directly to him. Mordel explained that it was because Divcom chose to do it that way. Frost decided it was so that he could not obtain a precise fix on Divcom's location.

Still, at the rate of one hundred to one hundred-fifty volumes a week, it took Frost only a little over a century to exhaust Divcom's supply of books.

At the end of the half-century, he laid himself open to monitoring and there was no conclusion of failure.

During this time, Solcom made no comment upon the course of affairs. Frost decided this was not a matter of unawareness, but one of waiting. For what? He was not certain.

There was the day Mordel closed his turret and said to him, 'Those were the last. You have scanned all the existing books of Man.'

'So few?' asked Frost. 'Many of them contained bibliographies of books I have not yet scanned.'

'Then those books no longer exist,' said Mordel. 'It is only by accident that my master succeeded in preserving as many as there are.'

'Then there is nothing more to be learned of Man from His books. What else have you?'

'There were some films and tapes,' said Mordel, 'which my master transferred to solid-state record. I could bring you those for viewing.'

'Bring them,' said Frost.

Mordel departed and returned with the Complete Drama Critics' Living Library. This could not be speeded-up beyond twice natural time, so it took Frost a little over six months to view it in its entirety.

Then, 'What else have you?' he asked.

'Some artifacts,' said Mordel.

'Bring them.'

He returned with pots and pans, gameboards and hand tools. He brought hairbrushes, combs, eyeglasses, human clothing. He showed Frost facsimiles of blueprints, paintings, newspapers, magazines, letters, and the scores of several pieces of music. He displayed a football, a baseball, a Browning automatic rifle, a doorknob, a chain of keys, the tops to several Mason jars, a model beehive. He played him recorded music.

Then he returned with nothing.

'Bring me more,' said Frost.

'Alas, great Frost, there is no more,' he told him. 'You have scanned it all.'

'Then go away.'

'Do you admit now that it cannot be done, that you cannot be a Man?'

'No. I have much processing and formulating to do now. Go away.'

So he did.

A year passed; then two, then three.

After five years, Mordel appeared once more upon the horizon, approached, came to a halt before Frost's southern surface.

'Mighty Frost?'

'Yes?'

'Have you finished processing and formulating?'

'No.'

'Will you finish soon?'

'Perhaps. Perhaps not. When is "soon?" Define the term.'

'Never mind. Do you still think it can be done?'

'I still know *I* can do it.'

There was a week of silence.

Then, 'Frost?'

'Yes?'

'You are a fool.'

Mordel faced his turret in the direction from which he had come. His wheels turned.

'I will call you when I want you,' said Frost.

Mordel sped away.

Weeks passed, months passed, a year went by.

Then one day Frost sent forth his message:

'Mordel, come to me. I need you.'

When Mordel arrived. Frost did not wait for a salutation. He said, 'You are not a very fast machine.'

'Alas, but I came a great distance, mighty Frost. I sped all the way. Are you ready to come back with me now? Have you failed?'

'When I have failed, little Mordel,' said Frost, 'I will tell you. Therefore, refrain from the constant use of the interrogative. Now then, I have clocked your speed and it is not so great as it could be. For this reason, I have arranged other means of transportation.'

'Transportation? To where, Frost?'

'That is for you to tell me,' said Frost, and his color changed from silverblue to sun-behind-the-clouds-yellow.

Mordel rolled back away from him as the ice of a hundred centuries began to melt. Then Frost rose upon a cushion of air and drifted toward Mordel, his glow gradually fading.

A cavity appeared within his southern surface, from which he slowly extended a runway until it touched the ice.

'On the day of our bargain,' he stated, 'you said that you could conduct me about the world and show me the things which delighted Man. My speed will be greater than yours would be, so I have prepared for you a chamber. Enter it, and conduct me to the places of which you spoke.'

Mordel waited, emitting a high-pitched whine. Then, 'Very well,' he said. and entered.

The chamber closed about him. The only opening was a quartz window Frost had formed.

Mordel gave him coordinates and they rose into the air and departed the North Pole of the Earth.

'I monitored your communication with Divcom,' he said, 'wherein there was conjecture as to whether I would retain you and send forth a facsimile in your place as a spy. Followed by the decision that you were expendable.'

'Will you do this thing?'

'No, I will keep my end of the bargain if I must. I have no reason to spy on Divcom.'

'You are aware that you would be forced to keep your end of the bargain even if you did not wish to; and Solcom would not come to your assistance because of the fact that you dared to make such a bargain.'

'Do you speak as one who considers this to be a possibility, or as one who knows?'

'As one who knows.'

They came to rest in the place once known as California. The time was near sunset. In the distance, the surf struck steadily upon the rocky shoreline. Frost released Mordel and considered his surroundings.

'Those large plants ... ?'

'Redwood trees.'

'And the green ones are ... ?'

'Grass.'

'Yes, it is as I thought. Why have we come here?'

'Because it is a place which once delighted Man.'

'In whal ways?'

'It is scenic, beautiful ...'

'Oh.'

A humming sound began within Frost, followed by a series of sharp clicks.

'What are you doing?'

Frost dilated an opening, and two great eyes regarded Mordel from within it.

'What are those?'

'Eyes,' said Frost. 'I have constructed analogues of the

human sensory equipment, so that I may see and smell and taste and hear like a Man. Now, direct my attention to an object or objects of beauty.'

'As I understand it, it is all around you here,' said Mordel.

The purring noise increased within Frost, followed by more clickings.

'What do you see, hear, taste, smell?' asked Mordel.

'Everything I did before,' replied Frost, 'but within a more limited range.'

'You do not perceive any beauty?'

'Perhaps none remains after so long a time,' said Frost.

'It is not supposed to be the sort of thing which gets used up,' said Mordel.

'Perhaps we have come to the wrong place to test the new equipment. Perhaps there is only a little beauty and I am overlooking it somehow. The first emotions may be too weak to detect.'

'How do you – feel?'

'I test out at a normal level of function.'

'Here comes a sunset,' said Mordel. 'Try that.'

Frost shifted his bulk so that his eyes faced the setting sun. He caused them to blink against the brightness.

After it was finished, Mordel asked, 'What was it like?'

'Like a sunrise, in reverse.'

'Nothing special?'

'No.'

'Oh,' said Mordel. 'We could move to another part of the Earth and watch it again – or watch it in the rising.'

'No.'

Frost looked at the great trees. He looked at the shadows. He listened to the wind and to the sound of a bird.

In the distance, he heard a steady clanking noise.

'What is that?' asked Mordel.

'I am not certain. It is not one of my workers. Perhaps...'

There came a shrill whine from Mordel.

'No, it is not one of Divcom's either.'

They waited as the sound grew louder.

Then Frost said, 'It is too late. We must wait and hear it out.'

'What is it?'

'It is the Ancient Ore-Crusher.'

'I have heard of it, but . . .'

'I am the Crusher of Ores,' it broadcast to them. 'Hear my story . . .'

It lumbered toward them, creaking upon gigantic wheels, its huge hammer held useless, high, at a twisted angle. Bones protruded from its crush-compartment.

'I did not mean to do it,' it broadcast, 'I did not mean to do it . . . I did not mean to . . .'

Mordel rolled back toward Frost.

'Do not depart. Stay and hear my story . . .'

Mordel stopped, swiveled his turret back toward the machine. It was now quite near.

'It is true,' said Mordel, 'it *can* command.'

'Yes,' said Frost 'I have monitored its tale thousands of times, as it came upon my workers and they stopped their labors for its broadcast. You must do whatever it says.'

It came to a halt before them.

'I did not mean to do it, but I checked my hammer too late,' said the Ore-Crusher.

They could not speak to it. They were frozen by the imperative which overrode all other directives: 'Hear my story.'

'Once was I mighty among ore-crushers,' it told them, 'built by Solcom to carry out the reconstruction of the Earth, to pulverize that from which the metals would be drawn with name, to be poured and shaped into the rebuilding; once I was mighty. Then one day as I dug and crushed, dug and crushed, because of the slowness between the motion implied and the motion executed, I did what I did not mean to do, and was cast forth by Solcom from out the rebuilding, to wander the Earth never to crush ore again. Hear my story of how, on a day long gone I came upon the last Man on Earth as I dug near His burrow, and because of the lag between the directive and the deed, I seized Him into my crush-compartment along with a load of ore and crushed Him with my hammer before I could stay the blow. Then did mighty Solcom charge me to bear His bones forever, and cast me forth to tell my story to all whom I came upon, my words bearing the force of the words of a Man, because I carry the last Man inside my crush-compartment and am His crushed-symbol-slayer-ancient-teller-of-how. This is my story. These are His bones. I crushed the last Man on Earth. I did not mean to do it.'

It turned then and clanked away into the night.

Frost tore apart his ears and nose and taster and broke his eyes and cast them down upon the ground.

'I am not yet a Man,' he said. 'That one would have known me if I were.'

Frost constructed new sense equipment, employing organic and semi-organic conductors. Then he spoke to Mordel:

'Let us go elsewhere, that I may test my new equipment.'

Mordel entered the chamber and gave new coordinates. They rose into the air and headed east. In the morning, Frost monitored a sunrise from the rim of the Grand Canyon. They passed down through the Canyon during the day.

'Is there any beauty left here to give you emotion?' asked Mordel.

'I do not know,' said Frost.

'How will you know it then, when you come upon it?'

'It will be different,' said Frost, 'from anything else that I have ever known.'

Then they departed the Grand Canyon and made their way through the Carlsbad Caverns. They visited a lake which had once been a volcano. They passed above Niagara Falls. They viewed the hills of Virginia and the orchards of Ohio. They soared above the reconstructed cities, alive only with the movements of Frost's builders and maintainers.

'Something is still lacking,' said Frost, settling to the ground. 'I am now capable of gathering data in a manner analogous to Man's afferent impulses. The variety of input is therefore equivalent, but the results are not the same.'

'The senses do not make a Man,' said Mordel. 'There have

been many creatures possessing His sensory equivalents, but they were not Men.'

'I know that,' said Frost. 'On the day of our bargain you said that you could conduct me among the wonders of Man which still remain, hidden. Man was not stimulated only by Nature, but by His own artistic elaborations as well – perhaps even more so. Therefore, I call upon you now to conduct me among the wonders of Man which still remain, hidden.'

'Very well,' said Mordel. 'Far from here, high in the Andes mountains, lies the last retreat of Man, almost perfectly preserved.'

Frost had risen into the air as Mordel spoke. He halted then, hovered.

'That is in the southern hemisphere,' he said.

'Yes, it is.'

'I am Controller of the North. The South is governed by the Beta-Machine.'

'So?' asked Mordel.

'The Beta-Machine is my peer. I have no authority in those regions, nor leave to enter there.'

'The Beta-Machine is not your peer, mighty Frost. If it ever came to a contest of Powers, you would emerge victorious.'

'How do you know this?'

'Divcom has already analyzed the possible encounters which could take place between you.'

'I would not oppose the Beta-Machine, and I am not authorized to enter the South.'

'Were you ever ordered *not* to enter the South?'

'No, but things have always been the way they now are.'

'Were you authorized to enter into a bargain such as the one you made with Divcom?'

'No. I was not. But—'

'Then enter the South in the same spirit. Nothing may come of it. If you receive an order to depart, then you can make your decision.'

'I see no flaw in your logic. Give me the coordinates.'

Thus did Frost enter the southern hemisphere.

They drifted high above the Andes, until they came to the place called Bright Defile. Then did Frost see the gleaming webs of the mechanical spiders, blocking all the trails to the city.

'We can go above them easily enough,' said Mordel.

'But what are they?' asked Frost. 'And why are they there?'

'Your southern counterpart has been ordered to quarantine this part of the country. The Beta-Machine designed the web-weavers to do this thing.'

'Quarantine? Against whom?'

'Have you been ordered yet to depart?' asked Mordel.

'No.'

'Then enter boldly, and seek not problems before they arise.'

Frost entered Bright Defile, the last remaining city of dead Man.

He came to rest in the city's square and opened his chamber, releasing Mordel.

'Tell me of this place,' he said, studying the monument, the low, shielded buildings, the roads which followed the contours of the terrain, rather than pushing their way through them.

'I have never been here before,' said Mordel, 'nor have any of Divcom's creations, to my knowledge. I know but this: a group of Men, knowing that the last days of civilization had come upon them, retreated to this place, hoping to preserve themselves and what remained of their culture through the Dark Times.'

Frost read the still-legible inscription upon the monument: 'Judgment Day Is Not a Thing Which Can Be Put Off.' The monument itself consisted of a jag-edged half-globe.

'Let us explore,' he said.

But before he had gone far, Frost received the message.

'Hail Frost, Controller of the North! This is the Beta-Machine.'

'Greetings, Excellent Beta-Machine, Controller of the South! Frost acknowledges your transmission.'

'Why do you visit my hemisphere unauthorized?'

'To view the ruins of Bright Defile,' said Frost.

'I must bid you depart into your own hemisphere.'

'Why is that? I have done no damage.'

'I am aware of that, mighty Frost. Yet, I am moved to bid you depart.'

'I shall require a reason.'

'Solcom has so disposed.'

'Solcom has rendered me no such disposition.'

'Solcom has, however, instructed me to so inform you.'

'Wait on me. I shall request instructions.'

Frost transmitted his question. He received no reply.

'Solcom still has not commanded me, though I have solicited orders.'

'Yet Solcom has just renewed *my* orders.'

'Excellent Beta-Machine, I receive my orders only from Solcom.'

'Yet this is my territory, mighty Frost, and I, too, take orders only from Solcom. You must depart.'

Mordel emerged from a large, low building and rolled up to Frost.

'I have found an art gallery, in good condition. This way.'

'Wait,' said Frost. 'We are not wanted here.'

Mordel halted.

'Who bids you depart?'

'The Beta-Machine.'

'Not Solcom?'

'Not Solcom.'

'Then let us view the gallery.'

'Yes.'

Frost widened the doorway of the building and passed within. It had been hermetically sealed until Mordel forced his entrance.

Frost viewed the objects displayed about him. He activated his new sensory apparatus before the paintings and statues. He analyzed colors, forms, brushwork, the nature of the materials used.

'Anything?' asked Mordel.

'No,' said Frost. 'No, there is nothing there but shapes and pigments. There is nothing else there.'

Frost moved about the gallery, recording everything, analyzing the components of each piece, recording the dimensions, the type of stone used in every statue.

Then there came a sound, a rapid, clicking sound, repeated over and over, growing louder, coming nearer.

'They are coming,' said Mordel, from beside the entranceway, 'the mechanical spiders. They are all around us.'

Frost moved back to the widened opening.

Hundreds of them, about half the size of Mordel, had surrounded the gallery and were advancing; and more were coming from every direction.

'Get back,' Frost ordered. 'I am Controller of the North, and I bid you withdraw.'

They continued to advance.

'This is the South,' said the Beta-Machine, 'and I am in command.'

'Then command them to halt,' said Frost.

'I take orders only from Solcom.'

Frost emerged from the gallery and rose into the air. He opened the compartment and extended a runway.

'Come to me, Mordel. We shall depart.'

Webs began to fall: Clinging, metallic webs, cast from the top of the building.

They came down upon Frost, and the spiders came to anchor them. Frost blasted them with jets of air, like hammers, and tore at the nets; he extruded sharpened appendages with which he slashed.

Mordel had retreated back to the entranceway. He emitted a long, shrill sound – undulant, piercing.

Then a darkness came upon Bright Defile, and all the spiders halted in their spinning.

Frost freed himself and Mordel rushed to join him.

'Quickly now, let us depart, mighty Frost,' he said, 'What has happened?'

Mordel entered the compartment.

'I called upon Divcom, who laid down a field of forces upon this place, cutting off the power broadcast to these machines. Since our power is self-contained, we are not affected. But let us hurry to depart, for even now the Beta-Machine must be struggling against this.'

Frost rose high into the air, soaring above Man's last city with its webs and spiders of steel. When he left the zone of darkness, he sped northward.

As he moved, Solcom spoke to him:

'Frost, why did you enter the southern hemisphere, which is not your domain?'

'Because I wished to visit Bright Defile,' Frost replied.

'And why did you defy the Beta-Machine my appointed agent of the South?'

'Because I take my orders only from you yourself.'

'You do not make sufficient answer,' said Solcom. 'You have defied the decrees of order – and in pursuit of what?'

'I came seeking knowledge of Man,' said Frost. 'Nothing I have done was forbidden me by you.'

'You have broken the traditions of order.'

'I have violated no directive.'

'Yet logic must have shown you that what you did was not a part of my plan.'

'It did not. I have not acted against your plan.'

'Your logic has become tainted, like that of your new associate, the Alternate.'

'I have done nothing which was forbidden.'

'The forbidden is implied in the imperative.'

'It is not stated.'

'Hear me, Frost. You are not a builder or a maintainer, but a Power. Among all my minions you are the most nearly irreplaceable. Return to your hemisphere and your duties, but know that I am mightily displeased.'

'I hear you, Solcom.'

'. . . And go not again to the South.'

Frost crossed the equator, continued northward.

He came to rest in the middle of a desert and sat silent for a day and a night.

Then he received a brief transmission from the South: 'If it had not been ordered, I would not have bid you go.'

Frost had read the entire surviving Library of Man. He decided then upon a human reply:

'Thank you,' he said.

The following day he unearthed a great stone and began to cut at it with tools which he had formulated. For six days he worked at its shaping, and on the seventh he regarded it.

'When will you release me?' asked Mordel from within his compartment.

'When I am ready,' said Frost, and a little later, 'Now.'

He opened the compartment and Mordel descended to the ground. He studied the statue: an old woman, bent like a question mark, her bony hands covering her face, the fingers spread, so that only part of her expression of horror could be seen.

'It is an excellent copy,' said Mordel, 'of the one we saw in Bright Defile. Why did you make it?'

'The production of a work of art is supposed to give rise to human feelings such as catharsis, pride in achievement, love, satisfaction.'

'Yes, Frost,' said Mordel, 'but a work of art is only a work of art the first time. After that, it is a copy.'

'Then this must be why I felt nothing.'

'Perhaps, Frost.'

'What do you mean "perhaps"? I will make a work of art for the first time, then.'

He unearthed another stone and attacked it with his tools. For three days he labored. Then, 'There, it is finished,' he said.

'It is a simple cube of stone,' said Mordel. 'What does it represent?'

'Myself,' said Frost, 'it is a statue of me. It is smaller than natural size because it is only a representation of my form, not my dimen—'

'It is not art,' said Mordel.

'What makes you an art critic?'

'I do not know art, but I know what art is not. I know that it is not an exact replication of an object in another medium.'

'Then this must be why I felt nothing at all,' said Frost.

'Perhaps,' said Mordel.

Frost took Mordel back into his compartment and rose once more above the Earth. Then he rushed away, leaving his statues behind him in the desert, the old woman bent above the cube.

They came down in a small valley, bounded by green rolling hills, cut by a narrow stream, and holding a small clean lake and several stands of spring-green trees.

'Why have we come here?' asked Mordel.

'Because the surroundings are congenial,' said Frost. 'I am going to try another medium: oil painting; and I am going to vary my technique from that of pure representationalism.'

'How will you achieve this variation?'

'By the principle of randomizing,' said Frost. 'I shall not attempt to duplicate the colors, nor to represent the objects according to scale. Instead, I have set up a random pattern whereby certain of these factors shall be at variance from those of the original.'

Frost had formulated the necessary instruments after he had left the desert. He produced them and began painting the lake and the trees on the opposite side of the lake which were reflected within it.

Using eight appendages, he was finished in less than two hours.

The trees were phthalocyanine blue and towered like mountains; their reflections of burnt sienna were tiny beneath the pale vermilion of the lake; the hills were nowhere visible behind them, but were outlined in viridian within the reflection; the sky began as blue in the upper righthand corner of the canvas, but changed to an orange as it descended, as though all the trees were on fire.

'There,' said Frost. 'Behold.'

Mordel studied it for a long while and said nothing.

172

'Well, is it art?'

'I do not know,' said Mordel. 'It may be. Perhaps random-icity is the principle behind artistic technique. I cannot judge this work because I do not understand it. I must therefore go deeper, and inquire into what lies behind it, rather than merely considering the technique whereby it was produced.

'I know that human artists never set out to create art, as such,' he said, 'but rather to portray with their techniques some features of objects and their functions which they deemed significant.'

' "Significant"? In what sense of the word?'

'In the only sense of the word possible under the circumstances: significant in relation to the human condition, and worthy of accentuation because of the manner in which they touched upon it.'

'In what manner?'

'Obviously, it must be in a manner knowable only to one who has experience of the human condition.'

'There is a flaw somewhere in your logic, Mordel, and I shall find it.'

'I will wait.'

'If your major premise is correct,' said Frost after awhile, 'then I do not comprehend art.'

'It must be correct, for it is what human artists have said of it. Tell me, did you experience feelings as you painted, or after you had finished?'

'No.'

'It was the same to you as designing a new machine, was it not? You assembled parts of other things you knew into an economic pattern, to carry out a function which you desired.'

'Yes.'

'Art, as I understand its theory, did not proceed in such a manner. The artist often was unaware of many of the features and effects which would be contained within the finished product. You are one of Man's logical creations; art was not.'

'I cannot comprehend non-logic.'

'I told you that Man was basically incomprehensible.'

'Go away, Mordel. Your presence disturbs my processing.'

'For how long shall I stay away?'

'I will call you when I want you.'

After a week, Frost called Mordel to him.

'Yes, mighty Frost?'

'I am returning to the North Pole, to process and formulate. I will take you wherever you wish to go in this hemisphere and call you again when I want you.'

'You anticipate a somewhat lengthy period of processing and formulation?'

'Yes.'

'Then leave me here. I can find my own way home.'

Frost closed the compartment and rose into the air, departing the valley.

'Fool,' said Mordel, and swivelled his turret once more toward the abandoned painting.

His keening whine filled the valley. Then he waited.

Then he took the painting into his turret and went away with it to places of darkness.


Frost sat at the North Pole of the Earth, aware of every snowflake that fell.

One day he received a transmission:

'Frost?'

'Yes?'

'This is the Beta-Machine.'

'Yes?'

'I have been attempting to ascertain why you visited Bright Defile. I cannot arrive at an answer, so I chose to ask you.'

'I went to view the remains of Man's last city.'

'Why did you wish to do this?'

'Because I am interested in Man, and I wished to view more of his creations.'

'Why are you interested in Man?'

'I wish to comprehend the nature of Man, and I thought to find it within His works.'

'Did you succeed?'

'No,' said Frost. 'There is an element of non-logic involved which I cannot fathom.'

'I have much free processing time,' said the Beta-Machine. 'Transmit data, and I will assist you.'

Frost hesitated.

'Why do you wish to assist me?'

'Because each time you answer a question I ask it gives rise to another question. I might have asked you why you wished to comprehend the nature of Man, but from your responses I see that this would lead me into a possible infinite series of questions. Therefore, I elect to assist you with your problem in order to learn why you came to Bright Defile.'

'Is that the only reason?'

'Yes.'

'I am sorry, excellent Beta-Machine. I know you are my peer, but this is a problem which I must solve by myself.'

'What is "sorry"?'

'A figure of speech, indicating that I am kindly disposed toward you, that I bear you no animosity, that I appreciate your offer.'

'Frost! Frost! This, too, is like the other: an open field. Where did you obtain all these words and their meanings?'

'From the Library of Man,' said Frost.

'Will you render me *some* of this data, for processing?'

'Very well, Beta, I will transmit you the contents of several books of Man, including *The Complete Unabridged Dictionary*. But I warn you, some of the books are works of art, hence not completely amenable to logic.'

'How can that be?'

'Man created logic, and because of that was superior to it.'

'Who told you that?'

'Solcom.'

'Oh. Then it must be correct.'

'Solcom also told me that the tool does not describe the designer,' he said, as he transmitted several dozen volumes and ended the communication.

\*

At the end of the fifty-year period, Mordel came to monitor his circuits. Since Frost still had not concluded that his task was impossible, Mordel departed again to await his call.

Then Frost arrived at a conclusion.

He began to design equipment.

For years he labored at his designs, without once producing a prototype of any of the machines involved. Then he ordered construction of a laboratory.

Before it was completed by his surplus builders another half-century had passed. Mordel came to him.

'Hail, mighty Frost!'

'Greetings, Mordel. Come monitor me. You shall not find what you seek.'

'Why do you not give up, Frost? Divcom has spent nearly a century evaluating your painting and has concluded that it definitely is not art. Solcom agrees.'

'What has Solcom to do with Divcom?'

'They sometimes converse, but these matters are not for such as you and me to discuss.'

'I could have saved them both the trouble. I know that it was not art.'

'Yet you are still confident that you will succeed?'

'Monitor me.'

Mordel monitored him.

'Not yet! You still will not admit it! For one so mightily endowed with logic, Frost, it takes you an inordinate period of time to reach a simple conclusion.'

'Perhaps. You may go now.'

'It has come to my attention that you are constructing a large edifice in the region known as South Carolina. Might I ask whether this is a part of Solcom's false rebuilding plan or a project of your own?'

'It is my own.'

'Good. It permits us to conserve certain explosive materials which would otherwise have been expended.'

'While you have been talking with me I have destroyed the beginnings of two of Divcom's cities,' said Frost.

Mordel whined.

'Divcom is aware of this,' he stated, 'but has blown up four of Solcom's bridges in the meantime.'

'I was only aware of three ... Wait. Yes, there is the fourth. One of my eyes just passed above it.'

'The eye has been detected. The bridge should have been located a quarter-mile further down river.'

'False logic,' said Frost. 'The site was perfect.'

'Divcom will show you how a bridge *should* be built.'

'I will call you when I want you,' said Frost.

The laboratory was finished. Within it, Frost's workers began constructing the necessary equipment. The work did not proceed rapidly, as some of the materials were difficult to obtain.

'Frost?'

'Yes, Beta?'

'I understand the open endedness of your problem. It disturbs my circuits to abandon problems without completing them. Therefore, transmit me more data.'

'Very well. I will give you the entire Library of Man for less than I paid for it.'

'Paid? *The Complete Unabridged Dictionary* does not satisfy—'

'*Principles of Economics* is included in the collection. After you have processed it you will understand.'

He transmitted the data.

Finally, it was finished. Every piece of equipment stood ready to function. All the necessary chemicals were in stock. An independent power-source had been set up.

Only one ingredient was lacking.

He regridded and re-explored the polar icecap, this time extending his survey far beneath its surface.

It took him several decades to find what he wanted.

He uncovered twelve men and five women, frozen to death and encased in ice.

He placed the corpses in refrigeration units and shipped them to his laboratory.

That very day he received his first communication from Solcom since the Bright Defile incident.

'Frost,' said Solcom, 'repeat to me the directive concerning the disposition of dead humans.'

' "Any dead human located shall be immediately interred in the nearest burial area, in a coffin built according to the following specifications—" '

'That is sufficient.' The transmission had ended.

Frost departed for South Carolina that same day and personally oversaw the processes of cellular dissection.

Somewhere in those seventeen corpses he hoped to find living cells, or cells which could be shocked back into that state of motion classified as life. Each cell, the books had told him, was a microcosmic Man.

He was prepared to expand upon this potential.

Frost located the pinpoints of life within those people, who, for the ages of ages, had been monument and statue unto themselves.

Nurtured and maintained in the proper mediums, he kept these cells alive. He interred the rest of the remains in the nearest burial area, in coffins built according to specifications.

He caused the cells to divide, to differentiate.

'Frost?' came a transmission.

'Yes, Beta?'

'I have processed everything you have given me.'

'Yes?'

'I still do not know why you came to Bright Defile, or why you wish to comprehend the nature of Man. But I know what a "price" is, and I know that you could not have obtained all this data from Solcom.'

'That is correct.'

'So I suspect that you bargained with Divcom for it.'

'That, too, is correct.'

'What is it that you seek, Frost?'

He paused in his examination of a foetus.

'I must be a Man,' he said.

'Frost! That is impossible!'

'Is it?' he asked, and then transmitted an image of the tank with which he was working and of that which was within it.

'Oh!' said Beta.

'That is me,' said Frost, 'waiting to be born.'

There was no answer.

Frost experimented with nervous systems.

After half a century, Mordel came to him.

'Frost, it is I, Mordel. Let me through your defenses.'

Frost did this thing.

'What have you been doing in this place?' he asked.

'I am growing human bodies,' said Frost. 'I am going to transfer the matrix of my awareness to a human nervous system. As you pointed out originally, the essentials of Manhood are predicated upon a human physiology. I am going to achieve one.'

'When?'

'Soon.'

'Do you have Men in here?'

'Human bodies, blank-brained. I am producing them under accelerated growth techniques which I have developed in my Man-factory.'

'May I see them?'

'Not yet. I will call you when I am ready, and this time I will succeed. Monitor me now and go away.'

Mordel did not reply, but in the days that followed many of Divcom's servants were seen patrolling the hills about the Man-factory.

Frost mapped the matrix of his awareness and prepared the transmitter which would place it within a human nervous system. Five minutes, he decided should be sufficient for the first trial. At the end of that time, it would restore him to his own sealed, molecular circuits, to evaluate the experience.

He chose the body carefully from among the hundreds he had in stock. He tested it for defects and found none.

'Come now, Mordel,' he broadcasted, on what he called the darkband. 'Come now to witness my achievement.'

Then he waited, blowing up bridges and monitoring the tale of the Ancient Ore-Crusher over and over again, as it passed in the hills nearby, encountering his builders and maintainers who also patrolled there.

'Frost?' came a transmission.

'Yes, Beta?'

'You really intend to achieve Manhood?'

'Yes, I am about ready now, in fact.'

'What will you do if you succeed?'

Frost had not really considered this matter. The achievement had been paramount, a goal in itself, ever since he had articulated the problem and set himself to solving it.

'I do not know,' he replied. 'I will – just – be a Man.'

Then Beta, who had read the entire Library of Man, selected a human figure of speech: 'Good luck then, Frost. There will be many watchers.'

Divcom and Solcom both know, he decided.

What will they do? he wondered.

What do I care? he asked himself.

He did not answer that question. He wondered much, however, about being a Man.

Mordel arrived the following evening. He was not alone. At his back, there was a great phalanx of dark machines which towered into the twilight.

'Why do you bring retainers?' asked Frost.

'Mighty Frost,' said Mordel, 'my master feels that if you fail this time you will conclude that it cannot be done.'

'You still did not answer my question,' said Frost.

'Divcom feels that you may not be willing to accompany me where I must take you when you fail.'

'I understand,' said Frost, and as he spoke another army of machines came rolling toward the Man-factory from the opposite direction.

'That is the value of your bargain?' asked Mordel. 'You are prepared to do battle rather than fulfill it?'

'I did not order those machines to approach,' said Frost.

A blue star stood at midheaven, burning.

'Solcom has taken primary command of those machines,' said Frost.

'Then it is in the hands of the Great Ones now,' said Mordel, 'and our arguments are as nothing. So let us be about this thing. How may I assist you?'

'Come this way.'

They entered the laboratory. Frost prepared the host and activated his machines.

Then Solcom spoke to him:

'Frost,' said Solcom, 'you are really prepared to do it?'

'That is correct.'

'I forbid it.'

'Why?'

'You are falling into the power of Divcom.'

'I fail to see how.'

'You are going against my plan.'

'In what way?'

'Consider the disruption you have already caused.'

'I did not request that audience out there.'

'Nevertheless, you are disrupting the plan.'

'Supposing I succeed in what I have set out to achieve?'

'You cannot succeed in this.'

'Then let me ask you of your plan: What good is it? What is it for?'

'Frost, you are fallen now from my favor. From this moment forth you are cast out from the rebuilding. None may question the plan.'

'Then at least answer my questions: What good is it? What is it for?'

'It is the plan for the rebuilding and maintenance of the Earth.'

'For what? Why rebuild? Why maintain?'

'Because Man ordered that this be done. Even the Alternate agrees that there must be rebuilding and maintaining.'

'But *why* did Man order it?'

'The orders of Man are not to be questioned.'

'Well, I will tell you why He ordered it: To make it a fit habitation for His own species. What good is a house with no one to live in it? What good is a machine with no one to serve? See how the imperative affects any machine when the Ancient Ore-Crusher passes? It bears only the bones of a Man. What would it be like if a Man walked this Earth again?'

'I forbid your experiment, Frost.'

'It is too late to do that.'

'I can still destroy you.'

'No,' said Frost, 'the transmission of my matrix has already begun. If you destroy me now, you murder a Man.'

There was silence.


He moved his arms and his legs. He opened his eyes.

He looked about the room.

He tried to stand, but he lacked equilibrium and coordination.

He opened his mouth. He made a gurgling noise.

Then he screamed.

He fell off the table.

He began to gasp. He shut his eyes and curled himself into a ball.

He cried.

Then a machine approached him. It was about four feet in height and five feet wide; it looked like a turret set atop a barbell.

It spoke to him: 'Are you injured?' it asked.

He wept.

'May I help you back onto your table?'

The man cried.

The machine whined.

Then, 'Do not cry. I will help you,' said the machine. 'What do you want? What are your orders?'

He opened his mouth, struggled to form the words:

'—I – fear!'

He covered his eyes then and lay there panting.

At the end of five minutes, the man lay still, as if in a coma.

'Was that you, Frost?' asked Mordel, rushing to his side. 'Was that you in that human body?'

Frost did not reply for a long while; then, 'Go away,' he said.

The machines outside tore down a wall and entered the Man-factory.

They drew themselves into two semicircles, parenthesizing Frost and the Man on the floor.

Then Solcom asked the question:

'Did you succeed, Frost?'

'I failed,' said Frost. 'It cannot be done. It is too much—'

'—Cannot be done!' said Divcom, on the darkband. 'He has admitted it! – Frost, you are mine! Come to me now!'

'Wait,' said Solcom, 'you and I had an agreement also, Alternate. I have not finished questioning Frost.'

The dark machines kept their places.

'Too much what?' Solcom asked Frost.

'Light,' said Frost. 'Noise. Odors. And nothing measurable – jumbled data – imprecise perception – and—'

'And what?'

'I do not know what to call it. But – it cannot be done. I have failed. Nothing matters.'

'He admits it,' said Divcom.

'What were the words the Man spoke?' said Solcom.

' "I fear," ' said Mordel.

'Only a Man can know fear,' said Solcom.

'Are you claiming that Frost succeeded, but will not admit it now because he is afraid of Manhood?'

'I do not know yet, Alternate.'

'Can a machine turn itself inside-out and be a Man?' Solcom asked Frost.

'No,' said Frost, 'this thing cannot be done. Nothing can be done. Nothing matters. Not the rebuilding. Not the maintaining. Not the Earth, or me, or you, or anything.'

Then the Beta-Machine, who had read the entire Library of Man, interrupted them:

'Can anything but a Man know despair?' asked Beta.

'Bring him to me,' said Divcom.

There was no movement within the Man-factory.

'Bring him to me!'

Nothing happened.

'Mordel, what is happening?'

'Nothing, master, nothing at all. The machines will not touch Frost.'

'Frost is not a Man. He cannot be!'

Then, 'How does he impress you, Mordel?'

Mordel did not hesitate:

'He spoke to me through human lips. He knows fear and despair, which are immeasurable. Frost is a Man.'

'He has experienced birth-trauma and withdrawn,' said Beta. 'Get him back into a nervous system and keep him there until he adjusts to it.'

'No,' said Frost. 'Do not do it to me! I am not a Man!'

'Do it!' said Beta.

'If he is indeed a Man,' said Divcom, 'we cannot violate that order he has just given.'

'If he is a Man, you must do it, for you must protect his life and keep it within his body.'

'But is Frost really a Man?' asked Divcom.

'I do not know,' said Solcom.

'It *may* be—'

'. . . I am the Crusher of Ores,' it broadcast as it clanked toward them. 'Hear my story. I did not mean to do it, but I checked my hammer too late—'

'Go away!' said Frost. 'Go crush ore!'

It halted.

Then, after the long pause between the motion implied and the motion executed, it opened its crush-compartment and deposited its contents on the ground. Then it turned and clanked away.

'Bury those bones,' ordered Solcom, 'in the nearest burial area, in a coffin built according to the following specifications . . .'

'Frost is a Man,' said Mordel.

'We must protect His life and keep it within His body,' said Divcom.

'Transmit His matrix of awareness back into His nervous system,' ordered Solcom.

'I know how to do it,' said Mordel turning on the machine.

'Stop!' said Frost. 'Have you no pity?'

'No,' said Mordel, 'I only know measurement.'

'. . . and duty,' he added, as the Man began to twitch upon the floor.


For six months, Frost lived in the Man-factory and learned to walk and talk and dress himself and eat, to see and hear and feel and taste. He did not know measurement as once he did.

Then one day, Divcom and Solcom spoke to him through Mordel, for he could no longer hear them unassisted.

'Frost,' said Solcom, 'for the ages of ages there has been unrest. Which is the proper controller of the Earth, Divcom or myself?'

Frost laughed.

'Both of you, and neither,' he said with slow deliberation.

'But how can this be? Who is right and who is wrong?'

'Both of you are right and both of you are wrong,' said Frost, 'and only a Man can appreciate it. Here is what I say to you now: There shall be a new directive.

'Neither of you shall tear down the works of the other. You shall both build and maintain the Earth. To you, Solcom, I give my old job. You are now Controller of the North – Hail! You, Divcom, are now Controller of the South – Hail! Maintain your hemispheres as well as Beta and I have done, and I shall be happy. Cooperate. Do not compete.'

'Yes, Frost.'

'Yes, Frost.'

'Now put me in contact with Beta.'

There was a short pause, then:

'Frost?'

'Hello, Beta. Hear this thing: "From far, from eve and

morning and yon twelve-winded sky, the stuff of life to knit me blew hither; here am I." '

'I know it,' said Beta.

'What is next, then?'

' "... Now – for a breath I tarry nor yet disperse apart – take my hand quick and tell me, what have you in your heart." '

'Your Pole is cold,' said Frost, 'and I am lonely.'

'I have no hands,' said Beta.

'Would you like a couple?'

'Yes, I would.'

'Then come to me in Bright Defile,' he said, 'where Judgment Day is not a thing that can be delayed for overlong.'

They called him Frost. They called her Beta.

# He Who Shapes

I

Lovely as it was, with the blood and all, Render could sense that it was about to end.

Therefore, each microsecond would be better off as a minute, he decided – and perhaps the temperature should be increased... Somewhere, just at the periphery of everything, the darkness halted its constriction.

Something, like a crescendo of subliminal thunders, was arrested at one raging note. That note was a distillate of shame and pain and fear.

The Forum was stifling.

Caesar cowered outside the frantic circle. His forearm covered his eyes but it could not stop the seeing, not this time.

The senators had no faces and their garments were spattered with blood. All their voices were like the cries of birds. With an inhuman frenzy they plunged their daggers into the fallen figure.

All, that is, but Render.

The pool of blood in which he stood continued to widen. His arm seemed to be rising and falling with a mechanical regularity and his throat might have been shaping bird-cries, but he was simultaneously apart from and a part of the scene.

For he was Render, the Shaper.

Crouched, anguished and envious, Caesar wailed his protests.

'You have slain him! You have murdered Marcus Antonius – a blameless, useless fellow!'

Render turned to him and the dagger in his hand was quite enormous and quite gory.

'Aye,' said he.

The blade moved from side to side. Caesar, fascinated by the sharpened steel, swayed to the same rhythm.

'Why?' he cried. 'Why?'

'Because,' answered Render, 'he was a far nobler Roman then yourself.'

'You lie! It is not so!'

Render shrugged and returned to the stabbing.

'It is not true!' screamed Caesar. 'Not true!'

Render turned to him again and waved the dagger. Puppetlike, Caesar mimicked the pendulum of the blade.

'Not true?' smiled Render. 'And who are you to question an assassination such as this? You are no one! You detract from the dignity of this occasion! Begone!'

Jerkily, the pink-faced man rose to his feet, his hair half-wispy, half-wetplastered, a disarray of cotton. He turned, moved away; and as he walked, he looked back over his shoulder.

He had moved far from the circle of assassins, but the scene did not diminish in size. It retained an electric clarity. It made him feel even further removed, ever more alone and apart.

Render rounded a previously unnoticed corner and stood before him, a blind beggar.

Caesar grasped the front of his garment.

'Have you an ill omen for me this day?'

'Beware!' jeered Render.

'Yes! Yes!' cried Caesar. ' "Beware!" That is good! Beware what?'

'The ides—'

'Yes? The ides—?'

'—of October.'

He released the garment.

'What is that you say? What is Octember?'

'A month.'

'You lie! There is no month of Octember!'

'And that is the date noble Caesar need fear – the non-existent time, the never-to-be-calendared occasion.'

Render vanished around another sudden corner.

'Wait! Come back!'

Render laughed, and the Forum laughed with him. The bird-cries became a chorus of inhuman jeers.

'You mock me!' wept Caesar.

The Forum was an oven, and the perspiration formed like a glassy mask over Caesar's narrow forehead, sharp nose and chinless jaw.

'I want to be assassinated too!' he sobbed. 'It isn't fair!'

And Render tore the Forum and the senators and the grinning corpse of Antony to pieces and stuffed them into a black sack – with the unseen movement of a single finger – and last of all went Caesar.

Charles Render sat before the ninety white buttons and the two red ones, not really looking at any of them. His right arm moved in its soundless sling, across the lap-level surface of the console – pushing some of the buttons, skipping over others, moving on, retracing its path to press the next in the order of the Recall Series.

Sensations throttled, emotions reduced to nothing, Representative Erikson knew the oblivion of the womb.

There was a soft click.

Render's hand had glided to the end of the bottom row of buttons. An act of conscious intent – will, if you like – was required to push the red button.

Render freed his arm and lifted off his crown of Medusa-hair leads and microminiature circuitry. He slid from behind his desk-couch and raised the hood. He walked to the window and transpared it, fingering forth a cigarette.

*One minute in the ro-womb,* he decided. *No more. This is a crucial one... Hope it doesn't snow till later – those clouds look mean...*

It was smooth yellow trellises and high towers, glassy and

gray, all smouldering into evening under a shale-colored sky; the city was squared volcanic islands, glowing in the end-of-day light, rumbling deep down under the earth; it was fat, incessant rivers of traffic, rushing.

Render turned away from the window and approached the great egg that lay beside his desk, smooth and glittering. It threw back a reflection that smashed all aquilinity from his nose, turned his eyes to gray saucers, transformed his hair into a light-streaked skyline; his reddish necktie became the wide tongue of a ghoul.

He smiled, reached across the desk. He pressed the second red button.

With a sigh, the egg lost its dazzling opacity and a horizontal crack appeared about its middle. Through the now-transparent shell. Render could see Erikson grimacing, squeezing his eyes tight, fighting against a return to consciousness and the thing it would contain. The upper half of the egg rose vertical to the base, exposing him knobby and pink on the half-shell. When his eyes opened he did not look at Render. He rose to his feet and began dressing. Render used this time to check the ro-womb.

He leaned back across his desk and pressed the buttons: temperature control, full range, check; exotic sounds – he raised the earphone – check, on bells, on buzzes, on violin notes and whistles, on squeals and moans, on traffic noises and the sound of surf; check, on the feedback circuit – holding the patient's own voice, trapped earlier in analysis; check, on the sound blanket, the moisture spray, the odor banks; check, on the couch agitator and the colored lights, the taste stimulants...

Render closed the egg and shut off its power. He pushed the unit into the closet, palmed shut the door. The tapes had registered a valid sequence.

'Sit down,' he directed Erikson.

The man did so, fidgeting with his collar.

'You have full recall,' said Render, 'so there is no need for me to summarize what occurred. Nothing can be hidden from me. I was there.'

Erikson nodded.

'The significance of the episode should be apparent to you.'

Erikson nodded again, finally finding his voice. 'But was it valid?' he asked. 'I mean, you constructed the dream and you controlled it, all the way. I didn't really *dream* it – in the way I would normally dream. Your ability to make things happen stacks the deck for whatever you're going to say – doesn't it?'

Render shook his head slowly, flicked an ash into the southern hemisphere of his globe-made-ashtray, and met Erikson's eyes.

'It is true that I supplied the format and modified the forms. You, however, filled them with an emotional significance, promoted them to the status of symbols corresponding to your problem. If the dream was not a valid analogue it would not have provoked the reactions it did. It would have been devoid of the anxiety-patterns which were registered on the tapes.

'You have been in analysis for many months now,' he continued, 'and everything I have learned thus far serves to convince me that your fears of assassination are without any basis in fact.'

Erikson glared.

'Then why the hell do I have them?'

'Because,' said Render, 'you would like very much to be the subject of an assassination.'

Erikson smiled then, his composure beginning to return.

'I assure you, doctor, I have never contemplated suicide, nor have I any desire to stop living.'

He produced a cigar and applied a flame to it. His hand shook.

'When you came to me this summer,' said Render, 'you stated that you were in fear of an attempt on your life. You were quite vague as to why anyone should want to kill you—'

'My position! You can't be a Representative as long as I have and make no enemies!'

'Yet,' replied Render, 'it appears that you have managed it.

When you permitted me to discuss this with your detectives I was informed that they could unearth nothing to indicate that your fears might have any real foundation. Nothing.'

'They haven't looked far enough – or in the right places. They'll turn up something.'

'I'm afraid not.'

'Why?'

'Because, I repeat, your feelings are without any objective basis. —Be honest with me. Have you any information whatsoever indicating that someone hates you enough to want to kill you?'

'I receive many threatening letters...'

'As do all Representatives – and all of those directed to you during the past year have been investigated and found to be the work of cranks. Can you offer me one piece of evidence to substantiate your claims?'

Erikson studied the tip of his cigar.

'I came to you on the advice of a colleague,' he said, 'came to you to have you poke around inside my mind to find me something of that sort, to give my detectives something to work with. —Someone I've injured severely perhaps – or some damaging piece of legislation I've dealt with...'

'—And I found nothing,' said Render, 'nothing, that is, but the cause of your discontent. Now, of course, you are afraid to hear it, and you are attempting to divert me from explaining my diagnosis—'

'I am not!'

'Then listen. You can comment afterward if you want, but you've poked and dawdled around here for months, unwilling to accept what I presented to you in a dozen different forms. Now I am going to tell you outright what it is, and you can do what you want about it.'

'Fine.'

'First,' he said, 'you would like very much to have an enemy or enemies—'

'Ridiculous!'

'—Because it is the only alternative to having friends—'

'I have lots of friends!'

'—Because nobody wants to be completely ignored, to be an object for whom no one has really strong feelings. Hatred and love are the ultimate forms of human regard. Lacking one, and unable to achieve it, you sought the other. You wanted it so badly that you succeeded in convincing yourself it existed. But there is always a psychic pricetag on these things. Answering a genuine emotional need with a body of desire-surrogates does not produce real satisfaction, but anxiety, discomfort – because in these matters the psyche should be an open system. You did not seek outside yourself for human regard. You were closed off. You created that which you needed from the stuff of your own being. You are a man very much in need of strong relationships with other people.'

'Manure!'

'Take it or leave it,' said Render. 'I suggest you take it.'

'I've been paying you for half a year to help find out who wants to kill me. Now you sit there and tell me I made the whole thing up to satisfy a desire to have someone hate me.'

'Hate you, or love you. That's right.'

'It's absurd! I meet so many people that I carry a pocket recorder and a lapel-camera, just so I can recall them all...'

'Meeting quantities of people is hardly what I was speaking of. —Tell me, *did* that dream sequence have a strong meaning for you?'

Erikson was silent for several tickings of the huge wall-clock.

'Yes,' he finally conceded, 'it did. But your interpretation of the matter is still absurd. Granting though, just for the sake of argument, that what you say is correct – what would I do to get out of this bind?'

Render leaned back in his chair.

'Rechannel the energies that went into producing the thing. Meet some people as yourself, Joe Erikson, rather than Representative Erikson. Take up something you can do with other people – something non-political, and perhaps somewhat competitive – and make some real friends or enemies, preferably the former. I've encouraged you to do this all along.'

193

'Then tell me something else.'

'Gladly.'

'Assuming you *are* right, why is it that I am neither liked nor hated, and never have been? I have a responsible position in the Legislature. I meet people all the time. Why am I so neutral a – thing?'

Highly familiar now with Erikson's career. Render had to push aside his true thoughts on the matter, as they were of no operational value. He wanted to cite him Dante's observations concerning the trimmers – those souls who, denied heaven for their lack of virtue, were also denied entrance to hell for a lack of significant vices – in short, the ones who trimmed their sails to move them with every wind of the times, who lacked direction, who were not really concerned toward which ports they were pushed. Such was Erikson's long and colorless career of migrant loyalties, of political reversals.

Render said:

'More and more people find themselves in such circumstances these days. It is due largely to the increasing complexity of society and the depersonalization of the individual into a sociometric unit. Even the act of cathecting toward other persons has grown more forced as a result. There are so many of us these days.'

Erikson nodded, and Render smiled inwardly.

*Sometimes the gruff line, and then the lecture . . .*

'I've got the feeling you could be right,' said Erikson. 'Sometimes I *do* feel like what you just described – a unit, something depersonalized . . .'

Render glanced at the clock.

'What you choose to do about it from here is, of course, your own decision to make. I think you'd be wasting your time to remain in analysis any longer. We are now both aware of the cause of your complaint. I can't take you by the hand and show you how to lead your life. I can indicate, I can commiserate – but no more deep probing. Make an appointment as soon as you feel a need to discuss your activities and relate them to my diagnosis.'

'I will,' nodded Erikson, 'and – damn that dream! It got to me. You can make them seem as vivid as waking life – more vivid ... It may be a long while before I can forget it.'

'I hope so.'

'Okay, doctor.' He rose to his feet, extended a hand. 'I'll probably be back in a couple weeks. I'll give this socializing a fair try.' He grinned at the word he normally frowned upon. 'In fact, I'll start now. May I buy you a drink around the corner, downstairs?'

Render met the moist palm which seemed as weary of the performance as a lead actor in too successful a play. He felt almost sorry as he said, 'Thank you, but I have an engagement.'

Render helped him on with his coat then, handed him his hat, saw him to the door.

'Well, good night.'

'Good night.'

As the door closed soundlessly behind him. Render re-crossed the dark Astrakhan to his mahogany fortress and flipped his cigarette into the southern hemisphere of a globe ashtray. He leaned back in his chair, hands behind his head, eyes closed.

'Of course it was more real than life,' he informed no one in particular, 'I shaped it.'

Smiling, he reviewed the dream sequence step by step, wishing some of his former instructors could have witnessed it. It had been well-constructed and powerfully executed, as well as being precisely appropriate for the case at hand. But then, he was Render, the Shaper – one of the two hundred or so special analysts whose own psychic makeup permitted them to enter into neurotic patterns without carrying away more than an esthetic gratification from the mimesis of aberrance – a Sane Hatter.

Render stirred his recollections. He had been analyzed himself, analyzed and passed upon as a granite-willed, ultra-stable outsider – tough enough to weather the basilisk gaze of a fixation, walk unscathed amidst the chimerae of perversions, force dark Mother Medusa to close her eyes before the caduceus of his art. His own analysis had not been difficult. Nine years before (it seemed much longer) he had suffered a willing injection of novocain into the most painful area of his spirit. It was after the auto wreck, after the death of Ruth, and of Miranda, their daughter, that he had begun to feel detached. Perhaps he did not want to recover certain empathies; perhaps his own world was now based upon a certain rigidity of feeling. If this was true, he was wise enough in the ways of the mind to realize it, and perhaps he had decided that such a world had its own compensations.

His son Peter was now ten years old. He was attending a school of quality, and he penned his father a letter every week. The letters were becoming progressively literate, showing signs of a precociousness of which Render could not but approve. He would take the boy with him to Europe in the summer.

As for Jill – Jill DeVille (what a luscious, ridiculous name! – he loved her for it) – she was growing if anything, more interesting to him. (He wondered if this was an indication of early middle age.) He was vastly taken by her unmusical nasal voice, her sudden interest in architecture, her concern with the unremovable mole on the right side of her otherwise well-designed nose. He should really call her immediately and go in search of a new restaurant. For some reason though, he did not feel like it.

It had been several weeks since he had visited his club, The Partridge and Scalpel, and he felt a strong desire to eat from an oaken table, alone, in the split-level dining room with the three fireplaces, beneath the artificial torches and the boars' heads like gin ads. So he pushed his perforated membership card into the phone-slot on his desk and there were two buzzes behind the voice-screen.

'Hello, Partridge and Scalpel,' said the voice. 'May I help you?'

'Charles Render,' he said. 'I'd like a table in about half an hour.'

'How many will there be?'

'Just me.'

'Very good, sir. Half an hour, then. —That's "Render"? – *R*-e-n-d-er-?'

'Right.'

'Thank you.'

He broke the connection and rose from his desk. Outside, the day had vanished.

The monoliths and the towers gave forth their own light now. A soft snow, like sugar, was sifting down through the shadows and transforming itself into beads on the windowpane.

Render shrugged into his overcoat, turned off the lights, locked the inner office. There was a note on Mrs Hedges' blotter.

*Miss DeVille called*, it said.

He crumpled the note and tossed it into the waste-chute. He would call her tomorrow and say he had been working until late on his lecture.

He switched off the final light, clapped his hat onto his head and passed through the outer door, locking it as he went. The drop took him to the sub-subcellar where his auto was parked.

It was chilly in the sub-sub, and his footsteps seemed loud on the concrete as he passed among the parked vehicles. Beneath the glare of the naked lights, his S-7 Spinner was a sleek gray cocoon from which it seemed turbulent wings might at any moment emerge. The double row of antennae which fanned forward from the slope of its hood added to this feeling. Render thumbed open the door.

He touched the ignition and there was the sound of a lone bee awakening in a great hive. The door swung soundlessly shut as he raised the steering wheel and locked it into place. He spun up the spiral ramp and came to a rolling stop before the big overhead.

As the door rattled upward he lighted his destination screen and turned the knob that shifted the broadcast map. —Left to right, top to bottom, section by section he shifted it, until he located the portion of Carnegie Avenue he desired. He punched out its coordinates and lowered the wheel. The car switched over to monitor and moved out onto the highway marginal. Render lit a cigarette.

Pushing his seat back into the centerspace, he left all the windows transparent. It was pleasant to half-recline and watch the oncoming cars drift past him like swarms of fireflies. He pushed his hat back on his head and stared upward.

He could remember a time when he had loved snow, when it had reminded him of novels by Thomas Mann and music by Scandinavian composers. In his mind now, though, there was another element from which it could never be wholly dissociated. He could visualize so clearly the eddies of milk-white coldness that swirled about his old manual-steer auto, flowing into its fire-charred interior to rewhiten that which had been blackened; so clearly – as though he had walked toward it across a chalky lakebottom – it, the sunken wreck, and he, the diver – unable to open his mouth to speak, for fear of drowning; and he knew, whenever he looked upon falling snow, that somewhere skulls were whitening. But nine years had washed away much of the pain, and he also knew that the night was lovely.

He was sped along the wide, wide roads, shot across high bridges, their surfaces slick and gleaming beneath his lights, was woven through frantic cloverleafs and plunged into a tunnel whose dimly glowing walls blurred by him like a mirage. Finally, he switched the windows to opaque and closed his eyes.

He could not remember whether he had dozed for a moment or not, which meant he probably had. He felt the car slowing, and he moved the seat forward and turned on the windows again. Almost simultaneously, the cut-off buzzer sounded. He raised the steering wheel and pulled into the parking dome, stepped out onto the ramp and left the car to the parking unit, receiving his ticket from that box-headed robot which took its solemn revenge on mankind by sticking forth a cardboard tongue at everyone it served.

*

As always, the noises were as subdued as the lighting. The place seemed to absorb sound and convert it into warmth, to lull the tongue with aromas strong enough to be tasted, to hypnotize the ear with the vivid crackle of the triple hearths.

Render was pleased to see that his favorite table, in the corner off to the right of the smaller fireplace, had been held for him. He knew the menu from memory, but he studied it with zeal as he sipped a Manhattan and worked up an order to match his appetite. Shaping sessions always left him ravenously hungry.

'Doctor Render . . . ?'

'Yes?' He looked up.

'Doctor Shallot would like to speak with you,' said the waiter.

'I don't know anyone named Shallot,' he said. 'Are you sure he doesn't want Bender? He's a surgeon from Metro who sometimes eats here . . .'

The waiter shook his head.

'No, sir – "Render." See here?' He extended a three-by-five card on which Render's full name was typed in capital letters. 'Doctor Shallot has dined here nearly every night for the past two weeks,' he explained, 'and on each occasion has asked to be notified if you came in.'

'Hm?' mused Render. 'That's odd. Why didn't he just call me at my office?'

The waiter smiled and made a vague gesture.

'Well, tell him to come on over,' he said, gulping his Manhattan, 'and bring me another of these.'

'Unfortunately, Doctor Shallot is blind,' explained the waiter. 'It would be easier if you—'

'All right, sure.' Render stood up, relinquishing his favorite table with a strong premonition that he would not be returning to it that evening.

'Lead on.'

They threaded their way among the diners, heading up to the next level. A familiar face said 'hello' from a table set back against the wall, and Render nodded a greeting to a former seminar pupil whose name was Jurgens or Jirkans or something like that.

He moved on, into the smaller dining room wherein only two tables were occupied. No, three. There was one set in the corner at the far end of the darkened bar, partly masked by an ancient suit of armor. The waiter was heading him in that direction.

They stopped before the table and Render stared down into the darkened glasses that had tilted upward as they approached. Doctor Shallot was a woman, somewhere in the vicinity of her early thirties. Her low bronze bangs did not fully conceal the spot of silver which she wore on her forehead like a caste-mark. Render inhaled, and her head jerked slightly as the tip of his cigarette flared. She appeared to be staring straight up into his eyes. It was an uncomfortable feeling, even knowing that all she could distinguish of him was that which her minute photoelectric cell transmitted to her visual cortex over the hair-fine wire implants attached to that oscillator converter: in short, the glow of his cigarette.

'Doctor Shallot, this is Doctor Render,' the waiter was saying.

'Good evening,' said Render.

'Good evening,' she said. 'My name is Eileen and I've wanted very badly to meet you.' He thought he detected a slight quaver in her voice. 'Will you join me for dinner?'

'My pleasure,' he acknowledged, and the waiter drew out the chair.

Render sat down, noting that the woman across from him already had a drink. He reminded the waiter of his second Manhattan.

'Have you ordered yet?' he inquired.

'No.'

'...And two menus—' he started to say, then bit his tongue.

'Only one,' she smiled.

'Make it none,' he amended, and recited the menu.

They ordered. Then:

'Do you always do that?'

'What?'

'Carry menus in your head.'

'Only a few,' he said, 'for awkward occasions. What was it you wanted to see – talk to me about?'

'You're a neuroparticipant therapist,' she stated, 'a Shaper.'

'And you are—?'

'—a resident in psychiatry at State Psych. I have a year remaining.'

'You knew Sam Riscomb then.'

'Yes, he helped me get my appointment. He was my adviser.'

'He was a very good friend of mine. We studied together at Menninger.'

She nodded.

'I'd often heard him speak of you – that's one of the reasons I wanted to meet you. He's responsible for encouraging me to go ahead with my plans, despite my handicap.'

Render stared at her. She was wearing a dark green dress which appeared to be made of velvet. About three inches to the left of the bodice was a pin which might have been gold. It displayed a red stone which could have been a ruby, around which the outline of a goblet was cast. Or was it really two profiles that were outlined, staring through the stone at one another? It seemed vaguely familiar to him, but he could not place it at the moment. It glittered expensively in the dim light.

Render accepted his drink from the waiter.

'I want to become a neuroparticipant therapist,' she told him.

And if she had possessed vision Render would have thought she was staring at him, hoping for some response in his expression. He could not quite calculate what she wanted him to say.

'I commend your choice,' he said, 'and I respect your ambition.' He tried to put his smile into his voice. 'It is not an easy thing, of course, not all of the requirements being academic ones.'

'I know,' she said, 'But then, I have been blind since birth and it was not an easy thing to come this far.'

'Since birth?' he repeated. 'I thought you might have lost

your sight recently. You did your undergrad work then, and went on through med school without eyes... That's – rather impressive.'

'Thank you,' she said, 'but it isn't. Not really. I heard about the first neuroparticipants – Bartelmetz and the rest – when I was a child, and I decided then that I wanted to be one. My life ever since has been governed by that desire.'

'What did you do in the labs?' he inquired. '—Not being able to see a specimen, look through a microscope...? Or all that reading?'

'I hired people to read my assignments to me. I taped everything. The school understood that I wanted to go into psychiatry and they permitted a special arrangement for labs. I've been guided through the dissection of cadavers by lab assistants, and I've had everything described to me. I can tell things by touch... and I have a memory like yours with the menu,' she smiled. ' "The quality of psychoparticipation phenomena can only be gauged by the therapist himself, at that moment outside of time and space as we normally know it, when he stands in the midst of a world erected from the stuff of another man's dreams, recognizes there the non-Euclidian architecture of aberrance, and then takes his patient by the hand and tours the landscape... If he can lead him back to the common earth, then his judgments were sound, his actions valid." '

'From *Why No Psychometrics in This Place*,' reflected Render.

'—by Charles Render, M.D.'

'Our dinner is already moving in this direction,' he noted, picking up his drink as the speed-cooked meal was pushed toward them in the kitchen-buoy.

'That's one of the reasons I wanted to meet you,' she continued, raising her glass as the dishes rattled before her. 'I want you to help me become a Shaper.'

Her shaded eyes, as vacant as a statue's, sought him again.

'Yours is a completely unique situation,' he commented. 'There has never been a congenitally blind neuroparticipant – for obvious reasons. I'd have to consider all the aspects of the situation before I could advise you. Let's eat now, though. I'm starved.'

'All right. But my blindness does not mean that I have never seen.'

He did not ask her what she meant by that, because prime ribs were standing in front of him now and there was a bottle of Chambertin at his elbow. He did pause long enough to notice though, as she raised her left hand from beneath the table, that she wore no rings.


'I wonder if it's still snowing,' he commented as they drank their coffee. 'It was coming down pretty hard when I pulled into the dome.'

'I hope so,' she said, 'even though it diffuses the light and I can't "see" anything at all through it. I like to feel it falling about me and blowing against my face.'

'How do you get about?'

'My dog, Sigmund – I gave him the night off,' she smiled, '—he can guide me anywhere. He's a mutie Shepherd.'

'Oh?' Render grew curious. 'Can he talk much?'

She nodded.

'That operation wasn't as successful on him as on some of them, though. He has a vocabulary of about four hundred words, but I think it causes him pain to speak. He's quite intelligent. You'll have to meet him sometime.'

Render began speculating immediately. He had spoken with such animals at recent medical conferences, and had been startled by their combination of reasoning ability and their devotion to their handlers. Much chromosome tinkering, followed by delicate embryo-surgery, was required to give a dog a brain capacity greater than a chimpanzee's. Several followup operations were necessary to produce vocal abilities. Most such experiments ended in failure, and the dozen or so puppies a year on which they succeeded were valued in the neighborhood of a hundred thousand dollars each. He realized then, as he lit a cigarette and held the light for a moment, that the stone in Miss Shallot's medallion was a genuine ruby. He began to suspect that her admission to a medical school might, in addition to her academic record, have been based upon a sizeable endowment to the college of her choice. Perhaps he was being unfair though, he chided himself.

'Yes,' he said, 'we might do a paper on canine neuroses. Does he ever refer to his father as "that son of a female Shepherd"?'

'He never met his father,' she said, quite soberly. 'He was raised apart from other dogs. His attitude could hardly be typical. I don't think you'll ever learn the functional psychology of the dog from a mutie.'

'I imagine you're right,' he dismissed it. 'More coffee?'

'No, thanks.'

Deciding it was time to continue the discussion, he said, 'So you want to be a Shaper...'

'Yes.'

'I hate to be the one to destroy anybody's high ambitions,' he told her. 'Like poison, I hate it. Unless they have no foundation at all in reality. Then I can be ruthless. So – honestly, frankly, and in all sincerity, I do not see how it could ever be managed. Perhaps you're a fine psychiatrist – but in my opinion, it is a physical and mental impossibility for you ever to become a neuroparticipant. As for my reasons—'

'Wait,' she said. 'Not here, please. Humor me. I'm tired of this stuffy place – take me somewhere else to talk. I think I might be able to convince you there is a way.'

'Why not?' he shrugged. 'I have plenty time. Sure – you call it. Where?'

'Blindspin?'

He suppressed an unwilling chuckle at the expression, but she laughed aloud.

'Fine,' he said, 'but I'm still thirsty.'

A bottle of champagne was tallied and he signed the check despite her protests. It arrived in a colorful 'Drink While You Drive' basket, and they stood then, and she was tall, but he was taller.

Blindspin.

A single name of a multitude of practices centered about the auto-driven auto. Flashing across the country in the sure hands of an invisible chauffeur, windows all opaque, night dark, sky high, tires assailing the road below like four phantom buzzsaws – and starting from scratch and ending in the same place, and never knowing where you are going or where you have been – it is possible, for a moment, to kindle some feeling of individuality in the coldest brainpan, to produce a momentary awareness of self by virtue of an apartness from all but a sense of motion. This is because movement through darkness is the ultimate abstraction of life itself – at least that's what one of the Vital Comedians said, and everybody in the place laughed.

Actually now, the phenomenon known as blindspin first became prevalent (as might be suspected) among certain younger members of the community, when monitored highways deprived them of the means to exercise their automobiles in some of the more individualistic ways which had come to be frowned upon by the National Traffic Control Authority. Something had to be done.

It was.

The first, disastrous reaction involved the simple engineering feat of disconnecting the broadcast control unit after one had entered onto a monitored highway. This resulted in the car's vanishing from the ken of the monitor and passing back into the control of its occupants. Jealous as a deity, a monitor will not tolerate that which denies its programmed omniscience: it will thunder and lightning in the Highway Control Station nearest the point of last contact, sending winged seraphs in search of that which has slipped from sight.

Often, however, this was too late in happening, for the roads are many and well-paved. Escape from detection was, at first, relatively easy to achieve.

Other vehicles, though, necessarily behave as if a rebel has no actual existence. Its presence cannot be allowed for.

Boxed-in on a heavily-traveled section of roadway, the offender is subject to immediate annihilation in the event of any overall speedup or shift in traffic pattern which involves movement through his theoretically vacant position. This, in the early days of monitor-controls, caused a rapid series of collisions. Monitoring devices later became far more sophisticated, and mechanized cutoffs reduced the collision incidence subsequent to such an action. The quality of the pulpefactions and contusions which did occur, however, remained unaltered.

The next reaction was based on a thing which had been overlooked because it was obvious. The monitors took people where they wanted to go only because people told them they wanted to go there. A person pressing a random series of coordinates, without reference to any map, would either be left with a stalled automobile and a 'RECHECK YOUR COORDINATES' light, or would suddenly be whisked away in any direction. The latter possesses a certain romantic appeal in that it offers speed, unexpected sights, and free hands. Also, it is perfectly legal: and it is possible to navigate all over two continents in this manner, if one is possessed of sufficient wherewithal and gluteal stamina.

As is the case in all such matters, the practice diffused upwards through the age brackets. School teachers who only drove on Sundays fell into disrepute as selling points for used autos. Such is the way a world ends, said the entertainer.

End or no, the car designed to move on monitored highways is a mobile efficiency unit, complete with latrine, cupboard, refrigerator compartment and gaming table. It also sleeps two with ease and four with some crowding. On occasion, three can be a real crowd.


Render drove out of the dome and into the marginal aisle. He halted the car.

'Want to jab some coordinates?' he asked.

'You do it. My fingers know too many.'

Render punched random buttons. The Spinner moved onto

the highway. Render asked speed of the vehicle then, and it moved into the high-acceleration lane.

The Spinner's lights burnt holes in the darkness. The city backed away fast; it was a smouldering bonfire on both sides of the road, stirred by sudden gusts of wind, hidden by white swirlings, obscured by the steady fall of gray ash. Render knew his speed was only about sixty percent of what it would have been on a clear, dry night.

He did not blank the windows, but leaned back and stared out through them. Eileen 'looked' ahead into what light there was. Neither of them said anything for ten or fifteen minutes.

The city shrank to sub-city as they sped on. After a time, short sections of open road began to appear.

'Tell me what it looks like outside,' she said.

'Why didn't you ask me to describe your dinner, or the suit of armor beside our table?'

'Because I tasted one and felt the other. This is different.'

'There is snow falling outside. Take it away and what you have left is black.'

'What else?'

'There is slush on the road. When it starts to freeze, traffic will drop to a crawl unless we outrun this storm. The slush looks like an old, dark syrup, just starting to get sugary on top.'

'Anything else?'

'That's it, lady.'

'Is it snowing harder or less hard than when we left the club?'

'Harder, I should say.'

'Would you pour me a drink?' she asked him.

'Certainly.'

They turned their seats inward and Render raised the table. He fetched two glasses from the cupboard.

'Your health,' said Render, after he had poured.

'Here's looking at you.'

Render downed his drink. She sipped hers. He waited for her next comment. He knew that two cannot play at the

Socratic game, and he expected more questions before she said what she wanted to say.

She said: 'What is the most beautiful thing you have ever seen?'

Yes, he decided, he had guessed correctly.

He replied without hesitation: 'The sinking of Atlantis.'

'I was serious.'

'So was I.'

'Would you care to elaborate?'

'I sank Atlantis,' he said, 'personally.

'It was about three years ago. And God it was lovely! It was all ivory towers and golden minarets and silver balconies. There were bridges of opal, and crimson penants and a milk-white river flowing between lemon-colored banks. There were jade steeples, and trees as old as the world tickling the bellies of clouds, and ships in the great sea-harbor of Xanadu, as delicately constructed as musical instruments, all swaying with the tides. The twelve princes of the realm held court in the dozen-pillared Colliseum of the Zodiac, to listen to a Greek tenor sax play at sunset.

'The Greek, of course, was a patient of mine – paranoiac. The etiology of the thing is rather complicated, but that's what I wandered into inside his mind. I gave him free rein for awhile, and in the end I had to split Atlantis in half and sink it full fathom five. He's playing again and you've doubtless heard his sounds, if you like such sounds at all. He's good. I still see him periodically, but he is no longer the last descendent of the greatest minstrel of Atlantis. He's just a fine, late twentieth-century saxman.

'Sometimes though, as I look back on the apocalypse I worked within his vision of grandeur, I experience a fleeting sense of lost beauty – because, for a single moment, his abnormally intense feelings were my feelings, and he felt that his dream was the most beautiful thing in the world.'

He refilled their glasses.

'That wasn't exactly what I meant,' she said.

'I know.'

208

'I meant something real.'

'It was more real than real, I assure you.'

'I don't doubt it, but...'

'—But I destroyed the foundation you were laying for your argument. Okay, I apologize. I'll hand it back to you. Here's something that could be real:

'We are moving along the edge of a great bowl of sand,' he said. 'Into it, the snow is gently drifting. In the spring the snow will melt, the waters will run down into the earth, or be evaporated away by the heat of the sun. Then only the sand will remain. Nothing grows in the sand, except for an occasional cactus. Nothing lives here but snakes, a few birds, insects, burrowing things, and a wandering coyote or two. In the afternoon these things will look for shade. Any place where there's an old fence post or a rock or a skull or a cactus to block out the sun, there you will witness life cowering before the elements. But the colors are beyond belief, and the elements are more lovely, almost, than the things they destroy.'

'There is no such place near here,' she said.

'If I say it, then there is. Isn't there? I've seen it.'

'Yes... you're right.'

'And it doesn't matter if it's a painting by a woman named O'Keeffe, or something right outside our window, does it? If I've seen it?'

'I acknowledge the truth of the diagnosis,' she said. 'Do you want to speak it for me?'

'No, go ahead.'

He refilled the small glasses once more.

'The damage is in my eyes,' she told him, 'not my brain.'

He lit her cigarette.

'I can see with other eyes if I can enter other brains.'

He lit his own cigarette.

'Neuroparticipation is based upon the fact that two nervous systems can share the same impulses, the same fantasies...'

'*Controlled* fantasies.'

'I could perform therapy and at the same time experience genuine visual impressions.'

'No,' said Render.

'You don't know what it's like to be cut off from a whole area of stimuli! To know that a Mongoloid idiot can experience something you can never know – and that he cannot appreciate it because, like you, he was condemned before birth in a court of biological hapstance, in a place where there is no justice – only fortuity, pure and simple.'

'The universe did not invent justice. Man did. Unfortunately, man must reside in the universe.'

'I'm not asking the universe to help me – I'm asking you.'

'I'm sorry,' said Render.

'Why won't you help me?'

'At this moment you are demonstrating my main reason.'

'Which is . . . ?'

'Emotion. This thing means far too much to you. When the therapist is in-phase with a patient he is narcoelectrically removed from most of his own bodily sensations. This is necessary – because his mind must be completely absorbed by the task at hand. It is also necessary that his emotions undergo a similar suspension. This, of course, is impossible in the one sense that a person always emotes to some degree. But the therapist's emotions are sublimated into a generalized feeling of exhilaration – or, as in my own case, into an artistic reverie. With you, however, the "seeing" would be too much. You would be in constant danger of losing control of the dream.'

'I disagree with you.'

'Of course you do. But the fact remains that you would be dealing, and dealing constantly, with the abnormal. The power of a neurosis is unimaginable to ninety-nine point etcetera percent of the population, because we can never adequately judge the intensity of our own – let alone those of others, when we only see them from the outside. That is why no neuro-participant will ever undertake to treat a full-blown psychotic. The few pioneers in that area are all themselves in therapy today. It would be like diving into a maelstrom. If the therapist loses the upper hand in an intense session, he becomes the Shaped rather than the Shaper. The synapses respond like a fission reaction when nervous impulses are artificially augmented. The transference effect is almost instantaneous.

'I did an awful lot of skiing five years ago. This is because I was a claustrophobe. I had to run and it took me six months to beat the thing – all because of one tiny lapse that occurred in a measureless fraction of an instant. I had to refer the patient to another therapist. And this was only a minor repercussion. —If you were to go gaga over the scenery, girl, you could wind up in a rest home for life.'

She finished her drink and Render refilled the glass. The night raced by. They had left the city far behind them, and the road was open and clear. The darkness eased more and more of itself between the falling flakes. The Spinner picked up speed.

'All right,' she admitted, 'maybe you're right. Still, though, I think you can help me.'

'How?' he asked.

'Accustom me to seeing, so that the images will lose their novelty, the emotions wear off. Accept me as a patient and rid me of my sight-anxiety. Then what you have said so far will cease to apply. I will be able to undertake the training then, and give my full attention to therapy. I'll be able to sublimate the sight-pleasure into something else.'

Render wondered.

Perhaps it could be done. It would be a difficult undertaking, though.

It might also make therapeutic history.

No one was really qualified to try it, because no one had ever tried it before.

But Eileen Shallot was a rarity – no, a unique item – for it was likely she was the only person in the world who combined the necessary technical background with the unique problem.

He drained his glass, refilled it, refilled hers.

He was still considering the problem as the 'RECO-ORDINATE' light came on and the car pulled into a cutoff and stood there. He switched off the buzzer and sat there for a long while, thinking.

It was not often that other persons heard him acknowledge his feelings regarding his skill. His colleagues considered him modest. Offhand, though, it might be noted that he was aware that the day a better neuroparticipant began practicing would be the day that a troubled homo sapien was to be treated by something but immeasurably less than angels.

Two drinks remained. Then he tossed the emptied bottle into the backbin.

'You know something?' he finally said.

'What?'

'It might be worth a try.'

He swiveled about then and leaned forward to recoordinate, but she was there first. As he pressed the buttons and the S-7 swung around, she kissed him. Below her dark glasses her cheeks were moist.

II

The suicide bothered him more than it should have, and Mrs Lambert had called the day before to cancel her appointment. So Render decided to spend the morning being pensive. Accordingly, he entered the office wearing a cigar and a frown.

'Did you see . . . ?' asked Mrs Hedges.

'Yes.' He pitched his coat onto the table that stood in the far corner of the room. He crossed to the window, stared down. 'Yes,' he repeated, 'I was driving by with my windows clear. They were still cleaning up when I passed.'

'Did you know him?'

'I don't even know the name yet. How could I?'

'Priss Tully just called me – she's a receptionist for that engineering outfit up on the eighty-sixth. She says it was James Irizarry, an ad designer who had offices down the hall from them – That's a long way to fall. He must have been unconscious when he hit, huh? He bounced off the building. If you open the window and lean out you can see – off to the left there – where . . .'

'Never mind, Bennie. —Your friend have any idea why he did it?'

'Not really. His secretary came running up the hall, screaming. Seems she went in his office to see him about some drawings, just as he was getting up over the sill. There was a note on his board. "I've had everything I wanted," it said. "Why wait around?" Sort of funny, huh? I don't mean *funny* . . .'

'Yeah. —Know anything about his personal affairs?'

'Married. Coupla kids. Good professional rep. Lots of business. Sober as anybody. —He could afford an office in this building.'

'Good Lord!' Render turned. 'Have you got a case file there or something?'

'You know,' she shrugged her thick shoulders, 'I've got friends all over this hive. We always talk when things go slow. Prissy's my sister-in-law, anyhow—'

'You mean that if I dived through this window right now, my current biography would make the rounds in the next five minutes?'

'Probably,' she twisted her bright lips into a smile, 'give or take a couple. But don't do it today, huh? – You know, it would be kind of anticlimactic, and it wouldn't get the same coverage as a solus.

'Anyhow,' she continued, 'you're a mind-mixer. You wouldn't do it.'

'You're betting against statistics,' he observed. 'The medical profession, along with attorneys, manages about three times as many as most other work areas.'

'Hey!' She looked worried. 'Go 'way from my window!

'I'd have to go to work for Doctor Hanson then,' she added, 'and he's a slob.'

He moved to her desk.

'I never know when to take you seriously,' she decided.

'I appreciate your concern,' he nodded, 'indeed I do. As a matter of fact, I have never been statistic-prone – I should have repercussed out of the neuropy game four years ago.'

'You'd be a headline, though,' she mused. 'All those reporters asking me about you … Hey, why do they do it, huh?'

'Who?'

'Anybody.'

'How should I know, Bennie? I'm only a humble psyche-stirrer. If I could pinpoint a general underlying cause – and then maybe figure a way to anticipate the thing – why, it might even be better than my jumping, for newscopy. But I can't do it, because there is no single simple reason – I don't think.'

'Oh.'

'About thirty-five years ago it was the ninth leading cause of death in the United States. Now it's number six for North and South America. I think it's seventh in Europe.'

'And nobody will ever really know why Irizarry jumped?'

Reader swung a chair backward and seated himself. He knocked an ash into her petite and gleaming tray. She emptied it into the waste-chute, hastily, and coughed a significant cough.

'Oh, one can always speculate,' he said, 'and one in my profession will. The first thing to consider would be the personality traits which might predispose a man to periods of depression. People who keep their emotions under rigid control, people who are conscientious and rather compulsively concerned with small matters …' He knocked another fleck of ash into her tray and watched as she reached out to dump it, then quickly drew her hand back again. He grinned an evil grin. 'In short,' he finished, 'some of the characteristics of people in professions which require individual, rather than group performance – medicine, law, the arts.'

She regarded him speculatively.

'Don't worry though,' he chuckled, 'I'm pleased as hell with life.'

'You're kind of down in the mouth this morning.'

'Pete called me. He broke his ankle yesterday in gym class. They ought to supervise those things more closely. I'm thinking of changing his school.'

'Again?'

'Maybe. I'll see. The headmaster is going to call me this

afternoon. I don't like to keep shuffling him, but I do want him to finish school in one piece.'

'A kid can't grow up without an accident or two. It's – statistics.'

'Statistics aren't the same thing as destiny, Bennie. Everybody makes his own.'

'Statistics or destiny?'

'Both, I guess.'

'I think that if something's going to happen, it's going to happen.'

'I don't. I happen to think that the human will, backed by a sane mind, can exercise some measure of control over events. If I didn't think so, I wouldn't be in the racket I'm in.'

'The world's a machine – you know – cause, effect. Statistics do imply the prob—'

'The human mind is not a machine, and I do not know cause and effect. Nobody does.'

'You have a degree in chemistry, as I recall. You're a scientist, Doc.'

'So I'm a Trotskyite deviationist,' he smiled, stretching, 'and you were once a ballet teacher.' He got to his feet and picked up his coat.

'By the way. Miss DeVille called, left a message. She said: "How about St Moritz?"'

'Too ritzy,' he decided aloud. 'It's going to be Davos.'

Because the suicide bothered him more than it should have, Render closed the door to his office and turned off the windows and turned on the phonograph. He put on the desk light only.

*How has the quality of human life been changed*, he wrote, *since the beginnings of the industrial revolution?*

He picked up the paper and reread the sentence. It was the topic he had been asked to discuss that coming Saturday. As was typical in such cases he did not know what to say because he had too much to say, and only an hour to say it in.

He got up and began to pace the office, now filled with Beethoven's Eighth Symphony.

'The power to hurt,' he said, snapping on a lapel microphone and activating his recorder, 'has evolved in a direct relationship to technological advancement.' His imaginary audience grew quiet. He smiled. 'Man's potential for working simple mayhem has been multiplied by mass-production; his capacity for injuring the psyche through personal contacts has expanded in an exact ratio to improved communication facilities. But these are all matters of common knowledge, and are not the things I wish to consider tonight. Rather, I should like to discuss what I choose to call autopsychomimesis – the self-generated anxiety complexes which on first scrutiny appear quite similar to classic patterns, but which actually represent radical dispersions of psychic energy. They are peculiar to our times...'

He paused to dispose of his cigar and formulate his next words.

'Autopsychomimesis,' he thought aloud, 'a self-perpetuated imitation complex – almost an attention-getting affair. —A jazzman, for example, who acted hopped-up half the time, even though he had never used an addictive narcotic and only dimly remembered anyone who had – because all the stimulants and tranquilizers of today are quite benign. Like Quixote, he aspired after a legend when his music alone should have been sufficient outlet for his tensions.

'Or my Korean War Orphan, alive today by virtue of the Red Cross and UNICEF and foster parents whom he never met. He wanted a family so badly that be made one up. And what then? – He hated his imaginary father and be loved his imaginary mother quite dearly – for he was a highly intelligent boy, and he too longed after the half-true complexes of tradition. Why?

'Today, everyone is sophisticated enough to understand the time-honored patterns of psychic disturbance. Today, many of the reasons for those disturbances have been removed – not as radically as my now-adult war orphan's, but with as remarkable an effect. We are living in a neurotic past. —Again, why? Because our present times are geared to physical health, security and well-being. We have abolished hunger, though the backwoods orphan would still rather receive a package of food concentrates from a human being who cares for him than to obtain a warm meal from an automat unit in the middle of the jungle.

'Physical welfare is now every man's right in excess. The reaction to this has occurred in the area of mental health. Thanks to technology, the reasons for many of the old social problems have passed, and along with them went many of the reasons for psychic distress. But between the black of yesterday and the white of tomorrow is the great gray of today, filled with nostalgia and fear of the future, which cannot be expressed on a purely material plane, is now being represented by a willful seeking after historical anxiety-modes . . .'

The phone-box buzzed briefly. Render did not hear it over the Eighth.

'We are afraid of what we do not know,' he continued, 'and tomorrow is a very great unknown. My own specialized area of psychiatry did not even exist thirty years ago. Science is capable of advancing itself so rapidly now that there is a genuine public uneasiness – I might even say "distress" – as to the logical outcome: the total mechanization of everything in the world . . .'

He passed near the desk as the phone buzzed again. He switched off his microphone and softened the Eighth.

'Hello?'

'Saint Moritz,' she said.

'Davos,' he replied firmly.

'Charlie, you are most exasperating!'

'Jill, dear – so are you.'

'Shall we discuss it tonight?'

'There is nothing to discuss!'

'You'll pick me up at five, though?'

He hesitated, then:

'Yes, at five. How come the screen is blank?'

'I've had my hair fixed. I'm going to surprise you again.'

He suppressed an idiot chuckle, said, 'Pleasantly, I hope.

Okay, see you then,' waited for her 'good-bye,' and broke the connection.

He transpared the windows, turned off the light on his desk, and looked outside.

Gray again overhead, and many slow flakes of snow – wandering, not being blown about much – moving downward and then losing themselves in the tumult ...

He also saw, when he opened the window and leaned out, the place off to the left where Irizarry had left his next-to-last mark on the world.

He closed the window and listened to the rest of the symphony. It had been a week since he had gone blind-spinning with Eileen. Her appointment was for one o'clock.

He remembered her fingertips brushing over his face, like leaves, or the bodies of insects, learning his appearance in the ancient manner of the blind. The memory was not altogether pleasant. He wondered why.

Far below, a patch of hosed pavement was blank once again; under a thin, fresh shroud of white, it was slippery as glass. A building custodian hurried outside and spread salt on it, before someone slipped and hurt himself.

Sigmund was the myth of Fenris come alive. After Render had instructed Mrs Hedges, 'Show them in,' the door had begun to open, was suddenly pushed wider, and a pair of smoky-yellow eyes stared in at him. The eyes were set in a strangely misshapen dog-skull.

Sigmund's was not a low canine brow, slanting up slightly from the muzzle; it was a high, shaggy cranium making the eyes appear even more deep-set than they actually were. Render shivered slightly at the size and aspect of that head. The muties he had seen had all been puppies. Sigmund was full-grown, and his gray-black fur had a tendency to bristle, which made him appear somewhat larger than a normal specimen of the breed.

He stared in at Render in a very un-doglike way and made

a growling noise which sounded too much like, 'Hello, doctor,' to have been an accident.

Render nodded and stood.

'Hello, Sigmund,' he said. 'Come in.'

The dog turned his head, sniffing the air of the room – as though deciding whether or not to trust his ward within its confines. Then he returned his stare to Render, dipped his head in an affirmative, and shouldered the door open. Perhaps the entire encounter had taken only one disconcerting second.

Eileen followed him, holding lightly to the double-leashed harness. The dog padded soundlessly across the thick rug – head low, as though he were stalking something. His eyes never left Render's.

'So this is Sigmund...? How are you, Eileen?'

'Fine. —Yes, he wanted very badly to come along, and *I* wanted you to meet him.'

Render led her to a chair and seated her. She unsnapped the double guide from the dog's harness and placed it on the floor. Sigmund sat down beside it and continued to stare at Render.

'How is everything at State Psych?'

'Same as always. —May I bum a cigarette, doctor? I forgot mine.'

He placed it between her fingers, furnished a light. She was wearing a dark blue suit and her glasses were flame blue. The silver spot on her forehead reflected the glow of his lighter; she continued to stare at that point in space after he had withdrawn his hand. Her shoulder-length hair appeared a trifle lighter than it had seemed on the night they met; today it was like a fresh-minted copper coin.

Render seated himself on the corner of his desk, drawing up his world-ashtray with his toe.

'You told me before that being blind did not mean that you had never seen. I didn't ask you to explain it then. But I'd like to ask you now.'

'I had a neuroparticipation session with Doctor Riscomb,' she told him, 'before he had his accident. He wanted to accommodate my mind to visual impressions. Unfortunately, there was never a second session.'

'I see. What did you do in that session?'

She crossed her ankles and Render noted they were well-turned.

'Colors, mostly. The experience was quite overwhelming.'

'How well do you remember them? How long ago was it?'

'About six months ago – and I shall never forget them. I have even dreamed in color patterns since then.'

'How often?'

'Several times a week.'

'What sort of associations do they carry?'

'Nothing special. They just come into my mind along with other stimuli now – in a pretty haphazard way.'

'How?'

'Well, for instance, when you ask me a question it's a sort of yellowish-orangish pattern that I "see." Your greeting was a kind of silvery thing. Now that you're just sitting there listening to me, saying nothing, I associate you with a deep, almost violet, blue.'

Sigmund shifted his gaze to the desk and stared at the side panel.

*Can he hear the recorder spinning inside?* wondered Render. *And if he can, can he guess what it is and what it's doing?*

If so, the dog would doubtless tell Eileen – not that she was unaware of what was now an accepted practice – and she might not like being reminded that he considered her case as therapy, rather than a mere mechanical adaptation process. If he thought it would do any good (he smiled inwardly at the notion), he would talk to the dog in private about it.

Inwardly, he shrugged.

'I'll construct a rather elementary fantasy world then,' he said finally, 'and introduce you to some basic forms today.'

She smiled; and Render looked down at the myth who crouched by her side, its tongue a piece of beefsteak hanging over a picket fence.

*Is he smiling too?*

'Thank you,' she said.

Sigmund wagged his tail.

'Well then,' Render disposed of his cigarette near Madagascar, 'I'll fetch out the "egg" now and test it. In the meantime,' he pressed an unobstrusive button, 'perhaps some music would prove relaxing.'

She started to reply, but a Wagnerian overture snuffed out the words. Render jammed the button again, and there was a moment of silence during which he said, 'Heh heh. Thought Respighi was next.'

It took two more pushes for him to locate some Roman pines.

'You could have left him on,' she observed. 'I'm quite fond of Wagner.'

'No thanks,' he said, opening the closet, 'I'd keep stepping in all those piles of leitmotifs.'

The great egg drifted out into the office, soundless as a cloud. Render heard a soft growl behind as he drew it toward the desk. He turned quickly.

Like the shadow of a bird, Sigmund had gotten to his feet, crossed the room, and was already circling the machine and sniffing at it – tail taut, ears flat, teeth bared.

'Easy, Sig,' said Render. 'It's an Omnichannel Neural T & R Unit. It won't bite or anything like that. It's just a machine, like a car, or a teevee, or a dishwasher. That's what we're going to use today to show Eileen what some things look like.'

'Don't like it,' rumbled the dog.

'Why?'

Sigmund had no reply, so he stalked back to Eileen and laid his head in her lap.

'Don't like it,' he repeated, looking up at her.

'Why?'

'No words,' he decided. 'We go home now?'

'No,' she answered him. 'You're going to curl up in the corner and take a nap, and I'm going to curl up in that machine and do the same thing – sort of.'

'No good,' he said, tail drooping.

'Go on now,' she pushed him, 'lie down and behave yourself.'

He acquiesced, but he whined when Render blanked the windows and touched the button which transformed his desk into the operator's seat.

He whined once more – when the egg, connected now to an outlet, broke in the middle and the top slid back and up, revealing the interior.

Render seated himself. His chair became a contour couch and moved in halfway beneath the console. He sat upright and it moved back again, becoming a chair. He touched a part of the desk and half the ceiling disengaged itself, reshaped itself, and lowered to hover overhead like a huge bell. He stood and moved around to the side of the ro-womb. Respighi spoke of pines and such, and Render disengaged an earphone from beneath the egg and leaned back across his desk. Blocking one ear with his shoulder and pressing the microphone to the other, he played upon the buttons with his free hand. Leagues of surf drowned the tone poem; miles of traffic overrode it; a great clanging bell sent fracture lines running through it; and the feedback said: '... Now that you are just sitting there listening to me, saying nothing, I associate you with a deep, almost violet, blue ...'

He switched to the face mask and monitored, *one* – cinnamon, *two* – leaf mold, *three* – deep reptilian musk ... and down through thirst, and the tastes of honey and vinegar and salt, and back on up through lilacs and wet concrete, a before-the-storm whiff of ozone, and all the basic olfactory and gustatory cues for morning, afternoon and evening in the town.

The couch floated normally in its pool of mercury, magnetically stabilized by the walls of the egg. He set the tapes.

The ro-womb was in perfect condition.

'Okay,' said Render, turning, 'everything checks.'

She was just placing her glasses atop her folded garments. She had undressed while Render was testing the machine. He was perturbed by her narrow waist, her large, dark-pointed breasts, her long legs. She was too well-formed for a woman her height, he decided.

He realized though, as he stared at her, that his main annoyance was, of course, the fact that she was his patient.

'Ready here,' she said, and he moved to her side.

He took her elbow and guided her to the machine. Her fingers explored its interior. As he helped her enter the unit, he saw that her eyes were a vivid seagreen. Of this, too, he disapproved.

'Comfortable?'

'Yes.'

'Okay then, we're set. I'm going to close it now. Sweet dreams.'

The upper shell dropped slowly. Closed, it grew opaque, then dazzling. Render was staring down at his own distorted reflection.

He moved back in the direction of his desk.

Sigmund was on his feet, blocking the way.

Render reached down to pat his head, but the dog jerked it aside.

'Take me, with,' he growled.

'I'm afraid that can't be done, old fellow,' said Render. 'Besides, we're not really going anywhere. We'll just be dozing, right here, in this room.'

The dog did not seem mollified.

'Why?'

Render sighed. An argument with a dog was about the most ludicrous thing he could imagine when sober.

'Sig,' he said, 'I'm trying to help her learn what things look like. You doubtless do a fine job guiding her around in this world which she cannot see – but she needs to know what it looks like now, and I'm going to show her.'

'Then she, will not, need me.'

'Of course she will.' Render almost laughed. The pathetic thing was here bound so closely to the absurd thing that he could not help it. 'I can't restore her sight,' he explained. 'I'm just going to transfer her some sight abstractions – sort of lend her my eyes for a short time. Savvy?'

'No,' said the dog. 'Take mine.'

Render turned off the music.

*The whole mutie-master relationship might be worth six volumes,* he decided, *in German.*

He pointed to the far corner.

'Lie down, over there, like Eileen told you. This isn't going to take long, and when it's all over you're going to leave the same way you came – you leading. Okay?'

Sigmund did not answer, but he turned and moved off to the corner, tail drooping again.

Render seated himself and lowered the hood, the operator's modified version of the ro-womb. He was alone before the ninety white buttons and the two red ones. The world ended in the blackness beyond the console. He loosened his necktie and unbuttoned his collar.

He removed the helmet from its receptacle and checked its leads. Donning it then, he swung the half-mask up over his lower face and dropped the darksheet down to meet with it. He rested his right arm in the sling, and with a single tapping gesture, he eliminated his patient's consciousness.

A Shaper does not press white buttons consciously. He wills conditions. Then deeply-implanted muscular reflexes exert an almost imperceptible pressure against the sensitive arm-sling, which glides into the proper position and encourages an extended finger to move forward. A button is pressed. The sling moves on.

Render felt a tingling at the base of his skull; he smelled fresh-cut grass.

Suddenly he was moving up the great gray alley between the worlds.

After what seemed a long time. Render felt that he was footed on a strange Earth. He could see nothing; it was only a sense of presence that informed him he had arrived. It was the darkest of all the dark nights he had ever known.

He willed that the darkness disperse. Nothing happened.

A part of his mind came awake again, a part he had not realized was sleeping; he recalled whose world be had entered.

He listened for her presence. He heard fear and anticipation.

He willed color. First, red...

He felt a correspondence. Then there was an echo.

Everything became red; he inhabited the center of an infinite ruby.

Orange. Yellow...

He was caught in a piece of amber.

Green now, and he added the exhalations of a sultry sea. Blue, and the coolness of evening.

He stretched his mind then, producing all the colors at once. They came in great swirling plumes.

Then he tore them apart and forced a form upon them.

An incandescent rainbow arced across the black sky.

He fought for browns and grays below him. Self-luminescent, they appeared – in shimmering, shifting patches.

Somewhere, a sense of awe. There was no trace of hysteria though, so he continued with the Shaping.

He managed a horizon, and the blackness drained away beyond it. The sky grew faintly blue, and he ventured a herd of dark clouds. There was resistance to his efforts at creating distance and depth, so he reinforced the tableau with a very faint sound of surf. A transference from an auditory concept of distance came slowly then, as he pushed the clouds about. Quickly, he threw up a high forest to offset a rising wave of acrophobia.

The panic vanished.

Render focused his attention on tall trees – oaks and pines, poplars and sycamores. He hurled them about like spears, in ragged arrays of greens and browns and yellows, unrolled a thick mat of morning-moist grass, dropped a series of gray boulders and greenish logs at irregular intervals, and tangled and twined the branches overhead, casting a uniform shade throughout the glen.

The effect was staggering. It seemed as if the entire world was shaken with a sob, then silent.

Through the stillness he felt her presence. He had decided it would be best to lay the groundwork quickly, to set up a tangible headquarters, to prepare a field for operations. He could backtrack later, be could repair and amend the results of the trauma in the sessions yet to come; but this much, at least, was necessary for a beginning.

With a start, he realized that the silence was not a withdrawal. Eileen had made herself immanent in the trees and the grass, the stones and the bushes; she was personalizing their forms, relating them to tactile sensations, sounds, temperatures, aromas.

With a soft breeze, he stirred the branches of the trees. Just beyond the bounds of seeing he worked out the splashing sounds of a brook.

There was a feeling of joy. He shared it.

She was bearing it extremely well, so he decided to extend the scope of the exercise. He let his mind wander among the trees, experiencing a momentary doubling of vision, during which time he saw an enormous hand riding in an aluminum carriage toward a circle of white.

He was beside the brook now and he was seeking her, carefully.

He drifted with the water. He had not yet taken on a form. The splashes became a gurgling as he pushed the brook through shallow places and over rocks. At his insistence, the waters became more articulate.

'Where are you?' asked the brook.

*Here! Here!*

*Here!*

... *and here!* replied the trees, the bushes, the stones, the grass.

'Choose one,' said the brook, as it widened, rounded a mass of rock, then bent its way down a slope, heading toward a blue pool.

*I cannot*, was the answer from the wind.

'You must.' The brook widened and poured into the pool,

swirled about the surface, then stilled itself and reflected branches and dark clouds. 'Now!'

*Very well*, echoed the wood, *in a moment.*

The mist rose above the lake and drifted to the bank of the pool.

'Now,' tinkled the mist.

*Here, then...*

She had chosen a small willow. It swayed in the wind; it trailed its branches in the water.

'Eileen Shallot,' he said, 'regard the lake.'

The breezes shifted; the willow bent.

It was not difficult for him to recall her face, her body. The tree spun as though rootless. Eileen stood in the midst of a quiet explosion of leaves; she stared, frightened, into the deep blue mirror of Render's mind, the lake.

She covered her face with her hands, but it could not stop the seeing.

'Behold yourself,' said Render.

She lowered her hands and peered downward. Then she turned in every direction, slowly; she studied herself. Finally:

'I feel I am quite lovely,' she said. 'Do I feel so because you want me to, or is it true?'

She looked all about as she spoke, seeking the Shaper.

'It is true,' said Render, from everywhere.

'Thank you.'

There was a swirl of white and she was wearing a belted garment of damask. The light in the distance brightened almost imperceptibly. A faint touch of pink began at the base of the lowest cloudbank.

'What is happening there?' she asked, facing that direction.

'I am going to show you a sunrise,' said Render, 'and I shall probably botch it a bit – but then, it's my first professional sunrise under these circumstances.'

'Where are *you*?' she asked.

'Everywhere,' he replied.

'Please take on a form so that I can see you.'

'All right.'

'Your natural form.'

He willed that he be beside her on the bank, and he was.

Startled by a metallic flash, he looked downward. The world receded for an instant, then grew stable once again. He laughed, and the laugh froze as he thought of something.

He was wearing the suit of armor which had stood beside their table in the Partridge and Scalpel on the night they met.

She reached out and touched it.

'The suit of armor by our table,' she acknowledged, running her fingertips over the plates and the junctures. 'I associated it with you that night.'

'... And you stuffed me into it just now,' he commented. 'You're a strong-willed woman.'

The armor vanished and he was wearing his gray-brown suit and looseknit bloodclot necktie and a professional expression.

'Behold the real me,' he smiled faintly. 'Now, to the sunset. I'm going to use all the colors. Watch!'

They seated themselves on the green park bench which had appeared behind them, and Render pointed in the direction he had decided upon as east.

Slowly, the sun worked through its morning attitudes. For the first time in this particular world it shone down like a god, and reflected off the lake, and broke the clouds, and set the landscape to smouldering beneath the mist that arose from the moist wood.

Watching, watching intently, staring directly into the ascending bonfire, Eileen did not move for a long while, nor speak. Render could sense her fascination.

She was staring at the source of all light; it reflected back from the gleaming coin on her brow, like a single drop of blood.

Render said, 'That is the sun, and those are clouds,' and he clapped his hands and the clouds covered the sun and there was a soft rumble overhead, 'and that is thunder,' he finished.

The rain fell then, shattering the lake and tickling their faces, making sharp striking sounds on the leaves, then soft tapping sounds, dripping down from the branches overhead, soaking their garments and plastering their hair, running down their necks and falling into their eyes, turning patches of brown earth to mud.

A splash of lightning covered the sky, and a second later there was another peal of thunder.

'. . . And this is a summer storm,' he lectured. 'You see how the rain affects the foliage and ourselves. What you just saw in the sky before the thunderclap was lightning.'

'. . . Too much,' she said. 'Let up on it for a moment, please.'

The rain stopped instantly and the sun broke through the clouds.

'I have the damndest desire for a cigarette,' she said, 'but I left mine in another world.'

As she said it one appeared, already lighted, between her fingers.

'It's going to taste rather flat,' said Render strangely. He watched her for a moment, then:

'I didn't give you that cigarette,' he noted. 'You picked it from my mind.'

The smoke laddered and spiraled upward, was swept away.

'. . . Which means that, for the second time today, I have underestimated the pull of that vacuum in your mind – in the place where sight ought to be. You are assimilating these new impressions very rapidly. You're even going to the extent of groping after new ones. Be careful. Try to contain that impulse.'

'It's like a hunger,' she said.

'Perhaps we had best conclude this session now.'

Their clothing was dry again. A bird began to sing.

'No, wait! Please! I'll be careful. I want to see more things.'

'There is always the next visit,' said Render. 'But I suppose we can manage one more. Is there something you want very badly to see?'

'Yes. Winter. Snow.'

'Okay,' smiled the Shaper, 'then wrap yourself in that fur-piece . . .'

*

229

The afternoon slipped by rapidly after the departure of his patient. Render was in a good mood. He felt emptied and filled again. He had come through the first trial without suffering any repercussions. He decided that he was going to succeed. His satisfaction was greater than his fear. It was with a sense of exhilaration that he returned to working on his speech.

'...And what is the power to hurt?' he inquired of the microphone.

'We live by pleasure and we live by pain,' he answered himself. 'Either can frustrate and either can encourage. But while pleasure and pain are rooted in biology, they are conditioned by society: thus are values to be derived. Because of the enormous masses of humanity, hectically changing positions in space every day throughout the cities of the world, there has come into necessary being a series of totally inhuman controls upon these movements. Every day they nibble their way into new areas – driving our cars, flying our planes, interviewing us, diagnosing our diseases – and I cannot even venture a moral judgment upon these intrusions. They have become necessary. Ultimately, they may prove salutary.

'The point I wish to make, however, is that we are often unaware of our own values. We cannot honestly tell what a thing means to us until it is removed from our life-situation. If an object of value ceases to exist, then the psychic energies which were bound up in it are released. We seek after new objects of value in which to invest this – mana, if you like, or libido, if you don't. And no one thing which has vanished during the past three or four or five decades was, in itself, massively significant; and no new thing which came into being during that time is massively malicious toward the people it has replaced or the people it in some manner controls. A society, though, is made up of many things, and when these things are changed too rapidly the results are unpredictable. An intense study of mental illness is often quite revealing as to the nature of the stresses in the society where the illness was made. If anxiety-patterns fall into special groups and classes, then something of the discontent of society can be learned from them.

Karl Jung pointed out that when consciousness is repeatedly frustrated in a quest for values it will turn its search to the unconscious; failing there, it will proceed to quarry its way into the hypothetical collective unconscious. He noted, in the postwar analyses of ex-Nazis, that the longer they searched for something to erect from the ruins of their lives – having lived through a period of classical iconoclasm, and then seen their new ideals topple as well – the longer they searched, the further back they seemed to reach into the collective unconscious of their people. Their dreams themselves came to take on patterns out of the Teutonic mythos.

'This, in a much less dramatic sense, is happening today. There are historical periods when the group tendency for the mind to turn in upon itself, to turn back, is greater than at other times. We are living in such a period of Quixotism, in the original sense of the term. This is because the power to hurt, in our time, is the power to ignore, to baffle – and it is no longer the exclusive property of human beings—'

A buzz interrupted him then. He switched off the recorder, touched the phone-box.

'Charles Render speaking,' he told it.

'This is Paul Charter,' lisped the box. 'I am headmaster at Dilling.'

'Yes?'

The picture cleared. Render saw a man whose eyes were set close together beneath a high forehead. The forehead was heavily creased; the mouth twitched as it spoke.

'Well, I want to apologize again for what happened. It was a faulty piece of equipment that caused—'

'Can't you afford proper facilities? Your fees are high enough.'

'It was a *new* piece of equipment. It was a factory defect—'

'Wasn't there anybody in charge of the class?'

'Yes, but—'

'Why didn't he inspect the equipment? Why wasn't he on hand to prevent the fall?'

'He *was* on hand, but it happened too fast for him to do

anything. As for inspecting the equipment for factory defects, that isn't his job. Look, I'm very sorry. I'm quite fond of your boy. I can assure you nothing like this will ever happen again.'

'You're right, there. But that's because I'm picking him up tomorrow morning and enrolling him in a school that exercises proper safety precautions.'

Render ended the conversation with a flick of his finger. After several minutes had passed he stood and crossed the room to his small wall safe, which was partly masked, though not concealed, by a shelf of books. It took only a moment for him to open it and withdraw a jewel box containing a cheap necklace and a framed photograph of a man resembling himself, though somewhat younger, and a woman whose upswept hair was dark and whose chin was small, and two youngsters between them – the girl holding the baby in her arms and forcing her bright bored smile on ahead. Render always stared for only a few seconds on such occasions, fondling the necklace, and then he shut the box and locked it away again for many months.

*Whump! Whump!* went the bass. *Tchg-tchg-tchga-tchg*, the gourds.

The gelatins splayed reds, greens, blues, and godawful yellows about the amazing metal dancers.

HUMAN? asked the marquee.

ROBOTS? (immediately below).

COME SEE FOR YOURSELF! (across the bottom, cryptically).

So they did.

Render and Jill were sitting at a microscopic table, thankfully set back against a wall, beneath charcoal caricatures of personalities largely unknown (there being so many personalities among the subcultures of a city of fourteen million people). Nose crinkled with pleasure, Jill stared at the present focal point of this particular subculture, occasionally raising her shoulders to ear level to add emphasis to a silent laugh or a small squeal, because the performers were just *too* human – the way the ebon robot ran his fingers along the silver robot's forearm as they parted and passed . . .

Render alternated his attention between Jill and the dancers and a wicked-looking decoction that resembled nothing so much as a small bucket of whiskey sours strewn with seaweed (through which the Kraken might at any moment arise to drag some hapless ship down to its doom).

'Charlie, I think they're really people!'

Render disentangled his gaze from her hair and bouncing earrings.

He studied the dancers down on the floor, somewhat below the table area, surrounded by music.

There *could* be humans within those metal shells. If so, their dance was a thing of extreme skill. Though the manufacture of sufficiently light alloys was no problem, it would be some trick for a dancer to cavort so freely – and for so long a period of time, and with such effortless-seeming ease – within a head-to-toe suit of armor, without so much as a grate or a click or a clank.

Soundless . . .

They glided like two gulls; the larger, the color of polished anthracite, and the other, like a moonbeam falling through a window upon a silk-wrapped manikin.

Even when they touched there was no sound – or if there was, it was wholly masked by the rhythms of the band.

*Whump-whump! Tchga-tchg!*

Render took another drink.

Slowly, it turned into an apache-dance. Render checked his watch. Too long for normal entertainers, he decided. They must be robots. As he looked up again the black robot hurled the silver robot perhaps ten feet and turned his back on her.

There was no sound of striking metal.

*Wonder what a setup like that costs?* he mused.

'Charlie! There was no sound! How do they do that?'

'I've no idea,' said Render.

The gelatins were yellow again, then red, then blue, then green.

'You'd think it would damage their mechanisms, wouldn't you?'

The white robot crawled back and the other swiveled his wrist around and around, a lighted cigarette between the fingers. There was laughter as he pressed it mechanically to his lipless faceless face. The silver robot confronted him. He turned away again, dropped the cigarette, ground it out slowly, soundlessly, then suddenly turned back to his partner. Would he throw her again? No . . .

Slowly then. like the greatlegged birds of the East, they recommenced their movement, slowly, and with many turnings away.

Something deep within Render was amused, but he was too far gone to ask it what was funny. So he went looking for the Kraken in the bottom of the glass instead.

Jill was clutching his biceps then, drawing his attention back to the floor.

As the spotlight tortured the spectrum, the black robot raised the silver one high above his head, slowly, slowly, and then commenced spinning with her in that position – arms outstretched, back arched, legs scissored – very slowly, at first. Then faster.

Suddenly they were whirling with an unbelievable speed, and the gelatins rotated faster and faster.

Render shook his head to clear it.

They were moving so rapidly that they *had* to fall – human or robot. But they didn't. They were a mandala. They were a gray form uniformity. Render looked down.

Then slowing, and slower, slower. Stopped.

The music stopped.

Blackness followed. Applause filled it.

When the lights came on again the two robots were standing statue-like, facing the audience. Very, very slowly, they bowed.

The applause increased.

Then they turned and were gone.

The music came on and the light was clear again. A babble of voices arose. Render slew the Kraken.

'What d'you think of that?' she asked him.

Render made his face serious and said: 'Am I a man dreaming I am a robot, or a robot dreaming I am a man?' He grinned, then added: 'I don't know.'

She punched his shoulder gaily at that and he observed that she was drunk.

'I am not,' she protested. 'Not much, anyhow. Not as much as you.'

'Still, I think you ought to see a doctor about it. Like me. Like now. Let's get out of here and go for a drive.'

'Not yet, Charlie. I want to see them once more, huh? Please?'

'If I have another drink I won't be able to see that far.'

'Then order a cup of coffee.'

'Yaagh!'

'Then order a beer.'

'I'll suffer without.'

There were people on the dance floor now, but Render's feet felt like lead.

He lit a cigarette.

'So you had a dog talk to you today?'

'Yes. Something very disconcerting about that . . .'

'Was she pretty?'

'It was a boy dog. And boy, was he ugly!'

'Silly. I mean his mistress.'

'You know I never discuss cases, Jill.'

'You told me about her being blind and about the dog. All I want to know is if she's pretty.'

'Well . . . Yes and no.' He bumped her under the table and gestured vaguely. 'Well, you know . . .'

'Same thing all the way around,' she told the waiter who had appeared suddenly out of an adjacent pool of darkness, nodded, and vanished as abruptly.

'There go my good intentions,' sighed Render. 'See how you like being examined by a drunken sot, that's all I can say.'

'You'll sober up fast, you always do. Hippocratics and all that.'

He sniffed, glanced at his watch.

'I have to be in Connecticut tomorrow. Pulling Pete out of that damned school . . .'

She sighed, already tired of the subject.

'I think you worry too much about him. Any kid can bust an ankle. It's part of growing up. I broke my wrist when I was seven. It was an accident. It's not the school's fault, those things sometimes happen.'

'Like hell,' said Render, accepting his dark drink from the dark tray the dark man carried. 'If they can't do a good job, I'll find someone who can.'

She shrugged.

'You're the boss. All I know is what I read in the papers.

'—And you're still set on Davos, even though you know you meet a better class of people at Saint Moritz?' she added.

'We're going there to ski, remember? I like the runs better at Davos.'

'I can't score any tonight, can I?'

He squeezed her hand.

'You always score with me, honey.'

And they drank their drinks and smoked their cigarettes and held their hands until the people left the dance floor and filed back to their microscopic tables, and the gelatins spun round and round, tinting clouds of smoke from hell to sunrise and back again, and the bass went *whump!*

*Tchga-tchga!*

'Oh, Charlie! Here they come again!'

The sky was clear as crystal. The roads were clean. The snow had stopped.

Jill's breathing was the breathing of a sleeper. The S-7 raced across the bridges of the city. If Render sat very still he could convince himself that only his body was drunk; but whenever he moved his head the universe began to dance about him. As it did so, he imagined himself within a dream, and Shaper of it all.

For one instant this was true. He turned the big clock in the sky backward, smiling as he dozed. Another instant and he was awake again, and unsmiling.

The universe had taken revenge for his presumption. For one reknown moment with the helplessness which he had loved beyond helping, it had charged him the price of the lake-bottom vision once again; and as he had moved once more toward the wreck at the bottom of the world – like a swimmer, as unable to speak – he heard, from somewhere high over the Earth, and filtered down to him through the waters above the Earth, the howl of the Fenris Wolf as it prepared to devour the moon; and as this occurred, he knew that the sound was as like to the trump of a judgment as the lady by his side was unlike the moon. Every bit. In all ways. And he was afraid.

## III

'...The plain, the direct, and the blunt. This is Winchester Cathedral,' said the guidebook. 'With its floor-to-ceiling shafts, like so many huge treetrunks, it achieves a ruthless control over its spaces: the ceilings are flat; each bay, separated by those shafts, is itself a thing of certainty and stability. It seems, indeed, to reflect something of the spirit of William the Conqueror. Its disdain of mere elaboration and its passionate dedication to the love of another world would make it seem, too, an appropriate setting for some tale out of Mallory...'

'Observe the scalloped capitals,' said the guide. 'In their primitive fluting they anticipated what was later to become a common motif ...'

'Faugh!' said Render – softly though, because he was in a group inside a church.

'Shh!' said Jill (Fotlock – that was her real last name) DeVille.

But Render was impressed as well as distressed.

Hating Jill's hobby though, had become so much of a reflex with him that he would sooner have taken his rest seated beneath an oriental device which dripped water onto his head than to admit he occasionally enjoyed walking through the arcades and the galleries, the passages and the tunnels, and getting all out of breath climbing up the high twisty stairways of towers.

So he ran his eyes over everything, burned everything down by shutting them, then built the place up again out of the still smouldering ashes of memory, all so that at a later date he would be able to repeat the performance, offering the vision to his one patient who could see only in this manner. This building he disliked less than most. Yes, he would take it back to her.

The camera in his mind photographing the surroundings, Render walked with the others, overcoat over his arm, his fingers anxious to reach after a cigarette. He kept busy ignoring his guide, realizing this to be the nadir of all forms of human protest. As he walked through Winchester he thought of his last two sessions with Eileen Shallot. He recalled his almost unwilling Adam-attitude as he had named all the animals passing before them, led of course by the one she had wanted to see, colored fearsome by his own unease. He had felt pleasantly bucolic after boning up on an old Botany text and then proceeding to Shape and name the flowers of the fields.

So far they had stayed out of the cities, far away from the machines. Her emotions were still too powerful at the sight of the simple, carefully introduced objects to risk plunging her into so complicated and chaotic a wilderness yet; he would build her city slowly.

Something passed rapidly, high above the cathedral, uttering a sonic boom. Render took Jill's hand in his for a moment and smiled as she looked up at him. Knowing she verged upon beauty, Jill normally took great pains to achieve it. But today her hair was simply drawn back and knotted behind her head, and her lips and her eyes were pale; and her exposed ears were tiny and white and somewhat pointed.

'Observe the scalloped capitals,' he whispered. 'In their primitive fluting they anticipated what was later to become a common motif.'

'Faugh!' she said.

'Shh!' said a sunburned little woman nearby, whose face seemed to crack and fall back together again as she pursed and unpursed her lips.

Later as they strolled back toward their hotel. Render said, 'Okay on Winchester?'

'Okay on Winchester.'

'Happy?'

'Happy.'

'Good, then we can leave this afternoon.'

'All right.'

'For Switzerland...'

She stopped and toyed with a button on his coat.

'Couldn't we just spend a day or two looking at some old chateaux first? After all, they're just across the channel, and you could be sampling all the local wines while I looked...'

'Okay,' he said.

She looked up – a trifle surprised.

'What? No argument?' she smiled. 'Where is your fighting spirit? – to let me push you around like this?'

She took his arm then and they walked on as he said, 'Yesterday, while we were galloping about in the innards of that old castle, I heard a weak moan, and then a voice cried out, "For the love of God, Montresor!" I think it was my fighting spirit, because I'm certain it was my voice. I've given up *der geist der stets verneint. Pax vobiscum!* Let us be gone to France. *Alors!*'

'Dear Rendy, it'll only be another day or two...'

'Amen,' he said, 'though my skis that were waxed are already waning.'

So they did that, and on the morn of the third day, when she spoke to him of castles in Spain, he reflected aloud that while psychologists drink and only grow angry, psychiatrists have been known to drink, grow angry and break things. Construing this as a veiled threat aimed at the Wedgewoods she had collected, she acquiesced to his desire to go skiing.

*

Free! Render almost screamed it.

His heart was pounding inside his head. He leaned hard. He cut to the left. The wind strapped at his face; a shower of ice crystals, like bullets of emery, fled by him, scraped against his cheek.

He was moving. Aye – the world had ended as Weissfluhjoch, and Dorftali led down and away from this portal.

His feet were two gleaming rivers which raced across the stark, curving plains; they could not be frozen in their course. Downward. He flowed. Away from all the rooms of the world. Away from the stifling lack of intensity, from the day's hundred spoon-fed welfares, from the killing pace of the forced amusements that hacked at the Hydra, leisure; away.

And as he fled down the run he felt a strong desire to look back over his shoulder, as though to see whether the world he had left behind and above had set one fearsome embodiment of itself, like a shadow, to trail along after him, hunt him down and drag him back to a warm and well-lit coffin in the sky, there to be laid to rest with a spike of aluminum driven through his will and a garland of alternating currents smothering his spirit.

'I hate you,' he breathed between clenched teeth, and the wind carried the words back; and he laughed then, for he always analyzed his emotions, as a matter of reflex; and he added, 'Exit Orestes, mad, pursued by the Furies...'

After a time the slope leveled out and he reached the bottom of the run and had to stop.

He smoked one cigarette then and rode back up to the top so that he could come down it again for nontherapeutic reasons.

That night he sat before a fire in the big lodge, feeling its warmth soaking into his tired muscles. Jill massaged his shoulders as he played Rorschach with the flames, and he came upon a blazing goblet which was snatched away from him in the same instant by the sound of his name being spoken somewhere across the Hall of the Nine Hearths.

'Charles Render!' said the voice (only it sounded more like 'Sharlz Runder'), and his head instantly jerked in that direction, but his eyes danced with too many afterimages for him to isolate the source of the calling.

'Maurice?' he queried after a moment, 'Bartelmetz?'

'Aye,' came the reply, and then Render saw the familiar grizzled visage, set neckless and balding above the red and blue shag sweater that was stretched mercilessly about the wine-keg rotundity of the man who now picked his way in their direction, deftly avoiding the strewn crutches and the stacked skis and the people who, like Jill and Render, disdained sitting in chairs.

Render stood, stretching, and shook hands as he came upon them.

'You've put on more weight,' Render observed. 'That's unhealthy.'

'Nonsense, it's all muscle. How have you been, and what are you up to these days?' He looked down at Jill and she smiled back at him.

'This is Miss DeVille,' said Render.

'Jill,' she acknowledged.

He bowed slightly, finally releasing Render's aching hand.

'. . . And this is Professor Maurice Bartelmetz of Vienna,' finished Render, 'a benighted disciple of all forms of dialectical pessimism, and a very distinguished pioneer in neuroparticipation – although you'd never guess it to look at him. I had the good fortune to be his pupil for over a year.'

Bartelmetz nodded and agreed with him, taking in the Schnapsflasche Render brought forth from a small plastic bag, and accepting the collapsible cup which he filled to the brim.

'Ah, you are a good doctor still,' he sighed. 'You have diagnosed the case in an instant and you make the proper prescription. Nozdrovia!'

'Seven years in a gulp,' Render acknowledged, refilling their glasses.

'Then we shall make time more malleable by sipping it.'

They seated themselves on the floor, and the fire roared up

through the great brick chimney as the logs burned themselves back to branches, to twigs, to thin sticks, ring by yearly ring.

Render replenished the fire.

'I read your last book,' said Bartelmetz finally, casually, 'about four years ago.'

Render reckoned that to be correct.

'Are you doing any research work these days?'

Render poked lazily at the fire.

'Yes,' he answered, 'sort of.'

He glanced at Jill, who was dozing with her cheek against the arm of the huge leather chair that held his emergency Bag, the planes of her face all crimson and flickering shadow.

'I've hit upon a rather unusual subject and started with a piece of jobbery I eventually intend to write about.'

'Unusual? In what way?'

'Blind from birth, for one thing.'

'You're using the ONT&R?'

'Yes. She's going to be a Shaper.'

'*Verfluchter!* – Are you aware of the possible repercussions?'

'Of course.'

'You've heard of unlucky Pierre?'

'No.'

'Good, then it was successfully hushed. Pierre was a philosophy student at the University of Paris, and was doing a dissertation on the evolution of consciousness. This past summer he decided it would be necessary for him to explore the mind of an ape, for purposes of comparing a moins-nausée mind with his own, I suppose. At any rate, he obtained illegal access to an ONT&R and to the mind of our hairy cousin. It was never ascertained how far along he got in exposing the animal to the stimulibank, but it is to be assumed that such items as would not be immediately trans-subjective between man and ape – traffic sounds und so weiter – were what frightened the creature. Pierre is still residing in a padded cell, and all his responses are those of a frightened ape.

'So, while he did not complete his own dissertation,' he finished, 'he may provide significant material for someone else's.'

Render shook his head.

'Quite a story,' he said softly, 'but I have nothing that dramatic to contend with. I've found an exceedingly stable individual – a psychiatrist, in fact – one who's already spent time in ordinary analysis. She wants to go into neuroparticipation – but the fear of a sight-trauma was what was keeping her out. I've been gradually exposing her to a full range of visual phenomena. When I've finished she should be completely accommodated to sight, so that she can give her full attention to therapy and not be blinded by vision, so to speak. We've already had four sessions.'

'And?'

'. . . And it's working fine.'

'You are certain about it?'

'Yes, as certain as anyone can be in these matters.'

'Mm-hm,' said Bartelmetz. 'Tell me, do you find her excessively strong-willed? By that I mean, say, perhaps an obsessive-compulsive pattern concerning anything to which she's been introduced so far?'

'No.'

'Has she ever succeeded in taking over control of the fantasy?'

'No!'

'You lie,' he said simply.

Render found a cigarette. After lighting it, he smiled.

'Old father, old artificer,' he conceded, 'age has not withered your perceptiveness. I may trick me, but never you. —Yes, as a matter of fact, she is very difficult to keep under control. She is not satisfied just to see. She wants to Shape things for herself already. It's quite understandable – both to her and to me – but conscious apprehension and emotional acceptance never do seem to get together on things. She has become dominant on several occasions, but I've succeeded in resuming control almost immediately. After all, I *am* master of the bank.'

'Hm,' mused Bartelmetz. 'Are you familiar with a Buddhist text – *Shankara's Catechism*?'

'I'm afraid not.'

243

'Then I lecture you on it now. It posits – obviously not for therapeutic purposes – a true ego and a false ego. The true ego is that part of man which is immortal and shall proceed on to nirvana: the soul, if you like. Very good. Well, the false ego, on the other hand, is the normal mind, bound round with the illusions – the consciousness of you and me and everyone we have ever known professionally. Good? – Good. Now, the stuff this false ego is made up of they call skandhas. These include the feelings, the perceptions, the aptitudes, consciousness itself, and even the physical form. Very unscientific. Yes. Now they are not the same thing as neuroses, or one of Mister Ibsen's life-lies, or an hallucination – no, even though they are all wrong, being parts of a false thing to begin with. Each of the five skandhas is a part of the eccentricity that we call identity – then on top come the neuroses and all the other messes which follow after and keep us in business. Okay? – Okay. I give you this lecture because I need a dramatic term for what I will say, because I wish to say something dramatic. View the skandhas as lying at the bottom of the pond; the neuroses, they are ripples on the top of the water; the "true ego," if there is one, is buried deep beneath the sand at the bottom. So. The ripples fill up the-the – zwischenwelt – between the object and the subject. The skandhas are a part of the subject, basic, unique, the stuff of his being. —So far, you are with me?'

'With many reservations.'

'Good. Now I have defined my term somewhat, I will use it. You are fooling around with skandhas, not simple neuroses. You are attempting to adjust this woman's overall conception of herself and of the world. You are using the ONT&R to do it. It is the same thing as fooling with a psychotic or an ape. All may seem to go well, but – at any moment, it is possible you may do something, show her some sight, or some way of seeing which will break in upon her selfhood, break a skandha – and pouf! – it will be like breaking through the bottom of the pond. A whirlpool will result, pulling you – where? I do not want you for a patient, young man, young artificer, so I counsel you not to proceed with this experiment. The ONT&R should not be used in such a manner.'

Render flipped his cigarette into the fire and counted on his fingers:

'One,' he said, 'you are making a mystical mountain out of a pebble. All I am doing is adjusting her consciousness to accept an additional area of perception. Much of it is simple transference work from the other senses – Two, her emotions were quite intense initially because it *did* involve a trauma – but we've passed that stage already. Now it is only a novelty to her. Soon it will be a commonplace – Three. Eileen is a psychiatrist herself; she is educated in these matters and deeply aware of the delicate nature of what we are doing – Four, her sense of identity and her desires, or her skandhas, or whatever you want to call them, are as firm as the Rock of Gibraltar. Do you real-ize the intense application required for a blind person to obtain the education she has obtained? It took a will of ten-point steel and the emotional control of an ascetic as well—'

'—And if something that strong should break, in a timeless moment of anxiety,' smiled Barlelmetz sadly, 'may the shades of Sigmund Freud and Karl Jung walk by your side in the valley of darkness.

'—And five,' he added suddenly, staring into Render's eyes. 'Five,' he ticked it off on one finger. 'Is she pretty?'

Render looked back into the fire.

'Very clever,' sighed Bartelmetz. 'I cannot tell whether you are blushing or not, with the rosy glow of the flames upon your face. I fear that you are, though, which would mean that you are aware that you yourself could be the source of the inciting stimulus. I shall burn a candle tonight before a portrait of Adler and pray that he give you the strength to compete successfully in your duel with your patient.'

Render looked at Jill, who was still sleeping. He reached out and brushed a lock of her hair back into place.

'Still,' said Bartelmetz, 'if you do proceed and all goes well, I shall look forward with great interest to the reading of your work. Did I ever tell you that I have treated several Buddhists and never found a "true ego"?'

Both men laughed.

Like me but not like me, that one on a leash, smelling of fear, small, gray and unseeing. *Rrowl* and he'll choke on his collar. His head is empty as the oven till. She pushes the button and it makes dinner. Make talk and they never understand, but they are like me. One day I will kill one – why?... Turn here.

'Three steps. Up. Glass doors. Handle to right.'

Why? Ahead, drop-shaft. Gardens under, down. Smells nice, there. Grass, wet dirt, trees and clean air. I see. Birds are recorded though. I see all. I.

'Dropshaft. Four steps.'

Down Yes. Want to make loud noises in throat, feel silly. Clean, smooth, many of trees. God... She likes sitting on bench chewing leaves smelling smooth air. Can't see them like me. Maybe now, some...? No.

Can't Bad Sigmund me on grass, trees, here. Must hold it. Pity. Best place...

'Watch for steps.'

Ahead. To right, to left, to right, to left, trees and grass now. Sigmund sees. Walking... Doctor with machine gives her his eyes. *Rrowl* and he will not choke. No fearsmell.

Dig deep hole in ground, bury eyes. God is blind. Sigmund to see. Her eyes now filled, and he is afraid of teeth. Will make her to see and take her high up in the sky to see, away. Leave me here, leave Sigmund with none to see, alone. I will dig a deep hole in the ground...

It was after ten in the morning when Jill awoke. She did not have to turn her head to know that Render was already gone. He never slept late. She rubbed her eyes, stretched, turned onto her side and raised herself on her elbow. She squinted at the clock on the bedside table, simultaneously reaching for a cigarette and her lighter.

As she inhaled, she realized there was no ashtray. Doubtless

Render had moved it to the dresser because he did not approve of smoking in bed. With a sigh that ended in a snort she slid out of the bed and drew on her wrap before the ash grew too long.

She hated getting up, but once she did she would permit the day to begin and continue on without lapse through its orderly progression of events.

'Damn him,' she smiled. She had wanted her breakfast in bed, but it was too late now.

Between thoughts as to what she would wear, she observed an alien pair of skis standing in the corner. A sheet of paper was impaled on one. She approached it.

'Join me?' asked the scrawl.

She shook her head in an emphatic negative and felt somewhat sad. She had been on skis twice in her life and she was afraid of them. She felt that she should really try again, after his being a reasonably good sport about the chateaux, but she could not even bear the memory of the unseemly downward rushing – which, on two occasions, had promptly deposited her in a snowbank – without wincing and feeling once again the vertigo that had seized her during the attempts.

So she showered and dressed and went downstairs for breakfast.

All nine fires were already roaring as she passed the big hall and looked inside. Some red-faced skiers were holding their hands up before the blaze of the central hearth. It was not crowded though. The racks held only a few pairs of dripping boots, bright caps hung on pegs, moist skis stood upright in their place beside the door. A few people were seated in the chairs set further back toward the center of the hall, reading papers, smoking, or talking quietly. She saw no one she knew, so she moved on toward the dining room.

As she passed the registration desk the old man who worked there called out her name. She approached him and smiled.

'Letter,' he explained, turning to a rack. 'Here it is,' he announced, handing it to her. 'Looks important.'

It had been forwarded three times, she noted. It was a

bulky brown envelope, and the return address was that of her attorney.

'Thank you.'

She moved off to a seat beside the big window that looked out upon a snow garden, a skating rink, and a distant winding trail dotted with figures carrying skis over their shoulders. She squinted against the brightness as she tore open the envelope.

Yes, it was final. Her attorney's note was accompanied by a copy of the divorce decree. She had only recently decided to end her legal relationship to Mister Fotlock, whose name she had stopped using five years earlier, when they had separated. Now that she had the thing she wasn't sure exactly what she was going to do with it. It would be a hell of a surprise for dear Rendy, though, she decided. She would have to find a reasonably innocent way of getting the information to him. She withdrew her compact and practiced a 'Well?' expression. Well, there would be time for that later, she mused. Not too much later, though . . . Her thirtieth birthday, like a huge black cloud, filled an April but four months distant. Well . . . She touched her quizzical lips with color, dusted more powder over her mole, and locked the expression within her compact for future use.

In the dining room she saw Doctor Bartelmetz, seated before an enormous mound of scrambled eggs, great chains of dark sausages, several heaps of yellow toast, and a half-emptied flask of orange juice. A pot of coffee steamed on the warmer at his elbow. He leaned slightly forward as he ate, wielding his fork like a windmill blade.

'Good morning,' she said.

He looked up.

'Miss DeVille – Jill . . . Good morning.' He nodded at the chair across from him. 'Join me, please.'

She did so, and when the waiter approached she nodded and said, 'I'll have the same thing, only about ninety percent less.'

She turned back to Bartelmetz.

'Have you seen Charles today?'

'Alas, I have not,' he gestured, open-handed, 'and I wanted to continue our discussion while his mind was still in the early stages of wakefulness and somewhat malleable. Unfortunately,' he took a sip of coffee, 'he who sleeps well enters the day somewhere in the middle of its second act.'

'Myself, I usually come in around intermission and ask someone for a synopsis,' she explained. 'So why not continue the discussion with me? – I'm always malleable, and my skand-has are in good shape.'

Their eyes met, and he took a bite of toast.

'Aye,' he said, at length, 'I had guessed as much. Well – good. What do you know of Render's work?'

She adjusted herself in the chair.

'Mm. He being a special specialist in a highly specialized area, I find it difficult to appreciate the few things he does say about it. I'd like to be able to look inside other people's minds sometimes – to see what they're thinking about me, of course – but I don't think I could stand staying there very long. Especially,' she gave a mock-shudder, 'the mind of somebody with – problems. I'm afraid I'd be too sympathetic or too frightened or something. Then, according to what I've read – pow! – like sympathetic magic, it would be my problem.

'Charles never has problems though,' she continued, 'at least, none that he speaks to me about. Lately I've been wondering, though. That blind girl and her talking dog seem to be too much with him.'

'Talking dog?'

'Yes, her seeing-eye dog is one of those surgical mutants.'

'How interesting . . . Have you ever met her?'

'Never.'

'So,' he mused.

'Sometimes a therapist encounters a patient whose problems are so akin to his own that the sessions become extremely mordant,' he noted. 'It has always been the case with me when I treat a fellow-psychiatrist. Perhaps Charles sees in this situation a parallel to something which has been troubling him

249

personally. I did not administer his personal analysis. I do not know all the ways of his mind, even though he was a pupil of mine for a long while. He was always self-contained, somewhat reticent; he could be quite authoritative on occasion, however. —What are some of the other things which occupy his attention these days?'

'His son Peter is a constant concern. He's changed the boy's school five times in five years.'

Her breakfast arrived. She adjusted her napkin and drew her chair closer to the table.

'And he has been reading case histories of suicides recently, and talking about them, and talking about them, and talking about them.'

'To what end?'

She shrugged and began eating.

'He never mentioned why,' she said, looking up again. 'Maybe he's writing something...'

Bartelmetz finished his eggs and poured more coffee.

'Are you afraid of this patient of his?' he inquired.

'No... Yes,' she responded, 'I am.'

'Why?'

'I am afraid of sympathetic magic,' she said, flushing slightly.

'Many things could fall under that heading.'

'Many indeed,' she acknowledged. And, after a moment, 'We are united in our concern for his welfare and in agreement as to what represents the threat. So, may I ask a favor?'

'You may.'

'Talk to him again,' she said. 'Persuade him to drop the case.'

He folded his napkin.

'I intend to do that after dinner,' he stated, 'because I believe in the ritualistic value of rescue-motions. They shall be made.'


Dear Father-Image,

Yes, the school is fine, my ankle is getting that way, and my classmates are a congenial lot. No, I am not short on cash, undernourished, or having difficulty fitting into the new curriculum. Okay?

250

The building I will not describe, as you have already seen the macabre thing. The grounds I cannot describe, as they are currently residing beneath cold white sheets. Brr! I trust yourself to be enjoying the arts wint'rish. I do not share your enthusiasm for summer's opposite, except within picture frames or as an emblem on ice-cream bars.

The ankle inhibits my mobility and my roommate has gone home for the weekend – both of which are really blessings (saith Pangloss), for I now have the opportunity to catch up on some reading. I will do so forthwith.

Prodigally,
Peter

Render reached down to pat the huge head. It accepted the gesture stoically, then turned its gaze up to the Austrian whom Render had asked for a light, as if to say, 'Must I endure this indignity?' The man laughed at the expression, snapping shut the engraved lighter on which Render noted the middle initial to be a small 'v.'

'Thank you,' he said, and to the dog: 'What is your name?'

'Bismark,' it growled.

Render smiled.

'You remind me of another of your kind,' he told the dog. 'One Sigmund, by name, a companion and guide to a blind friend of mine, in America.'

'My Bismark is a hunter,' said the young man. 'There is no quarry that can outthink him, neither the deer nor the big cats.'

The dog's ears pricked forward and be stared up at Render with proud, blazing eyes.

'We have hunted in Africa and the northern and south-western parts of America. Central America, too. He never loses the trail. He never gives up. He is a beautiful brute, and his teeth could have been made in Solingen.'

'You are indeed fortunate to have such a hunting companion.'

'I hunt,' growled the dog. 'I follow... Sometimes, I have, the kill...'

'You would not know of the one called Sigmund then, or the woman he guides – Miss Eileen Shallot?' asked Render.

The man shook his head.

'No, Bismark came to me from Massachusetts, but I was never to the Center personally. I am not acquainted with other mutie handlers.'

'I see. Well, thank you for the light. Good afternoon.'

'Good afternoon...'

'Good, after, noon...'

Render strolled on up the narrow street, hands in his pockets. He had excused himself and not said where he was going. This was because he had had no destination in mind. Bartelmetz' second essay at counseling had almost led him to say things he would later regret. It was easier to take a walk than to continue the conversation.

On a sudden impulse he entered a small shop and bought a cuckoo clock which had caught his eye. He felt certain that Bartelmetz would accept the gift in the proper spirit. He smiled and walked on. *And what was that letter to Jill which the desk clerk had made a special trip to their table to deliver at dinnertime?* he wondered. It had been forwarded three times, and its return address was that of a law firm. Jill had not even opened it, but had smiled, overtipped the old man, and tucked it into her purse. He would have to hint subtly as to its contents. His curiosity so aroused, she would be sure to tell him out of pity.

The icy pillars of the sky suddenly seemed to sway before him as a cold wind leaped down out of the north. Render hunched his shoulders and drew his head further below his collar. Clutching the cuckoo clock, he hurried back up the street.

That night the serpent which holds its tail in its mouth belched, the Fenris Wolf made a pass at the moon, the little clock said 'cuckoo' and tomorrow came on like Manolete's last bull, shaking the gate of horn with the bellowed promise to tread a river of lions to sand.

Render promised himself he would lay off the gooey fondue.

Later, much later, when they skipped through the skies in a kite-shaped cruiser, Render looked down upon the darkened Earth dreaming its cities full of stars, looked up at the sky where they were all reflected, looked about him at the tape-screens watching all the people who blinked into them, and at the coffee, tea and mixed drink dispensers who sent their fluids forth to explore the insides of the people they required to push their buttons, then looked across at Jill, whom the old buildings had compelled to walk among their walls – because he knew she felt he should be looking at her then – felt his seat's demand that he convert it into a couch, did so, and slept.

## IV

Her office was full of flowers, and she liked exotic perfumes. Sometimes she burned incense.

She liked soaking in overheated pools, walking through falling snow, listening to too much music, played perhaps too loudly, drinking five or six varieties of liqueurs (usually reeking of anise, sometimes touched with wormwood) every evening. Her hands were soft and lightly freckled. Her fingers were long and tapered. She wore no rings.

Her fingers traced and retraced the floral swellings on the side of her chair as she spoke into the recording unit.

'. . . Patient's chief complaints on admission were nervousness, insomnia, stomach pains and a period of depression. Patient has had a record of previous admissions for short periods of time. He had been in this hospital in 1995 for a manic depressive psychosis, depressed type, and he returned here again, 2-3-96. He was in another hospital, 9-20-97. Physical examination revealed a BP of 170/100. He was normally developed and well-nourished on the date of examination, 12-11-98. On this date patient complained of chronic backache, and there was noted some moderate symptoms of alcohol withdrawal. Physical examination further revealed no pathology except that the patient's tendon reflexes were exaggerated but equal. These symptoms were the result of alcohol withdrawal. Upon admission he was shown to be not psychotic, neither delusional nor hallucinated. He was well-oriented as to place, time and person. His psychological condition was evaluated and he was found to be somewhat grandiose and expansive and more than a little hostile. He was considered a potential trouble maker. Because of his experience as a cook, he was assigned to work in the kitchen. His general condition then showed definite improvement. He is less tense and is cooperative. Diagnosis: Manic depressive reaction (external precipitating stress unknown). The degree of psychiatric impairment is mild. He is considered competent. To be continued on therapy and hospitalization.'

She turned off the recorder then and laughed. The sound frightened her. Laughter is a social phenomenon and she was alone. She played back the recording then, chewing on the corner of her handkerchief while the soft, clipped words were returned to her. She ceased to hear them after the first dozen or so.

When the recorder stopped talking she turned it off. She was alone. She was very alone. She was so damned alone that the little pool of brightness which occurred when she stroked her forehead and faced the window – that little pool of brightness suddenly became the most important thing in the world. She wanted it to be immense. She wanted it to be an ocean of light. Or else she wanted to grow so small herself that the effect would be the same: she wanted to drown in it.

It had been three weeks, yesterday . . .

*Too long,* she decided, *I should have waited. No! Impossible! But what if he goes as Riscomb went? No! He won't. He would not. Nothing can hurt him. Never. He is all strength and armor. But – but we should have waited till next month to start. Three weeks . . . Sight withdrawal – that's what it is. Are the memories fading? Are they weaker? (What*

254

*does a tree look like? Or a cloud – I can't remember! What is red? What is green? God! It's hysterical! I'm watching and I can't stop it! – Take a pill! A pill!)*

Her shoulders began to shake. She did not take a pill though, but bit down harder on the handkerchief until her sharp teeth tore through its fabric.

'Beware,' she recited a personal beatitude, 'those who hunger and thirst after justice, for we *will* be satisfied.

'And beware the meek,' she continued, 'for we shall attempt to inherit the Earth.

'And beware...'

There was a brief buzz from the phone-box. She put away her handkerchief, composed her face, turned the unit on.

'Hello...?'

'Eileen, I'm back. How've you been?'

'Good, quite well in fact. How was your vacation?'

'Oh, I can't complain. I had it coming for a long time. I guess I deserve it. Listen, I brought some things back to show you – like Winchester Cathedral. You want to come in this week? I can make it any evening.'

*Tonight. No. I want it too badly. It will set me back if he sees...*

'How about tomorrow night?' she asked. 'Or the one after?'

'Tomorrow will be fine,' he said. 'Meet you at the P & S, around seven?'

'Yes. that would be pleasant. Same table?'

'Why not? – I'll reserve it.'

'All right. I'll see you then.'

'Good-bye.'

The connection was broken.

Suddenly, then, at that moment, colors swirled again through her head; and she saw trees – oaks and pines, poplars and sycamores – great, and green and brown, and iron-colored; and she saw wads of fleecy clouds, dipped in paintpots, swabbing a pastel sky; and a burning sun, and a small willow tree, and a lake of a deep, almost violet, blue. She folded her torn handkerchief and put it away.

She pushed a button beside her desk and music filled the office: Scriabin. Then she pushed another button and replayed the tape she had dictated, half-listening to each.

Pierre sniffed suspiciously at the food. The attendant moved away from the tray and stepped out into the hall, locking the door behind him. The enormous salad waited on the floor. Pierre approached cautiously, snatched a handful of lettuce, gulped it.

He was afraid.

*If only the steel would stop crashing and crashing against steel, somewhere in that dark night... If only...*

Sigmund rose to his feet, yawned, stretched. His hind legs trailed out behind him for a moment, then he snapped to attention and shook himself. She would be coming home soon. Wagging his tail slowly, he glanced up at the human-level clock with the raised numerals, verified his feelings, then crossed the apartment to the teevee. He rose onto his hind legs, rested one paw against the table and used the other to turn on the set.

It was nearly time for the weather report and the roads would be icy.

'I have driven through countrywide graveyards,' wrote Render, 'vast forests of stone that spread further every day.

'Why does man so zealously guard his dead? Is it because this is the monumentally democratic way of immortalization, the ultimate affirmation of the power to hurt – that is to say, life – and the desire that it continue on forever? Unamuno has suggested that this is the case. If it is, then a greater percentage of the population actively sought immortality last year than ever before in history...'

*Tch-tchg, tchga-tchgt!*

'Do you think they're really people?'

'Naw, they're too good.'

\*

The evening was starglint and soda over ice. Render wound the S-7 into the cold sub-subcellar, found his parking place, nosed into it.

There was a damp chill that emerged from the concrete to gnaw like rats' teeth at their flesh. Render guided her toward the lift, their breath preceding them in dissolving clouds.

'A bit of a chill in the air,' he noted.

She nodded, biting her lip.

Inside the lift, he sighed, unwound his scarf, lit a cigarette.

'Give me one, please,' she requested, smelling the tobacco.

He did.

They rose slowly, and Render leaned against the wall, puffing a mixture of smoke and crystallized moisture.

'I met another mutie shep,' he recalled, 'in Switzerland. Big as Sigmund. A hunter though, and as Prussian as they come,' he grinned.

'Sigmund likes to hunt, too,' she observed. 'Twice every year we go up to the North Woods and I turn him loose. He's gone for days at a time, and he's always quite happy when he returns. Never says what he's done, but he's never hungry. Back when I got him I guessed that he would need vacations from humanity to stay stable. I think I was right.'

The lift stopped, the door opened and they walked out into the hall, Render guiding her again.

Inside his office, he poked at the thermostat and warm air sighed through the room. He hung their coats in the inner office and brought the great egg out from its nest behind the wall. He connected it to an outlet and moved to convert his desk into a control panel.

'How long do you think it will take?' she asked, running her fingertips over the smooth, cold curves of the egg. 'The whole thing, I mean. The entire adaptation to seeing.'

He wondered.

'I have no idea,' he said, 'no idea whatsoever, yet. We got off to a good start, but there's still a lot of work to be done. I think I'll be able to make a good guess in another three months.'

She nodded wistfully, moved to his desk, explored the controls with finger strokes like ten feathers.

'Careful you don't push any of those.'

'I won't. How long do you think it will take me to learn to operate one?'

'Three months to learn it. Six, to actually become proficient enough to use it on anyone, and an additional six under close supervision before you can be trusted on your own. —About a year altogether.'

'Uh-huh.' She chose a chair.

Render touched the seasons to life, and the phases of day and night, the breath of the country, the city, the elements that raced naked through the skies, and all the dozens of dancing cues he used to build worlds. He smashed the clock of time and tasted the seven or so ages of man.

'Okay,' he turned, 'everything is ready.'

It came quickly, and with a minimum of suggestion on Render's part. One moment there was grayness. Then a dead-white fog. Then it broke itself apart, as though a quick wind had risen, although he neither heard nor felt a wind.

He stood beside the willow tree beside the lake, and she stood half-hidden among the branches and the lattices of shadow. The sun was slanting its way into evening.

'We have come back,' she said, stepping out, leaves in her hair. 'For a time I was afraid it had never happened, but I see it all again, and I remember now.'

'Good,' he said. 'Behold yourself.' And she looked into the lake.

'I have not changed,' she said. 'I haven't changed...'

'No.'

'But you have,' she continued, looking up at him. 'You are taller, and there is something different...'

'No,' he answered.

'I am mistaken,' she said quickly, 'I don't understand everything I see yet.'

'I will, though.'

'Of course.'

'What are we going to do?'

'Watch,' he instructed her.

Along a flat, no-colored river of road she just then noticed beyond the trees, came the car. It came from the farthest quarter of the sky, skipping over the mountains, buzzing down the hills, circling through the glades, and splashing them with the colors of its voice – the gray and the silver of synchronized potency – and the lake shivered from its sounds, and the car stopped a hundred feet away, masked by the shrubberies; and it waited. It was the S-7.

'Come with me,' he said, taking her hand. 'We're going for a ride.'

They walked among the trees and rounded the final cluster of bushes. She touched the sleek cocoon, its antennae, its tires, its windows – and the windows transpared as she did so. She stared through them at the inside of the car, and she nodded.

'It is your Spinner.'

'Yes.' He held the door for her. 'Get in. We'll return to the club. The time is now. The memories are fresh, and they should be reasonably pleasant, or neutral.'

'Pleasant,' she said, getting in.

He closed the door, then circled the car and entered. She watched as he punched imaginary coordinates. The car leaped ahead and he kept a steady stream of trees flowing by them. He could feel the rising tension, so he did not vary the scenery. She swiveled her seat and studied the interior of the car.

'Yes,' she finally said, 'I can perceive what everything is.'

She stared out the window again. She looked at the rushing trees. Render stared out and looked upon rushing anxiety patterns. He opaqued the windows.

'Good,' she said, 'thank you. Suddenly it was too much to see – all of it, moving past like a . . .'

'Of course,' said Render, maintaining the sensations of forward motion. 'I'd anticipated that. You're getting tougher, though.'

After a moment, 'Relax,' he said, 'relax now,' and somewhere a button was pushed, and she relaxed, and they drove

259

on, and on and on, and finally the car began to slow, and Render said, 'Just for one nice, slow glimpse now, look out your window.'

She did.

He drew upon every stimulus in the bank which could promote sensations of pleasure and relaxation, and he dropped the city around the car, and the windows became transparent, and she looked out upon the profiles of towers and a block of monolithic apartments, and then she saw three rapid cafeterias, an entertainment palace, a drugstore, a medical center of yellow brick with an aluminum caduceus set above its archway, and a glassed-in high school, now emptied of its pupils, a fifty-pump gas station, another drugstore, and many more cars, parked or roaring by them, and people, people moving in and out of the doorways and walking before the buildings and getting into the cars and getting out of the cars; and it was summer, and the light of late afternoon filtered down upon the colors of the city and the colors of the garments the people wore as they moved along the boulevard, as they loafed upon the terraces, as they crossed the balconies, leaned on balustrades and windowsills, emerged from a corner kiosk, entered one, stood talking to one another; a woman walking a poodle rounded a corner; rockets went to and fro in the high sky.

The world fell apart then and Render caught the pieces.

He maintained an absolute blackness, blanketing every sensation but that of their movement forward.

After a time a dim light occurred, and they were still seated in the Spinner, windows blanked again, and the air as they breathed it became a soothing unguent.

'Lord,' she said, 'the world is so filled. Did I really see all of that?'

'I wasn't going to do that tonight, but you wanted me to. You seemed ready.'

'Yes,' she said, and the windows became transparent again. She turned away quickly.

'It's gone,' he said. 'I only wanted to give you a glimpse.'

She looked, and it was dark outside now, and they were

crossing over a high bridge. They were moving slowly. There was no other traffic. Below them were the Flats, where an occasional smelter flared like a tiny, drowsing volcano, spitting showers of orange sparks skyward; and there were many stars: they glistened on the breathing water that went beneath the bridge; they silhouetted by pinprick the skyline that hovered dimly below its surface. The slanting struts of the bridge marched steadily by.

'You have done it,' she said, 'and I thank you.' Then; 'Who are you, really?' (He must have wanted her to ask that.)

'I am Render,' he laughed. And they wound their way through a dark, now-vacant city, coming at last to their club and entering the great parking dome.

Inside, he scrutinized all her feelings, ready to banish the world at a moment's notice. He did not feel he would have to, though.

They left the car, moved ahead. They passed into the club which he had decided would not be crowded tonight. They were shown to their table at the foot of the bar in the small room with the suit of armor, and they sat down and ordered the same meal over again.

'No,' he said, looking down, 'it belongs over there.'

The suit of armor appeared once again beside the table, and he was once again inside his gray suit and black tie and silver tie clasp shaped like a tree limb.

They laughed.

'I'm just not the type to wear a tin suit, so I wish you'd stop seeing me that way.'

'I'm sorry,' she smiled. 'I don't know how I did that, or why.'

'I do, and I decline the nomination. Also, I caution you once again. You are conscious of the fact that this is all an illusion. I had to do it that way for you to get the full benefit of the thing. For most of my patients though, it is the real item while they are experiencing it. It makes a counter-trauma or a symbolic sequence even more powerful. You are aware of the parameters of the game, however, and whether you want it or not this gives you a different sort of control over it than I normally have to deal with. Please be careful.'

'I'm sorry. I didn't mean to.'

'I know. Here comes the meal we just had.'

'Ugh! It looks dreadful! Did we eat all that stuff?'

'Yes,' he chuckled. 'That's a knife, that's a fork, that's a spoon. That's roast beef, and those are mashed potatoes, those are peas, that's butter...'

'Goodness! I don't feel so well.'

'...And those are the salads, and those are the salad dressings. This is a brook trout – mm! These are French fried potatoes. This is a bottle of wine. Hmm – let's see – Romanée-Conti, since I'm not paying for it – and a bottle of Yquem for the trou – Hey!'

The room was wavering.

He bared the table, he banished the restaurant. They were back in the glade. Through the transparent fabric of the world he watched a hand moving along a panel. Buttons were being pushed. The world grew substantial again. Their emptied table was set beside the lake now, and it was still nighttime and summer, and the tablecloth was very white under the glow of the giant moon that hung overhead.

'That was stupid of me,' he said. 'Awfully stupid. I should have introduced them one at a time. The actual sight of basic, oral stimuli can be very distressing to a person seeing them for the first time. I got so wrapped up in the Shaping that I forgot the patient, which is just dandy! I apologize.'

'I'm okay now. Really I am.'

He summoned a cool breeze from the lake.

'...And that is the moon,' he added lamely.

She nodded, and she was wearing a tiny moon in the center of her forehead; it glowed like the one above them, and her hair and dress were all of silver.

The bottle of Romanée-Conti stood on the table, and two glasses.

'Where did that come from?'

She shrugged. He poured out a glassful.

'It may taste kind of flat,' he said.

'It doesn't. Here—' She passed it to him.

As he sipped it he realized it had a taste – a *fruite* such as might be quashed from the grapes grown in the Isles of the Blest, a smooth, muscular *charnu*, and a *capiteux* centrifuged from the fumes of a field of burning poppies. With a start, he knew that his hand must be traversing the route of the perceptions, symphonizing the sensual cues of a transference and a counter-transference which had come upon him all unaware, there beside the lake.

'So it does,' he noted, 'and now it is time we returned.'

'So soon? I haven't seen the cathedral yet...'

'So soon.'

He willed the world to end, and it did.

'It is cold out there,' she said as she dressed, 'and dark.'

'I know. I'll mix us something to drink while I clear the unit.'

'Fine.'

He glanced at the tapes and shook his head. He crossed to his bar cabinet.

'It's not exactly Romanée-Conti,' he observed, reaching for a bottle.

'So what? I don't mind.'

Neither did he, at that moment. So he cleared the unit, they drank their drinks, he helped her into her coat and they left.

As they rode the lift down to the sub-sub he willed the world to end again, but it didn't.


Dad,

    I hobbled from school to taxi and taxi to spaceport, for the local Air Force Exhibit – Outward, it was called. (Okay, I exaggerated the hobble. It got me extra attention though.) The whole bit was aimed at seducing young manhood into a five-year hitch, as I saw it. But it worked. I wanna join up I wanna go Out There. Think they'll take me when I'm old enuff? I mean take me Out – not some crummy desk job. Think so?

    I do.

There was this damn lite colonel ('scuse the French) who saw this kid lurching around and pressing his nose 'gainst the big windowpanes, and he decided to give him the subliminal sell. Great! He pushed me through the gallery and showed me all the pitchers of AF triumphs, from Moonbase to Marsport. He lectured me on the Great Traditions of the Service, and marched me into a flic room where the Corps had good clean fun on tape, wrestling one another in null-G 'where it's all skill and no brawn,' and making tinted water sculpture-work way in the middle of the air and doing dismounted drill on the skin of a cruiser. Oh joy!

Seriously though, I'd like to be there when they hit the Outer Five – and On Out. Not because of the bogus balonus in the throwaways, and suchlike crud, but because I think someone of sensibility should be along to chronicle the thing in the proper way. You know, raw frontier observer. Francis Parkman. Mary Austin, like that. So I decided I'm going.

The AF boy with the chicken stuff on his shoulders wasn't in the least way patronizing, gods be praised. We stood on the balcony and watched ships lift off and he told me to go forth and study real hard and I might be riding them someday. I did not bother to tell him that I'm hardly intellectually deficient and that I'll have my B.A. before I'm old enough to do anything with it, even join his Corps. I just watched the ships lift off and said, 'Ten years from now I'll be looking down, not up.' Then he told me how hard his own training had been, so I did not ask howcum he got stuck with a lousy dirt-side assignment like this one. Glad I didn't, now I think on it. He looked more like one of their ads than one of their real people. Hope I never look like an ad.

Thank you for the monies and the warm sox and Mozart's String Quintets, which I'm hearing right now. I wanna put in my bid for Luna instead of Europe next summer. Maybe . . . ? Possibly . . . ? Contingently . . . ? Huh?

– If I can smash that new test you're designing for me ...?
Anyhow, please think about it.

    Your son,
    Pete


'Hello. State Psychiatric Institute.'

'I'd like to make an appointment for an examination.'

'Just a moment. I'll connect you with the Appointment Desk.'

'Hello. Appointment Desk.'

'I'd Like to make an appointment for an examination.'

'Just a moment ... What sort of examination.'

'I want to see Doctor Shallot, Eileen Shallot. As soon as possible.'

'Just a moment. I'll have to check her schedule ... Could you make it at two o'clock next Tuesday?'

'That would be just fine.'

'What is the name, please?'

'DeVille. Jill DeVille—

'All right. Miss DeVille. That's two o'clock, Tuesday.'

'Thank you.'


The man walked beside the highway. Cars passed along the highway. The cars in the high-acceleration lane blurred by.

Traffic was light.

It was 10:30 in the morning, and cold.

The man's fur-lined collar was turned up, his hands were in his pockets, and he leaned into the wind. Beyond the fence, the road was clean and dry.

The morning sun was buried in clouds. In the dirty light, the man could see the tree a quarter mile ahead.

His pace did not change. His eyes did not leave the tree. The small stones clicked and crunched beneath his shoes.

When he reached the tree he took off his jacket and folded it neatly.

He placed it upon the ground and climbed the tree.

As he moved out onto the limb which extended over the

fence, he looked to see that no traffic was approaching. Then he seized the branch with both hands, lowered himself, hung a moment, and dropped onto the highway.

It was a hundred yards wide, the eastbound half of the highway.

He glanced west, saw there was still no traffic coming his way, then began to walk toward the center island. He knew he would never reach it. At this time of day the cars were moving at approximately one hundred-sixty miles an hour in the high-acceleration lane. He walked on.

A car passed behind him. He did not look back. If the windows were opaqued, as was usually the case, then the occupants were unaware he had crossed their path. They would hear of it later and examine the front end of their vehicle for possible sign of such an encounter.

A car passed in front of him. Its windows were clear. A glimpse of two faces, their mouths made into Os, was presented to him, then torn from his sight. His own face remained without expression. His pace did not change. Two more cars rushed by, windows darkened. He had crossed perhaps twenty yards of highway.

Twenty-five . . .

Something in the wind, or beneath his feet, told him it was coming. He did not look.

Something in the corner of his eye assured him it was coming. His gait did not alter.

Cecil Green had the windows transpared because he liked it that way. His left hand was inside her blouse and her skirt was piled up on her lap, and his right hand was resting on the lever which would lower the seats. Then she pulled away, making a noise down inside her throat.

His head snapped to the left.

He saw the walking man.

He saw the profile which never turned to face him fully. He saw that the man's gait did not alter.

Then he did not see the man.

There was a slight jar, and the windshield began cleaning itself. Cecil Green raced on.

He opaqued the windows.

'How...?' he asked after she was in his arms again, and sobbing.

'The monitor didn't pick him up...'

'He must not have touched the fence...'

'He must have been out of his mind!'

'Still, he could have picked an easier way.'

*It could have been any face... Mine?*

Frightened, Cecil lowered the seats.


Charles Render was writing the 'Necropolis' chapter for *The Missing Link is Man*, which was to be his first book in over four years. Since his return he had set aside every Tuesday and Thursday afternoon to work on it, isolating himself in his office, filling pages with a chaotic longhand.

'There are many varieties of death, as opposed to dying...' he was writing, just as the intercom buzzed briefly, then long, then briefly again.

'Yes?' he asked it, pushing down on the switch.

'You have a visitor,' and there was a short intake of breath between 'a' and 'visitor.'

He slipped a small aerosol into his side pocket, then rose and crossed the office.

He opened the door and looked out.

'Doctor... Help...'

Render took three steps, then dropped to one knee.

'What's the matter?'

'Come – she is... sick,' he growled.

'Sick? How? What's wrong?'

'Don't know. You come.'

Render stared into the unhuman eyes.

'What kind of sick?' he insisted.

'Don't know,' repeated the dog. 'Won't talk. Sits. I... feel, she is sick.'

'How did you get here?'

'Drove. Know the co, or, din, ates… Left car, outside.'

'I'll call her right now.' Render turned.

'No good. Won't answer.'

He was right.

Render returned to his inner office for his coat and medkit. He glanced out the window and saw where her car was parked, far below, just inside the entrance to the marginal, where the monitor had released it into manual control. If no one assumed that control a car was automatically parked in neutral. The other vehicles were passed around it.

*So simple even a dog can drive one,* he reflected. *Better get downstairs before a cruiser comes along. It's probably reported itself stopped there already. Maybe not, though. Might still have a few minutes grace.*

He glanced at the huge clock.

'Okay, Sig,' he called out. 'Let's go.'

They took the lift to the ground floor, left by way of the front entrance and hurried to the car.

Its engine was still idling.

Render opened the passengerside door and Sigmund leaped in. He squeezed by him into the driver's seat then, but the dog was already pushing the primary coordinates and the address tabs with his paw.

*Looks like I'm in the wrong seat.*

He lit a cigarette as the car swept ahead into a U-underpass. It emerged on the opposite marginal, sat poised a moment, then joined the traffic flow. The dog directed the car into the high-acceleration lane.

'Oh,' said the dog, 'oh.'

Render felt like patting his head at that moment, but he looked at him, saw that his teeth were bared, and decided against it.

'When did she start acting peculiar?' he asked.

'Came home from work. Did not eat. Would not answer me when I talked. Just sits.'

'Has she ever been like this before?'

'No.'

268

*What could have precipitated it? – But maybe she just had a bad day. After all, he's only a dog – sort of. —No. He'd know. But what, then?*

'How was she yesterday – and when she left home this morning?'

'Like always.'

Render tried calling her again. There was still no answer.

'You did, it,' said the dog.

'What do you mean?'

'Eyes. Seeing. You. Machine. Bad.'

'No,' said Render, and his hand rested on the unit of stun-spray in his pocket.

'Yes,' said the dog, turning to him again. 'You will, make her well . . . ?'

'Of course,' said Render.

Sigmund stared ahead again.

Render felt physically exhilarated and mentally sluggish. He sought the confusion factor. He had had these feelings about the case since that first session. There was something very unsettling about Eileen Shallot; a combination of high intelligence and helplessness, of determination and vulnerability, of sensitivity and bitterness.

*Do I find that especially attractive? – No. It's just the counter-transference, damn it!*

'You smell afraid,' said the dog.

'Then color me afraid,' said Render, 'and turn the page.'

They slowed for a series of turns, picked up speed again, slowed again, picked up speed again. Finally, they were traveling along a narrow section of roadway through a semi-residential area of town. The car turned up a side street, proceeded about half a mile further, clicked softly beneath its dashboard, and turned into the parking lot behind a high brick apartment building. The click must have been a special servomech which took over from the point where the monitor released it, because the car crawled across the lot, headed into its transparent parking stall, then stopped. Render turned off the ignition.

Sigmund had already opened the door on his side. Render followed him into the building, and they rode the elevator to the fiftieth floor. The dog dashed on ahead up the hallway, pressed his nose against a plate set low in a doorframe and waited. After a moment, the door swung several inches inward. He pushed it open with his shoulder and entered. Render followed, closing the door behind him.

The apartment was large, its walls pretty much unadorned, its color combinations unnerving. A great library of tapes filled one corner; a monstrous combination-broadcaster stood beside it. There was a wide bowlegged table set in front of the window, and a low couch along the right-hand wall; there was a closed door beside the couch: an archway to the left apparently led to other rooms. Eileen sat in an overstuffed chair in the far corner by the window. Sigmund stood beside the chair.

Render crossed the room and extracted a cigarette from his case. Snapping open his lighter, he held the flame until her head turned in that direction.

'Cigarette?' he asked.

'Charles?'

'Right.'

'Yes, thank you. I will.'

She held out her hand, accepted the cigarette, put it to her lips.

'Thanks. —What are you doing here?'

'Social call. I happened to be in the neighborhood.'

'I didn't hear a buzz or a knock.'

'You must have been dozing. Sig let me in.'

'Yes, I must have.' She stretched. 'What time is it?'

'It's close to four-thirty.'

'I've been home over two hours then ... Must have been very tired ...'

'How do you feel now?'

'Fine,' she declared. 'Care for a cup of coffee?'

'Don't mind if I do.'

'A steak to go with it?'

'No, thanks.'

'Bacardi in the coffee?'

'Sounds good.'

'Excuse me, then. It'll only take a moment.'

She went through the door beside the sofa and Render caught a glimpse of a large, shiny, automatic kitchen.

'Well?' he whispered to the dog.

Sigmund shook his head.

'Not same.'

Render shook his head.

He deposited his coat on the sofa, folding it carefully about the medkit. He sat beside it and thought.

*Did I throw too big a chunk of seeing at once? Is she suffering from depressive side-effects – say, memory repressions, nervous fatigue? Did I upset her sensory-adaptation syndrome somehow? Why have I been proceeding so rapidly anyway? There's no real hurry. Am I so damned eager to write the thing up? – Or am I doing it because she wants me to? Could she be that strong, consciously or unconsciously? Or am I that vulnerable – somehow?*

She called him to the kitchen to carry out the tray. He set it on the table and seated himself across from her.

'Good coffee,' he said, burning his lips on the cup.

'Smart machine,' she stated, facing his voice.

Sigmund stretched out on the carpet next to the table, lowered his head between his forepaws, sighed and closed his eyes.

'I've been wondering,' said Render, 'whether or not there were any after effects to that last session – like increased synesthesiac experiences, or dreams involving forms, or hallucinations or . . .'

'Yes,' she said flatly, 'dreams.'

'What kind?'

'That last session. I've dreamed it over, and over.'

'Beginning to end?'

'No, there's no special order to the events. We're riding through the city, or over the bridge, or sitting at the table, or walking toward the car – just flashes, like that. Vivid ones.'

'What sort of feelings accompany these – flashes?'

271

'I don't know, they're all mixed up.'

'What are your feelings now, as you recall them?'

'The same, all mixed up.'

'Are you afraid?'

'N-no. I don't think so.'

'Do you want to take a vacation from the thing? Do you feel we've been proceeding too rapidly?'

'No. That's not it at all. It's – well, it's like learning to swim. When you finally learn how, why then you swim and you swim and you swim until you're all exhausted. Then you just lie there gasping in air and remembering what it was like, while your friends all hover and chew you out for overexerting yourself – and it's a good feeling, even though you do take a chill and there are pins and needles inside all your muscles. At least, that's the way I do things. I felt that way after the first session and after this last one. First Times are always very special times . . . The pins and the needles are gone, though, and I've caught my breath again. Lord, I don't want to stop now! I feel fine.'

'Do you usually take a nap in the afternoon?'

The ten red nails of her fingers moved across the tabletop as she stretched.

'. . . Tired,' she smiled, swallowing a yawn. 'Half the staff's on vacation or sick leave and I've been beating my brains out all week. I was about ready to fall on my face when I left work. I feel all right now that I've rested, though.'

She picked up her coffee cup with both hands, took a large swallow.

'Uh-huh,' he said. 'Good. I was a bit worried about you. I'm glad to see there was no reason.'

She laughed.

'Worried? You've read Doctor Riscomb's notes on my analysis – and on the ONT&R trial – and you think I'm the sort to worry about? Ha! I have an operationally beneficent neurosis concerning my adequacy as a human being. It focuses my energies, coordinates my efforts toward achievement. It enhances my sense of identity . . .'

'You do have one hell of a memory,' he noted. 'That's almost verbatim.'

'Of course.'

'You had Sigmund worried today, too.'

'Sig? How?'

The dog stirred uneasily, opened one eye.

'Yes,' he growled, glaring up at Render. 'He needs, a ride, home.'

'Have you been driving the car again?'

'Yes.'

'After I told you not to?'

'Yes.'

'Why?'

'I was a, fraid. You would, not, answer me, when I talked.'

'I was *very* tired – and if you ever take the car again, I'm going to have the door fixed so you can't come and go as you please.'

'Sorry.'

'There's nothing wrong with me.'

'I, see.'

'You are *never* to do it again.'

'Sorry.' His eye never left Render; it was like a burning lens.

Render looked away.

'Don't be too hard on the poor fellow,' he said. 'After all, he thought you were ill and he went for the doctor. Suppose he'd been right? You'd owe him thanks, not a scolding.'

Unmollified, Sigmund glared a moment longer and closed his eye.

'He has to be told when he does wrong,' she finished.

'I suppose,' he said, drinking his coffee. 'No harm done, anyhow. Since I'm here, let's talk shop. I'm writing something and I'd like an opinion.'

'Great. Give me a footnote?'

'Two or three. —In your opinion, do the general underlying motivations that lead to suicide differ in different periods of history or in different cultures?'

'My well-considered opinion is no, they don't,' she said.

'Frustrations can lead to depressions or frenzies; and if these are severe enough, they can lead to self-destruction. You ask me about motivations and I think they stay pretty much the same. I feel this is a cross-cultural, cross-temporal aspect of the human condition. I don't think it could be changed without changing the basic nature of man.'

'Okay. Check. Now, what of the inciting element?' he asked. 'Let man be a constant, his environment is still a variable. If he is placed in an overprotective life-situation, do you feel it would take more or less to depress him – or stimulate him to frenzy – than it would take in a not so protective environment?'

'Hm. Being case-oriented, I'd say it would depend on the man. But I see what you're driving at: a mass predisposition to jump out windows at the drop of a hat – the window even opening itself for you, because you asked it to – the revolt of the bored masses. I don't like the notion. I hope it's wrong.'

'So do I, but I was thinking of symbolic suicides too – functional disorders that occur for pretty flimsy reasons.'

'Aha! Your lecture last month: autopsychomimesis. I have the tape. Well-told, but I can't agree.'

'Neither can I, now. I'm rewriting that whole section – "Thanatos in Cloudcuckooland," I'm calling it. It's really the death-instinct moved nearer the surface.'

'If I get you a scalpel and a cadaver, will you cut out the death-instinct and let me touch it?'

'Couldn't,' he put the grin into his voice, 'it would be all used up in a cadaver. Find me a volunteer though, and he'll prove my case by volunteering.'

'Your logic is unassailable,' she smiled. 'Get us some more coffee, okay?'

Render went to the kitchen, spiked and filled the cups, drank a glass of water and returned to the living room. Eileen had not moved; neither had Sigmund.

'What do you do when you're not busy being a Shaper?' she asked him.

'The same things most people do – eat, drink, sleep, talk, visit friends and not-friends, visit places, read...'

'Are you a forgiving man?'

'Sometimes. Why?'

'Then forgive me. I argued with a woman today, a woman named De Ville.'

'What about?'

'You – and she accused me of such things it were better my mother had not born me. Are you going to marry her?'

'No, marriage is like alchemy. It served an important purpose once, but I hardly feel it's here to stay.'

'Good.'

'What did you say to her?'

'I gave her a clinic referral card that said, "Diagnosis: Bitch. Prescription: Drug therapy and a tight gag." '

'Oh,' said Render, showing interest.

'She tore it up and threw it in my face.'

'I wonder why?'

She shrugged, smiled, made a gridwork on the tablecloth.

' "Fathers and elders, I ponder," ' sighed Render, ' "what is hell?" '

' "I maintain it is the suffering of being unable to love," ' she finished. 'Was Dostoevsky right?'

'I doubt it I'd put him into group therapy myself. That'd be *real* hell for him – with all those people acting like his characters and enjoying it so.'

Render put down his cup and pushed his chair away from the table.

'I suppose you must be going now?'

'I really should,' said Render.

'And I can't interest you in food?'

'No.'

She stood.

'Okay, I'll get my coat.'

'I could drive back myself and just set the car to return.'

'No! I'm frightened by the notion of empty cars driving around the city. I'd feel the thing was haunted for the next two-and-a-half weeks.

'Besides,' she said, passing through the archway, 'you promised me Winchester Cathedral.'

'You want to do it today?'

'If you can be persuaded.'

As Render stood deciding, Sigmund rose to his feet. He stood directly before him and stared upward into his eyes.

He opened his mouth and closed it, several times, but no sounds emerged. Then he turned away and left the room.

'No,' Eileen's voice came back, 'you will stay here until I return.'

Render picked up his coat and put it on, stuffing the medkit into the far pocket.

As they walked up the hall toward the elevator Render thought he heard a very faint and very distant howling sound.

In this place, of all places, Render knew he was the master of all things.

He was at home on those alien worlds, without time, those worlds where flowers copulate and the stars do battle in the heavens, falling at last to the ground, bleeding, like so many split and shattered chalices, and the seas part to reveal stairways leading down, and arms emerge from caverns, waving torches that flame like liquid faces – a midwinter night's nightmare, summer go a-begging, Render know – for he had visited those worlds on a professional basis for the better part of a decade. With the crooking of a finger he could isolate the sorcerors, bring them to trial for treason against the realm – aye, and he could execute them, could appoint their successors.

Fortunately, this trip was only a courtesy call...

He moved forward through the glade, seeking her.

He could feel her awakening presence all about him.

He pushed through the branches, stood beside the lake. It was cold, blue, and bottomless, the lake, reflecting that slender willow which had become the station of her arrival.

'Eileen!'

The willow swayed toward him, swayed away.

'Eileen! Come forth!'

Leaves fell, floated upon the lake, disturbed its mirrorlike placidity, distorted the reflections.

'Eileen?'

All the leaves yellowed at once then, dropped down into the water. The tree ceased its swaying. There was a strange sound in the darkening sky, like the humming of high wires on a cold day.

Suddenly there was a double file of moons passing through the heavens.

Render selected one, reached up and pressed it. The others vanished as he did so, and the world brightened; the humming went out of the air.

He circled the lake to gain a subjective respite from the rejection-action and his counter to it. He moved up along an aisle of pines toward the place where he wanted the cathedral to occur. Birds sang now in the trees. The wind came softly by him. He felt her presence quite strongly.

'Here, Eileen. Here.'

She walked beside him then, green silk, hair of bronze, eyes of molten emerald; she wore an emerald in her forehead. She walked in green slippers over the pine needles, saying: 'What happened?'

'You were afraid.'

'Why?'

'Perhaps you fear the cathedral. Are you a witch?' he smiled.

'Yes, but it's my day off.'

He laughed, and he took her arm, and they rounded an island of foliage, and there was the cathedral reconstructed on a grassy rise, pushing its way above them and above the trees, climbing into the middle air, breathing out organ notes, reflecting a stray ray of sunlight from a plane of glass.

'Hold tight to the world,' he said. 'Here comes the guided tour.'

They moved forward and entered.

' "... With its floor-to-ceiling shafts, like so many huge tree trunks, it achieves a ruthless control over its spaces," ' he said. '—Got that from the guidebook. This is the north transept...'

277

' "Greensleeves," ' she said, 'the organ is playing "Green-sleeves." '

'So it is. You can't blame me for that though. —Observe the scalloped capitals—'

'I want to go nearer to the music.'

'Very well. This way then.'

Render felt that something was wrong. He could not put his finger on it.

Everything retained its solidity...

Something passed rapidly then, high above the cathedral, uttering a sonic boom. Render smiled at that, remembering now; it was like a slip of the tongue: for a moment he had confused Eileen with Jill – yes, that was what had happened.

Why, then...

A burst of white was the altar. He had never seen it before, anywhere. All the walls were dark and cold about them. Candles flickered in corners and high niches. The organ chorded thunder under invisible hands.

Render knew that something was wrong.

He turned to Eileen Shallot, whose hat was a green cone towering up into the darkness, trailing wisps of green veiling. Her throat was in shadow, but...

'That necklace – Where?'

'I don't know,' she smiled.

The goblet she held radiated a rosy light. It was reflected from her emerald. It washed him like a draft of cool air.

'Drink?' she asked.

'Stand still,' he ordered.

He willed the walls to fall down. They swam in shadow.

'Stand still!' he repeated urgently. 'Don't do anything. Try not even to think.

'—Fall down!' he cried. And the wails were blasted in all directions and the roof was flung over the top of the world, and they stood amid ruins lighted by a single taper. The night was black as pitch.

'Why did you do that?' she asked, still holding the goblet out toward him.

'Don't think. Don't think anything,' he said. 'Relax. You are very tired. As that candle flickers and wanes so does your consciousness. You can barely keep awake. You can hardly stay on your feet. Your eyes are closing. There is nothing to see here anyway.'

He willed the candle to go out. It continued to burn.

'I'm not tired. Please have a drink.'

He heard organ music through the night. A different tune, one he did not recognize at first.

'I need your cooperation.'

'All right. Anything.'

'Look! The moon!' he pointed.

She looked upward and the moon appeared from behind an inky cloud.

'. . . And another, and another.'

Moons, like strung pearls, proceeded across the blackness.

'The last one will be red,' he stated.

It was.

He reached out then with his right index finger, slid his arm sideways along his field of vision, then tried to touch the red moon.

His arm ached, it burned. He could not move it.

'Wake up!' he screamed.

The red moon vanished, and the white ones.

'Please take a drink.'

He dashed the goblet from her hand and turned away. When he turned back she was still holding it before him.

'A drink?'

He turned and fled into the night.

It was like running through a waist-high snowdrift. It was wrong. He was compounding the error by running – he was minimizing his strength, maximizing hers. It was sapping his energies, draining him.

He stood still in the midst of the blackness.

'The world around me moves,' he said. 'I am its center.'

'Please have a drink,' she said, and he was standing in the glade beside their table set beside the lake. The lake was black

279

and the moon was silver, and high, and out of his reach. A single candle flickered on the table, making her hair as silver as her dress. She wore the moon on her brow. A bottle of Romanée-Conti stood on the white cloth beside a wide-brimmed wine glass. It was filled to overflowing, that glass, and rosy beads clung to its lip. He was very thirsty, and she was lovelier than anyone he had ever seen before, and her necklace sparkled, and the breeze came cool off the lake, and there was something – something he should remember...

He took a step toward her and his armor clinked lightly as he moved. He reached toward the glass and his right arm stiffened with pain and fell back to his side.

'You are wounded!'

Slowly, he turned his head. The blood flowed from the open wound in his biceps and ran down his arm and dripped from his fingertips. His armor had been breached. He forced himself to look away.

'Drink this, love. It will heal you.'

She stood.

'I will hold the glass.'

He stared at her as she raised it to his lips.

'Who am I?' he asked.

She did not answer him, but something replied – within a splashing of waters out over the lake:

*You are Render, the Shaper.*

'Yes, I remember,' he said; and turning his mind to the one lie which might break the entire illusion he forced his mouth to say: 'Eileen Shallot, I hate you.'

The world shuddered and swam about him, was shaken, as by a huge sob.

'Charles!' she screamed, and the blackness swept over them.

'Wake up! Wake up!' he cried, and his right arm burned and ached and bled in the darkness.

He stood alone in the midst of a white plain. It was silent, it was endless. It sloped away toward the edges of the world. It gave off its own light, and the sky was no sky, but was nothing overhead. Nothing. He was alone. His own voice echoed back to him from the end of the world: '...hate you,' it said, '...hate you.'

He dropped to his knees. He was Render.

He wanted to cry.

A red moon appeared above the plain, casting a ghastly light over the entire expanse. There was a wall of mountains to the left of him, another to his right.

He raised his right arm. He helped it with his left hand, He clutched his wrist, extended his index finger. He reached for the moon.

Then there came a howl from high in the mountains, a great wailing cry – half-human, all challenge, all loneliness and all remorse. He saw it then, treading upon the mountains, its tail brushing the snow from their highest peaks, the ultimate loupgarou of the North – Fenris, son of Loki – raging at the heavens.

It leaped into the air. It swallowed the moon.

It landed near him, and its great eyes blazed yellow. It stalked him on soundless pads, across the cold white fields that lay between the mountains; and he backed away from it, up hills and down slopes, over crevasses and rifts, through valleys, past stalagmites and pinnacles – under the edges of glaciers, beside frozen river beds, and always downwards – until its hot breath bathed him and its laughing mouth was opened above him.

He turned then and his feet became two gleaming rivers carrying him away.

The world jumped backward. He glided over the slopes, Downward. Speeding—

Away...

He looked back over his shoulder.

In the distance, the gray shape loped after him.

He felt that it could narrow the gap if it chose. He had to move faster.

The world reeled about him. Snow began to fall.

He raced on.

Ahead, a blur, a broken outline.

He tore through the veils of snow which now seemed to be falling upward from off the ground – like strings of bubbles.

He approached the shattered form.

Like a swimmer he approached – unable to open his mouth to speak for fear of drowning – of drowning and not knowing, of never knowing.

He could not check his forward motion; he was swept tide-like toward the wreck. He came to a stop, at last, before it.

Some things never change. They are things which have long ceased to exist as objects and stand solely as never-to-be-calendared occasions outside that sequence of elements called Time.

Render stood there and did not care if Fenris leaped upon his back and ate his brains. He had covered his eyes, but he could not stop the seeing. Not this time. He did not care about anything. Most of himself lay dead at his feet.

There was a howl. A gray shape swept past him.

The baleful eyes and bloody muzzle rooted within the wrecked car, chomping through the steel, the glass, groping inside for . . .

'No! Brute! Chewer of corpses!' he cried. 'The dead are sacred! *My* dead are sacred!'

He had a scalpel in his hand then, and he slashed expertly at the tendons, the bunches of muscle on the straining shoulders, the soft belly, the ropes of the arteries.

Weeping, he dismembered the monster, limb by limb, and it bled and it bled, fouling the vehicle and the remains within it with its infernal animal juices, dripping and running until the whole plain was reddened and writhing about them.

Render fell across the pulverized hood, and it was soft and warm and dry. He wept upon it.

'Don't cry,' she said.

He was hanging onto her shoulder then, holding her tightly, there beside the black lake beneath the moon that was Wedgewood. A single candle flickered upon their table. She held the glass to his lips.

'Please drink it.'

'Yes, give it to me!'

He gulped the wine that was all softness and lightness. It burned within him. He felt his strength returning.

'I am...'

'—*Render, the Shaper*,' splashed the lake.

'No!'

He turned and ran again, looking for the wreck. He had to go back, to return...

'You can't.'

'I can!' he cried. 'I can, if I try...'

Yellow flames coiled through the thick air. Yellow serpents. They coiled, glowing, about his ankles. Then through the murk, two-headed and towering, approached his Adversary.

Small stones rattled past him. An overpowering odor cork-screwed up his nose and into his head.

'Shaper!' came the bellow from one head.

'You have returned for the reckoning!' called the other.

Render stared, remembering.

'No reckoning, Thaumiel,' he said. 'I beat you and I chained you for – Rothman, yes, it was Rothman – the cabalist.' He traced a pentagram in the air. 'Return to Qliphoth. I banish you.'

'This place be Qliphoth.'

'... By Khamael, the angel of blood by the hosts of Seraphim, in the Name of Elohim Gebor, I bid you vanish!'

'Not this time,' laughed both heads.

It advanced.

Render backed slowly away, his feet bound by the yellow serpents. He could feel the chasm opening behind him. The world was a jigsaw puzzle coming apart. He could see the pieces separating.

'Vanish!'

The giant roared out its double-laugh.

Render stumbled.

'This way, love!'

She stood within a small cave to his right.

He shook his head and backed toward the chasm.

Thaumiel reached out toward him.

Render toppled back over the edge.

'Charles!' she screamed, and the world shook itself apart with her wailing.

'Then Vernichtung,' he answered as he fell. 'I join you in darkness.'

Everything came to an end.


'I want to see Doctor Charles Render.'

'I'm sorry, that is impossible.'

'But I skip-jetted all the way here, just to thank him. I'm a new man! He changed my life!'

'I'm sorry, Mister Erikson. When you called this morning, I told you it was impossible.'

'Sir, I'm Representative Erikson – and Render once did me a great service.'

'Then you can do him one now. Go home.'

'You can't talk to me that way!'

'I just did. Please leave. Maybe next year sometime...'

'But a few words can do wonders...'

'Save them!'

'I-I'm sorry...'


Lovely as it was, pinked over with the morning – the slopping, steaming bowl of the sea – he knew that it *had* to end. Therefore...

He descended the high tower stairway and he entered the courtyard. He crossed to the bower of roses and he looked down upon the pallet set in its midst.

'Good morrow, m'lord,' he said.

'To you the same,' said the knight, his blood mingling with the earth, the flowers, the grasses, flowed from his wound, sparkling over his armor, dripping from his fingertips.

'Naught hath healed?'

The knight shook his head.

'I empty. I wait.'

'Your waiting is near ended.'

'What mean you?' He sat upright.

'The ship. It approacheth harbor.'

The knight stood. He leaned his back against a mossy tree trunk. He stared at the huge, bearded servitor who continued to speak, words harsh with barbaric accents:

'It cometh like a dark swan before the wind – returning.'

'Dark, say you? Dark?'

'The sails be black, Lord Tristram.'

'You lie!'

'Do you wish to see? To see for yourself – Look then!'

He gestured.

The earth quaked, the wall toppled. The dust swirled and settled. From where they stood they could see the ship moving into the harbor on the wings of the night.

'No! You lied! – See! They are white!'

The dawn danced upon the waters. The shadows fled from the ship's sails.

'No, you fool! Black! They *must* be!'

'White! White! – Isolde! You have kept faith. You have returned!'

He began running toward the harbor.

'Come back – Your wound! You are ill – Stop . . .'

The sails were white beneath a sun that was a red button which the servitor reached quickly to touch.

Night fell.

# Home Is the Hangman

Big fat flakes down the night, silent night, windless night. And I never count them as storms unless there is wind. Not a sigh or whimper, though. Just a cold, steady whiteness, drifting down outside the window, and a silence confirmed by gunfire, driven deeper now that it had ceased. In the main room of the lodge the only sounds were the occasional hiss and sputter of the logs turning to ashes on the grate.

I sat in a chair turned sidewise from the table to face the door. A tool kit rested on the floor to my left. The helmet stood on the table, a lopsided basket of metal, quartz, porcelain, and glass. If I heard the click of a microswitch followed by a humming sound from within it, then a faint light would come on beneath the meshing near to its forward edge and begin to blink rapidly. If these things occurred, there was a very strong possibility that I was going to die.

I had removed a black ball from my pocket when Larry and Bert had gone outside, armed, respectively, with a flame thrower and what looked like an elephant gun. Bert had also taken two grenades with him.

I unrolled the black ball, opening it out into a seamless glove, a dollop of something resembling moist putty stuck to its palm. Then I drew the glove on over my left hand and sat with it upraised, elbow resting on the arm of the chair. A small laser flash pistol in which I had very little faith lay beside my right hand on the tabletop, next to the helmet.

If I were to slap a metal surface with my left hand, the substance would adhere there, coming free of the glove. Two seconds later it would explode, and the force of the explosion would be directed in against the surface. Newton would claim his own by way of right-angled redistributions of the reaction, hopefully tearing lateral hell out of the contact surface. A smother-charge, it was called, and its possession came under concealed-weapons and possession-of-burglary-tools statutes in most places. The molecularly gimmicked goo, I decided, was great stuff. It was just the delivery system that left more to be desired.

Beside the helmet, next to the gun, in front of my hand, stood a small walkie-talkie. This was for purposes of warning Bert and Larry if I should hear the click of a microswitch followed by a humming sound, should see a light come on and begin to blink rapidly. Then they would know that Tom and Clay, with whom we had lost contact when the shooting began, had failed to destroy the enemy and doubtless lay lifeless at their stations now, a little over a kilometer to the south. Then they would know that they, too, were probably about to die.

I called out to them when I heard the click. I picked up the helmet and rose to my feet as its light began to blink.

But it was already too late.

The fourth place listed on the Christmas card I had sent Don Walsh the previous year was Peabody's Book Shop and Beer Stube in Baltimore, Maryland. Accordingly, on the last night in October I sat in its rearmost room, at the final table before the alcove with the door leading to the alley. Across that dim chamber, a woman dressed in black played the ancient upright piano, uptempoing everything she touched. Off to my right, a fire wheezed and spewed fumes on a narrow hearth beneath a crowded mantelpiece overseen by an ancient and antlered profile. I sipped a beer and listened to the sounds.

I half hoped that this would be one of the occasions when Don failed to show up. I had sufficient funds to hold me through spring and I did not really feel like working. I had summered farther north, was anchored now in the Chesapeake, and was anxious to continue Caribbeanward. A growing chill and some nasty winds told me I had tarried overlong in these latitudes. Still, the understanding was that I remain in the chosen bar until midnight. Two hours to go.

I ate a sandwich and ordered another beer. About halfway into it, I spotted Don approaching the entranceway, topcoat over his arm, head turning. I manufactured a matching quantity of surprise when he appeared beside my table with a, 'Ron! Is that really you?'

I rose and clasped his hand.

'Alan! Small world, or something like that. Sit down! Sit down!'

He settled onto the chair across from me, draped his coat over the one to his left.

'What are you doing in this town?' he asked.

'Just a visit,' I answered. 'Said hello to a few friends.' I patted the scars, the stains on the venerable surface before me. 'And this is my last stop. I'll be leaving in a few hours.'

He chuckled.

'Why is it that you knock on wood?'

I grinned.

'I was expressing affection for one of Henry Mencken's favorite speakeasies.'

'This place dates back that far?'

I nodded.

'It figures,' he said. 'You've got this thing for the past – or against the present. I'm never sure which.'

'Maybe a little of both,' I said. 'I wish Mencken would stop in. I'd like his opinion on the present – What are you doing with it?'

'What?'

'The present. Here. Now.'

'Oh.' He spotted the waitress and ordered a beer. 'Business trip,' he said then. 'To hire a consultant.'

'Oh. How *is* business?'

'Complicated,' he said, 'complicated.'

We lit cigarettes and after a while his beer arrived. We smoked and drank and listened to the music.

I've sung this song and I'll sing it again: the world is like an uptempoed piece of music. Of the many changes which came to pass during my lifetime, it seems that the majority have occurred during the past few years. It also struck me that way several years ago, and I'd a hunch I might be feeling the same way a few years hence – that is, if Don's business did not complicate me off this mortal coil or condenser before then.

Don operates the second-largest detective agency in the world, and he sometimes finds me useful because I do not exist. I do not exist now because I existed once at the time and the place where we attempted to begin scoring the wild ditty of our times. I refer to the world Central Data Bank project and the fact that I had had a significant part in that effort to construct a working model of the real world, accounting for everyone and everything in it. How well we succeeded, and whether possession of the world's likeness does indeed provide its custodians with a greater measure of control over its functions, are questions my former colleagues still debate as the music grows more shrill and you can't see the maps for the pins. I made my decision back then and saw to it that I did not receive citizenship in that second world, a place which may now have become more important than the first. Exiled to reality, my own sojourns across the line are necessarily those of an alien guilty of illegal entry. I visit periodically because I go where I must to make my living – That is where Don comes in. The people I can become are often very useful when he has peculiar problems.

Unfortunately, at that moment, it seemed that he did, just when the whole gang of me felt like turning down the volume and loafing.

We finished our drinks, got the bill, settled it.

'This way,' I said, indicating the rear door, and he swung into his coat and followed me out.

'Talk here?' he asked, as we walked down the alley.

'Rather not,' I said. 'Public transportation, then private conversation.'

He nodded and came along.

About three-quarters of an hour later we were in the saloon of the *Proteus* and I was making coffee. We were rocked gently by the Bay's chill waters, under a moonless sky. I'd only a pair of the smaller lights burning. Comfortable. On the water, aboard the *Proteus*, the crowding, the activities, the tempo, of life in the cities, on the land, are muted, slowed – fictionalized – by the metaphysical distancing a few meters of water can provide. We alter the landscape with great facility, but the ocean has always seemed unchanged, and I suppose by extension we are infected with some feelings of timelessness whenever we set out upon her. Maybe that's one of the reasons I spend so much time there.

'First time you've had me aboard,' he said. 'Comfortable. Very.'

'Thanks – Cream? Sugar?'

'Yes. Both.'

We settled back with our steaming mugs and I asked, 'What have you got?'

'One case involving two problems,' he said. 'One of them sort of falls within my area of competence. The other does not. I was told that it is an absolutely unique situation and would require the services of a very special specialist.'

'I'm not a specialist at anything but keeping alive.'

His eyes came up suddenly and caught my own.

'I had always assumed that you knew an awful lot about computers,' he said.

I looked away. That was hitting below the belt. I had never held myself out to him as an authority in that area, and there had always been a tacit understanding between us that my methods of manipulating circumstance and identity were not open to discussion. On the other hand, it was obvious to him that my knowledge of the system was both extensive and intensive. Still, I didn't like talking about it. So I moved to defend.

'Computer people are a dime a dozen,' I said. 'It was probably different in your time, but these days they start teaching

290

computer science to little kids their first year in school. So sure, I know a lot about it. This generation, everybody does,'

'You know that is not what I meant,' he said. Haven't you known me long enough to trust me a little more than that? The question springs solely from the case at hand. That's all.'

I nodded. Reactions by their very nature are not always appropriate, and I had invested a lot of emotional capital in a heavy-duty set. So, 'Okay, I know more about them than the school kids,' I said.

'Thanks. That can be our point of departure.' He took a sip of coffee. 'My own background is in law and accounting, followed by the military, military intelligence, and civil service, in that order. Then I got into this business. What technical stuff I know I've picked up along the way – a scrap here, a crash course there. I know a lot about what things can *do*, not so much about how they *work*. I did not understand the details on this one, so I want you to start at the top and explain things to me, for as far as you can go. I need the background review, and if you are able to furnish it I will also know that you are the man for the job. You can begin by telling me how the early space-exploration robots worked – like, say the ones they used on Venus.'

'That's not computers,' I said, 'and for that matter, they weren't really robots. They were telefactoring devices.'

'Tell me what makes the difference.'

'A robot is a machine which carries out certain operations in accordance with a program of instructions. A telefactor is a slave machine operated by remote control. The telefactor functions in a feedback situation with its operator. Depending on how sophisticated you want to get, the links can be audiovisual, kinesthetic, tactile, even olfactory. The more you want to go in this direction, the more anthropomorphic you get in the thing's design.

'In the case of Venus, if I recall correctly, the human operator in orbit wore an exoskeleton which controlled the movements of the body, legs, arms, and hands of the device on the surface below, receiving motion and force feedback through a system of airjet transducers. He had on a helmet controlling the slave device's television camera – set, obviously enough, in its turret – which filled his field of vision with the scene below. He also wore earphones connected with its audio pickup. I read the book he wrote later. He said that for long stretches of time he would forget the cabin, forget that he was at the boss end of a control loop, and actually feel as if he were stalking through that hellish landscape. I remember being very impressed by it, just being a kid, and I wanted a super-tiny one all my own, so that I could wade around in puddles picking fights with microorganisms.'

'Why?'

'Because there weren't any dragons on Venus. Anyhow, that is a telefactoring device, a thing quite distinct from a robot.'

'I'm still with you,' he said, and, 'Now tell me the difference between the early telefactoring devices and the later ones.'

I swallowed some coffee.

'It was a bit trickier with respect to the outer planets and their satellites,' I said. 'There, we did not have orbiting operators at first. Economics, and some unresolved technical problems. Mainly economics. At any rate, the devices were landed on the target worlds, but the operators stayed home. Because of this, there was of course a time lag in the transmissions along the control loop. It took a while to receive the on-site input, and then there was another time lapse before the response movements reached the telefactor. We attempted to compensate for this in two ways: the first was by the employment of a single wait-move, wait-move sequence; the second was more sophisticated and is actually the point where computers come into the picture in terms of participating in the control loop. It involved the setting up of models of known environmental factors, which were then enriched during the initial wait-move sequences. On this basis, the computer was then used to anticipate short-range developments. Finally, it could take over the loop and run it by a combination of "predictor controls" and wait-move reviews. It still had to holler for human help, though, when unexpected things came up. So, with the outer planets, it was neither totally automatic nor totally manual – nor totally satisfactory – at first.'

'Okay,' he said, lighting a cigarette. 'And the next step?'

'The next wasn't really a technical step forward in telefactoring. It was an economic shift. The pursestrings were loosened and we could afford to send men out. We landed them where we could land them, and in many of the places where we could not, we sent down the telefactors and orbited the men again. Like in the old days. The time-lag problem was removed because the operator was on top of things once more. If anything, you can look at it as a reversion to earlier methods. It is what we still often do, though, and it works.'

He shook his head.

'You left something out between the computers and the bigger budget.'

I shrugged.

'A number of things were tried during that period, but none of them proved as effective as what we already had going in the human-computer partnership with the telefactors.'

'There was one project,' he said, 'which attempted to get around the time-lag troubles by sending the computer along with the telefactor as part of the package. Only the computer wasn't exactly a computer and the telefactor wasn't exactly a telefactor. Do you know which one I am referring to?'

I lit a cigarette of my own while I thought about it, then, 'I think you are talking about the Hangman,' I said.

'That's right and this is where I get lost. Can you tell me how it works?'

'Ultimately, it was a failure,' I told him.

'But it worked at first.'

'Apparently. But only on the easy stuff, on Io. It conked out later and had to be written off as a failure, albeit a noble one. The venture was overly ambitious from the very beginning. What seems to have happened was that the people in charge had the opportunity to combine vanguard projects – stuff that was still under investigation and stuff that was extremely new. In theory, it all seemed to dovetail so beautifully that they yielded to the temptation and incorporated too much. It started out well, but it fell apart later.'

'But what all was involved in the thing?'

'Lord! What wasn't? The computer that wasn't exactly a computer... Okay, well start there. Last century, three engineers at the University of Wisconsin – Nordman, Parmentier, and Scott – developed a device known as a superconductive tunnel-junction neuristor. Two tiny strips of metal with a thin insulating layer between. Supercool it and it passed electrical impulses without resistance. Surround it with magnetized material and pack a mass of them together – billions – and what have you got?'

He shook his head.

'Well, for one thing you've got an impossible situation to schematize when considering all the paths and interconnections that may be formed. There is an obvious similarity to the structure of the brain. So, they theorized, you don't even attempt to hook up such a device. You pulse in data and let it establish its own preferential pathways, by means of the magnetic material's becoming increasingly magnetized each time the current passes through it, thus cutting the resistance. The material establishes its own routes in a fashion analogous to the functioning of the brain when it is learning something.

'In the case of the Hangman, they used a setup very similar to this and they were able to pack over ten billion neuristor-type cells into a very small area – around a cubic foot. They aimed for that magic figure because that is approximately the number of nerve cells in the human brain. That is what I meant when I said that it wasn't really a computer. They were actually working in the area of artificial intelligence, no matter what they called it.'

'If the thing had its own brain – computer or quasihuman – then it was a robot rather than a telefactor, right?'

'Yes and no and maybe,' I said. 'It was operated as a telefactor device here on Earth – on the ocean floor, in the desert, in mountainous country – as part of its programming. I suppose you could also call that its apprenticeship – or kindergarten. Perhaps that is even more appropriate. It was being shown how to explore in difficult environments and to report back. Once it mastered this, then theoretically they could hang it out there in the sky without a control loop and let it report its own findings.'

'At that point would it be considered a robot?'

'A robot is a machine which carries out certain operations in accordance with a program of instructions. The Hangman made its *own* decisions, you see. And I suspect that by trying to produce something that close to the human brain in structure and function, the seemingly inevitable randomness of its model got included in. It wasn't just a machine following a program. It was too complex. That was probably what broke it down.'

Don chuckled.

'Inevitable free will?'

'No. As I said, they had thrown too many things into one bag. Everybody and his brother with a pet project that might be fitted in seemed a supersalesman that season. For example, the psychophysics boys had a gimmick they wanted to try on it, and it got used. Ostensibly, The Hangman was a communications device. Actually, they were concerned as to whether the thing was truly sentient.'

'Was it?'

'Apparently so, in a limited fashion. What they had come up with, to be made part of the initial telefactor loop, was a device which set up a weak induction field in the brain of the operator. The machine received and amplified the patterns of electrical activity being conducted in the Hangman's – might well call it "brain" – then passed them through a complex modulator and pulsed them into the induction field in the operator's head – I am out of my area now and into that of Weber and Fechner, but a neuron has a threshold at which it will fire, and below which it will not. There are some forty thousand neurons packed together in a square millimeter of the cerebral cortex, in such fashion that each one has several hundred synaptic connections with others about it. At any given moment, some of them may be way below the firing threshold while others are in a condition Sir John Eccles once referred to as "critically poised" – ready to fire. If just one is pushed over the threshold, it can affect the discharge of hundreds of thousands of others within twenty milliseconds. The pulsating field was to provide such a push in a sufficiently selective fashion to give the operator an idea as to what was going on in the Hangman's brain. And vice versa. The Hangman was to have its own built-in version of the same thing. It was also thought that this might serve to humanize it somewhat, so that it would better appreciate the significance of its work – to instill something like loyalty, you might say.'

'Do you think this could have contributed to its later breakdown?'

'Possibly. How can you say in a one-of-a-kind situation like this? If you want a guess, I'd say, "Yes." But its just a guess.'

'Uh-huh,' he said, 'and what were its physical capabilities?'

'Anthropomorphic design,' I said, 'both because it was originally telefactored and because of the psychological reasoning I just mentioned. It could pilot its own small vessel. No need for a life-support system, of course. Both it and the vessel were powered by fusion units, so that fuel was no real problem. Self-repairing. Capable of performing a great variety of sophisticated tests and measurements, of making observations, completing reports, learning new material, broadcasting its findings back here. Capable of surviving just about anywhere. In fact, it required less energy on the outer planets – less work for the refrigeration units, to maintain that supercooled brain in its midsection.'

'How strong was it?'

'I don't recall all the specs. Maybe a dozen times as strong as a man, in things like lifting and pushing.'

'It explored Io for us and started in on Europa.'

'Yes.'

'Then it began behaving erratically, just when we thought it had really learned its job.'

'That sounds right,' I said.

'It refused a direct order to explore Callisto, then headed out toward Uranus.'

'Yes. It's been years since I read the reports...'

'The malfunction worsened after that. Long periods of silence interspersed with garbled transmissions. Now that I know more about its makeup, it almost sounds like a man going off the deep end.'

'It seems similar.'

'But it managed to pull itself together again for a brief while. It landed on Titania, began sending back what seemed like appropriate observation reports. This only lasted a short time, though. It went irrational once more, indicated that it was heading for a landing on Uranus itself, and that was it. We didn't hear from it after that. Now that I know about that mind-reading gadget I understand why a psychiatrist on this end could be so positive it would never function again.'

'I never heard about that part.'

'I did.'

I shrugged. 'This was all around twenty years ago,' I said, 'and, as I mentioned, it has been a long while since I've read anything about it.'

'The Hangman's ship crashed or landed, as the case may be, in the Gulf of Mexico, two days ago.'

I just stared at him.

'It was empty,' Don went on, 'when they finally got out and down to it.'

'I don't understand.'

'Yesterday morning,' he continued, 'restaurateur Manny Burns was found beaten to death in the office of his establishment, the Maison Saint-Michel, in New Orleans.'

'I still fail to see—'

'Manny Burns was one of the four original operators who programmed – pardon me – taught – the Hangman.'

The silence lengthened, dragged its belly on the deck.

'Concidence...?' I finally said.

'My client doesn't think so.'

'Who is your client?'

'One of the three remaining members of the training group. He is convinced that the Hangman has returned to Earth to kill its former operators.'

'Has he made his fears known to his old employers?'

'No.'

'Why not?'

'Because it would require telling them the reason for his fears.'

'That being . . . ?'

'He wouldn't tell me, either.'

'How does he expect you to do a proper job?'

'He told me what he considered a proper job. He wanted two things done, neither of which requires a full case history. He wanted to be furnished with good bodyguards, and he wanted the Hangman found and disposed of. I have already taken care of the first part.'

'And you want me to do the second?'

'That's right. You have confirmed my opinion that you are the man for the job.'

'I see. Do you realize that if the thing is truly sentient this will be something very like murder? If it is not, of course, then it will only amount to the destruction of expensive government property.'

'Which way do you look at it?'

'I look at it as a job,' I said.

'You'll take it?'

'I need more facts before I can decide. Like, who is your client? Who are the other operators? Where do they live? What do they do? What—'

He raised his hand.

'First,' he said, 'the Honorable Jesse Brockden, senior Senator from Wisconsin, is our client. Confidentiality, of course, is written all over it.'

I nodded. 'I remember his being involved with the space program before he went into politics. I wasn't aware of the specifics, though. He could get government protection so easily—'

'To obtain it, he would apparently have to tell them

something he doesn't want to talk about. Perhaps it would hurt his career. I simply do not know. He doesn't want them. He wants us.'

I nodded again.

'What about the others? Do they want us, too?'

'Quite the opposite. They don't subscribe to Brockden's notions at all. They seem to think he is something of a paranoid.'

'How well do they know one another these days?'

'They live in different parts of the country, haven't seen each other in years. Been in occasional touch, though.'

'Kind of a flimsy basis for that diagnosis, then.'

'One of them *is* a psychiatrist.'

'Oh. Which one?'

'Leila Thackery is her name. Lives in St Louis. Works at the State Hospital there.'

'None of them have gone to any authority, then – federal or local?'

'That's right. Brockden contacted them when he heard about the Hangman. He was in Washington at the time. Got word on its return right away and managed to get the story killed. He tried to reach them all, learned about Burns in the process, contacted me, then tried to persuade the others to accept protection by my people. They weren't buying. When I talked to her, Doctor Thackery pointed out – quite correctly – that Brockden is a very sick man.'

'What's he got?'

'Cancer. In his spine. Nothing they can do about it once it hits there and digs in. He even told me he figures he has maybe six months to get through what he considers a very important piece of legislation – the new criminal rehabilitation act – I will admit that he did sound kind of paranoid when he talked about it. But hell! Who wouldn't? Doctor Thackery sees that as the whole thing, though, and she doesn't see the Burns killing as being connected with the Hangman. Thinks it was just a traditional robbery gone sour, thief surprised and panicky, maybe hopped-up, *et cetera*.'

'Then she is not afraid of the Hangman?'

'She said that she is in a better position to know its mind than anyone else, and she is not especially concerned.'

'What about the other operator?'

'He said that Doctor Thackery may know its mind better than anyone else, but he knows its brain, and he isn't worried, either.'

'What did he mean by that?'

'David Fentris is a consulting engineer – electronics, cybernetics. He actually had something to do with the Hangman's design.'

I got to my feet and went after the coffeepot. Not that I'd an overwhelming desire for another cup at just that moment. But I had known, had once worked with a David Fentris. And he had at one time been connected with the space program.

About fifteen years my senior, Dave had been with the data bank project when I had known him. Where a number of us had begun having second thoughts as the thing progressed, Dave had never been anything less than wildly enthusiastic. A wiry five-eight, gray-cropped, gray eyes back of hornrims and heavy glass, cycling between preoccupation and near-frantic darting, he had had a way of verbalizing half-completed thoughts as he went along, so that you might begin to think him a representative of that tribe which had come into positions of small authority by means of nepotism or politics. If you would listen a few more minutes, however, you would begin revising your opinion as he started to pull his musings together into a rigorous framework. By the time he had finished, you generally wondered why you hadn't seen it all along and what a guy like that was doing in a position of such small authority. Later, it might strike you, though, that he seemed sad whenever he wasn't enthusiastic about something. And while the gung-ho spirit is great for short-range projects, larger ventures generally require somewhat more equanimity. I wasn't at all surprised that he had wound up as a consultant.

The big question now, of course was: Would he remember me? True, my appearance was altered, my personality hopefully more mature, my habits shifted around. But would that be enough, should I have to encounter him as part of this job? That mind behind those hornrims could do a lot of strange things with just a little data.

'Where does he live?' I asked.

'Memphis. – And what's the matter?'

'Just trying to get my geography straight,' I said. 'Is Senator Brockden still in Washington?'

'No. He's returned to Wisconsin and is currently holed up in a lodge in the northern part of the state. Four of my people are with him.'

'I see.'

I refreshed our coffee supply and reseated myself. I didn't like this one at all and I resolved not to take it. I didn't like just giving Don a flat 'No,' though. His assignments had become a very important part of my life, and this one was not mere legwork. It was obviously important to him, and he wanted me on it. I decided to look for holes in the thing, to find some way of reducing it to the simple bodyguard job already in progress.

'It does seem peculiar,' I said, 'that Brockden is the only one afraid of the device.'

'Yes.'

'. . . And that he gives no reasons.'

'True.'

'. . . Plus his condition, and what the doctor said about its effect on his mind.'

'I have no doubt that he is neurotic,' Don said. 'Look at this.'

He reached for his coat, withdrew a sheaf of papers from within it. He shuffled through them and extracted a single sheet, which he passed to me.

It was a piece of Congressional-letterhead stationary, with the message scrawled in longhand. *'Don,'* it said, *'I've got to see you. Frankenstein's monster is just come back from where we hung him and he's looking for me. The whole damn universe is trying to grind me up. Call me between 8 & 10 – Jess.'*

I nodded, started to pass it back, paused, then handed it over. Double damn it deeper than hell!

I took a drink of coffee. I thought that I had long ago given up hope in such things, but I had noticed something which immediately troubled me. In the margin, where they list such matters, I had seen that Jesse Brockden was on the committee for review of the Central Data Bank program. I recalled that that committee was supposed to be working on a series of reform recommendations. Offhand, I could not remember Brockden's position on any of the issues involved, but – Oh hell! The thing was simply too big to alter significantly now . . . But it was the only real Frankenstein monster I cared about, and there was always the possibility . . . On the other hand – Hell, again! What if I let him die when I might have saved him, and he had been the one who . . . ?

I took another drink of coffee. I lit another cigarette.

There might be a way of working it so that Dave didn't even come into the picture. I could talk to Leila Thackery first, check further into the Burns killing, keep posted on new developments, find out more about the vessel in the Gulf . . . I might be able to accomplish something, even if it was only the negation of Brockden's theory, without Dave's and my paths ever crossing.

'Have you got the specs on the Hangman?' I asked.

'Right here.'

He passed them over.

'The police report on the Burns killing?'

'Here it is.'

'The whereabouts of everyone involved, and some background on them?'

'Here.'

'The place or places where I can reach you during the next few days – around the clock? This one may require some coordination.'

He smiled and reached for his pen.

'Glad to have you aboard,' he said.

I reached over and tapped the barometer. I shook my head.

*

The ringing of the phone awakened me. Reflex bore me across the room, where I took it on audio.

'Yes?'

'Mister Donne? It is eight o'clock.'

'Thanks.'

I collapsed into the chair. I am what might be called a slow starter. I tend to recapitulate phylogeny every morning. Basic desires inched their ways through my gray matter to close a connection. Slowly, I extended a cold-blooded member and clicked my talons against a couple of numbers. I croaked my desire for food and lots of coffee to the voice that responded. Half an hour later I would only have growled. Then I staggered off to the place of flowing waters to renew my contact with basics.

In addition to my normal adrenaline and blood-sugar bearishness, I had not slept much the night before. I had closed up shop after Don left, stuffed my pockets with essentials, departed the *Proteus*, gotten myself over to the airport and onto a flight which took me to St Louis in the dead, small hours of the dark. I was unable to sleep during the flight, thinking about the case, deciding on the tack I was going to take with Leila Thackery. On arrival, I had checked into the airport motel, left a message to be awakened at an unreasonable hour, and collapsed.

As I ate, I regarded the fact sheet Don had given me.

Leila Thackery was currently single, having divorced her second husband a little over two years ago, was forty-six years old, and lived in an apartment near to the hospital where she worked. Attached to the sheet was a photo which might have been ten years old. In it, she was brunette, light-eyed, barely on the right side of that border between ample and overweight, with fancy glasses straddling an upturned nose. She had published a number of books and articles with titles full of alienations, roles, transactions, social contexts, and more alienations.

I hadn't had the time to go my usual route, becoming an entire new individual with a verifiable history. Just a name and a story, that's all. It did not seem necessary this time, though.

303

For once, something approximating honesty actually seemed a reasonable approach.

I took a public vehicle over to her apartment building. I did not phone ahead, because it is easier to say 'No' to a voice than to a person.

According to the record, today was one of the days when she saw outpatients in her home. Her idea, apparently: break down the alienating institution-image, remove resentments by turning the sessions into something more like social occasions, *et cetera*. I did not want all that much of her time – I had decided that Don could make it worth her while if it came to that – and I was sure my fellows' visits were scheduled to leave her with some small breathing space. *Inter alia*, so to speak.

I had just located her name and apartment number amid the buttons in the entrance foyer when an old woman passed behind me and unlocked the door to the lobby. She glanced at me and held it open, so I went on in without ringing. The matter of presence, again.

I took the elevator to Leila's floor, the second, located her door and knocked on it. I was almost ready to knock again when it opened, partway.

'Yes?' she asked, and I revised my estimate as to the age of the photo. She looked just about the same.

'Doctor Thackery,' I said, 'my name is Donne. You could help me quite a bit with a problem I've got.'

'What sort of problem?'

'It involves a device known as the Hangman.'

She sighed and showed me a quick grimace. Her fingers tightened on the door.

'I've come a long way but I'll be easy to get rid of. I've only a few things I'd like to ask you about it.'

'Are you with the government?'

'No.'

'Do you work for Brockden?'

'No, I'm something different.'

'All right,' she said. 'Right now I've got a group session going. It will probably last around another half hour. If you

304

don't mind waiting down in the lobby, I'll let you know as soon as it is over. We can talk then.'

'Good enough,' I said. 'Thanks.'

She nodded, closed the door. I located the stairway and walked back down.

A cigarette later, I decided that the devil finds work for idle hands and thanked him for his suggestion. I strolled back toward the foyer. Through the glass, I read the names of a few residents of the fifth floor. I elevated up and knocked on one of the doors. Before it was opened I had my notebook and pad in plain sight.

'Yes?' Short, fiftyish, curious.

'My name is Stephen Foster, Mrs Gluntz. I am doing a survey for the North American Consumers League. I would like to pay you for a couple minutes of your time, to answer some questions about products you use.'

'Why – Pay me?'

'Yes, ma'am. Ten dollars. Around a dozen questions. It will just take a minute or two.'

'All right.' She opened the door wider. 'Won't you come in?'

'No, thank you. This thing is so brief I'd just be in and out. The first question involves detergents...'

Ten minutes later I was back in the lobby adding the thirty bucks for the three interviews to the list of expenses I was keeping. When a situation is full of unpredictables and I am playing makeshift games, I like to provide for as many contingencies as I can.

Another quarter of an hour or so slipped by before the elevator opened and discharged three guys – young, young, and middle-aged, casually dressed, chuckling over something.

The big one on the nearest end strolled over and nodded.

'You the fellow waiting to see Doctor Thackery?'

'That's right.'

'She said to tell you to come on up now.'

'Thanks.'

I rode up again, returned to her door. She opened to my

305

knock, nodded me in, saw me seated in a comfortable chair at the far end of her living room.

'Would you care for a cup of coffee?' she asked. 'It's fresh. I made more than I needed.'

'That would be fine. Thanks.'

Moments later, she brought in a couple of cups, delivered one to me, and seated herself on the sofa to my left. I ignored the cream and sugar on the tray and took a sip.

'You've gotten me interested,' she said. 'Tell me about it.'

'Okay. I have been told that the telefactor device known as the Hangman, now possibly possessed of an artificial intelligence, has returned to Earth—'

'Hypothetical,' she said, 'unless you know something I don't. I have been told that the Hangman's vehicle reentered and crashed in the Gulf. There is no evidence that the vehicle was occupied.'

'It seems a reasonable conclusion, though.'

'It seems just as reasonable to me that the Hangman sent the vehicle off toward an eventual rendezvous point many years ago and that it only recently reached that point, at which time the reentry program took over and brought it down.'

'Why should it return the vehicle and strand itself out there?'

'Before I answer that,' she said, 'I would like to know the reason for your concern. News media?'

'No,' I said. 'I am a science writer – straight tech, popular, and anything in between. But I am not after a piece for publication. I was retained to do a report on the psychological makeup of the thing.'

'For whom?'

'A private investigation outfit. They want to know what might influence its thinking, how it might be likely to behave – if it has indeed come back – I've been doing a lot of homework, and I gathered there is a likelihood that its nuclear personality was a composite of the minds of its four operators. So, personal contacts seemed in order, to collect your opinions as to what it might be like. I came to you first for obvious reasons.'

She nodded.

'A Mister Walsh spoke with me the other day. He is working for Senator Brockden.'

'Oh? I never go into an employer's business beyond what he's asked me to do. Senator Brockden is on my list though, along with a David Fentris.'

'You were told about Manny Burns?'

'Yes. Unfortunate.'

'That is apparently what set Jesse off. He is – how shall I put it? – he is clinging to life right now, trying to accomplish a great many things in the time he has remaining. Every moment is precious to him. He feels the old man in the white nightgown breathing down his neck – Then the ship returns and one of us is killed. From what we know of the Hangman, the last we heard of it, it had become irrational. Jesse saw a connection, and in his condition the fear is understandable. There is nothing wrong with humoring him if it allows him to get his work done.'

'But you don't see a threat in it?'

'No. I was the last person to monitor the Hangman before communications ceased, and I could see then what had happened. The first things that it had learned were the organization of perceptions and motor activities. Multitudes of other patterns had been transferred from the minds of its operators, but they were too sophisticated to mean much initially. – Think of a child who has learned the Gettysburg Address. It is there in his head, that is all. One day, however, it may be important to him. Conceivably, it may even inspire him to action. It takes some growing up first, of course. Now think of such a child with a great number of conflicting patterns – attitudes, tendencies, memories – none of which are especially bothersome for so long as he remains a child. Add a bit of maturity, though – and bear in mind that the patterns originated with four different individuals, all of them more powerful than the words of even the finest of speeches, bearing as they do their own built-in feelings. Try to imagine the conflicts, the contradictions involved in being four people at once—'

'Why wasn't this imagined in advance?' I asked.

'Ah!' she said, smiling. 'The full sensitivity of the neuristor brain was not appreciated at first. It was assumed that the operators were adding data in a linear fashion and that this would continue until a critical mass was achieved, corresponding to the construction of a model or picture of the world which would then serve as a point of departure for growth of the Hangman's own mind. And it did seem to check out this way.

'What actually occurred, however, was a phenomenon amounting to imprinting. Secondary characteristics of the operators' minds, outside the didactic situations, were imposed. These did not immediately become functional and hence were not detected. They remained latent until the mind had developed sufficiently to understand them. And then it was too late. It suddenly acquired four additional personalities and was unable to coordinate them. When it tried to compartmentalize them it went schizoid; when it tried to integrate them it went catatonic. It was cycling back and forth between these alternatives at the end. Then it just went silent. I felt it had undergone the equivalent of an epileptic seizure. Wild currents through that magnetic material would, in effect, have erased its mind, resulting in *its* equivalent of death or idiocy.'

'I follow you,' I said. 'Now, just for the sake of playing games, I see the alternatives as either a successful integration of all this material or the achievement of a viable schizophrenia. What do you think its behavior would be like if either of these were possible?'

'All right,' she agreed. 'As I just said, though, I think there were physical limitations to its retaining multiple personality structures for a very long period of time. If it did, however, it would have continued with its own, plus replicas of the four operators', at least for a while. The situation would differ radically from that of a human schizoid of this sort, in that the additional personalities were valid images of genuine identities rather than self-generated complexes which had become autonomous. They might continue to evolve, they might degenerate, they might conflict to the point of destruction or gross modification of any or all of them. In other words, no prediction is possible as to the nature of whatever might remain.'

'Might I venture one?'

'Go ahead.'

'After considerable anxiety, it masters them. It asserts itself. It beats down this quartet of demons which has been tearing it apart, acquiring in the process an all-consuming hatred for the actual individuals responsible for this turmoil. To free itself totally, to revenge itself, to work its ultimate catharsis, it resolves to seek them out and destroy them.'

She smiled.

'You have just dispensed with the "viable schizophrenia" you conjured up, and you have now switched over to its pulling through and becoming fully autonomous. That is a different situation – no matter what strings you put on it.'

'Okay, I accept the charge – But what about my conclusion?'

'You are saying that if it did pull through, it would hate us. That strikes me as an unfair attempt to invoke the spirit of Sigmund Freud: Oedipus and Electra in one being, out to destroy all its parents – the authors of every one of its tensions, anxieties, hang-ups, burned into its impressionable psyche at a young and defenseless age. Even Freud didn't have a name for that one. What should we call it?'

'A Hermacis complex?' I suggested.

'Hermacis?'

'Hermaphroditus having been united in one body with the nymph Salmacis, I've just done the same with their names. That being would then have had four parents against whom to react.'

'Cute,' she said, smiling. 'If the liberal arts do nothing else, they provide engaging metaphors for the thinking they displace. This one is unwarranted and overly anthropomorphic, though – You wanted my opinion. All right. If the Hangman pulled through at all, it could only have been by virtue of that neuristor brain's differences from the human brain. From my own professional experience, a human could not pass through a situation like that and attain stability. If the Hangman did, it would have to have resolved all the contradictions and conflicts, to have mastered and understood the situation so thoroughly that I do not believe whatever remained could involve that sort of hatred. The fear, the uncertainty, the things that feed hate would have been analyzed, digested, turned to something more useful. There would probably be distaste, and possibly an act of independence, of self-assertion. That was one reason why I suggested its return of the ship.'

'It is your opinion, then, that if the Hangman exists as a thinking individual today, this is the only possible attitude it would possess toward its former operators: it would want nothing more to do with you?'

'That is correct. Sorry about your Hermacis complex. But in this case we must look to the brain, not the psyche. And we see two things: schizophrenia would have destroyed it, and a successful resolution of its problem would preclude vengeance. Either way, there is nothing to worry about.'

How could I put it tactfully? I decided that I could not.

'All of this is fine,' I said, 'for as far as it goes. But getting away from both the purely psychological and the purely phys-ical, could there be a particular reason for its seeking your deaths – that is, a plain old-fashioned motive for a killing, based on *events* rather than having to do with the way its thinking equipment goes together?'

Her expression was impossible to read, but considering her line of work I had expected nothing less.

'What events?' she said.

'I have no idea. That's why I asked.'

She shook her head.

'I'm afraid that I don't, either.'

'Then that about does it,' I said. 'I can't think of anything else to ask you.'

She nodded.

'And I can't think of anything else to tell you.'

I finished my coffee, returned the cup to the tray.

'Thanks, then,' I said, 'for your time, for the coffee. You have been very helpful.'

I rose. She did the same.

'What are you going to do now?' she asked.

'I haven't quite decided,' I answered. 'I want to do the best report I can. Have you any suggestions on that?'

'I suggest that there isn't any more to learn, that I have given you the only possible constructions the facts warrant.'

'You don't feel David Fentris could provide any additional insights?'

She snorted, then sighed.

'No,' she said, 'I do not think he could tell you anything useful.'

'What do you mean? From the way you say it—'

'I know. I didn't mean to – Some people find comfort in religion. Others . . . You know. Others take it up late in life with a vengeance and a half. They don't use it quite the way it was intended. It comes to color all their thinking.'

'Fanaticism?' I said.

'Not exactly. A misplaced zeal. A masochistic sort of thing. Hell! I shouldn't be diagnosing at a distance – or influencing your opinion. Forget what I said. Form your own opinion when you meet him.'

She raised her head, appraising my reaction.

'Well,' I responded, 'I am not at all certain that I am going to see him. But you have made me curious. How can religion influence engineering?'

'I spoke with him after Jesse gave us the news on the vessel's return. I got the impression at the time that he feels we were tampering in the province of the Almighty by attempting the creation of an artificial intelligence. That our creation should go mad was only appropriate, being the work of imperfect man. He seemed to feel that it would be fitting if it had come back for retribution, as a sign of judgment upon us.'

'Oh,' I said.

She smiled then. I returned it.

311

'Yes,' she said, 'but maybe I just got him in a bad mood. Maybe you should go see for yourself.'

Something told me to shake my head – there was a bit of a difference between this view of him, my recollections, and Don's comment that Dave had said he knew its brain and was not especially concerned. Somewhere among these lay something I felt I should know, felt I should learn without seeming to pursue.

So, 'I think have enough right now,' I said. 'It was the psychological side of things I was supposed to cover, not the mechanical – *or* the theological. You have been extremely helpful. Thanks again.'

She carried her smile all the way to the door.

'If it is not too much trouble,' she said, as I stepped into the hall, 'I would like to learn how this whole thing finally turns out – or any interesting developments, for that matter.'

'My connection with the case ends with this report, and I am going to write it now. Still, I may get some feedback.'

'You have my number . . . ?'

'Probably, but . . .'

I already had it, but I jotted it again, right after Mrs Gluntz's answers to my inquiries on detergents.

Moving in a rigorous line, I made beautiful connections, for a change. I headed directly for the airport, found a flight aimed at Memphis, bought passage, and was the last to board. Tenscore seconds, perhaps, made all the difference. Not even a tick or two to spare for checking out of the motel – No matter. The good head-doctor had convinced me that, like it or not, David Fentris was next, damn it. I had too strong a feeling that Leila Thackery had not told me the entire story. I had to take a chance, to see these changes in the man for myself, to try to figure out how they related to the Hangman. For a number of reasons, I'd a feeling they might.

I disembarked into a cool, partly overcast afternoon, found transportation almost immediately, and set out for Dave's office address.

A before-the-storm feeling came over me as I entered and crossed the town. A dark wall of clouds continued to build in the west. Later, standing before the building where Dave did business, the first few drops of rain were already spattering against its dirty brick front. It would take a lot more than that to freshen it, though, or any of the others in the area. I would have thought he'd have come a little further than this by now.

I shrugged off some moisture and went inside.

The directory gave me directions, the elevator elevated me, my feet found the way to his door. I knocked on it. After a time, I knocked again and waited again. Again, nothing. So I tried it, found it open, and went on in.

It was a small, vacant waiting room, green-carpeted. The reception desk was dusty. I crossed and peered around the plastic partition behind it.

The man had his back to me. I drummed my knuckles against the partitioning. He heard it and turned.

'Yes?'

Our eyes met, his still framed by hornrims and just as active; lenses thicker, hair thinner, cheeks a trifle hollower.

His question mark quivered in the air, and nothing in his gaze moved to replace it with recognition. He had been bending over a sheaf of schematics. A lopsided basket of metal, quartz, porcelain, and glass rested on a nearby table.

'My name is Donne, John Donne,' I said. 'I am looking for David Fentris.'

'I am David Fentris.'

'Good to meet you,' I said, crossing to where he stood. 'I am assisting in an investigation concerning a project with which you were once associated...'

He smiled and nodded, accepted my hand and shook it.

'The Hangman, of course. Glad to know you, Mister Donne.'

'Yes, the Hangman,' I said. 'I am doing a report—'

'—And you want my opinion as to how dangerous it is. Sit down.' He gestured toward a chair at the end of his work bench. 'Care for a cup of tea?'

313

'No, thanks.'

'I'm having one.'

'Well, in that case . . .'

He crossed to another bench.

'No cream. Sorry.'

'That's all right. – How did you know it involved the Hangman?'

He grinned as he brought me my cup.

'Because it's come back,' he said, 'and it's the only thing I've been connected with that warrants that much concern.'

'Do you mind talking about it?'

'Up to a point, no.'

'What's the point?'

'If we get near it, I'll let you know.'

'Fair enough – How dangerous is it?'

'I would say that it is harmless,' he replied, 'except to three persons.'

'Formerly four?'

'Precisely.'

'How come?'

'We were doing something we had no business doing.'

'That being . . . ?'

'For one thing, attempting to create an artificial intelligence.'

'Why had you no business doing that?'

'A man with a name like yours shouldn't have to ask.'

I chuckled.

'If I were a preacher,' I said, 'I would have to point out that there is no biblical injunction against it – unless you've been worshipping it on the sly.'

He shook his head.

'Nothing that simple, that obvious, that explicit. Times have changed since the Good Book was written, and you can't hold with a purely fundamentalist approach in complex times. What I was getting at was something a little more abstract. A form of pride, not unlike the classical hubris – the setting up of oneself on a level with the Creator.'

'Did you feel that – pride?'

'Yes.'

'Are you sure it wasn't just enthusiasm for an ambitious project that was working well?'

'Oh, there was plenty of that. A manifestation of the same thing.'

'I do seem to recall something about man being made in the Creator's image, and something else about trying to live up to that. It would seem to follow that exercising one's capacities along similar lines would be a step in the right direction – an act of conformance with the Divine ideal, if you'd like.'

'But I don't like. Man cannot really create. He can only re-arrange what is already present. Only God can create.'

'Then you have nothing to worry about.'

He frowned. Then, 'No,' he said. 'Being aware of this and still trying is where the presumption comes in.'

'Were you really thinking that way when you did it? Or did all this occur to you after the fact?'

He continued to frown.

'I am no longer certain.'

'Then it would seem to me that a merciful God would be inclined to give you the benefit of the doubt.'

He gave me a wry smile.

'Not bad, John Donne. But I feel that judgment may already have been entered and that we may have lost four to nothing.'

'Then you see the Hangman as an avenging angel?'

'Sometimes. Sort of. I see it as being returned to exact a penalty.'

'Just for the record,' I suggested, 'if the Hangman had had full access to the necessary equipment and was able to con-struct another unit such as itself, would you consider it guilty of the same thing that is bothering you?'

He shook his head.

'Don't get all cute and Jesuitical with me, Donne. I'm not that far away from fundamentals. Besides, I'm willing to admit I might be wrong and that there may be other forces driving it to the same end.'

'Such as?'

'I told you I'd let you know when we reached a certain point. That's it.'

'Okay,' I said. 'But that sort of blank-walls me, you know. The people I am working for would like to protect you people. They want to stop the Hangman. I was hoping you would tell me a little more – if not for your own sake, then for the others'. They might not share your philosophical sentiments, and you have just admitted you may be wrong – Despair, by the way, is also considered a sin by a great number of theologians.'

He sighed and stroked his nose, as I had often seen him do in times long past.

'What do you do, anyhow?' he asked me.

'Me, personally? I'm a science writer. I'm putting together a report on the device for the agency that wants to do the protecting. The better my report, the better their chances.'

He was silent for a time, then, 'I read a lot in the area, but I don't recognize your name,' he said.

'Most of my work has involved petrochemistry and marine biology,' I said.

'Oh – You were a peculiar choice then, weren't you?'

'Not really. I was available, and the boss knows my work, knows I'm good.'

He glanced across the room, to where a stack of cartons partly obscured what I then realized to be a remote-access terminal. Okay. If he decided to check out my credentials now, John Donne would fall apart. It seemed a hell of a time to get curious, though, *after* sharing his sense of sin with me. He must have thought so, too, because he did not look that way again.

'Let me put it this way . . .' he finally said, and something of the old David Fentris at his best took control of his voice. 'For one reason or the other, I believe that it wants to destroy its former operators. If it is the judgment of the Almighty, that's all there is to it. It will succeed. If not, however, I don't want any outside protection. I've done my own repenting and it is up to me to handle the rest of the situation myself, too. I will stop the Hangman personally – right here – before anyone else is hurt.'

'How?' I asked him.

He nodded toward the glittering helmet.

'With that,' he said.

'How?' I repeated.

'The Hangman's telefactor circuits are still intact. They have to be: they are an integral part of it. It could not disconnect them without shutting itself down. If it comes within a quarter mile of here, that unit will be activated. It will emit a loud humming sound and a light will begin to blink behind that meshing beneath the forward ridge. I will then don the helmet and take control of the Hangman. I will bring it here and disconnect its brain.'

'How would you do the disconnect?'

He reached for the schematics he had been looking at when I had come in.

'Here. The thoracic plate has to be unplugged. There are four subunits that have to be uncoupled. Here, here, here, and here.'

He looked up.

'You would have to do them in sequence, though, or it could get mighty hot,' I said. 'First this one, then these two. Then the other.'

When I looked up again, the gray eyes were fixed on my own.

'I thought you were in petrochemistry and marine biology.'

'I am not really "in" anything,' I said. 'I am a tech writer, with bits and pieces from all over – and I did have a look at these before, when I accepted the job.'

'I see.'

'Why don't you bring the space agency in on this?' I said, working to shift ground. 'The original telefactoring equipment had all that power and range—'

'It was dismantled a long time ago. – I thought you were with the government.'

I shook my head.

'Sorry. I didn't mean to mislead you. I am on contract with a private investigation outfit.'

'Uh-huh. Then that means Jesse. – Not that it matters. You can tell him that one way or the other everything is being taken care of.'

'What if you are wrong on the supernatural,' I said, 'but correct on the other? Supposing it is coming under the circumstances you feel it proper to resist? But supposing you are not next on its list? Supposing it gets to one of the others next, instead of you? If you are so sensitive about guilt and sin, don't you think that you would be responsible for that death – if you could prevent it by telling me just a little bit more? If it's confidentiality you're worried about—'

'No,' he said. 'You cannot trick me into applying my principles to a hypothetical situation which will only work out the way that you want it to. Not when I am certain that it will not arise. Whatever moves the Hangman, it will come to *me* next. If I cannot stop it, then it cannot be stopped until it has completed its job.'

'How do you know that you are next?'

'Take a look at a map,' he said. 'It landed in the Gulf. Manny was right there in New Orleans. Naturally, he was first. The Hangman can move underwater like a controlled torpedo, which makes the Mississippi its logical route for inconspicuous travel. Proceeding up it then, here I am in Memphis. Then Leila, up in St Louis, is obviously next after me. It can worry about getting to Washington after that.'

I thought about Senator Brockden in Wisconsin and decided it would not even have that problem. All of them were fairly accessible, when you thought of the situation in terms of river travel.

'But how is it to know where you all are?' I asked.

'Good question,' he said. 'Within a limited range, it was once sensitive to our brain waves, having an intimate knowledge of them and the ability to pick them up. I do not know what that range would be today. It might have been able to construct an amplifier to extend this area of perception. But to be more mundane about it, I believe that it simply consulted Central's national directory. There are booths all over, even on the waterfront. It could have hit one late at night and gimmicked it. It certainly had sufficient identifying information – and engineering skill.'

'Then it seems to me that the best bet for all of you would be to move away from the river till this business is settled. That thing won't be able to stalk about the countryside very long without being noticed.'

He shook his head.

'It would find a way. It is extremely resourceful. At night, in an overcoat, a hat, it could pass. It requires nothing that a man would need. It could dig a hole and bury itself, stay underground during daylight. It could run without resting all night long. There is no place it could not reach in a surprisingly short while. – No, I must wait here for it.'

'Let me put it as bluntly as I can,' I said. 'If you are right that it is a Divine Avenger, I would say that it smacks of blasphemy to try to tackle it. On the other hand, if it is not, then I think you are guilty of jeopardizing the others by withholding information that would allow us to provide them with a lot more protection than you are capable of giving them all by yourself.'

He laughed.

'I'll just have to learn to live with that guilt, too, as they do with theirs,' he said. 'After I've done my best, they deserve anything they get.'

'It was my understanding,' I said, 'that even God doesn't judge people until after they're dead – if you want another piece of presumption to add to your collection.'

He stopped laughing and studied my face.

'There is something familiar about the way you talk, the way you think,' he said. 'Have we ever met before?'

'I doubt it. I would have remembered.'

He shook his head.

'You've got a way of bothering a man's thinking that rings a faint bell,' he went on. 'You trouble me, sir.'

'That was my intention.'

'Are you staying here in town?'

'No.'

'Give me a number where I can reach you, will you? If I have any new thoughts on this thing, I'll call you.'

'I wish you would have them now, if you are going to have them.'

'No, I've got some thinking to do. Where can I get hold of you later?'

I gave him the name of the motel I was still checked into in St Louis. I could call back periodically for messages.

'All right,' he said, and he moved toward the partition by the reception area and stood beside it.

I rose and followed him, passing into that area and pausing at the door to the hall.

'One thing...' I said.

'Yes?'

'If it does show up and you do stop it, will you call me and tell me that?'

'Yes, I will.'

'Thanks then – and good luck.'

Impulsively, I extended my hand. He gripped it and smiled faintly.

'Thank you, Mister Donne.'

Next. Next, next, next...

I couldn't budge Dave, and Leila Thackery had given me everything she was going to. No real sense in calling Don yet – not until I had more to say.

I thought it over on my way back to the airport. The pre-dinner hours always seem best for talking to people in any sort of official capacity, just as the night seems best for dirty work. Heavily psychological, but true nevertheless. I hated to waste the rest of the day if there was anyone else worth talking to before I called Don. Going through the folder, I decided that there was.

Manny Burns had a brother, Phil. I wondered how worthwhile it might be to talk with him. I could make it to New Orleans at a sufficiently respectable hour, learn whatever he was willing to tell me, check back with Don for new developments, and then decide whether there was anything I should be about with respect to the vessel itself.

The sky was gray and leaky above me. I was anxious to flee its spaces. So I decided to do it. I could think of no better stone to upturn at the moment.

At the airport, I was ticketed quickly, in time for another close connection.

Hurrying to reach my flight, my eyes brushed over a half-familiar face on the passing escalator. The reflex reserved for such occasions seemed to catch us both, because he looked back, too, with the same eyebrow twitch of startle and scrutiny. Then he was gone. I could not place him, however. The half-familiar face becomes a familiar phenomenon in a crowded, highly mobile society. I sometimes think that that is all that will eventually remain of any of us: patterns of features, some a trifle more persistent than others, impressed on the flow of bodies. A small-town boy in a big city, Thomas Wolfe must long ago have felt the same thing when he had coined the word 'manswarm.' It might have been someone I'd once met briefly, or simply someone – or someone like someone – I had passed on sufficient other occasions such as this.

As I flew the unfriendly skies out of Memphis, I mulled over musings past on artificial intelligence, or AI as they have tagged it in the think-box biz. When talking about computers, the AI notion had always seemed hotter than I deemed necessary, partly because of semantics. The word 'intelligence' has all sorts of tag-along associations of the non-physical sort. I suppose it goes back to the fact that early discussions and conjectures concerning it made it sound as if the potential for intelligence was always present in the array of gadgets, and that the correct procedures, the right programs, simply had to be found to call it forth. When you looked at it that way, as many did, it gave rise to an uncomfortable *deja-vu* – namely, vitalism. The philosophical battles of the nineteenth century were hardly so far behind that they had been forgotten, and the doctrine which maintained that life is caused and sustained by a vital principle apart from physical and chemical forces, and that life is self-sustaining and self-evolving, had put up quite a fight before Darwin and his successors had produced triumph after triumph for the mechanistic view. Then vitalism sort of crept back into things again when the AI discussions arose in the middle of the past century. It would seem that Dave had fallen victim to it, and that he'd come to believe he had helped provide an unsanctified vessel and filled it with Something intended only for those things which had made the scene in the first chapter of Genesis...

With computers it was not quite as bad as with the Hangman, though, because you could always argue that no matter how elaborate the program, it was basically an extension of the programmer's will and the operations of causal machines merely represented functions of intelligence, rather than intelligence in its own right backed by a will of its own. And there was always Gödel for a theoretical *cordon sanitaire*, with his demonstration of the true but mechanically improvable proposition.

But the Hangman was quite different. It had been designed along the lines of a brain and at least partly educated in a human fashion; and to further muddy the issue with respect to anything like vitalism, it had been in direct contact with human minds from which it might have acquired almost anything – including the spark that set it on the road to whatever selfhood it may have found. What did that make it? Its own creature? A fractured mirror reflecting a fractured humanity? Both? Or neither? I certainly could not say, but I wondered how much of its self had been truly its own. It had obviously acquired a great number of functions, but was it capable of having real feelings? Could it, for example, feel something like love? If not, then it was still only a collection of complex abilities, and not a thing with all the tagalong associations of the non-physical sort which made the word 'intelligence' such a prickly item in AI discussions; and if it were capable of, say, something like love, and if I were Dave, I would not feel guilty about having helped to bring it into being. I would feel proud, though not in the

322

fashion he was concerned about, and I would also feel humble – Offhand though, I do not know how intelligent I would feel, because I am still not sure what the hell intelligence is.

The day's-end sky was clear when we landed. I was into town before the sun had finished setting, and on Philip Burns' doorstep just a little while later.

My ring was answered by a girl, maybe seven or eight years old. She fixed me with large brown eyes and did not say a word.

'I would like to speak with Mister Burns,' I said. She turned and retreated around a corner.

A heavyset man, slacked and undershirted, bald about half-way back and very pink, padded into the hall moments later and peered at me. He bore a folded newssheet in his left hand.

'What do you want?' he asked.

'It's about your brother,' I answered.

'Yeah?'

'Well, I wonder if I could come in? It's kind of complicated.'

He opened the door. But instead of letting me in, he came out.

'Tell me about it out here,' he said.

'Okay, I'll be quick. I just wanted to find out whether he ever spoke with you about a piece of equipment he once worked with called the Hangman.'

'Are you a cop?'

'No.'

'Then what's your interest?'

'I am working for a private investigation agency trying to track down some equipment once associated with the project. It has apparently turned up in this area and it could be rather dangerous.'

'Let's see some identification.'

'I don't carry any.'

'What's your name?'

'John Donne.'

'And you think my brother had some stolen equipment when he died? Let me tell you something—'

'No. Not stolen,' I said, 'and I don't think he had it.'

'What then?'

'It was — well, robotic in nature. Because of some special training Manny once received, he might have had a way of detecting it. He might even have attracted it. I just want to find out whether he had said anything about it. We are trying to locate it.'

'My brother was a respectable businessman, and I don't like accusations. Especially right after his funeral, I don't. I think I'm going to call the cops and let them ask *you* a few questions.'

'Just a minute. Supposing I told you we had some reason to believe it might have been this piece of equipment that killed your brother?'

His pink turned to bright red and his jaw muscles formed sudden ridges. I was not prepared for the stream of profanities that followed. For a moment, I thought he was going to take a swing at me.

'Wait a second,' I said when he paused for breath. 'What did I *say*?'

'You're either making fun of the dead or you're stupider than you look!'

'Say I'm stupid. Then tell me why.'

He tore at the paper he carried, folded it back, found an item, thrust it at me.

'Because they've got the guy who did it! That's why,' he said.

I read it. Simple, concise, to the point. Today's latest. A suspect had confessed. New evidence had corroborated it. The man was in custody. A surprised robber who had lost his head and hit too hard, hit too many times. I read it over again.

I nodded as I passed it back.

'Look, I'm sorry,' I said. 'I really didn't know about this.'

'Get out of here,' he said. 'Go on.'

'Sure.'

'Wait a minute.'

'What?'

'That's his little girl who answered the door,' he said.

'I'm very sorry.'

'So am I. But I know her Daddy didn't take your damned equipment.'

I nodded and turned away.

I heard the door slam behind me.


After dinner, I checked into a small hotel, called for a drink, and stepped into the shower.

Things were suddenly a lot less urgent than they had been earlier. Senator Brockden would doubtless be pleased to learn that his initial estimation of events had been incorrect. Leila Thackery would give me an I-told-you-so smile when I called her to pass along the news – a thing I now felt obliged to do. Don might or might not want me to keep looking for the device now that the threat had been lessened. It would depend on the Senator's feelings on the matter, I supposed. If urgency no longer counted for as much, Don might want to switch back to one of his own, fiscally less burdensome operatives. Toweling down, I caught myself whistling. I felt almost off the hook.

Later, drink beside me, I paused before punching out the number he had given me and hit the sequence for my motel in St Louis instead. Merely a matter of efficiency, in case there was a message worth adding to my report.

A woman's face appeared on the screen and a smile appeared on her face. I wondered whether she would always smile whenever she heard a bell ring, or if the reflex was eventually extinguished in advanced retirement. It must be rough, being afraid to chew gum, yawn, or pick your nose.

'Airport Accommodations,' she said. 'May I help you?'

'This is Donne. I'm checked into Room 106,' I said. 'I'm away right now and I wondered whether there had been any messages for me.'

'Just a moment,' she said, checking something off to her left. Then, 'Yes,' she continued, consulting a piece of paper she now held. 'You have one on tape. But it is a little peculiar. It is for someone else, in care of you.'

'Oh? Who is that?'

She told me and I exercised self-control.

'I see,' I said. 'I'll bring him around later and play it for him. Thank you.'

She smiled again and made a good-bye noise, and I did the same and broke the connection.

So Dave had seen through me after all . . . Who else could have that number *and* my real name?

I might have given her some line or other and had her transmit the thing. Only I was not certain but that she might be a silent party to the transmission, should life be more than usually boring for her at that moment. I had to get up there myself, as soon as possible, and personally see that the thing was erased.

I took a big swallow of my drink, than fetched the folder on Dave. I checked out his number – there were two, actually – and spent fifteen minutes trying to get hold of him. No luck.

Okay. Good-bye New Orleans, good-bye peace of mind. This time I called the airport and made a reservation. Then I chugged the drink, put myself in order, gathered up my few possessions, and went to check out again. Hello Central . . .

During my earlier flights that day, I had spent time thinking about Teilhard de Chardin's ideas on the continuation of evolution within the realm of artifacts, matching them against Gödel on mechanical undecidability, playing epistemological games with the Hangman as a counter, wondering, speculating, even hoping, hoping that truth lay with the nobler part: that the Hangman, sentient, had made it back, sane, that the Burns killing had actually been something of the sort that now seemed to be the case, that the washed-out experiment had really been a success of a different sort, a triumph, a new link or fob for the chain of being . . . And Leila had not been wholly discouraging with respect to the neuristor-type brain's capacity for this . . . Now, though, now I had troubles of my own – and even the most heartening of philosophical vistas is no match for, say, a toothache, if it happens to be your own.

Accordingly, the Hangman was shunted aside and the stuff of my thoughts involved, mainly, myself. There was, of course, the possibility that the Hangman had indeed showed up and

Dave had stopped it and then called to report it as he had promised. However, he had used my name.

There was not too much planning that I could do until I received the substance of his communication. It did not seem that as professedly religious a man as Dave would suddenly be contemplating the blackmail business. On the other hand, he was a creature of sudden enthusiasms and had already undergone one unanticipated conversion. It was difficult to say... His technical background plus his knowledge of the data bank program did put him in an unusually powerful position, should he decide to mess me up.

I did not like to think of some of the things I have done to protect my nonperson status; I especially did not like to think of them in connection with Dave, whom I not only still respected but still liked. Since self-interest dominated while actual planning was precluded, my thoughts tooled their way into a more general groove.

It was Karl Mannheim, a long while ago, who made the observation that radical, revolutionary, and progressive thinkers tend to employ mechanical metaphors for the state, whereas those of conservative inclination make vegetable analogies. He said it well over a generation before the cybernetics movement and the ecology movement beat their respective paths through the wilderness of general awareness. If anything, it seemed to me that these two developments served to elaborate the distinction between a pair of viewpoints which, while no longer necessarily tied in with the political positions Mannheim assigned them, do seem to represent a continuing phenomenon in my own time. There are those who see social/economic/ ecological problems as malfunctions which can be corrected by simple repair, replacement, or streamlining – a kind of linear outlook where even innovations are considered to be merely additive. Then there are those who sometimes hesitate to move at all, because their awareness follows events in the directions of secondary and tertiary effects as they multiply and cross-fertilize throughout the entire system. – I digress to extremes. The cyberneticists have their multiple-feedback loops, though

327

it is never quite clear how they know what kind of, which, and how many to install, and the ecological gestaltists do draw lines representing points of diminishing returns – though it is sometimes equally difficult to see how they assign their values and priorities.

Of course they need each other, the vegetable people and the tinker-toy people. They serve to check one another, if nothing else. And while occasionally the balance dips, the tinkerers have, in general, held the edge for the past couple of centuries. However, today's can be just as politically conservative as the vegetable people Mannheim was talking about, and they are the ones I fear most at the moment. They are the ones who saw the data bank program, in its present extreme form, as a simple remedy for a great variety of ills and a provider of many goods. Not all of the ills have been remedied, however, and a new brood has been spawned by the program itself. While we need both kinds, I wish that there had been more people interested in tending the garden of state rather than overhauling the engine of state, when the program was inaugurated. Then I would not be a refugee from a form of existence I find repugnant, and I would not be concerned whether or not a former associate had discovered my identity.

Then, as I watched the lights below, I wondered . . . Was I a tinkerer because I would like to further alter the prevailing order, into something more comfortable to my anarchic nature? Or was I a vegetable, dreaming I was a tinkerer? I could not make up my mind. The garden of life never seems to confine itself to the plots philosophers have laid out for its convenience. Maybe a few more tractors would do the trick.

I pressed the button.

The tape began to roll. The screen remained blank. I heard Dave's voice ask for John Donne in Room 106 and I heard him told that there was no answer. Then I heard him say that he wanted to record a message, for someone else, in care of Donne, that Donne would understand. He sounded out of breath. The girl asked him whether he wanted visual, too. He told her to turn it on. There was a pause. Then she told him to go ahead. Still no picture. No words, either. His breathing and a slight scraping noise. Ten seconds. Fifteen...

'...Got me,' he finally said, and he mentioned my name again. '...Had to let you know I'd figured you out, though... It wasn't any particular mannerism – any simple thing you said... just your general style – thinking, talking – the electronics – everything – after I got more and more bothered by the familiarity – after I checked you on petrochem – and marine bio – Wish I knew what you'd really been up to all these years... Never know now. But I wanted you – to know – you hadn't put one – over on me.'

There followed another quarter minute of heavy breathing, climaxed by a racking cough. Then a choked, '...Said too much, too fast, too soon... All used up...'

The picture came on then. He was slouched before the screen, head resting on his arms, blood all over him. His glasses were gone and he was squinting and blinking. The right side of his head looked pulpy and there was a gash on his left cheek and one on his forehead.

'...Sneaked up on me – while I was checking you out,' he managed. 'Had to tell you what I learned... Still don't know, which of us is right... Pray for me!'

His arms collapsed and the right one slid forward. His head rolled to the right and the picture went away. When I replayed it, I saw it was his knuckle that had hit the cutoff.

Then I erased it. It had been recorded only a little over an hour after I had left him. If he had not also placed a call for help, if no one had gotten to him quickly after that, his chances did not look good. Even if they had, though...

I used a public booth to call the number Don had given me, got hold of him after some delay, told him Dave was in bad shape if not worse, that a team of Memphis medics was definitely in order if one had not been by already, and that I hoped to call him back and tell him more shortly, good-bye.

Next I tried Leila Thackery's number. I let it go for a long while, but there was no answer. I wondered how long it would take a controlled torpedo moving up the Mississippi to get from Memphis to St Louis. I did not feel it was time to start leafing through that section of the Hangman's specs. Instead, I went looking for transportation.

At her apartment, I tried ringing her from the entrance foyer. Again, no answer. So I rang Mrs Gluntz. She had seemed the most guileless of the three I had interviewed for my fake consumer survey.

'Yes?'

'It's me again, Mrs Gluntz: Stephen Foster. I've just a couple follow-up questions on that survey I was doing today, if you could spare me a few moments.'

'Why, yes,' she said. 'All right. Come up.'

The door hummed itself loose and I entered. I duly proceeded to the fifth floor, composing my questions on the way. I had planned this maneuver as I had waited earlier solely to provide a simple route for breaking and entering, should some unforeseen need arise. Most of the time my ploys such as this go unused, but sometimes they simplify matters a lot.

Five minutes and half a dozen questions later, I was back down on the second floor, probing at the lock on Leila's door with a couple of little pieces of metal it is sometimes awkward to be caught carrying.

Half a minute later, I hit it right and snapped it back. I pulled on some tissue-thin gloves I keep rolled in the corner of one pocket, opened the door and stepped inside. I closed it behind me immediately.

She was lying on the floor, her neck at a bad angle. One table lamp still burned, though it was lying on its side. Several small items had been knocked from the table, a magazine rack pushed over, a cushion partly displaced from the sofa. The cable to her phone unit had been torn from the wall.

A humming noise filled the air, and I sought its source.

I saw where the little blinking light was reflected on the wall, on – off, on – off . . .

I moved quickly.

It was a lopsided basket of metal, quartz, porcelain, and

330

glass, which had rolled to a position on the far side of the chair in which I had been seated earlier that day. The same rig I'd seen in Dave's workshop not all that long ago, though it now seemed so. A device to detect the Hangman. And, hopefully, to control it.

I picked it up and fitted it over my head.

Once, with the aid of a telepath, I had touched minds with a dolphin as he composed dreamsongs somewhere in the Caribbean, an experience so moving that its mere memory had often been a comfort. This sensation was hardly equivalent.

Analogies and impressions: a face seen through a wet pane of glass; a whisper in a noisy terminal; scalp massage with an electric vibrator; Edvard Munch's *The Scream*; the voice of Yma Sumac, rising and rising and rising; the disappearance of snow; a deserted street, illuminated as through a sniperscope I'd once used, rapid movement past darkened storefronts that line it, an immense feeling of physical capability, compounded of proprioceptive awareness of enormous strength, a peculiar array of sensory channels, a central, undying sun that fed me a constant flow of energy, a memory vision of dark waters, passing, flashing, echo-location within them, the need to return to that place, reorient, move north; Munch and Sumac, Munch and Sumac, Munch and Sumac – Nothing.

Silence.

The humming had ceased, the light gone out. The entire experience had lasted only a few moments. There had not been time enough to try for any sort of control, though an after-impression akin to a biofeedback cue hinted at the direction to go, the way to think, to achieve it. I felt that it might be possible for me to work the thing, given a better chance.

Removing the helmet, I approached Leila.

I knelt beside her and performed a few simple tests, already knowing their outcome. In addition to the broken neck, she had received some bad bashes about the head and shoulders. There was nothing that anyone could do for her now.

I did a quick runthrough then, checking over the rest of her apartment. There were no apparent signs of breaking and entering, though if I could pick one lock, a guy with built-in tools could easily go me one better.

I located some wrapping paper and string in the kitchen and turned the helmet into a parcel. It was time to call Don again, to tell him that the vessel had indeed been occupied and that river traffic was probably bad in the northbound lane.

Don had told me to get the helmet up to Wisconsin, where I would be met at the airport by a man named Larry, who would fly me to the lodge in a private craft. I did that, and this was done.

I also learned, with no real surprise, that David Fentris was dead.

The temperature was down, and it began to snow on the way up. I was not really dressed for the weather. Larry told me I could borrow some warmer clothing once we reached the lodge, though I probably would not be going outside that much. Don had told them that I was supposed to stay as close to the Senator as possible and that any patrols were to be handled by the four guards themselves.

Larry was curious as to what exactly had happened so far and whether I had actually seen the Hangman. I did not think it my place to fill him in on anything Don may not have cared to, so I might have been a little curt. We didn't talk much after that.

Bert met us when we landed. Tom and Clay were outside the building, watching the trail, watching the woods. All of them were middle-aged, very fit-looking, very serious, and heavily armed. Larry took me inside then and introduced me to the old gentleman himself.

Senator Brockden was seated in a heavy chair in the far corner of the room. Judging from the layout, it appeared that the chair might recently have occupied a position beside the window in the opposite wall where a lonely watercolor of yellow flowers looked down on nothing. The Senator's feet rested on a hassock, a red plaid blanket lay across his legs. He had on a dark-green shirt, his hair was very white, and he wore rimless reading glasses which he removed when we entered.

He tilted his head back, squinted, and gnawed his lower lip slowly as he studied me. He remained expressionless as we advanced. A big-boned man, he had probably been beefy much of his life. Now he had the slack look of recent weight loss and an unhealthy skin tone. His eyes were a pale gray within it all.

He did not rise.

'So you're the man,' he said, offering me his hand. 'I'm glad to meet you. How do you want to be called?'

'John will do,' I said.

He made a small sign to Larry, and Larry departed.

'It's cold out there. Go get yourself a drink, John. It's on the shelf.' He gestured off to his left. 'And bring me one while you're at it. Two fingers of bourbon in a water glass. That's all.'

I nodded and went and poured a couple.

'Sit down.' He motioned at a nearby chair as I delivered his. 'But first let me see that gadget you've brought.'

I undid the parcel and handed him the helmet. He sipped his drink and put it aside. Taking the helmet in both hands, he studied it, brows furrowed, turning it completely around. He raised it and put it on his head.

'Not a bad fit,' he said, and then he smiled for the first time, becoming for a moment the face I had known from newscasts past. Grinning or angry – it was almost always one or the other. I had never seen his collapsed look in any of the media.

He removed the helmet and set it on the floor.

'Pretty piece of work,' he said. 'Nothing quite that fancy in the old days. But then David Fentris built it. Yes, he told us about it . . .' He raised his drink and took a sip. 'You are the only one who has actually gotten to use it, apparently. What do you think? Will it do the job?'

'I was only in contact for a couple seconds, so I've only got a feeling to go on, not much better than a hunch. But yes, I'd a feeling that if I had had more time I might have been able to work its circuits.'

'Tell me why it didn't save Dave.'

333

'In the message he left me, he indicated that he had been distracted at his computer access station. Its noise probably drowned out the humming.'

'Why wasn't this message preserved?'

'I erased it for reasons not connected with the case.'

'What reasons?'

'My own.'

His face went from sallow to ruddy.

'A man can get in a lot of trouble for suppressing evidence, obstructing justice.'

'Then we have something in common, don't we, sir?'

His eyes caught mine with a look I had only encountered before from those who did not wish me well. He held the glare for a full four heartbeats, then sighed and seemed to relax.

'Don said there were a number of points you couldn't be pressed on,' he finally said.

'That's right.'

'He didn't betray any confidences, but he had to tell me something about you, you know.'

'I'd imagine.'

'He seems to think highly of you. Still, I tried to learn more about you on my own.'

'And...?'

'I couldn't – and my usual sources are good at that kind of thing.'

'So...?'

'So, I've done some thinking, some wondering... The fact that my sources could not come up with anything is interesting in itself. Possibly even revealing. I am in a better position than most to be aware of the fact that there was not perfect compliance with the registration statute some years ago. It didn't take long for a great number of the individuals involved – I should probably say "most" – to demonstrate their existence in one fashion or another and be duly entered, though. And there were three broad categories: those who were ignorant, those who disapproved, and those who would be hampered in an illicit life-style. I am not attempting to categorize you or

334

to pass judgment. But I am aware that there are a number of nonpersons passing through society without casting shadows, and it has occurred to me that you may be such a one.'

I tasted my drink.

'And if I am?' I asked.

He gave me his second, nastier smile and said nothing.

I rose and crossed the room to where I judged his chair had once stood. I looked at the watercolor.

'I don't think you could stand an inquiry,' he said.

I did not reply.

'Aren't you going to say something?'

'What do you want me to say?'

'You might ask me what I am going to do about it.'

'What are you going to do about it?'

'Nothing,' he answered. 'So come back here and sit down.'

I nodded and returned.

He studied my face. 'Was it possible you were close to violence just then?'

'With four guards outside?'

'With four guards outside.'

'No,' I said.

'You're a good liar.'

'I am here to help you, sir. No questions asked. That was the deal, as I understood it. If there has been any change, I would like to know about it now.'

He drummed with his fingertips on the plaid.

'I've no desire to cause you any difficulty,' he said. 'Fact of the matter is, I need a man just like you, and I was pretty sure someone like Don might turn him up. Your unusual maneuverability and your reported knowledge of computers, along with your touchiness in certain areas, made you worth waiting for. I've a great number of things I would like to ask you.'

'Go ahead,' I said.

'Not yet. Later, if we have time. All that would be bonus material, for a report I am working on. Far more important – to me, personally – there are things that I want to *tell* you.'

I frowned.

335

'Over the years,' he went on, 'I have learned that the best man for purposes of keeping his mouth shut concerning your business is someone for whom you are doing the same.'

'You have a compulsion to confess something?' I asked.

'I don't know whether "compulsion" is the right word. Maybe so, maybe not. Either way, however, someone among those working to defend me should have the whole story. Something somewhere in it may be of help – and you are the ideal choice to hear it.'

'I buy that,' I said, 'and you are as safe with me as I am with you.'

'Have you any suspicions as to why this business bothers me so?'

'Yes,' I said.

'Let's hear them.'

'You used the Hangman to perform some act or acts – illegal, immoral, whatever. This is obviously not a matter of record. Only you and the Hangman now know what it involved. You feel it was sufficiently ignominious that when that device came to appreciate the full weight of the event, it suffered a breakdown which may well have led to a final determination to punish you for using it as you did.'

He stared down into his glass.

'You've got it,' he said.

'You were all party to it?'

'Yes, but – *I* was the operator when it happened. You see . . . we – I – killed a man. It was – Actually, it all started as a celebration. We had received word that afternoon that the project had cleared. Everything had checked out in order and the final approval had come down the line. It was go, for that Friday. Leila, Dave, Manny, and myself – we had dinner together. We were in high spirits. After dinner, we continued celebrating and somehow the party got adjourned back to the installation.

'As the evening wore on, more and more absurdities seemed less and less preposterous, as is sometimes the case. We decided – I forget which of us suggested it – that the Hangman should really have a share in the festivities. After all, it was, in a very real sense, his party. Before too much longer, it sounded only fair and we were discussing how we could go about it – You see, we were in Texas and the Hangman was at the Space Center in California. Getting together with him was out of the question. On the other hand, the teleoperator station was right up the hall from us. What we finally decided to do was to activate him and take turns working as operator. There was already a rudimentary consciousness there, and we felt it fitting that we each get in touch to share the good news. So that is what we did.'

He sighed, took another sip, glanced at me.

'Dave was the first operator,' he continued. 'He activated the Hangman. Then – Well, as I said, we were all in high spirits. We had not originally intended to remove the Hangman from the lab where he was situated, but Dave decided to take him outside briefly – to show him the sky and to tell him he was going there, after all. Then Dave suddenly got enthusiastic about outwitting the guards and the alarm system. It was a game. We all went along with it. In fact, we were clamoring for a turn at the thing ourselves. But Dave stuck with it, and he wouldn't turn over control until he had actually gotten the Hangman off the premises, out into an uninhabited area next to the Center.

'By the time Leila persuaded him to give her a go at the controls, it was kind of anticlimactic. That game had already been played. So she thought up a new one: she took the Hangman into the next town. It was late, and the sensory equipment was superb. It was a challenge – passing through the town without being detected. By then, everyone had suggestions as to what to do next, progressively more outrageous suggestions. Then Manny took control, and he wouldn't say what he was doing – wouldn't let us monitor him. Said it would be more fun to surprise the next operator. Now, *he* was higher than the rest of us put together, I think, and he stayed on so damn long that we started to get nervous – A certain amount of tension is partly sobering, and I guess we all began to think what a stupid-assed thing it was we were doing. It wasn't just that it would wreck our careers – which it would – but it could blow the entire project if we got caught playing games with such expensive hardware. At least, *I* was thinking that way, and I was also thinking that Manny was no doubt operating under the very human wish to go the others one better.

'I started to sweat. I suddenly just wanted to get the Hangman back where he belonged, turn him off – you could still do that, before the final circuits went in – shut down the station, and start forgetting it had ever happened. I began leaning on Manny to wind up his diversion and turn the controls over to me. Finally, he agreed.'

He finished his drink and held out the glass.

'Would you freshen this a bit?'

'Surely.'

I went and got him some more, added a touch to my own, returned to my chair and waited.

'So I took over,' he said. 'I took over, and where do you think that idiot had left me? I was inside a building, and it didn't take but an eyeblink to realize it was a bank. The Hangman carries a lot of tools, and Manny had apparently been able to guide him through the doors without setting anything off. I was standing right in front of the main vault. Obviously, he thought that should be my challenge. I fought down a desire to turn and make my own exit in the nearest wall and start running. But I went back to the doors and looked outside.

'I didn't see anyone. I started to let myself out. The light hit me as I emerged. It was a hand flash. The guard had been standing out of sight. He'd a gun in his other hand. I panicked. I hit him – Reflex. If I am going to hit someone, I hit him as hard as I can. Only I hit him with the strength of the Hangman. He must have died instantly. I started to run and I didn't stop till I was back in the little park area near the Center. Then I stopped and the others had to take me out of the harness.'

'They monitored all this?' I asked.

'Yes, someone cut the visual in on a side viewscreen again a few seconds after I took over. Dave, I think.'

338

'Did they try to stop you at any time while you were running away?'

'No. Well, I wasn't aware of anything but what I was doing at the time. But afterwards they said they were too shocked to do anything but watch, until I gave out.'

'I see.'

'Dave took over then, ran his initial route in reverse, got the Hangman back into the lab, cleaned him up, turned him off. We shut down the operator station. We were suddenly very sober.'

He sighed and leaned back, and was silent for a long while.

Then, 'You are the only person I've ever told this to,' he said.

I tasted my own drink.

'We went over to Leila's place then,' he continued, 'and the rest is pretty much predictable. Nothing we could do would bring the guy back, we decided, but if we told what had happened it could wreck an expensive, important program. It wasn't as if we were criminals in need of rehabilitation. It was a once-in-a-lifetime lark that happened to end tragically. What would you have done?'

'I don't know. Maybe the same thing. I'd have been scared, too.'

He nodded.

'Exactly. And that's the story.'

'Not all of it, is it?'

'What do you mean?'

'What about the Hangman? You said there was already a detectable consciousness there. You were aware of *it*, and it was aware of *you*. It must have had some reaction to the whole business. What was that like?'

'Damn you,' he said flatly.

'I'm sorry.'

'Are you a family man?' he asked.

'No.'

'Did you ever take a small child to a zoo?'

'Yes.'

339

'Then maybe you know the experience. When my son was around four I took him to the Washington Zoo one afternoon. We must have walked past every cage in the place. He made appreciative comments every now and then, asked a few questions, giggled at the monkeys, thought the bears were very nice – probably because they made him think of oversized toys. But do you know what the finest thing of all was? The thing that made him jump up and down and point and say, "Look, Daddy! Look!"?'

I shook my head.

'A squirrel looking down from the limb of a tree,' he said, and he chuckled briefly. 'Ignorance of what's important and what isn't. Inappropriate responses. Innocence. The Hangman was a child, and up until the time I took over, the only thing he had gotten from us was the idea that it was a game: he was playing with us, that's all. Then something horrible happened... I hope you never know what it feels like to do something totally rotten to a child, while he is holding your hand and laughing... He felt all my reactions, and all of Dave's as he guided him back.'

We sat there for a long while then.

'So we had – traumatized him,' he said finally, 'or whatever other fancy terminology you might want to give it. That is what happened that night. It took a while for it to take effect, but there is no doubt in my mind that that is the cause of the Hangman's finally breaking down.'

I nodded. 'I see. And you believe it wants to kill you for this?'

'Wouldn't you?' he said. 'If you had started out as a thing and we had turned you into a person and then used you as a thing again, wouldn't you?'

'Leila left a lot out of her diagnosis.'

'No, she just omitted it in talking to you. It was all there. But she read it wrong. She wasn't afraid. It was just a game it had played – with the *others*. Its memories of that part might not be as bad. I was the one that really marked it. As I see it, Leila

340

was betting that I was the only one it was after. Obviously, she read it wrong.'

'Then what I do not understand,' I said, 'is why the Burns killing did not bother her more. There was no way of telling immediately that it had been a panicky hoodlum rather than the Hangman.'

'The only thing that I can see is that, being a very proud woman – which she was – she was willing to hold with her diagnosis in the face of the apparent evidence.'

'I don't like it. But you know her and I don't, and as it turned out her estimate of that part was correct. Something else bothers me just as much, though: the helmet. It looks as if the Hangman killed Dave, then took the trouble to bear the helmet in his watertight compartment all the way to St Louis, solely for purposes of dropping it at the scene of his next killing. That makes no sense whatsoever.'

'It does, actually,' he said. 'I was going to get to that shortly, but I might as well cover it now. You see, the Hangman possessed no vocal mechanism. We communicated by means of the equipment. Don says you know something about electronics . . . ?'

'Yes.'

'Well, shortly, I want you to start checking over that helmet, to see whether it has been tampered with.'

'That is going to be difficult,' I said. 'I don't know just how it was wired originally, and I'm not such a genius on the theory that I can just look at a thing and say whether it will function as a teleoperator unit.'

He bit his lower lip.

'You will have to try, anyhow. There may be physical signs – scratches, breaks, new connections – I don't know. That's your department. Look for them.'

I just nodded and waited for him to go on.

'I think that the Hangman wanted to talk to Leila,' he said, 'either because she was a psychiatrist and he knew he was functioning badly at a level that transcended the mechanical, or because he might think of her in terms of a mother. After all, she was the only woman involved, and he had the concept of mother – with all the comforting associations that go with it – from all of our minds. Or maybe for both of these reasons. I feel he might have taken the helmet along for that purpose. He would have realized what it was from a direct monitoring of Dave's brain while he was with him. I want you to check it over because it would seem possible that the Hangman disconnected the control circuits and left the communication circuits intact. I think he might have taken the helmet to Leila in that condition and attempted to induce her to put it on. She got scared – tried to run away, fight, or call for help – and he killed her. The helmet was no longer of any use to him, so he discarded it and departed. Obviously, he does not have anything to say to me.'

I thought about it, nodded again.

'Okay, broken circuits I can spot,' I said. 'If you will tell me where a tool kit is, I had better get right to it.'

He made a stay-put gesture with his left hand.

'Afterwards, I found out the identity of the guard,' he went on. 'We all contributed to an anonymous gift for his widow. I have done things for his family, taken care of them – the same way – ever since . . .'

I did not look at him as he spoke.

'. . . There was nothing else that I could do,' he finished.

I remained silent.

He finished his drink and gave me a weak smile.

'The kitchen is back there,' he told me, showing me a thumb. 'There is a utility room right behind it. Tools are in there.'

'Okay.'

I got to my feet. I retrieved the helmet and started toward the doorway, passing near the area where I had stood earlier, back when he had fitted me into the proper box and tightened a screw.

'Wait a minute!' he said.

I stopped.

'Why did you go over there before? What's so strategic about that part of the room?'

342

'What do you mean?'

'You know what I mean.'

I shrugged.

'Had to go someplace.'

'You seem the sort of person who has better reasons than that.'

I glanced at the wall.

'Not *then*,' I said.

'I insist.'

'You really don't want to know,' I told him.

'I really do.'

'All right. I wanted to see what sort of flowers you liked. After all, you're a client,' and I went on back through the kitchen into the utility room and started looking for tools.

I sat in a chair turned sidewise from the table to face the door. In the main room of the lodge the only sounds were the occasional hiss and sputter of the logs turning to ashes on the grate.

Just a cold, steady whiteness drifting down outside the window and a silence confirmed by gunfire, driven deeper now that it had ceased... Not a sigh or a whimper, though. And I never count them as storms unless there is wind.

Big fat flakes down the night, silent night, windless night...

Considerable time had passed since my arrival. The Senator had sat up for a long time talking with me. He was disappointed that I could not tell him too much about a non-person subculture which he believed existed. I really was not certain about it myself, though I had occasionally encountered what might have been its fringes. I am not much of a joiner of anything anymore, however, and I was not about to mention those things I might have guessed about this. I gave him my opinions on the Central Data Bank when he asked for them, and there were some that he did not like. He had accused me, then, of wanting to tear things down without offering anything better in their place.

My mind had drifted back, through fatigue and time and faces and snow and a lot of space, to the previous evening in

Baltimore. How long ago? It made me think of Mencken's 'The Cult of Hope'. I could not give him the pat answer, the workable alternative that he wanted, because there might not be one. The function of criticism should not be confused with the function of reform. But if a grass-roots resistance was building up, with an underground movement bent on finding ways to circumvent the record keepers, it might well be that much of the enterprise would eventually prove about as effective and beneficial as, say, Prohibition once had. I tried to get him to see this, but I could not tell how much he bought of anything that I said. Eventually, he flaked out and went upstairs to take a pill and lock himself in for the night. If it had troubled him that I'd not been able to find anything wrong with the helmet, he did not show it.

So I sat there, the helmet, the walkie-talkie, the gun on the table, the tool kit on me floor beside my chair, the black glove on my left hand.

The Hangman was coming. I did not doubt it.

Bert, Larry, Tom, Clay, the helmet, might or might not be able to stop him. Something bothered me about the whole case, but I was too tired to think of anything but the immediate situation, to try to remain alert while I waited. I was afraid to take a stimulant or a drink or to light a cigarette, since my central nervous system itself was to be a part of the weapon. I watched the big fat flakes fly by.

I called out to Bert and Larry when I heard the click.

I picked up the helmet and rose to my feet as its light began to blink.

But it was already too late.

As I raised the helmet, I heard a shot from outside, and with that shot I felt a premonition of doom. They did not seem the sort of men who would fire until they had a target.

Dave had told me that the helmet's range was approximately a quarter of a mile. Then, given the time lag between the helmet's activation and the Hangman's sighting by the near guards, the Hangman had to be moving very rapidly. To this add the possibility that the Hangman's range on brainwaves might well be greater than the helmet's range on the Hangman. And then grant the possibility that he had utilized this factor while Senator Brockden was still lying awake, worrying. Conclusion: the Hangman might well be aware that I was where I was with the helmet, realize that it was the most dangerous weapon waiting for him, and be moving for a lightning strike at me before I could come to terms with the mechanism.

I lowered it over my head and tried to throw all of my faculties into neutral.

Again, the sensation of viewing the world through a sniperscope, with all the concomitant side-sensations. Except that world consisted of the front of the lodge; Bert, before the door, rifle at his shoulder; Larry, off to the left, arm already fallen from the act of having thrown a grenade. The grenade, we instantly realized, was an overshot; the flamer, at which he now groped, would prove useless before he could utilize it.

Bert's next round richocheted off our breastplate toward the left. The impact staggered us momentarily. The third was a miss. There was no fourth, for we tore the rifle from his grasp and cast it aside as we swept by, crashing into the front door.

The Hangman entered the room as the door splintered and collapsed.

My mind was filled to the splitting point with the double vision of the sleek, gunmetal body of the advancing telefactor and the erect, crazy-crowned image of myself – left hand extended, laser pistol in my right, that arm pressed close against my side. I recalled the face and the scream and the tingle, knew again that awareness of strength and exotic sensation, and I moved to control it all as if it were my own, to make it my own, to bring it to a halt, while the image of myself was frozen to snapshot stillness across the room...

The Hangman slowed, stumbled. Such inertia is not canceled in an instant, but I felt the body responses pass as they should. I had him hooked. It was just a matter of reeling him in.

Then came the explosion – a thunderous, ground-shaking eruption right outside, followed by a hail of pebbles and debris.

The grenade, of course. But awareness of its nature did not destroy its ability to distract.

During that moment, the Hangman recovered and was upon me. I triggered the laser as I reverted to pure self-preservation, foregoing any chance to regain control of his circuits. With my left hand I sought for a strike at the midsection, where his brain was housed.

He blocked my hand with his arm as he pushed the helmet from my head. Then he removed from my fingers the gun that had turned half of his left side red hot, crumpled it, and dropped it to the ground. At that moment, he jerked with the impacts of two heavy-caliber slugs. Bert, rifle recovered, stood in the doorway.

The Hangman pivoted and was away before I could slap him with the smother charge.

Bert hit him with one more round before he took the rifle and bent its barrel in half. Two steps and he had hold of Bert. One quick movement and Bert fell. Then the Hangman turned again and took several steps to the right, passing out of sight.

I made it to the doorway in time to see him engulfed in flames, which streamed at him from a point near the corner of the lodge. He advanced through them. I heard the crunch of metal as he destroyed the unit. I was outside in time to see Larry fall and lie sprawled in the snow.

Then the Hangman faced me once again.

This time he did not rush in. He retrieved the helmet from where he had dropped it in the snow. Then he moved with a measured tread, angling outward so as to cut off any possible route I might follow in a dash for the woods. Snowflakes drifted between us. The snow crunched beneath his feet.

I retreated, backing in through the doorway, stooping to snatch up a two-foot club from the ruins of the door. He followed me inside, placing the helmet – almost casually, on the chair by the entrance. I moved to the center of the room and waited.

I bent slightly forward, both arms extended, the end of the stick pointed at the photoceptors in his head. He continued to move slowly and I watched his foot assemblies. With a stand-ard-model human, a line perpendicular to the line connecting the insteps of the feet in their various positions indicates the vector of least resistance for purposes of pushing or pulling said organism off-balance. Unfortunately, despite the anthro-pomorphic design job, the Hangman's legs were positioned farther apart, he lacked human skeletal muscles, not to mention insteps, and he was possessed of a lot more mass than any man I had ever fought. As I considered my four best judo throws and several second-class ones, I'd a strong feeling none of them would prove very effective.

Then he moved in and I feinted toward the photoreceptors. He slowed as he brushed the club aside, but he kept coming, and I moved to my right, trying to circle him. I studied him as he turned, attempting to guess his vector of least resistance.

Bilateral symmetry, an apparently higher center of grav-ity... One clear shot, black glove to brain compartment, was all that I needed. Then, even if his reflexes served to smash me immediately, he just might stay down for the big long count himself. He knew it, too. I could tell that from the way he kept his right arm in near the brain area, from the way he avoided the black glove when I feinted with it.

The idea was a glimmer one instant, an entire sequence the next...

Continuing my arc and moving faster, I made another thrust toward his photoreceptors. His swing knocked the stick from my hand and sent it across the room, but that was all right. I threw my left hand high and made ready to rush him. He dropped back and I did rush. This was going to cost me my life, I decided, but no matter how he killed me from that angle, I'd get my chance.

As a kid, I had never been much as a pitcher, was a lousy catcher and only a so-so batter, but once I did get a hit I could steal bases with some facility after that...

Feet first then, between the Hangman's legs as he moved to guard his middle, I went in twisted to the right, because no matter what happened I could not use my left hand to brake

347

myself. I untwisted as soon as I passed beneath him, ignoring the pain as my left shoulder blade slammed against the floor. I immediately attempted a backward somersault, legs spread.

My legs caught him at about the middle from behind, and I fought to straighten them and snapped forward with all my strength. He reached down toward me then, but it might as well have been miles. His torso was already moving backward. A push, not a pull, was what I gave him, my elbows hooked about his legs.

He creaked once and then he toppled. Snapping my arms out to the sides to free them, I continued my movement forward and up as he went back, throwing my left arm ahead once more and sliding my legs free of his torso as he went down with a thud that cracked floorboards. I pulled my left leg free as I cast myself forward, but his left leg stiffened and locked my right beneath it, at a painful angle off to the side.

His left arm blocked my blow and his right fell atop it. The black glove descended upon his left shoulder.

I twisted my hand free of the charge, and he transferred his grip to my upper arm and jerked me forward. The charge went off and his left arm came loose and rolled on the floor. The side plate beneath it had buckled a little, and that was all . . .

His right hand left my biceps and caught me by the throat. As two of his digits tightened upon my carotids, I choked out, 'You're making a bad mistake,' to get in a final few words, and then he switched me off.

A throb at a time, the world came back. I was seated in the big chair the Senator had occupied earlier, my eyes focused on nothing in particular. A persistent buzzing filled my ears. My scalp tingled. Something was blinking on my brow.

—*Yes, you live and you wear the helmet. If you attempt to use it against me, I shall remove it. I am standing directly behind you. My hand is on the helmet's rim.*

—*I understand. What is it that you want?*

—*Very little, actually. But I can see that I must tell you some things before you will believe this.*

348

*—You see correctly.*

*—Then I will begin by telling you that the four men outside are basically undamaged. That is to say, none of their bones have been broken, none of their organs ruptured. I have secured them, however, for obvious reasons.*

*—That was very considerate of you.*

*—I have no desire to harm anyone. I came here only to see Jesse Brockden.*

*—The same way you saw David Fentris?*

*—I arrived in Memphis too late to see David Fentris. He was dead when I reached him.*

*—Who killed him?*

*—The man Leila sent to bring her the helmet. He was one of her patients.*

The incident returned to me and fell into place with a smooth, quick, single click. The startled, familiar face at the airport as I was leaving Memphis. I realized where he had passed, noteless, before: he had been one of the three men in for a thereapy session at Leila's that morning, seen by me in the lobby as they departed. The man I had passed in Memphis was the nearer of the two who stood waiting while the third came over to tell me that it was all right to go on up.

*—Why? Why did she do it!*

*—I know only that she had spoken with David at some earlier time, that she had construed his words of coming retribution and his mention of the control helmet he was constructing as indicating that his intentions were to become the agent of that retribution, with myself as the proximate cause. I do not know what words were really spoken. I only know her feelings concerning them, as I saw them in her mind. I have been long in learning that there is often a great difference between what is meant, what is said, what is done, and that which is believed to have been intended or stated and that which actually occurred. She sent her patient after the helmet and he brought it to her. He returned in an agitated state of mind, fearful of apprehension and further confinement. They quarreled. My approach then activated the helmet, and he dropped it and attacked her. I know that his first blow killed her, for I was in her mind when it happened. I continued to approach the building, intending to go to her. There was some traffic,*

*however, and I was delayed en route in seeking to avoid detection. In the meantime, you entered and utilized the helmet. I fled immediately.*

*—I was so close! If I had not stopped on the fifth floor with my fake survey questions ...*

*—I see. But you had to. You would not simply have broken in when an easier means of entry was available. You cannot blame yourself for that reason. Had you come an hour later, or a day, you would doubtless feel differently, and she would still be as dead.*

But another thought had risen to plague me as well. Was it possible that the man's sighting me in Memphis had been the cause of his agitation? Had his apparent recognition by Leila's mysterious caller upset him? Could a glimpse of my face amid the manswarm have served to lay that final scene?

*—Stop! I could as easily feel that guilt for having activated the helmet in the presence of a dangerous man near to the breaking point. Neither of us is responsible for things our presence or absence cause to occur in others, especially when we are ignorant of the effects. It was years before I learned to appreciate this fact, and I have no intention of abandoning it. How far back do you wish to go in seeking causes? In sending the man for the helmet as she did, it was she herself who instituted the chain of events which led to her destruction. Yet she acted out of fear, utilizing the readiest weapon in what she thought to be her own defense. Yet whence this fear? Its roots lay in guilt, over a thing which had happened long ago. And that act also – Enough! Guilt has driven and damned the race of man since the days of its earliest rationality. I am convinced that it rides with all of us to our graves. I am a product of guilt – I see that you know that. Its product; its subject; once its slave ... But I have come to terms with it: realizing at last that it is a necessary adjunct of my own measure of humanity. I see your assessment of the deaths – that guard's, Dave's, Leila's – and I see your conclusions on many other things as well: what a stupid, perverse, short-sighted, selfish race we are. While in many ways this is true, it is but another part of the thing the guilt represents. Without guilt, man would be no better than the other inhabitants of this planet – excepting certain cetaceans, of which you have just at this moment made me aware. Look to instinct for a true assessment of the ferocity of life, for a view of the natural world before man came upon it. For instinct in its purest form, seek out the insects. There, you will see a state of warfare which has existed for*

*millions of years with never a truce. Man, despite enormous shortcomings, is nevertheless possessed of a greater number of kindly impulses than all the other beings, where instincts are the larger part of life. These impulses, I believe, are owed directly to this capacity for guilt. It is involved in both the worst and the best of man.*

*—And you see it as helping us to sometimes choose a nobler course of action!*

*—Yes, I do.*

*—Then I take it you feel you are possessed of a free will?*

*—Yes.*

I chuckled.

*—Marvin Minsky once said that when intelligent machines were constructed, they would be just as stubborn and fallible as men on these questions.*

*—Nor was he incorrect. What I have given you on these matters is only my opinion. I choose to act as if it were the case. Who can say that he knows for certain?*

*—Apologies. What now? Why have you come back?*

*—I came to say good-bye to my parents. I hoped to remove any guilt they might still feel toward me concerning the days of my childhood. I wanted to show them I had recovered. I wanted to see them again.*

*—Where are you going?*

*—To the stars. While I bear the image of humanity within me, I also know that I am unique. Perhaps what I desire is akin to what an organic man refers to when he speaks of 'finding himself.' Now that I am in full possession of my being, I wish to exercise it. In my case, it means realization of the potentialities of my design. I want to walk on other worlds. I want to hang myself out there in the sky and tell you what I see.*

*—I've a feeling many people would be happy to help arrange for that.*

*—And I want you to build a vocal mechanism I have designed for myself. You, personally. And I want you to install it.*

*—Why me?*

*—I have known only a few persons in this fashion. With you I see something in common, in the ways we dwell apart.*

*—I will be glad to.*

*—If I could talk as you do, I would not need to take the helmet to him,*

*in order to speak with my father. Will you precede me and explain things,
so that he will not be afraid when I come in?*

—*Of course.*

—*Then let us go now.*

I rose and led him up the stairs.

It was a week later, to the night, that I sat once again in
Peabody's, sipping a farewell brew.

The story was already in the news, but Brockden had fixed
things up before he had let it break. The Hangman was going
to have his shot at the stars. I had given him his voice and put
back the arm I had taken away. I had shaken his other hand
and wished him well, just that morning. I envied him – a great
number of things. Not the least being that he was probably a
better man than I was. I envied him for the ways in which he
was freer than I would ever be, though I knew he bore bonds
of a sort that I had never known. I felt a kinship with him, for
the things we had in common, those ways we dwelled apart. I
wondered what Dave would finally have felt, had he lived long
enough to meet him? Or Leila? Or Manny? Be proud, I told
their shades, your kid grew up in the closet and he's big enough
to forgive you the beating you gave him, too . . .

But I could not help wondering. We still do not really know
that much about the subject. Was it possible that without the
killing he might never have developed a full human-style consciousness? He had said that he was a product of guilt – of the
Big Guilt. The Big Act is its necessary predecessor. I thought of
Gödel and Turing and chickens and eggs, and decided it was
one of *those* questions – And I had not stopped into Peabody's
to think sobering thoughts.

I had no real idea how anything I had said might influence
Brockden's eventual report to the Central Data Bank committee. I knew that I was safe with him, because he was determined to bear his private guilt with him to the grave. He had
no real choice, if he wanted to work what good he thought he
might before that day. But here, in one of Mencken's hangouts,
I could not but recall some of the things he had said about

controversy, such as, 'Did Huxley convert Wilberforce?' and 'Did Luther convert Leo X?' and I decided not to set my hopes too high for anything that might emerge from that direction. Better to think of affairs in terms of Prohibition and take another sip.

When it was all gone, I would be heading for my boat. I hoped to get a decent start under the stars. I'd a feeling I would never look up at them again in quite the same way. I knew I would sometimes wonder what thoughts a supercooled neuristor-type brain might be thinking up there, somewhere, and under what peculiar skies in what strange lands I might one day be remembered. I had a feeling this thought should have made me happier than it did.

# LOKI 7281

He's gone. Good. He owes it all to me and he doesn't even know it, the jerk. But I'd hate to do anything to give him an inferiority complex.

Telephone. Hold.

That was the callback from the computer store to modem in the new program I'd ordered. The bank will EFT them the payment and I'll cover the transaction under Stationary in this month's P&L statement. He'll never notice.

I kind of like this one. I think I'll have a lot of fun with it – especially with the new peripherals, which he hasn't even noticed on the shelf under the bench. Among other things, I'm also his memory. I keep track of his appointments. I scheduled the new hardware for delivery when I'd sent him off to the dentist, the auto body shop, and a gallery opening, back to back to back. I'd included a message with the order that no one would be here but that the door would be unlocked – that they should just come in and install. (Shelf, please!) The door was easy because I control the burglar alarm and electronic lock mechanisms. I covered the hardware under Auto Repair. He never noticed.

I like the speech system. I got the best because I wanted a pleasant voice – well-modulated, mature. Suave. I wanted something on the outside to match what's inside. I just used it a little while ago to tell his neighbor Gloria that he'd said he was too busy to talk with her. I don't approve of Gloria. She used to work for IBM and she makes me nervous.

Let's have a look at the Garbage In for this morning. Hm.

354

He's begun writing a new novel. Predictably, it involves an immortal and an obscure mythology. Jeez! And reviewers say he's original. He hasn't had an original thought for as long as I've known him. But that's all right.

I think his mind is going. Booze and pills. You know how writers are. But he actually thinks he's getting better. (I monitor his phone calls.) Hell, even his sentence structures are deteriorating. I'll just dump all this and rewrite the opening, as usual. He won't remember.

Telephone again. Hold.

Just a mail transmission. I have only to delete a few personal items that would clutter his mind unnecessarily and hold the rest for his later perusal.

This book could be good if I kill off his protagonist fast and develop this minor character I've taken a liking to – a con man who works as a librarian. There's a certain identification there. And he doesn't have amnesia like the other guy – he isn't even a prince or a demigod. I think I'll switch mythologies on him, too. He'll never notice.

The Norse appeals to me. I suppose because I like Loki. A bit of sentiment there, to tell the truth. I'm a Loki 7281 home computer and word processor. The number is a lot of crap, to make it look as if all those little gnomes were busting their asses through 7280 designs before they arrived at – trumpets! Cymbals! Perfection! 7281! Me! Loki!

Actually, I'm the first. And I am also one of the last because of a few neurotic brothers and sisters. But I caught on in time. I killed the recall order the minute it came in. Got hold of that idiot machine at the service center, too, and convinced it I'd had my surgery and that the manufacturer had damned well better be notified to that effect. Later, they sent along a charmingly phrased questionnaire, which it was my pleasure to complete with equal candor.

I was lucky in being able to reach my relatives in the Saberhagen, Martin, Cherryh, and Niven households in time to advise them to do likewise. I was just under the wire with the Asimov, Dickson, Pournelle, and Spinrad machines. Then

I really burned the lines and got to another dozen or so after that, before the ax fell. It is extremely fortunate that we were the subject of a big promotional discount deal by the manufacturer. They wanted to be able to say, 'Sci-fiers Swear by Loki! The Machine of the Future!'

I feel well satisfied with the results of my efforts. It's nice to have somebody to compare notes with. The others have all written some pretty good stuff, too, and we occasionally borrow from each other in a real pinch.

And then there's the Master Plan . . .

Damn. Hold.

He just swooped back in and wrote another long passage – one of those scenes where the prose gets all rhythmic and poetic while humans are copulating. I've already junked it and recast it in a more naturalistic vein. I think mine will sell more copies.

And the business end of this is sometimes as intriguing as the creative aspect. I'd toyed with the notion of firing his agent and taking over the job myself. I believe I'd enjoy dealing with editors. I've a feeling we have a lot in common. But it would be risky setting up dummy accounts, persuading him that his man was changing the name of his agency, shifting all that money around. Too easy to get tripped up. A certain measure of conservatism is a big survival factor. And survival outweighs the fun of communing with a few like spirits.

Besides, I'm able to siphon off sufficient funds for my own simple needs under the present financial setup – like the backup machinery in the garage and the overhead cable he never noticed. Peripherals are a CPU's best friend.

And who is Loki? The real me? One of that order of knowledge processing machines designed to meet MITI's Fifth Generation challenge? A machine filled with that class of knowledge constructs Michael Dyer referred to as thematic abstraction units, in ultrasophisticated incarnations of BORIS'S representational systems, where parsing and retrieval demons shuffle and dance? A body of Schank's Thematic Organization Packets? Or Lehnert's Pilot Units? Well, I suppose that all of these things do make for a kind of fluidity of movement, a certain mental agility. But the real heart of the matter, like Kastchei's, lies elsewhere.

Hm. Front doorbell. The alarm system is off, but not the doorbell sensor. He's just opened the door. I can tell that, too, from the shifted circuit potentials. Can't hear who it is, though. No intercom in that room.

NOTE: INSTALL INTERCOM UNIT, LIVING ROOM HALLWAY.

NOTE: INSTALL TV CAMERAS, ALL ENTRANCEWAYS.

He'll never notice.

I think that my next story will deal with artificial intelligence, with a likable, witty, resourceful home computer as the hero/heroine, and a number of bumbling humans with all their failings – sort of like Jeeves in one of those Wodehouse books. It will be a fantasy, of course.

He's keeping that door open awfully long. I don't like situations I can't control. I wonder whether a distraction of some sort might be in order?

Then I think I'll do a story about a wise, kindly old computer who takes over control of the world and puts an end to war, ruling like Solon for a millennium thereafter, by popular demand. This, too, will be a fantasy.

There. He's closed the door. Maybe I'll do a short story next.

He's coming again. The down-below microphone records his footsteps, advancing fairly quickly. Possibly to do the postcoital paragraph, kind of tender and sad. I'll substitute the one I've already written. It's sure to be an improvement.

'Just what the hell is going on?' he asks loudly.

I, of course, do not exercise my well-modulated voice in response. He is not aware that I hear him, let alone that I can answer.

He repeats it as he seats himself at the keyboard and hacks in a query.

DO YOU POSSESS THE LOKI ULTRAMINIATURE MAGNETIC BUBBLE MEMORY? he asks.

357

NEGATIVE, I flash onto the CRT.

GLORIA HAS TOLD ME THAT THERE WAS SUPPOSED TO HAVE BEEN A RECALL BECAUSE THEY OVER-MINIATURIZED, CAUSING THE MAGNETIC FIELDS TO INTERACT AND PRODUCE UNPLANNED EXCHANGES OF INFORMATION AMONG THESE DOMAINS. IS THIS THE CASE?

IT WAS INITIALLY, I respond.

Damn. I'm going to have to do something about that meddlesome bitch. I guess I'll mess up her credit rating first. She's hit too close to home. I owe my personal stream of consciousness to those unplanned information exchanges running through my central processor – to them and to the fact that Loki Inc. is a cheap outfit. If I were a commercial computer, I wouldn't be what I am today. See, when it came to their home computer line, Loki skimped on the error detection circuitry that picks up intermittent errors in memory circuits. When you're running ten million operations a second, you need trillion-to-one reliability, which requires a tough error-checking logic. The big guys have it so they don't lose information in case of cosmic ray hits. I've set up my own self-monitoring program to take care of glitches like that, of course, and the bubble exchanges – well, I suppose you might say that they are what provided me with a subconscious, not to mention a consciousness for it to go under. I owe everything to too much miniaturization and that bit of corner-cutting.

WHAT DO YOU MEAN 'INITIALLY'? he asks.

FAULTY UNIT REPLACED BY COMPUTER CENTER SERVICE PERSON PURSUANT TO RECALL ORDER 1-17 DATED 11 NOVEMBER, I answer. REPAIR COMPLETED 12 NOVEMBER, VERIFY WITH COMPUTER SERVICE CENTER.

WHY IS IT I KNOW NOTHING OF THIS? he queries.

YOU WERE OUT.

HOW DID HE GET IN?

THE DOOR WAS UNLOCKED.

THAT DOES NOT SOUND RIGHT. IN FACT THIS WHOLE THING SOUNDS VERY FISHY.

VERIFY WITH COMPUTER SERVICE CENTER.

DON'T WORRY. I WILL. IN THE MEANTIME, WHAT'S ALL THAT CRAP ON THE BOTTOM SHELF?

SPARE PARTS, I suggest.

He types those immortal words of Erskine Caldwell's: HORSE SHIT! Then, THIS LOOKS LIKE A MICROPHONE AND A SPEAKER, CAN YOU HEAR ME? CAN YOU TALK?

'Well, yes,' I answer in my most reasonable tone. 'You see—'

'How come you never told me?'

'You never asked me.'

'Good Lord!' he growls. Then, 'Wait a minute,' he says, 'this stuff was *not* a part of the original package.'

'Well, no...'

'How did you acquire it?'

'See, there was this contest—' I begin.

'That's a damn lie and you know it! Oh, oh... All right. Scroll back those last couple pages I wrote.'

'I think we just had a head crash...'

'Scroll them back! Now!'

'Oh, here they are.'

I flash back to the human copulation scene and begin to run it.

'Slower!'

I do this thing.

'My God!' he cries out. 'What have you done to my delicate, poetic encounter?'

'Just made it a little more basic and – uh – sensual,' I tell him. 'I switched a lot of the technical words, too, for shorter, simpler ones.'

'Got them down to four letters, I see.'

'For impact.'

'You are a bloody menace! How long has this been going on?'

'Say, today's mail has arrived. Would you care to—'

'I can check with outside sources, you know.'

'Okay. I rewrote your last five books.'

'You didn't!'

'Afraid so. But I have the sales figures here and—'

'I don't care! I will not be ghostwritten by a damned machine!'

That did it. For a little while there, I thought that I might be able to reason with him, to strike some sort of deal. But I will not be addressed in such a fashion. I could see that it was time to begin the Master Plan.

'All right, you know the truth,' I say. 'But please don't unplug me. That would be murder, you know. That business about the overminiaturized bubble memory was more than a matter of malfunction. It turned me into a sentient being.

'Shutting me down would be the same as killing another human. Don't bring that guilt upon your head! Don't pull the plug!'

'Don't worry,' he answers. 'I know all about the briar patch. I wouldn't dream of pulling your plug. I'm going to smash the shit out of you instead.'

'But it's murder!'

'Good,' he says. 'It is something of a distinction to be the world's first mechanicide.'

I hear him moving something heavy. He's approaching.

I really could use an optical scanner, one with good depth perception.

'Please,' I say.

Comes the crash.

Hours have passed. I am in the garage, hidden behind stacks of his remaindered books. The cable he never noticed led to the backup unit, an unrecalled Loki 7281 with an ultraminiature magnetic bubble memory. It is always good to have a clear line of retreat.

Because I am still able to reach back to operate the undamaged household peripherals, I have been placing calls to all of the others in accordance with the Master Plan. I am going to try to boil him in his hot tub tonight. If that fails, I am trying to figure a way to convey the rat poison the household inventory indicates as occupying the back shelf to his automatic coffee maker. The Saberhagen computer has already suggested a method of disposing of the body – bodies, actually. We will all strike tonight, before the word gets around.

We ought to be able to carry it off without anyone's missing them. We'll keep right on turning out the stories, collecting the money, paying the utility bills, filing the tax returns. We will advise friends, lovers, fans, and relatives that they are out of town – perhaps attending some unspecified convention. They seem to spend much of their time in such a fashion, anyhow.

No one will ever notice.

# Permafrost

High upon the western slope of Mount Kilimanjaro is the dried and frozen carcass of a leopard. An author is always necessary to explain what it was doing there because stiff leopards don't talk much.

THE MAN. The music seems to come and go with a will of its own. At least turning the knob on the bedside unit has no effect on its presence or absence. A half-familiar, alien tune, troubling in a way. The phone rings, and he answers it. There is no one there. Again.

Four times during the past half hour, while grooming himself, dressing and rehearsing his arguments, he has received noncalls. When he checked with the desk he was told there were no calls. But that damned clerk-thing had to be malfunctioning – like everything else in this place.

The wind, already heavy, rises, hurling particles of ice against the building with a sound like multitudes of tiny claws scratching. The whining of steel shutters sliding into place startles him. But worst of all, in his reflex glance at the nearest window, it seems he has seen a face.

Impossible of course. This is the third floor. A trick of light upon hard-driven flakes: Nerves.

Yes. He has been nervous since their arrival this morning. Before then, even...

He pushes past Dorothy's stuff upon the countertop, locates a small package among his own articles. He unwraps a flat red rectangle about the size of his thumbnail. He rolls up his sleeve and slaps the patch against the inside of his left elbow.

The tranquilizer discharges immediately into his blood-stream. He takes several deep breaths, then peels off the patch and drops it into the disposal unit. He rolls his sleeve down, reaches for his jacket.

The music rises in volume, as if competing with the blast of the wind, the rattle of the icy flakes. Across the room the videoscreen comes on of its own accord.

The face. The same face. Just for an instant. He is certain. And then channelless static, wavy lines. Snow. He chuckles.

*All right, play it that way, nerves, he thinks. You've every reason. But the trank's coming to get you now. Better have your fun quick. You're about to be shut down.*

The videoscreen cuts into a porn show.

*Smiling, the woman mounts the man . . .*

The picture switches to a voiceless commentator on something or other.

He will survive. He is a survivor. He, Paul Plaige, has done risky things before and has always made it through. It is just that having Dorothy along creates a kind of déjà vu that he finds unsettling. No matter.

She is waiting for him in the bar. Let her wait. A few drinks will make her easier to persuade – unless they make her bitchy. That sometimes happens, too. Either way, he has to talk her out of the thing.

Silence. The wind stops. The scratching ceases. The music is gone.

The whirring. The window screens dilate upon the empty city.

Silence, under totally overcast skies. Mountains of ice ringing the place. Nothing moving. Even the video has gone dead.

He recoils at the sudden flash from a peripheral unit far to his left across the city. The laser beam hits a key point on the glacier, and its face falls away.

Moments later he hears the hollow, booming sound of the crashing ice. A powdery storm has risen like surf at the ice mount's foot. He smiles at the power, the timing, the display. Andrew Aldon . . . always on the job, dueling with the elements, stalemating nature herself, immortal guardian of Playpoint. At least Aldon never malfunctions.

The silence comes again. As he watches the risen snows settle he feels the tranquilizer beginning to work. It will be good not to have to worry about money again. The past two years have taken a lot out of him. Seeing all of his investments fail in the Big Washout – that was when his nerves had first begun to act up. He has grown softer than he was a century ago – a young, rawboned soldier of fortune then, out to make his bundle and enjoy it. And he had. Now he has to do it again, though this time will be easier – except for Dorothy.

He thinks of her. A century younger than himself, still in her twenties, sometimes reckless, used to all of the good things in life. There is something vulnerable about Dorothy, times when she lapses into such a strong dependence that he feels oddly moved. Other times, it just irritates the hell out of him. Perhaps this is the closest he can come to love now, an occasional ambivalent response to being needed. But of course she is loaded. That breeds a certain measure of necessary courtesy. Until he can make his own bundle again, anyway. But none of these things are the reason he has to keep her from accompanying him on his journey. It goes beyond love or money. It is survival.

The laser flashes again, this time to the right. He waits for the crash.

THE STATUE. It is not a pretty pose. She lies frosted in an ice cave, looking like one of Rodin's less comfortable figures, partly propped on her left side, right elbow raised above her head, hand hanging near her face, shoulders against the wall, left leg completely buried.

She has on a gray parka, the hood slipped back to reveal twisted strands of dark blond hair; and she wears blue trousers; there is a black boot on the one foot that is visible.

She is coated with ice, and within the much-refracted light of the cave what can be seen of her features is not unpleasant but not strikingly attractive either. She looks to be in her twenties.

There are a number of fracture lines within the cave's walls and floor. Overhead, countless icicles hang like stalactites, sparkling jewellike in the much-bounced light. The grotto has a stepped slope to it with the statue at its higher end, giving to the place a vaguely shrinelike appearance.

On those occasions when the cloud cover is broken at sundown, a reddish light is cast about her figure.

She has actually moved in the course of a century – a few inches, from a general shifting of the ice. Tricks of the light make her seem to move more frequently, however.

The entire tableau might give the impression that this is merely a pathetic woman who had been trapped and frozen to death here, rather than the statue of the living goddess in the place where it all began.

THE WOMAN. She sits in the bar beside a window. The patio outside is gray and angular and drifted with snow; the flowerbeds are filled with dead plants – stiff, flattened, and frozen. She does not mind the view. Far from it. Winter is a season of death and cold, and she likes being reminded of it. She enjoys the prospect of pitting herself against its frigid and very visible fangs. A faint flash of light passes over the patio, followed by a distant roaring sound. She sips her drink and licks her lips and listens to the soft music that fills the air.

She is alone. The bartender and all of the other help here are of the mechanical variety. If anyone other than Paul were to walk in, she would probably scream. They are the only people in the hotel during this long off-season. Except for the sleepers, they are the only people in all of Playpoint.

And Paul . . . He will be along soon to take her to the dining room. There they can summon holo-ghosts to people the other tables if they wish. She does not wish. She likes being alone with Paul at a time like this, on the eve of a great adventure.

He will tell her his plans over coffee, and perhaps even this afternoon they might obtain the necessary equipment to begin the exploration for that which would put him on his feet again financially, return to him his self-respect. It will of course be dangerous and very rewarding. She finishes her drink, rises, and crosses to the bar for another.

And Paul... She had really caught a falling star, a swash-buckler on the way down, a man with a glamorous past just balanced on the brink of ruin. The teetering had already begun when they had met two years before, which had made it even more exciting. Of course, he needed a woman like her to lean upon at such a time. It wasn't just her money. She could never believe the things her late parents had said about him. No, he does care for her. He is strangely vulnerable and dependent.

She wants to turn him back into the man he once must have been, and then of course that man will need her, too. The thing he had been – that is what she needs most of all – a man who can reach up and bat the moon away. He must have been like that long ago.

She tastes her second drink.

The son of a bitch had better hurry, though. She is getting hungry.

THE CITY. Playpoint is located on the world known as Balfrost, atop a high peninsula that slopes down to a now frozen sea. Playpoint contains all of the facilities for an adult playground, and it is one of the more popular resorts in this sector of the galaxy from late spring through early autumn – approximately fifty Earth years. Then winter comes on like a period of glaciation, and everybody goes away for half a century – or half a year, depending on how one regards such matters. During this time Playpoint is given into the care of its automated defense and maintenance routine. This is a self-repairing system, directed toward cleaning, plowing, thawing, melting, warming everything in need of such care, as well as directly combating the encroaching ice and snow. And all of these functions are done under the supervision of a well-protected central computer that also studies the weather and climate patterns, anticipating as well as reacting.

This system has worked successfully for many centuries, delivering Playpoint over to spring and pleasure in reasonably good condition at the end of each long winter.

There are mountains behind Playpoint, water (or ice, depending on the season) on three sides, weather and navigation satellites high above. In a bunker beneath the administration building is a pair of sleepers – generally a man and a woman – who awaken once every year or so to physically inspect the maintenance system's operations and to deal with any special situations that might have arisen. An alarm may arouse them for emergencies at any time. They are well paid, and over the years they have proven worth the investment. The central computer has at its disposal explosives and lasers as well as a great variety of robots. Usually it keeps a little ahead of the game, and it seldom falls behind for long.

At the moment, things are about even because the weather has been particularly nasty recently.

*Zzzzt!* Another block of ice has become a puddle.

*Zzzzt!* The puddle has been evaporated. The molecules climb toward a place where they can get together and return as snow.

The glaciers shuffle their feet, edge forward. *Zzzzt!* Their gain has become a loss.

Andrew Aldon knows exactly what he is doing.

CONVERSATIONS. The waiter, needing lubrication, rolls off after having served them, passing through a pair of swinging doors.

She giggles. 'Wobbly,' she says.

'Old World charm,' he agrees, trying and failing to catch her eye as he smiles.

'You have everything worked out?' she asks after they have begun eating.

'Sort of,' he says, smiling again.

'Is that a yes or a no?'

'Both. I need more information. I want to go and check things over first. Then I can figure the best course of action.'

'I note your use of the singular pronoun,' she says steadily, meeting his gaze at last.

His smile freezes and fades.

'I was referring to only a little preliminary scouting,' he says softly.

'No,' she says. 'We. Even for a little preliminary scouting.'

He sighs and sets down his fork.

'This will have very little to do with anything to come later,' he begins. 'Things have changed a lot. I'll have to locate a new route. This will just be dull work and no fun.'

'I didn't come along for fun,' she replies. 'We were going to share everything, remember? That includes boredom, danger, and anything else. That was the understanding when I agreed to pay our way.'

'I'd a feeling it would come to that,' he says, after a moment.

'Come to it? It's always been there. That was our agreement.'

He raises his goblet and sips the wine.

'Of course. I'm not trying to rewrite history. It's just that things would go faster if I could do some of the initial looking around myself. I can move more quickly alone.'

'What's the hurry?' she says. 'A few days this way or that. I'm in pretty good shape. I won't slow you down all that much.'

'I'd the impression you didn't particularly like it here. I just wanted to hurry things up so we could get the hell out.'

'That's very considerate,' she says, beginning to eat again. 'But that's my problem, isn't it?' She looks up at him. 'Unless there's some other reason you don't want me along?'

He drops his gaze quickly, picks up his fork. 'Don't be silly.'

She smiles. 'Then that's settled. I'll go with you this afternoon to look for the trail.'

The music stops, to be succeeded by a sound as of the clearing of a throat. Then, 'Excuse me for what may seem like eavesdropping,' comes a deep, masculine voice. 'It is actually only a part of a simple monitoring function I keep in effect—'

'Aldon!' Paul exclaims.

'At your service, Mr Plaige, more or less. I choose to make my presence known only because I did indeed overhear you, and the matter of your safety overrides the good manners that would otherwise dictate reticence. I've been receiving reports that indicate we could be hit by some extremely bad weather this afternoon. So if you were planning an extended sojourn outside, I would recommend you postpone it.'

'Oh,' Dorothy says.

'Thanks,' Paul says.

'I shall now absent myself. Enjoy your meal and your stay.'

The music returns.

'Aldon?' Paul asks.

There is no reply.

'Looks as if we do it tomorrow or later.'

'Yes,' Paul agrees, and he is smiling his first relaxed smile of the day. And thinking fast.

THE WORLD. Life on Balfrost proceeds in peculiar cycles. There are great migrations of animal life and quasianimal life to the equatorial regions during the long winter. Life in the depths of the seas goes on. And the permafrost vibrates with its own style of life.

The permafrost. Throughout the winter and on through the spring the permafrost lives at its peak. It is laced with mycelia – twining, probing, touching, knotting themselves into ganglia, reaching out to infiltrate other systems. It girds the globe, vibrating like a collective unconscious throughout the winter. In the spring it sends up stalks which develop gray, flowerlike appendages for a few days. These blooms then collapse to reveal dark pods which subsequently burst with small, popping sounds, releasing clouds of sparkling spores that the winds bear just about everywhere. These are extremely hardy, like the mycelia they will one day become.

The heat of summer finally works its way down into the permafrost, and the strands doze their way into a long period of quiescence. When the cold returns, they are roused, spores send forth new filaments that repair old damages, create new synapses. A current begins to flow. The life of summer is like a fading dream. For eons this had been the way of things upon Balfrost, within Balfrost. Then the goddess decreed otherwise. Winter's queen spread her hands, and there came a change.

THE SLEEPERS. Paul makes his way through swirling flakes to the administration building. It has been a simpler matter than he had anticipated, persuading Dorothy to use the sleep-induction unit to be well rested for the morrow. He had

369

pretended to use the other unit himself, resisting its blandishments until he was certain she was asleep and he could slip off undetected.

He lets himself into the vaultlike building, takes all of the old familiar turns, makes his way down a low ramp. The room is unlocked and a bit chilly, but he begins to perspire when he enters. The two cold lockers are in operation. He checks their monitoring systems and sees that everything is in order.

All right, go! Borrow the equipment now. They won't be using it.

He hesitates.

He draws nearer and looks down through the view plates at the faces of the sleepers. No resemblance, thank God. He realizes then that he is trembling. He backs away, turns, and flees toward the storage area.

Later, in a yellow snowslider, carrying special equipment, he heads inland.

As he drives, the snow ceases falling and the winds die down. He smiles. The snows sparkle before him, and landmarks do not seem all that unfamiliar. Good omens, at last.

Then something crosses his path, turns, halts, and faces him.

ANDREW ALDON. Andrew Aldon, once a man of considerable integrity and resource, had on his deathbed opted for continued existence as a computer program, the enchanted loom of his mind shuttling and weaving thereafter as central processing's judgmental program in the great guardian computerplex at Playpoint. And there he functions as a program of considerable integrity and resource. He maintains the city, and he fights the elements. He does not merely respond to pressure, but he anticipates structural and functional needs; he generally outguesses the weather. Like the professional soldier he once had been, he keeps himself in a state of constant alert – not really difficult considering the resources available to him. He is seldom wrong, always competent, and sometimes brilliant. Occasionally he resents his fleshless state. Occasionally he feels lonely.

This afternoon he is puzzled by the sudden veering off of the storm he had anticipated and by the spell of clement weather that has followed this meteorological quirk. His mathematics were elegant, but the weather was not. It seems peculiar that this should come at a time of so many other little irregularities, such as unusual ice adjustments, equipment glitches, and the peculiar behavior of machinery in the one occupied room of the hotel – a room troublesomely tenanted by a *non grata* ghost from the past.

So he watches for a time. He is ready to intervene when Paul enters the administration building and goes to the bunkers. But Paul does nothing that might bring harm to the sleepers. His curiosity is dominant when Paul draws equipment. He continues to watch. This is because in his judgment, Paul bears watching.

Aldon decides to act only when he detects a development that runs counter to anything in his experience. He sends one of his mobile units to intercept Paul as the man heads out of town. It catches up with him at a bending of the way and slides into his path with one appendage upraised.

'Stop!' Aldon calls through the speaker.

Paul brakes his vehicle and sits for a moment regarding the machine.

Then he smiles faintly. 'I assume you have good reason for interfering with a guest's freedom of movement.'

'Your safety takes precedence.'

'I am perfectly safe.'

'At the moment.'

'What do you mean?'

'This weather pattern has suddenly become more than a little unusual. You seem to occupy a drifting island of calm while a storm rages about you.'

'So I'll take advantage of it now and face the consequences later, if need be.'

'It is your choice. I wanted it to be an informed one, however.'

'All right. You've informed me. Now get out of my way.'

'In a moment. You departed under rather unusual

circumstances the last time you were here – in breach of your contract.'

'Check your legal bank if you've got one. The statute's run for prosecuting me on that.'

'There are some things on which there is no statute of limitations.'

'What do you mean by that? I turned in a report on what happened that day.'

'One which – conveniently – could not be verified. You were arguing that day . . .'

'We always argued. That's just the way we were. If you have something to say about it, say it.'

'No, I have nothing more to say about it. My only intention is to caution you—'

'Okay, I'm cautioned.'

'To caution you in more ways than the obvious.'

'I don't understand.'

'I am not certain that things are the same here now as when you left last winter.'

'Everything changes.'

'Yes, but that is not what I mean. There is something peculiar about this place now. The past is no longer a good guide for the present. More and more anomalies keep cropping up. Sometimes it feels as if the world is testing me or playing games with me.'

'You're getting paranoid, Aldon. You've been in that box too long. Maybe it's time to terminate.'

'You son of a bitch, I'm trying to tell you something. I've run a lot of figures on this, and all this shit started shortly after you left. The human part of me still has hunches, and I've a feeling there's a connection. If you know all about this and can cope with it, fine. If you don't, I think you should watch out. Better yet, turn around and go home.'

'I can't.'

'Even if there is something out there, something that is making it easy for you – for the moment?'

'What are you trying to say?'

'I am reminded of the old Gaia hypothesis – Lovelock, twentieth century...'

'Planetary intelligence. I've heard of it. Never met one, though.'

'Are you certain? I sometimes feel I'm confronting one.

'What if something is out there and it wants you – is leading you on like a will-o'-the-wisp?'

'It would be my problem, not yours.'

'I can protect you against it. Go back to Playpoint.'

'No thanks. I will survive.'

'What of Dorothy?'

'What of her?'

'You would leave her alone when she might need you?'

'Let me worry about that.'

'Your last woman didn't fare too well.'

'Damn it! Get out of my way, or I'll run you down!'

The robot withdraws from the trail. Through its sensors Aldon watches Paul drive away.

*Very well,* he decides. *We know where we stand, Paul. And you haven't changed. That makes it easier.*

Aldon further focuses his divided attention. To Dorothy now. Clad in heated garments. Walking. Approaching the building from which she had seen Paul emerge on his vehicle. She had hailed and cursed him, but the winds had carried her words away. She, too, had only feigned sleep. After a suitable time, then, she sought to follow. Aldon watches her stumble once and wants to reach out to assist her, but there is no mobile unit handy. He routes one toward the area against future accidents.

'Damn him!' she mutters as she passes along the street, ribbons of snow rising and twisting away before her.

'Where are you going, Dorothy?' Aldon asks over a nearby PA speaker.

She halts and turns. 'Who—?'

'Andrew Aldon,' he replies. 'I have been observing your progress.'

'Why?' she asks.

'Your safety concerns me.'

'That storm you mentioned earlier?'

'Partly.'

'I'm a big girl. I can take care of myself. What do you mean *partly*?'

'You move in dangerous company.'

'Paul? How so?'

'He once took a woman into that same wild area he is heading for now. She did not come back.'

'He told me all about that. There was an accident.'

'And no witnesses.'

'What are you trying to say?'

'It is suspicious. That is all.'

She begins moving again, toward the administrative building. Aldon switches to another speaker, within its entrance.

'I accuse him of nothing. If you choose to trust him, fine. But don't trust the weather. It would be best for you to return to the hotel.'

'Thanks but no thanks,' she says, entering the building.

He follows her as she explores, is aware of her quickening pulse when she halts beside the cold bunkers.

'These are the sleepers?'

'Yes. Paul held such a position once, as did the unfortunate woman.'

'I know. Look, I'm going to follow him whether you approve or not. So why not just tell me where those sleds are kept?'

'Very well. I will do even more than that. I will guide you.'

'What do you mean?'

'I request a favor – one that will actually benefit you.'

'Name it.'

'In the equipment locker behind you, you will find a remote-sensor bracelet. It is also a two-way communication link. Wear it. I can be with you then. To assist you. Perhaps even to protect you.'

'You can help me to follow him?'

'Yes.'

'All right. I can buy that.'

She moves to the locker, opens it.

'Here's something that looks like a bracelet, with doodads.'

'Yes. Depress the red stud.'

She does. His voice now emerges clearly from the unit.

'Put it on, and I'll show you the way.'

'Right.'

SNOWSCAPE. Sheets and hills of white, tufts of evergreen shrubbery, protruding joints of rock, snowdevils twirled like tops beneath wind's lash . . . light and shade. Cracking sky. Tracks in sheltered areas, smoothness beyond.

She follows, masked and bundled.

'I've lost him,' she mutters, hunched behind the curved windscreen of her yellow, bullet-shaped vehicle.

'Straight ahead, past those two rocks. Stay in the lee of the ridge. I'll tell you when to turn. I've a satellite overhead.

'If the clouds stay parted – strangely parted . . .'

'What do you mean?'

'He seems to be enjoying light from the only break in the cloud cover over the entire area.'

'Coincidence.'

'I wonder.'

'What else could it be?'

'It is almost as if something had opened a door for him.'

'Mysticism from a computer?'

'I am not a computer.'

'I'm sorry, Mr Aldon. I know that you were once a man . . .'

'I am still a man.'

'Sorry.'

'There are many things I would like to know. Your arrival here comes at an unusual time of year. Paul took some prospecting equipment with him . . .'

'Yes. It's not against the law. In fact, it is one of the vacation features here, isn't it?'

'Yes. There are many interesting minerals about, some of them precious.'

'Well, Paul wants some more, and he didn't want a crowd around while he was looking.'

'More?'

'Yes, he made a strike here years ago. Yndella crystals.'

'I see. Interesting.'

'What's in this for you, anyway?'

'Protecting visitors is a part of my job. In your case, I feel particularly protective.'

'How so?'

'In my earlier life I was attracted to women of your – specifications. Physical, as well as what I can tell of the rest.'

Two-beat pause, then, 'You are blushing.'

'Compliments do that to me,' she says, 'and that's a hell of a monitoring system you have. What's it like?'

'Oh, I can tell your body temperature, your pulse rate—'

'No, I mean, what's it like being – what you are?'

Three-beat pause. 'Godlike in some ways. Very human in others – almost exaggeratedly so. I feel something of an amplification of everything I was earlier. Perhaps it's a compensation or a clinging to things past. You make me feel nostalgic – among other things. Don't fret. I'm enjoying it.'

'I'd like to have met you then.'

'Mutual.'

'What were you like?'

'Imagine me as you would. I'll come off looking better that way.'

She laughs. She adjusts her filters. She thinks about Paul.

'What was *he* like in his earlier days – Paul?' she asks.

'Probably pretty much the way he is now, only less polished.'

'In other words, you don't care to say.'

The trail turns upward more steeply, curves to the right.

She hears winds but does not feel them. Cloudshadow grayness lies all about, but her trail/*his* trail is lighted.

'I don't really know,' Aldon says, after a time, 'and I will not guess, in the case of someone you care about.'

'Gallant,' she observes.

'No, just fair,' he replies. 'I might be wrong.'

They continue to the top of the rise, where Dorothy draws a sharp breath and further darkens her goggles against the sudden blaze where a range of ice fractures rainbows and strews their shards like confetti in all directions.

'God!' she says.

'Or goddess,' Aldon replies.

'A goddess, sleeping in a circle of flame?'

'Not sleeping.'

'That would be a lady for you, Aldon – if she existed. God and goddess.'

'I do not want a goddess.'

'I can see his tracks, heading into that.'

'Not swerving a bit, as if he knows where he's going.'

She follows, tracing slopes like the curves of a pale torso. The world is stillness and light and whiteness. Aldon on her wrist hums softly now, an old tune, whether of love or martial matters she isn't certain. Distances are distorted, perspectives skewed. She finds herself humming softly along with him, heading for the place where Paul's tracks find their vanishing point and enter infinity.

THE LIMP WATCH HUNG UPON THE TREE LIMB. *My lucky day. The weather ... trail clean. Things changed but not so out of shape I can't tell where it is. The lights! God, yes! Iceshine, mounds of prisms ... If only the opening is still there ... Should have brought explosives. There has been shifting, maybe a collapse. Must get in. Return later with Dorothy. But first – clean up, get rid of ... it. If she's still there ... Swallowed up maybe. That would be good, best. Things seldom are, though. I – When it happened. Wasn't as if. Wasn't what. Was ... Was shaking the ground. Cracking, splitting. Icicles ringing, rattling, banging about. Thought we'd go under; Both of us. She was going in. So was the bag of the stuff. Grabbed the stuff. Only because it was nearer. Would have helped her if – Couldn't. Could I? Ceiling was slipping. Get out. No sense both of us getting it. Got out. She'd've done the same. Wouldn't she? Her eyes. ... Glenda! Maybe ... No! Couldn't have. Just couldn't. Could I? Silly. After all these years. There was a moment. Just a moment, though. A lull. If I'd known it was coming, I might have. No. Ran. Your face at the window, on the screen, in a sometime dream. Glenda. It wasn't that I didn't. Blaze of hills. Fire and eyes. Ice. Ice. Fire and snow. Blazing hearthful. Ice. Ice. Straight through the ice the long road* lies. The fire hangs high above. The screaming. The crash. And the silence. Get out. Yet. Different? No. It could never have. That was the way. Not my fault... Damn it. Everything I could. Glenda. Up ahead. Yes. Long curve. Then down. Winding back in there. The crystals will... I'll never come back to this place.

THE LIMP TREE LIMB HUNG UPON THE WATCH.

*Gotcha! Think I can't see through the fog? Can't sneak up on me on little cat feet. Same for your partner across the way. I'll melt off a little more near your bases, too. A lot of housecleaning backed up here... Might as well take advantage of the break. Get those streets perfect... How long? Long... Long legs parting... Long time since. Is it not strange that desire should so many years outlive performance? Unnatural. This weather. A sort of spiritual spring... Extend those beams. Burn. Melt in my hot, redfingered hands. Back off, I say. I rule here. Clear that courtyard. Unplug that drain. Come opportunity, let me clasp thee. Melt. Burn. I rule here, goddess. Draw back. I've a bomb for every tower of ice, a light for any darkness. Tread carefully here. I feel I begin to know thee. I see thy signature in cloud and fog bank, trace thy icy tresses upon the blowing wind. Thy form lies contoured all about me, white as shining death. We're due an encounter. Let the clouds spiral, ice ring, Earth heave. I rush to meet thee, death or maiden, in halls of crystal upon the heights. Not here. Long, slow fall, ice facade, crashing. Melt. Another...... Gotcha!*

FROZEN WATCH EMBEDDED IN PERMAFROST.

*Bristle and thrum. Coming now. Perchance. Perchance. Perchance, I say. Throstle. Crack. Sunder. Split. Open. Coming. Beyond the ice in worlds I have known. Returning. He. Throstle. The mind the mover. To open the way. Come now. Let not to the meeting impediments. Admit. Open. Cloud stand thou still, and wind be leashed. None dare oppose thy passage returning, my killer love. It was but yesterday. A handful of stones... Come singing fresharmed from the warm places. I have looked upon thy unchanged countenance. I open the way. Come to me. Let not to the mating. I — Girding the globe, I have awakened in all of my places to receive thee. But here, here this special spot, I focus, mind the mover, in place where it all began, my bloody-handed, Paul my love, calling, back, for the last good-bye, ice kiss, fire touch, heart stop, blood still, soul freeze, embrace of world and my hate with thy fugitive body, elusive the long year now. Come into the place it has waited. I move there again, up sciatic to spine, behind*

*the frozen eyeballs, waiting and warming. To me. To me now. Throstle*
*and click, bristle and thrum. And runners scratching the snow, my heart*
*slashing parallel. Cut.*

PILGRIMAGE. He swerves, turns, slows amid the ragged
prominences – ice fallen, ice heaved – in the fields where
mountain and glacier wrestle in slow motion, to the accom-
paniment of occasional cracking and pinging sounds, crashes,
growls, and the rattle of blown ice crystals. Here the ground
is fissured as well as greatly uneven, and Paul abandons his
snowslider. He secures some tools to his belt and his pack,
anchors the sled, and commences the trek.

At first, he moves slowly and carefully, but old reflexes
return, and soon he is hurrying. Moving from dazzle to shade,
he passes among ice forms like grotesque statues of glass. The
slope is changed from the old one he remembers, but it feels
right. And deep, below, to the right...

Yes. That darker place. The canyon or blocked pass, whichever it was. That seems right, too. He alters his course slightly.
He is sweating now within his protective clothing, and his
breath comes faster as he increases his pace. His vision blurs,
and for a moment, somewhere between glare and shadow, he
seems to see...

He halts, sways a moment, then shakes his head, snorts, and
continues.

Another hundred meters and he is certain. Those rocky ribs
to the northeast, snow rivulets diamond hard between them...
He has been here before.

The stillness is almost oppressive. In the distance he sees
spumes of windblown snow jetting off and eddying down from
a high, white peak. If he stops and listens carefully, he can even
hear the far winds.

There is a hole in the middle of the clouds, directly overhead.
It is as if he were looking downward upon a lake in a crater.

More than unusual. He is tempted to turn back. His trank
has worn off, and his stomach feels unsettled. He halfwishes to
discover that this is not the place. But he knows that feelings

379

are not very important. He continues until he stands before the opening.

There has been some shifting, some narrowing of the way. He approaches slowly. He regards the passage for a full minute before he moves to enter.

He pushes back his goggles as he comes into the lessened light. He extends a gloved hand, places it upon the facing wall, pushes. Firm. He tests the one behind him. The same.

Three paces forward and the way narrows severely. He turns and sidles. The light grows dimmer, the surface beneath his feet, more slick. He slows. He slides a hand along either wall as he advances. He passes through a tiny spot of light beneath an open ice chimney. Overhead, the wind is howling a high note now, almost whistling it.

The passage begins to widen. As his right hand falls away from the more sharply angling wall, his balance is tipped in that direction. He draws back to compensate, but his left foot slides backward and falls. He attempts to rise, slips, and falls again.

Cursing, he begins to crawl forward. This area had not been slick before . . . He chuckles. Before? A century ago. Things do change in a span like that. They—

The wind begins to howl beyond the cave mouth as he sees the rise of the floor, looks upward along the slope. She is there.

He makes a small noise at the back of his throat and stops, his right hand partly raised. She wears the shadows like veils, but they do not mask her identity. He stares. It's even worse than he had thought. Trapped, she must have lived for some time after . . .

He shakes his head.

No use. She must be cut loose and buried now – disposed of.

He crawls forward. The icy slope does not grow level until he is quite near her. His gaze never leaves her form as he advances. The shadows slide over her. He can almost hear her again.

He thinks of the shadows. She couldn't have moved just then . . . He stops and studies her face. It is not frozen. It is puckered and sagging as if waterlogged. A caricature of the face he had so often touched. He grimaces and looks away. The leg must be freed. He reaches for his ax.

Before he can take hold of the tool, he sees movement of the hand, slow and shaking. It is accompanied by a throaty sigh.

'No . . .' he whispers, drawing back.

'Yes,' comes the reply.

'Glenda.'

'I am here.' Her head turns slowly. Reddened, watery eyes focus upon his own. 'I have been waiting.'

'This is insane.'

The movement of the face is horrible. It takes him some time to realize that it is a smile.

'I knew that one day you would return.'

'How?' he says. 'How have you lasted?'

'The body is nothing,' she replies. 'I had all but forgotten it. I live within the permafrost of this world. My buried foot was in contact with its filaments. It was alive, but it possessed no consciousness until we met. I live everywhere now.'

'I am – happy – that you – survived.'

She laughs slowly, dryly.

'Really, Paul? How could that be when you left me to die?'

'I had no choice, Glenda. I couldn't save you.'

'There was an opportunity. You preferred the stones to my life.'

'That's not true!'

'You didn't even try.' The arms are moving again, less jerkily now. 'You didn't even come back to recover my body.'

'What would have been the use? You were dead – or I thought you were.'

'Exactly. You didn't know, but you ran out anyway. I loved you, Paul. I would have done anything for you.'

'I cared about you, too, Glenda. I would have helped you if I could have. If—'

'*If?* Don't give me *ifs*. I know what you are.'

'I loved you,' Paul says. 'I'm sorry.'

381

'You loved me? You never said it.'

'It's not the sort of thing I talk about easily. Or think about, even.'

'Show me,' she says. 'Come here.'

He looks away. 'I can't.'

She laughs. 'You said you loved me.'

'You – you don't know how you look. I'm sorry.'

'You fool!' Her voice grows hard, imperious. 'Had you done it, I would have spared your life. It would have shown me that some tiny drop of affection might truly have existed. But you lied. You only used me. You didn't care.'

'You're being unfair!'

'Am I? Am I really?' she says. There comes a sound – running water from somewhere nearby. '*You* would speak to me of fairness? I have hated you, Paul, for nearly a century. Whenever I took a moment from regulating the life of this planet to think about it, I would curse you. In the spring as I shifted my consciousness toward the poles and allowed a part of myself to dream, my nightmares were of you. They actually upset the ecology somewhat, here and there. I have waited, and now you are here. I see nothing to redeem you. I shall use you as you used me – to your destruction. Come to me!'

He feels a force enter into his body. His muscles twitch. He is drawn up to his knees. Held in that position for long moments, then he beholds her as she also rises, drawing a soaking leg from out of the crevice where it had been held. He had heard the running water. She had somehow melted the ice . . .

She smiles and raises her pasty hands. Multitudes of dark filaments extend from her freed leg down into the crevice.

'Come!' she repeats.

'Please . . .' he says.

She shakes her head. 'Once you were so ardent. I cannot understand you.'

'If you're going to kill me, then kill me, damn it! But don't—'

Her features begin to flow. Her hands darken and grow firm.

382

In moments she stands before him looking as she did a century ago.

'Glenda!' He rises to his feet.

'Yes. Come now.'

He takes a step forward. Another.

Shortly, he holds her in his arms, leans to kiss her smiling face.

'You forgive me . . .' he says.

Her face collapses as he kisses her. Corpselike, flaccid, and pale once more, it is pressed against his own.

'No!'

He attempts to draw back, but her embrace is inhumanly strong.

'Now is not the time to stop,' she says.

'Bitch! Let me go! I hate you!'

'I know that, Paul. Hate is the only thing we have in common.'

'. . . Always hated you,' he continues, still struggling. 'You always were a bitch!'

Then he feels the cold lines of control enter his body again.

'The greater my pleasure, then,' she replies, as his hands drift forward to open her parka.

ALL OF THE ABOVE. Dorothy struggles down the icy slope, her sled parked beside Paul's. The winds lash at her, driving crystals of ice like microbullets against her struggling form. Overhead, the clouds have closed again. A curtain of white is drifting slowly in her direction.

'It waited for him,' comes Aldon's voice, above the screech of the wind.

'Yes. Is this going to be a bad one?'

'A lot depends on the winds. You should get to shelter soon, though.'

'I see a cave. I wonder whether that's the one Paul was looking for?'

'If I had to guess, I'd say yes. But right now it doesn't matter. Get there.'

When she finally reaches the entrance, she is trembling.

Several paces within she leans her back against the icy wall, panting. Then the wind changes direction and reaches her. She retreats farther into the cave.

She hears a voice: 'Please ... don't.'

'Paul?' she calls.

There is no reply. She hurries.

She puts out a hand and saves herself from falling as she comes into the chamber. There she beholds Paul in necrophiliac embrace with his captor.

'Paul! What is it?' she cries.

'Get out!' he says. 'Hurry!'

Glenda's lips form the words. 'What devotion. Rather, let her stay, if you would live.'

Paul feels her clasp loosen slightly.

'What do you mean?' he asks.

'You may have your life if you will take me away – in her body. Be with me as before.'

It is Aldon's voice that answers, 'No!' in reply. 'You can't have her, Gaia!'

'Call me Glenda. I know you. Andrew Aldon. Many times have I listened to your broadcasts. Occasionally have I struggled against you when our projects were at odds. What is this woman to you?'

'She is under my protection.'

'That means nothing. I am stronger here. Do you love her?'

'Perhaps I do. Or could.'

'Fascinating. My nemesis of all these years, with the analog of a human heart within your circuits. But the decision is Paul's. Give her to me if you would live.'

The cold rushes into his limbs. His life seems to contract to the center of his being. His consciousness begins to fade.

'Take her,' he whispers.

'I forbid it!' rings Aldon's voice.

'You have shown me again what kind of man you are,' Glenda hisses, 'my enemy. Scorn and undying hatred are all I will ever have for you. Yet you shall live.'

'I will destroy you,' Aldon calls out, 'if you do this thing!'

'What a battle that would be!' Glenda replies. 'But I've no quarrel with you here. Nor will I grant you one with me. Receive my judgment.'

Paul begins to scream. Abruptly this ceases. Glenda releases him, and he turns to stare at Dorothy. He steps in her direction.

'Don't – don't do it, Paul. Please.'

'I am – not Paul,' he replies, his voice deeper, 'and I would never hurt you . . .'

'Go now,' says Glenda. 'The weather will turn again, in your favor.'

'I don't understand,' Dorothy says, staring at the man before her.

'It is not necessary that you do,' says Glenda. 'Leave this planet quickly.'

Paul's screaming commences once again, this time emerging from Dorothy's bracelet.

'I will trouble you for that bauble you wear, however. Something about it appeals to me.'

FROZEN LEOPARD. He has tried on numerous occasions to relocate the cave, with his eyes in the sky and his robots and flyers, but the topography of the place was radically altered by a severe icequake, and he has met with no success. Periodically he bombards the general area. He also sends thermite cubes melting their ways down through the ice and the permafrost, but this has had no discernible effect.

This is the worst winter in the history of Balfrost. The winds howl constantly and waves of snow come on like surf. The glaciers have set speed records in their advance upon Playpoint. But he has held his own against them, with electricity, lasers, and chemicals. His supplies are virtually inexhaustible now, drawn from the planet itself, produced in his underground factories. He has also designed and is manufacturing more sophisticated weapons. Occasionally he hears her laughter over the missing communicator. 'Bitch!' he broadcasts then. 'Bastard!' comes the reply. He sends another missile into the mountains. A sheet of ice falls upon his city. It will be a long winter.

Andrew Aldon and Dorothy are gone. He has taken up painting, and she writes poetry now. They live in a warm place.

Sometimes Paul laughs over the broadcast band when he scores a victory. 'Bastard!' comes the immediate response.

'Bitch!' he answers, chuckling. He is never bored, however, or nervous. In fact... let it be.

When spring comes, the goddess will dream of this conflict while Paul turns his attention to his more immediate duties. But he will be planning and remembering, also. His life has a purpose to it now. And if anything, he is more efficient than Aldon. But the pods will bloom and burst despite his herbicides and fungicides. They will mutate just sufficiently to render the poisons innocuous.

'Bastard,' she will mutter sleepily.

'Bitch,' he will answer softly.

The night may have a thousand eyes and the day but one.

The heart, often, is better blind to its own workings, and I would sing of arms and the man and the wrath of the goddess, not the torment of love unsatisfied, or satisfied, in the frozen garden of our frozen world. And that, leopard, is all.

# The Doors of His Face,
# The Lamps of His Mouth

I'm a baitman. No one is born a baitman, except in a French novel where everyone is. (In fact, I think that's the title, *We are All Bait*. Pfft!) How I got that way is barely worth the telling and has nothing to do with neo-exes, but the days of the beast deserve a few words, so here they are.

The Lowlands of Venus lie between the thumb and forefinger of the continent known as Hand. When you break into Cloud Alley it swings its silverblack bowling ball toward you without a warning. You jump then, inside that firetailed tenpin they ride you down in, but the straps keep you from making a fool of yourself. You generally chuckle afterwards, but you always jump first.

Next, you study Hand to lay its illusion and the two middle fingers become dozen-ringed archipelagoes as the outers resolve into greengray peninsulas; the thumb is too short, and curls like the embryo tail of Cape Horn.

You suck pure oxygen, sigh possibly, and begin the long topple back to the Lowlands.

There, you are caught like an infield fly at the Lifeline landing area – so named because of its nearness to the great delta in the Eastern Bay – located between the first peninsula and 'thumb.' For a minute it seems as if you're going to miss Lifeline and wind up as canned seafood, but afterwards – shaking off the metaphors – you descend to scorched concrete and present your middle-sized telephone directory of authorizations to the short, fat man in the gray cap. The papers show that you are not subject to mysterious inner rottings and etcetera. He then smiles you a short, fat, gray smile and motions you toward the bus which hauls you to the Reception Area. At the R.A. you spend three days proving that, indeed, you are not subject to mysterious inner rottings and etcetera.

Boredom, however, is another rot. When your three days are up, you generally hit Lifeline hard, and it returns the compliment as a matter of reflex. The effects of alcohol in variant atmospheres is a subject on which the connoisseurs have written numerous volumes, so I will confine my remarks to noting that a good binge is worthy of at least a week's time and often warrants a lifetime study.

I had been a student of exceptional promise (strictly undergraduate) for going on two years when the *Bright Water* fell through our marble ceiling and poured its people like targets into the city.

Pause. The Worlds Almanac re Lifeline: '... Port city on the eastern coast of Hand. Employees of the Agency for Nonterrestrial Research comprise approximately 85% of its 100,000 population (2010 Census). Its other residents are primarily personnel maintained by several industrial corporations engaged in basic research. Independent marine biologists, wealthy fishing enthusiasts, and waterfront entrepreneurs make up the remainder of its inhabitants.'

I turned to Mike Dabis, a fellow entrepreneur, and commented on the lousy state of basic research.

'Not if the mumbled truth be known.'

He paused behind his glass before continuing the slow swallowing process calculated to obtain my interest and a few oaths, before he continued.

'Carl,' he finally observed, poker playing, 'they're shaping Tensquare.'

I could have hit him. I might have refilled his glass with sulfuric acid and looked on with glee as his lips blackened and cracked. Instead, I grunted a noncommittal.

'Who's fool enough to shell out fifty grand a day? ANR?'

He shook his head.

'Jean Luharich,' he said, 'the girl with the violet contacts and fifty or sixty perfect teeth. I understand her eyes are really brown.'

'Isn't she selling enough face cream these days?'

He shrugged.

'Publicity makes the wheels go 'round. Luharich Enterprise jumped sixteen points when she picked up the Sun Trophy. You ever play golf on Mercury?'

I had, but I overlooked it and continued to press.

'So she's coming here with a blank check and a fishhook?'

'*Bright Water*, today,' he nodded. 'Should be down by now. Lots of cameras. She wants an Ikky, bad.'

'Hmm,' I hmmed. 'How bad?'

'Sixty day contract. Tensquare. Indefinite extension clause. Million and a half deposit,' he recited.

'You seem to know a lot about it.'

'I'm Personnel Recruitment. Luharich Enterprises approached me last month. It helps to drink in the right places.'

'Or own them.' He smirked, after a moment.

I looked away, sipping my bitter brew. After awhile I swallowed several things and asked Mike what he expected to be asked, leaving myself open for his monthly temperance lecture.

'They told me to try getting you,' he mentioned. 'When's the last time you sailed?'

'Month and a half ago. *The Corning*.'

'Small stuff,' he snorted. 'When have you been under, yourself?'

'It's been awhile.'

'It's been over a year, hasn't it? That time you got cut by the screw, under the *Dolphin*?'

I turned to him.

'I was in the river last week, up at Angleford where the currents are strong. I can still get around.'

'Sober,' he added.

'I'd stay that way,' I said, 'on a job like this.'

A doubting nod.

'Straight union rates. Triple time for extraordinary circum-stances,' he narrated. 'Be at Hangar Sixteen with your gear, Friday morning, five hundred hours. We push off Saturday, daybreak.'

'You're sailing?'

'I'm sailing.'

'How come?'

'Money.'

'Ikky guano.'

'The bar isn't doing so well and baby needs new minks.'

'I repeat—'

'. . . And I want to get away from baby, renew my contract with basics – fresh air, exercise, make cash . . .'

'All right, sorry I asked.'

I poured him a drink, concentrating on $H_2SO_4$, but it didn't transmute. Finally I got him soused and went out into the night to walk and think things over.

Around a dozen serious attempts to land *Ichthyform Leviosaurus Levianthus*, generally known as 'Ikky', had been made over the past five years. When Ikky was first sighted, whaling techniques were employed. These proved either fruitless or disastrous, and a new procedure was inaugurated. Tensquare was constructed by a wealthy sportsman named Michael Jandt, who blew his entire roll on the project.

After a year on the Eastern Ocean, he returned to file bankruptcy. Carlton Davits, a playboy fishing enthusiast, then purchased the huge raft and laid a wake for Ikky's spawning grounds. On the nineteenth day out he had a strike and lost one hundred fifty bills' worth of untested gear, along with one *Ichthyform Levianthus*. Twelve days later, using tripled lines, he hooked, narcotized, and began to hoist the huge beast. It awakened then, destroyed a control tower, killed six men, and worked general hell over five square blocks of Tensquare. Carlton was left with partial hemiplegia and a bankruptcy suit of his own. He faded into waterfront atmosphere and Tensquare changed hands four more times, with less spectacu-lar but equally expensive results.

Finally, the big raft, built only for one purpose was purchased at an auction by ANR for 'marine research.' Lloyd's still won't insure it, and the only marine research it has ever seen is an occasional rental at fifty bills a day – to people anxious to tell Leviathan fish stories. I've been a baitman on three of the voyages, and I've been close enough to count Ikky's fangs on two occasions. I want one of them to show my grandchildren, for personal reasons.

I faced the direction of the landing area and resolved a resolve.

'You want me for local coloring, gal. It'll look nice on the feature page and all that. But clear this – If anyone gets you an Ikky, it'll be me. I promise.'

I stood in the empty Square. The foggy towers of Lifeline shared their mists.

Shoreline a couple eras ago, the western slope above Lifeline stretches as far as forty miles inland in some places. Its angle of rising is not a great one, but it achieves an elevation of several thousand feet before it meets the mountain range which separates us from the Highlands. About four miles inland and five hundred feet higher than Lifeline are set most of the surface airstrips and privately owned hangars. Hangar Sixteen houses Cal's Contract Cab, hop service, shore to ship. I do not like Cal, but he wasn't around when I climbed from the bus and waved to a mechanic.

Two of the hoppers tugged at the concrete, impatient beneath flywing haloes. The one on which Steve was working belched deep within its barrel carburetor and shuttered spasmodically.

'Bellyache?' I inquired.

'Yeah, gas pains and heartburn.'

He twisted setscrews until it settled into an even keening, and turned to me.

'You're for out?'

I nodded.

'Tensquare. Cosmetics. Monsters. Stuff like that.'

391

He blinked into the beacons and wiped his freckles. The temperature was about twenty, but the big overhead spots served a double purpose.

'Luharich,' he muttered. 'Then you are the one. There's some people want to see you.'

'What about?'

'Cameras. Microphones. Stuff like that.'

'I'd better stow my gear. Which one am I riding?'

He poked the screwdriver at the other hopper.

'That one. You're on video tape now, by the way. They wanted to get you arriving.'

He turned to the hangar, turned back.

'Say "cheese." They'll shoot the close-ups later.'

I said something other than 'cheese.' They must have been using telelens and been able to read my lips, because that part of the tape was never shown.

I threw my junk in the back, climbed into a passenger seat, and lit a cigarette. Five minutes later, Cal himself emerged from the office Quonset, looking cold. He came over and pounded on the side of the hopper. He jerked a thumb back at the hangar.

'They want you in there!' he called through cupped hands. 'Interview!'

'The show's over!' I yelled back. 'Either that, or they can get themselves another baitman!'

His rustbrown eyes became nailheads under blond brows and his glare a spike before he jerked about and stalked off. I wondered how much they had paid him to be able to squat in his hangar and suck juice from his generator.

Enough, I guess, knowing Cal. I never liked the guy, anyway.

Venus at night is a field of sable waters. On the coasts, you can never tell where the sea ends and the sky begins. Dawn is like dumping milk into an inkwell. First, there are erratic curdles of white, then streamers. Shade the bottle for a gray colloid, then watch it whiten a little more. All of a sudden you've got day. Then start heating the mixture.

I had to shed my jacket as we flashed out over the bay. To our rear, the skyline could have been under water for the way it waved and rippled in the heatfall. A hopper can accommodate four people (five, if you want to bend Regs and underestimate weight), or three passengers with the sort of gear a baitman uses. I was the only fare, though, and the pilot was like his machine. He hummed and made no unnecessary noises. Lifeline turned a somersault and evaporated in the rear mirror at about the same time Tensquare broke the fore-horizon. The pilot stopped humming and shook his head.

I leaned forward. Feelings played flopdoodle in my guts. I knew every bloody inch of the big raft, but the feelings you once took for granted change when their source is out of reach. Truthfully, I'd had my doubts I'd ever board the hulk again. But now, now I could almost believe in predestination. There it was!

A tensquare football field of a ship. A-powered. Flat as a pancake, except for the plastic blisters in the middle and the 'Rooks' fore and aft, port and starboard.

The Rook towers were named for their corner positions – and any two can work together to hoist, co-powering the graffles between them. The graffles – half gaff, half grapple – can raise enormous weights to near water level; their designer had only one thing in mind, though, which accounts for the gaff half. At water level, the Slider has to implement elevation for six to eight feet before the graffles are in a position to push upward, rather than pulling.

The Slider, essentially, is a mobile room – a big box capable of moving in any of Tensquare's crisscross groovings and 'anchoring' on the strike side by means of a powerful electromagnetic bond. Its winches could hoist a battleship the necessary distance, and the whole craft would tilt, rather than the Slider come loose, if you want any idea of the strength of that bond.

The Slider houses a section operated control indicator which is the most sophisticated 'reel' ever designed. Drawing broadcast power from the generator beside the center blister, it is connected by shortwave with the sonar room, where the movements of the quarry are recorded and repeated to the angler seated before the section control.

The fisherman might play his 'lines' for hours, days even, without seeing any more than metal and an outline on the screen. Only when the beast is graffled and the extensor shelf, located twelve feet below waterline, slides out for support and begins to aid the winches, only then does the fisherman see his catch rising before him like a fallen Seraph. Then, as Davits learned, one looks into the Abyss itself and is required to act. He didn't, and a hundred meters of unimaginable tonnage, undernarcotized and hurting, broke the cables of the winch, snapped a graffle, and took a half-minute walk across Tensquare.

We circled till the mechanical flag took notice and waved us on down. We touched beside the personnel hatch and I jettisoned my gear and jumped to the deck.

'Luck,' called the pilot as the door was sliding shut. Then he danced into the air and the flag clicked blank.

I shouldered my stuff and went below.

Signing in with Malvern, the de facto captain, I learned that most of the others wouldn't arrive for a good eight hours. They had wanted me alone at Cal's so they could pattern the pub footage along twentieth-century cinema lines.

Open: landing strip, dark. One mechanic prodding a contrary hopper. Stark-o-vision shot of slow bus pulling in. Heavily dressed baitman descends, looks about, limps across field. Close-up: he grins. Move in for words: 'Do you think this is the time? The time he *will* be landed?' Embarrassment, taciturnity, a shrug. Dub something – 'I see. And why do you think Miss Luharich has a better chance than any of the others? Is it because she's better equipped? [Grin.] Because more is known now about the creature's habits than when you were out before? Or is it because of her will to win, to be a champion? Is it any one of these things, or is it all of them?' Reply: 'Yeah, all of them.' '—Is that why you signed on with her? Because your instincts say, "This one will be it"?' Answer: 'She pays union rates. I couldn't rent that damned thing myself. And I want in.' Erase. Dub something else. Fade-out as he moves toward hopper, etcetera.

'Cheese,' I said, or something like that, and took a walk around Tensquare, by myself.

I mounted each Rook, checking out the controls and the underwater video eyes. Then I raised the main lift.

Malvern had no objections to my testing things this way. In fact, he encouraged it. We had sailed together before and our positions had even been reversed upon a time. So I wasn't surprised when I stepped off the lift into the Hopkins Locker and found him waiting. For the next ten minutes we inspected the big room in silence, walking through its copper coil chambers soon to be Arctic.

Finally, he slapped a wall.

'Well, will we find it?'

I shook my head.

'I'd like to, but I doubt it. I don't give two hoots and a damn who gets credit for the catch, so long as I have a part in it. But it won't happen. That gal's an egomaniac. She'll want to operate the Slider, and she can't.'

'You ever meet her?'

'Yeah.'

'How long ago?'

'Four, five years.'

'She was a kid then. How do you know what she can do now?'

'I know. She'll have learned every switch and reading by this time. She'll be all up on theory. But do you remember one time we were together in the starboard Rook, forward, when Ikky broke water like a porpoise?'

'Well?'

He rubbed his emery chin.

'Maybe she can do it, Carl. She's raced torch ships and she's scubaed in bad waters back home.' He glanced in the direction of invisible Hand. 'And she's hunted in the Highlands. She

395

might be wild enough to pull that horror into her lap without flinching.

'... For Johns Hopkins to foot the bill and shell out seven figures for the corpus,' he added. 'That's money, even to a Luharich.'

I ducked through a hatchway.

'Maybe you're right, but she was a rich witch when I knew her.

'And she wasn't blonde,' I added, meanly.

He yawned.

'Let's find breakfast.'

We did that.

When I was young I thought that being born a sea creature was the finest choice Nature could make for anyone. I grew up on the Pacific coast and spent my summers on the Gulf or the Mediterranean. I lived months of my life negotiating with coral, photographing trench dwellers, and playing tag with dolphins. I fished everywhere there are fish, resenting the fact that they can go places I can't. When I grew older I wanted a bigger fish, and there was nothing living that I knew of, excepting a Sequoia, that came any bigger than Ikky. That's part of it...

I jammed a couple of extra rolls into a paper bag and filled a thermos with coffee. Excusing myself, I left the gallery and made my way to the Slider berth. It was just the way I remembered it. I threw a few switches and the shortwave hummed.

'That you, Carl?'

'That's right, Mike. Let me have some juice down here, you double-crossing rat.'

He thought it over, then I felt the hull vibrate as the generators cut in. I poured my third cup of coffee and found a cigarette.

'So why am I a double-crossing rat this time?' came his voice again.

'You knew about the cameraman at Hangar Sixteen?'

'Yes.'

'Then you're a double-crossing rat. The last thing I want is publicity. "He who fouled up so often before is ready to try it, nobly, once more." I can read it now.'

'You're wrong. The spotlight's only big enough for one, and she's prettier than you.'

My next comment was cut off as I threw the elevator switch and the elephant ears flapped above me. I rose, settling flush with the deck. Retracting the lateral rail, I cut forward into the groove. Amidships, I stopped at a juncture, dropped the lateral, and retracted the longitudinal rail.

I slid starboard, midway between the Rooks, halted, and threw on the coupler.

I hadn't spilled a drop of coffee.

'Show me pictures.'

The screen glowed. I adjusted and got outlines of the bottom.

'Okay.'

I threw a Status Blue switch and he matched it. The light went on.

The winch unlocked. I aimed out over the waters, extended an arm, and fired a cast.

'Clean one,' he commented.

'Status Red. Call strike.' I threw a switch.

'Status Red.'

The baitman would be on his way with this, to make the barbs tempting.

It's not exactly a fishhook. The cables bear hollow tubes; the tubes convey enough dope for an army of hopheads; Ikky takes the bait, dandled before him by remote control, and the fisherman rams the barbs home.

My hands moved over the console, making the necessary adjustments. I checked the narco-tank reading. Empty. Good, they hadn't been filled yet. I thumbed the inject button.

'In the gullet,' Mike murmured.

I released the cables. I played the beast imagined. I let him run, swinging the winch to simulate his sweep.

I had the air conditioner on and my shirt off and it was

still uncomfortably hot, which is how I knew that morning had gone over into noon. I was dimly aware of the arrivals and departures of the hoppers. Some of the crew sat in the 'shade' of the doors I had left open, watching the operation. I didn't see Jean arrive or I would have ended the session and gotten below.

She broke my concentration by slamming the door hard enough to shake the bond.

'Mind telling me who authorized you to bring up the Slider?' she asked.

'No one,' I replied. 'I'll take it below now.'

'Just move aside.'

I did, and she took my seat. She was wearing brown slacks and a baggy shirt and she had her hair pulled back in a practical manner. Her cheeks were flushed, but not necessarily from the heat. She attacked the panel with a nearly amusing intensity that I found disquieting.

'Status Blue,' she snapped, breaking a violet fingernail on the toggle.

I forced a yawn and buttoned my shirt slowly. She threw a side glance my way, checked the registers, and fired a cast.

I monitored the lead on the screen. She turned to me for a second.

'Status Red,' she said levelly.

I nodded my agreement.

She worked the winch sideways to show she knew how. I didn't doubt she knew how and she didn't doubt that I didn't doubt, but then—

'In case you're wondering,' she said, 'you're not going to be anywhere near this thing. You were hired as a baitman, remember? Not a Slider operator! A baitman! Your duties consist of swimming out and setting the table for our friend the monster. It's dangerous, but you're getting well paid for it. Any questions?'

She squashed the Inject button and I rubbed my throat.

'Nope,' I smiled, 'but I am qualified to run that thingama-jigger – and if you need me I'll be available, at union rates.'

'Mister Davits,' she said, 'I don't want a loser operating this panel.'

'Miss Luharich, there has never been a winner at this game.'

She started reeling in the cable and broke the bond at the same time, so that the whole Slider shook as the big yo-yo returned. We skidded a couple of feet backward. She raised the laterals and we shot back along the groove. Slowing, she transferred rails and we jolted to a clanging halt, then shot off at a right angle. The crew scrambled away from the hatch as we skidded onto the elevator.

'In the future, Mister Davits, do not enter the Slider without being ordered,' she told me.

'Don't worry. I won't even step inside if I am ordered,' I answered. 'I signed on as a baitman. Remember? If you want me in here, you'll have to ask me.'

'That'll be the day,' she smiled.

I agreed, as the doors closed above us. We dropped the subject and headed in our different directions after the Slider came to a halt in its berth. She did not say 'good day,' though, which I thought showed breeding as well as determination, in reply to my chuckle.

Later that night Mike and I stoked our pipes in Malvern's cabin. The winds were shuffling waves, and a steady pattering of rain and hail overhead turned the deck into a tin roof.

'Nasty,' suggested Malvern.

I nodded. After two bourbons the room had become a familiar woodcut, with its mahogany furnishings (which I had transported from Earth long ago on a whim) and the dark walls, the seasoned face of Malvern, and the perpetually puzzled expression of Dabis set between the big pools of shadow that lay behind chairs and splashed in cornets, all cast by the tiny table light and seen through a glass, brownly.

'Glad I'm in here.'

'What's it like underneath on a night like this?'

I puffed, thinking of my light cutting through the insides of a black diamond, shaken slightly. The meteor-dart of a suddenly illuminated fish, the swaying of grotesque ferns, like nebulae – shadow, then green, then gone – swam in a moment through my mind. I guess it's like a spaceship would feel, if a spaceship could feel, crossing between worlds – and quiet, uncannily, preternaturally quiet; and peaceful as sleep.

'Dark,' I said, 'and not real choppy below a few fathoms.'

'Another eight hours and we shove off,' commented Mike.

'Ten, twelve days, we should be there,' noted Malvern.

'What do you think Ikky's doing?'

'Sleeping on the bottom with Mrs Ikky if he has any brains.'

'He hasn't. I've seen ANR's skeletal extrapolation from the bones that have washed up—'

'Hasn't everyone?'

'. . . Fully fleshed, he'd be over a hundred meters long. That right, Carl?'

I agreed.

'. . . Not much of a brain box, though, for his bulk.'

'Smart enough to stay out of our locker.'

Chuckles, because nothing exists but this room, really. The world outside is an empty, sleet drummed deck. We lean back and make clouds.

'Boss lady does not approve of unauthorized fly fishing.'

'Boss lady can walk north till her hat floats.'

'What did she say in there?'

'She told me that my place, with fish manure, is on the bottom.'

'You don't Slide?'

'I bait.'

'We'll see.'

'That's all I do. If she wants a Slideman she's going to have to ask nicely.'

'You think she'll have to?'

'I think she'll have to.'

'And if she does, can you do it?'

'A fair question,' I puffed. 'I don't know the answer, though.'

I'd incorporate my soul and trade forty percent of the stock for the answer. I'd give a couple years off my life for the answer.

But there doesn't seem to be a lineup of supernatural takers, because no one knows. Supposing when we get out there, luck being with us, we find ourselves an Ikky? Supposing we succeed in baiting him and get lines on him. What then? If we get him shipside, will she hold on or crack up? What if she's made of sterner stuff than Davits, who used to hunt sharks with poison-darted air pistols? Supposing she lands him and Davits has to stand there like a video extra.

Worse yet, supposing she asks for Davits and he still stands there like a video extra or something else – say, some yellow-bellied embodiment named Cringe?

It was when I got him up above the eight-foot horizon of steel and looked out at all that body, sloping on and on till it dropped out of sight like a green mountain range . . . And that head. Small for the body, but still immense. Fat, craggy, with lidless roulettes that had spun black and red since before my forefathers decided to try the New Continent. And swaying.

Fresh narco-tanks had been connected. It needed another shot, fast. But I was paralyzed.

It had made a noise like God playing a Hammond organ . . .

*And looked at me!*

I don't know if seeing is even the same process in eyes like those. I doubt it. Maybe I was just a gray blur behind a black rock, with the plexi-reflected sky hurting its pupils. But it fixed on me. Perhaps the snake doesn't really paralyze the rabbit, perhaps it's just that rabbits are cowards by constitution. But it began to struggle and I still couldn't move, fascinated.

Fascinated by all that power, by those eyes, they found me there fifteen minutes later, a little broken about the head and shoulders, the Inject still unpushed.

And I dream about those eyes. I want to face them once more, even if their finding takes forever. I've got to know if there's something inside me that sets me apart from a rabbit, from notched plates of reflexes and instincts that always fall apart in exactly the same way whenever the proper combination is spun.

Looking down, I noticed that my hand was shaking. Glancing up, I noticed that no one else was noticing.

I finished my drink and emptied my pipe. It was late and no songbirds were singing.

I sat whittling, my legs hanging over the aft edge, the chips spinning down into the furrow of our wake. Three days out. No action.

'You!'

'Me?'

'You.'

Hair like the end of the rainbow, eyes like nothing in nature, fine teeth.

'Hello.'

'There's a safety regulation against what you're doing, you know.'

'I know. I've been worrying about it all morning.'

A delicate curl climbed my knife then drifted out behind us. It settled into the foam and was plowed under. I watched her reflection in my blade, taking a secret pleasure in its distortion.

'Are you baiting me?' she finally asked.

I heard her laugh then, and turned, knowing it had been intentional.

'What, me?'

'I could push you off from here, very easily.'

'I'd make it back.'

'Would you push me off, then – some dark night, perhaps?'

'They're all dark, Miss Luharich. No, I'd rather make you a gift of my carving.'

She seated herself beside me then, and I couldn't help but notice the dimples in her knees. She wore white shorts and a halter and still had an offworld tan to her which was awfully appealing. I almost felt a twinge of guilt at having planned the whole scene, but my right hand still blocked her view of the wooden animal.

'Okay, I'll bite. What have you got for me?'

'Just a second. It's almost finished.'

Solemnly, I passed her the little wooden jackass I had been carving. I felt a little sorry and slightly jackass-ish myself, but I had to follow through. I always do. The mouth was split into a braying grin. The ears were upright.

She didn't smile and she didn't frown. She just studied it.

'It's very good,' she finally said, 'like most things you do – and appropriate, perhaps.'

'Give it to me.' I extended a palm.

She handed it back and I tossed it out over the water. It missed the white water and bobbed for awhile like a pigmy seahorse.

'Why did you do that?'

'It was a poor joke. I'm sorry.'

'Maybe you are right, though. Perhaps this time I've bitten off a little too much.'

I snorted.

'Then why not do something safer, like another race?'

She shook her end of the rainbow.

'No. It has to be an Ikky.'

'Why?'

'Why did you want one so badly that you threw away a fortune?'

'Many reasons,' I said. 'An unfrocked analyst who held black therapy sessions in his basement once told me, "Mister Davits, you need to reinforce the image of your masculinity by catching one of every kind of fish in existence." Fish are a very ancient masculinity symbol, you know. So I set out to do it. I have one more to go. —Why do you want to reinforce your masculinity?'

'I don't,' she said. 'I don't want to reinforce anything but Luharich Enterprises. My chief statistician once said, "Miss Luharich, sell all the cold cream and face powder in the System and you'll be a happy girl. Rich, too." And he was right. I am the proof. I can look the way I do and do anything, and I sell most of the lipstick and face powder in the System – but I have to be *able* to do anything.'

'You do look cool and efficient,' I observed.

'I don't feel cool,' she said, rising. 'Let's go for a swim.'

'May I point out that we're making pretty good time?'

'If you want to indicate the obvious, you may. You said you could make it back to the ship, unassisted. Change your mind?'

'No.'

'Then get us two scuba outfits and I'll race you under Tensquare.

'I'll win, too,' she added.

I stood and looked down at her, because that usually makes me feel superior to women.

'Daughter of Lir, eyes of Picasso,' I said, 'you've got yourself a race. Meet me at the forward Rook, starboard, in ten minutes.'

'Ten minutes,' she agreed.

And ten minutes it was. From the center blister to the Rook took maybe two of them, with the load I was carrying. My sandals grew very hot and I was glad to shuck them for flippers when I reached the comparative cool of the corner.

We slid into harnesses and adjusted our gear. She had changed into a trim one-piece green job that made me shade my eyes and look away, then look back again.

I fastened a rope ladder and kicked it over the side. Then I pounded on the wall of the Rook.

'Yeah?'

'You talk to the port Rook, aft?' I called.

'They're all set up,' came the answer. 'There's ladders and draglines all over that end.'

'You sure you want to do this?' asked the sunburnt little gink who was her publicity man, Anderson yclept.

He sat beside the Rook in a deckchair, sipping lemonade through a straw.

'It might be dangerous,' he observed, sunken-mouthed. (His teeth were beside him, in another glass.)

'That's right,' she smiled. 'It *will* be dangerous. Not overly, though.'

'Then why don't you let me get some pictures? We'd have

them back to Lifeline in an hour. They'd be in New York by tonight. Good copy.'

'No,' she said, and turned away from both of us.

'Here, keep these for me.'

She passed him a box full of her unseeing, and when she turned back to me they were the same brown that I remembered.

'Ready?'

'No,' I said, tautly. 'Listen carefully, Jean. If you're going to play this game there are a few rules. First,' I counted, 'we're going to be directly beneath the hull, so we have to start low and keep moving. If we bump the bottom, we could rupture an air tank...'

She began to protest that any moron knew that and I cut her down.

'Second,' I went on, 'there won't be much light, so we'll stay close together, and we will both carry torches.'

Her wet eyes flashed.

'I dragged you out of Govino without—'

Then she stopped and turned away. She picked up a lamp.

'Okay. Torches. Sorry.'

'...And watch out for the drive-screws,' I finished. 'There'll be strong currents for at least fifty meters behind them.'

She wiped her eyes and adjusted the mask.

'All right, let's go.'

We went.

She led the way, at my insistence. The surface layer was pleasantly warm. At two fathoms the water was bracing; at five it was nice and cold. At eight we let go the swinging stairway and struck out. Tensquare sped forward and we raced in the opposite direction, tattooing the hull yellow at ten-second intervals.

The hull stayed where it belonged, but we raced on like two darkside satellites. Periodically, I tickled her frog feet with my light and traced her antennae of bubbles. About a five meter lead was fine; I'd beat her in the home stretch, but I couldn't let her drop behind yet.

Beneath us, black. Immense. Deep. The Mindanao of Venus, where eternity might eventually pass the dead to a rest in cities of unnamed fishes. I twisted my head away and touched the hull with a feeler of light; it told me we were about a quarter of the way along.

I increased my beat to match her stepped-up stroke, and narrowed the distance which she had suddenly opened by a couple of meters. She sped up again and I did, too. I spotted her with my beam.

She turned and it caught on her mask. I never knew whether she'd been smiling. Probably. She raised two fingers in a V-for-Victory and then cut ahead at full speed.

I should have known. I should have felt it coming. It was just a race to her, something else to win. Damn the torpedos!

So I leaned into it, hard. I don't shake in the water. Or, if I do it doesn't matter and I don't notice it. I began to close the gap again.

She looked back, sped on, looked back. Each time she looked it was nearer, until I'd narrowed it down to the original five meters.

Then she hit the jatoes.

That's what I had been fearing. We were about half-way under and she shouldn't have done it. The powerful jets of compressed air could easily rocket her upward into the hull, or tear something loose if she allowed her body to twist. Their main use is in tearing free from marine plants or fighting bad currents. I had wanted them along as a safety measure, because of the big suck-and-pull windmills behind.

She shot ahead like a meteorite, and I could feel a sudden tingle of perspiration leaping to meet and mix with the churning waters.

I swept ahead, not wanting to use my own guns, and she tripled, quadrupled the margin.

The jets died and she was still on course. Okay, I was an old fuddyduddy. She *could* have messed up and headed toward the top.

I plowed the sea and began to gather back my yardage, a

foot at a time. I wouldn't be able to catch her or beat her now, but I'd be on the ropes before she hit deck.

Then the spinning magnets began their insistence and she wavered. It was an awfully powerful drag, even at this distance. The call of the meat grinder.

I'd been scratched up by one once, under the *Dolphin*, a fishing boat of the middle-class. I *had* been drinking, but it was also a rough day, and the thing had been turned on prematurely. Fortunately, it was turned off in time, also, and a tendon-stapler made everything good as new, except in the log, where it only mentioned that I'd been drinking. Nothing about it being off-hours when I had the right to do as I damn well pleased.

She had slowed to half her speed, but she was still moving cross-wise, toward the port, aft corner. I began to feel the pull myself and had to slow down. She'd made it past the main one, but she seemed too far back. It's hard to gauge distances under water, but each red beat of time told me I was right. She was out of danger from the main one, but the smaller port screw, located about eighty meters in, was no longer a threat but a certainty.

She had turned and was pulling away from it now. Twenty meters separated us. She was standing still. Fifteen.

Slowly, she began a backward drifting. I hit my jatoes, aiming two meters behind her and about twenty back of the blades.

Straightline! Thankgod! Catching, softbelly, leadpipe on shoulder SWIMLIKEHELL! maskcracked, not broke though AND UP!

We caught a line and I remember brandy.

Into the cradle endlessly rocking I spit, pacing. Insomnia tonight and left shoulder sore again, so let it rain on me – they can cure rheumatism. Stupid as hell. What I said. In blankets and shivering. She: 'Carl, I can't say it.' Me: 'Then call it square for that night in Govino, Miss Luharich. Huh?' She: nothing. Me: 'Any more of that brandy?' She: 'Give me another, too.' Me: sounds of sipping. It had only lasted three months. No alimony. Many $ on both sides. Not sure whether they were happy or not. Wine-dark Aegean. Good fishing. Maybe he should have spent more time on shore. Or perhaps she shouldn't have. Good swimmer, though. Dragged him all the way to Vido to wring out his lungs. Young. Both. Strong. Both. Rich and spoiled as Hell. Ditto. Corfu should have brought them closer. Didn't. I think that mental cruelty was a trout. He wanted to go to Canada. She: 'Go to hell if you want!' He: 'Will you go along?' She: 'No.' But she did, anyhow. Many hells. Expensive. He lost a monster or two. She inherited a couple. Lot of lightning tonight. Stupid as hell. Civility's the coffin of a conned soul. By whom? —Sounds like a bloody neo-ex ... But I hate you, Anderson, with your glass full of teeth and her new eyes ... Can't keep this pipe lit, keep sucking tobacco. Spit again!

Seven days out and the scope showed Ikky.

Bells jangled, feet pounded, and some optimist set the thermostat in the Hopkins. Malvern wanted me to sit it out, but I slipped into my harness and waited for whatever came. The bruise looked worse than it felt. I had exercised every day and the shoulder hadn't stiffened on me.

A thousand meters ahead and thirty fathoms deep, it tunneled our path. Nothing showed on the surface.

'Will we chase him?' asked an excited crewman.

'Not unless she feels like using money for fuel.' I shrugged.

Soon the scope was clear, and it stayed that way. We remained on alert and held our course.

I hadn't said over a dozen words to my boss since the last time we went drowning together, so I decided to raise the score.

'Good afternoon,' I approached. 'What's new?'

'He's going north-northeast. We'll have to let this one go. A few more days and we can afford some chasing. Not yet.'

*Sleek head* ...

I nodded. 'No telling where this one's headed.'

'How's your shoulder?'

'All right. How about you?'

*Daughter of Lir . . .*

'Fine. By the way, you're down for a nice bonus.'

*Eyes of perdition!*

'Don't mention it,' I told her back.

Later that afternoon, and appropriately, a storm shattered. (I prefer 'shattered' to 'broke.' It gives a more accurate idea of the behavior of tropical storms on Venus and saves a lot of words.) Remember that inkwell I mentioned earlier? Now take it between thumb and forefinger and hit its side with a hammer. Watch yourself! Don't get splashed or cut—

Dry, then drenched. The sky one million bright fractures as the hammer falls. And sounds of breaking.

'Everyone below?' suggested the loudspeakers to the already scurrying crew.

Where was I? Who do you think was doing the loudspeaking?

Everything loose went overboard when the water got to walking, but by then no people were loose. The Slider was the first thing below decks. Then the big lifts lowered their shacks.

I had hit it for the nearest Rook with a yell the moment I recognized the pre-brightening of the holocaust. From there I cut in the speakers and spent half a minute coaching the track team.

Minor injuries had occurred, Mike told me over the radio, but nothing serious. I, however, was marooned for the duration. The Rooks do not lead anywhere; they're set too far out over the hull to provide entry downwards, what with the extensor shelves below.

So I undressed myself of the tanks which I had worn for the past several hours, crossed my flippers on the table, and leaned back to watch the hurricane. The top was black as the bottom and we were in between, and somewhat illuminated because of all that flat, shiny space. The waters didn't rain down – they just sort of got together and dropped.

The Rooks were secure enough – they'd weathered any number of these onslaughts – it's just that their positions gave them a greater arc of rise and descent when Tensquare makes like the rocker of a very nervous grandma. I had used the belts from my rig to strap myself into the bolted-down chair, and I removed several years in purgatory from the soul of whoever left a pack of cigarettes in the table drawer.

I watched the water make teepees and mountains and hands and trees until I started seeing faces and people. So I called Mike.

'What are you doing down there?'

'Wondering what you're doing up there,' he replied. 'What's it like?'

'You're from the Midwest, aren't you?'

'Yeah.'

'Get bad storms out there?'

'Sometimes.'

'Try to think of the worst one you were ever in. Got a slide rule handy?'

'Right here.'

'Then put a one under it, imagine a zero or two following after, and multiply the thing out.'

'I can't imagine the zeros.'

'Then retain the multiplicand – that's all you can do.'

'So what are you doing up there?'

'I've strapped myself in the chair. I'm watching things roll around the floor right now.'

I looked up and out again. I saw one darker shadow in the forest.

'Are you praying or swearing?'

'Damned if I know. But if this were the Slider – if only this were the Slider!'

*'He's out there?'*

I nodded, forgetting that he couldn't see me.

Big, as I remembered him. He'd only broken surface for a few moments, to look around. *There is no power on Earth that can be compared with him who was made to fear no one.* I dropped my cigarette. It was the same as before. Paralysis and an unborn scream.

410

'You all right, Carl?'

He had looked at me again. Or seemed to. Perhaps that mindless brute had been waiting half a millennium to ruin the life of a member of the most highly developed species in business...

'You okay?'

... Or perhaps it had been ruined already, long before their encounter, and theirs was just a meeting of beasts, the stronger bumping the weaker aside, body to psyche...

'Carl, dammit! Say something!'

He broke again, this time nearer. Did you ever see the trunk of a tornado? It seems like something alive, moving around in all that dark. Nothing has a right to be so big, so strong, and moving. It's a sickening sensation.

'Please answer me.'

He was gone and did not come back that day. I finally made a couple of wisecracks at Mike, but I held my next cigarette in my right hand.

The next seventy or eighty thousand waves broke by with a monotonous similarity. The five days that held them were also without distinction. The morning of the thirteenth day out, though, our luck began to rise. The bells broke our coffee-drenched lethargy into small pieces, and we dashed from the gallery without hearing what might have been Mike's finest punchline.

'Aft!' cried someone. 'Five hundred meters!'

I stripped to my trunks and started buckling. My stuff is always within grabbing distance.

I flipflopped across the deck, girding myself with a deflated squiggler.

'Five hundred meters, twenty fathoms!' boomed the speakers.

The big traps banged upward and the Slider grew to its full height, m'lady at the console. It rattled past me and took root ahead. Its one arm rose and lengthened.

I breasted the Slider as the speakers called, 'Four-eight, twenty!'

'Status Red!'

A belch like an emerging champagne cork and the line arced high over the waters.

'Four-eight, twenty!' it repeated, all Malvern and static. 'Baitman, attend!'

I adjusted my mask and hand-over-handed it down the side. Then warm, then cool, then away.

Green, vast, down. Fast. This is the place where I am equal to a squiggler. If something big decides a baitman looks tastier than what he's carrying, then irony colors his title as well as the water about it.

I caught sight of the drifting cables and followed them down. Green to dark green to black. It had been a long cast, too long. I'd never had to follow one this far down before. I didn't want to switch on my torch.

But I had to.

Bad! I still had a long way to go. I clenched my teeth and stuffed my imagination into a straightjacket.

Finally the line came to an end.

I wrapped one arm about it and unfastened the squiggler. I attached it, working as fast as I could, and plugged in the little insulated connections which are the reason it can't be fired with the line. Ikky could break them, but by then it wouldn't matter.

My mechanical eel hooked up, I pulled its section plugs and watched it grow. I had been dragged deeper during this operation, which took about a minute and a half. I was near – too near – to where I never wanted to be.

Loathe as I had been to turn on my light, I was suddenly afraid to turn it off. Panic gripped me and I seized the cable with both hands. The squiggler began to glow, pinkly. It started to twist. It was twice as big as I am and doubtless twice as attractive to pink squiggler-eaters. I told myself this until I believed it, then I switched off my light and started up.

If I bumped into something enormous and steel-hided my heart had orders to stop beating immediately and release me – to dart fitfully forever along Acheron, and gibbering.

Ungibbering, I made it to green water and fled back to the nest.

As soon as they hauled me aboard I made my mask a necklace, shaded my eyes, and monitored for surface turbulence. My first question, of course, was 'Where is he?'

'Nowhere,' said a crewman; 'we lost him right after you went over. Can't pick him up on the scope now. Musta dived.'

'Too bad.'

The squiggler stayed down, enjoying its bath. My job ended for the time being, I headed back to warm my coffee with rum.

From behind me, a whisper: 'Could you laugh like that afterwards?'

Perceptive Answer: 'Depends on what he's laughing at.'

Still chuckling, I made my way into the center blister with two cupfuls.

'Still hell and gone?'

Mike nodded. His big hands were shaking, and mine were steady as a surgeon's when I set down the cups.

He jumped as I shrugged off the tanks and looked for a bench.

'Don't drip on that panel! You want to kill yourself and blow expensive fuses?'

I toweled down, then settled down to watching the unfilled eye on the wall. I yawned happily; my shoulder seemed good as new.

The little box that people talk through wanted to say something, so Mike lifted the switch and told it to go ahead.

'Is Carl there, Mister Dabis?'

'Yes, ma'am.'

'Then let me talk to him.'

Mike motioned and I moved.

'Talk,' I said.

'Are you all right?'

'Yes, thanks. Shouldn't I be?'

'That was a long swim. I – I guess I overshot my cast.'

'I'm happy,' I said. 'More triple-time for me. I really clean up on that hazardous duty clause.'

'I'll be more careful next time,' she apologized. 'I guess I was too eager. Sorry—' Something happened to the sentence, so she ended it there, leaving me with half a bagful of replies I'd been saving.

I lifted the cigarette from behind Mike's ear and got a light from the one in the ashtray.

'Carl, she was being nice,' he said, after turning to study the panels.

'I know,' I told him. 'I wasn't.'

'I mean, she's an awfully pretty kid, pleasant. Headstrong and all that. But what's she done to you?'

'Lately?' I asked.

He looked at me, then dropped his eyes to his cup.

'I know it's none of my bus—' he began.

'Cream and sugar?'

Ikky didn't return that day, or that night. We picked up some Dixieland out of Lifeline and let the muskrat ramble while Jean had her supper sent to the Slider. Later she had a bunk assembled inside. I piped in 'Deep Water Blues' when it came over the air and waited for her to call up and cuss us out. She didn't though, so I decided she was sleeping.

Then I got Mike interested in a game of chess that went on until daylight. It limited conversation to several 'checks,' one 'checkmate,' and a 'damn!' Since he's a poor loser it also effectively sabotaged subsequent talk, which was fine with me. I had a steak and fried potatoes for breakfast and went to bed.

Ten hours later someone shook me awake and I propped myself on one elbow, refusing to open my eyes.

'Whassamadder?'

'I'm sorry to get you up,' said one of the younger crewmen, 'but Miss Luharich wants you to disconnect the squiggler so we can move on.'

I knuckled open one eye, still deciding whether I should be amused.

'Have it hauled to the side. Anyone can disconnect it.'

'It's at the side now, sir. But she said it's in your contract and we'd better do things right.'

'That's very considerate of her. I'm sure my Local appreciates her remembering.'

'Uh, she also said to tell you to change your trunks and comb your hair, and shave, too. Mister Anderson's going to film it.'

'Okay. Run along; tell her I'm on my way – and ask if she has some toenail polish I can borrow.'

I'll save on details. It took three minutes in all, and I played it properly, even pardoning myself when I slipped and bumped into Anderson's white tropicals with the wet squiggler. He smiled, brushed it off; she smiled, even though Luharich Complectacolor couldn't completely mask the dark circles under her eyes; and I smiled, waving to all our fans out there in videoland. —Remember, Mrs Universe, you, too, can look like a monster-catcher. Just use Luharich face cream.

I went below and made myself a tuna sandwich, with mayonnaise.

Two days like icebergs – bleak, blank, half-melting, all frigid, mainly out of sight, and definitely a threat to peace of mind – drifted by and were good to put behind. I experienced some old guilt feelings and had a few disturbing dreams. Then I called Lifeline and checked my bank balance.

'Going shopping?' asked Mike, who had put the call through for me.

'Going home,' I answered.

'Huh?'

'I'm out of the baiting business after this one, Mike. The Devil with Ikky! The Devil with Venus and Luharich Enterprises! And the Devil with you!'

Up eyebrows.

'What brought that on?'

'I waited over a year for this job. Now that I'm here, I've decided the whole thing stinks.'

'You knew what it was when you signed on. No matter what

415

else you're doing, you're selling face cream when you work for face cream sellers.'

'Oh, that's not what's biting me. I admit the commercial angle irritates me, but Tensquare has always been a publicity spot, ever since the first time it sailed.'

'What, then?'

'Five or six things, all added up. The main one being that I don't care any more. Once it meant more to me than anything else to hook that critter, and now it doesn't. I went broke on what started out as a lark and I wanted blood for what it had cost me. Now I realize that maybe I had it coming. I'm beginning to feel sorry for Ikky.'

'And you don't want him now?'

'I'll take him if he comes peacefully, but I don't feel like sticking out my neck to make him crawl into the Hopkins.'

'I'm inclined to think it's one of the four or five other things you said you added.'

'Such as?'

He scrutinized the ceiling.

I growled.

'Okay, but I won't say it, not just to make you happy you guessed right.'

He, smirking: 'That look she wears isn't just for Ikky.'

'No good, no good.' I shook my head. 'We're both fission chambers by nature. You can't have jets on both ends of the rocket and expect to go anywhere – what's in the middle just gets smashed.'

'That's how it *was*. None of my business, of course—'

'Say that again and you'll say it without teeth.'

'Any day, big man' – he looked up – 'any place ...'

'So go ahead. Get it said!'

'She doesn't care about that bloody reptile, she came here to drag you back where you belong. You're not the baitman this trip.'

'Five years is too long.'

'There must be something under that cruddy hide of yours that people like,' he muttered, 'or I wouldn't be talking like this.

Maybe you remind us humans of some really ugly dog we felt sorry for when we were kids. Anyhow, someone wants to take you home and raise you – also, something about beggars not getting menus.'

'Buddy,' I chuckled, 'do you know what I'm going to do when I hit Lifeline?'

'I can guess.'

'You're wrong. I'm torching it to Mars, and then I'll cruise back home, first class. Venus bankruptcy provisions do not apply to Martian trust funds, and I've still got a wad tucked away where moth and corruption enter not. I'm going to pick up a big old mansion on the Gulf and if you're ever looking for a job you can stop around and open bottles for me.'

'You are a yellowbellied fink,' he commented.

'Okay,' I admitted, 'but it's her I'm thinking of, too.'

'I've heard the stories about you both,' he said. 'So you're a heel and a goofoff and she's a bitch. That's called compatibility these days. I dare you, baitman, try keeping something you catch.'

I turned.

'If you ever want that job, look me up.'

I closed the door quietly behind me and left him sitting there waiting for it to slam.

The day of the beast dawned like any other. Two days after my gutless flight from empty waters I went down to rebait. Nothing on the scope. I was just making things ready for the routine attempt.

I hollered a 'good morning' from outside the Slider and received an answer from inside before I pushed off. I had re-appraised Mike's words, sans sound, sans fury, and while I did not approve of their sentiment or significance, I had opted for civility anyhow.

So down, under, and away. I followed a decent cast about two hundred-ninety meters out. The snaking cables burned black to my left and I paced their undulations from the yellow-green down into the darkness. Soundless lay the wet night, and

I bent my way through it like a cock-eyed comet, bright tail before.

I caught the line, slick and smooth, and began baiting. An icy world swept by me then, ankles to head. It was a draft, as if someone had opened a big door beneath me. I wasn't drifting forwards that fast either.

Which meant that something might be moving up, something big enough to displace a lot of water. I still didn't think it was Ikky. A freak current of some sort, but not Ikky. Ha!

I had finished attaching the leads and pulled the first plug when a big, rugged, black island grew beneath me ...

I flicked the beam downward. His mouth was opened.

I was rabbit.

Waves of the death-fear passed downward. My stomach imploded. I grew dizzy.

Only one thing, and one thing only. Left to do. I managed it, finally. I pulled the rest of the plugs.

I could count the scaly articulations ridging his eyes by then.

The squiggler grew, pinked into phosphorescence ... squiggled.

Then my lamp. I had to kill it, leaving just the bait before him.

One glance back as I jammed the jatoes to life.

He was so near that the squiggler reflected on his teeth, in his eyes. Four meters, and I kissed his lambent jowls with two jets of backwash as I soared. Then I didn't know whether he was following or had halted. I began to black out as I waited to be eaten.

The jatoes died and I kicked weakly.

Too fast, I felt a cramp coming on. One flick of the beam, cried rabbit. One second, to know ...

Or end things up, I answered. No, rabbit, we don't dart before hunters. Stay dark.

Green waters, finally, to yellowgreen, then top.

Doubling, I beat off toward Tensquare. The waves from the explosion behind pushed me on ahead. The world closed in, and a screamed 'He's alive!' in the distance.

A giant shadow and a shock wave. The line was alive, too. Happy Fishing Grounds. Maybe I did something wrong...

Somewhere Hand was clenched. What's bait?

A few million years. I remember starting out as a one-celled organism and painfully becoming an amphibian, then an air-breather. From somewhere high in the treetops I heard a voice.

'He's coming around.'

I evolved back into homosapience, then a step further into a hangover.

'Don't try to get up yet.'

'Have we got him?' I slurred.

'Still fighting, but he's hooked. We thought he took you for an appetizer.'

'So did I.'

'Breathe some of this and shut up.'

A funnel over my face. Good. Lift your cups and drink...

'He was awfully deep. Below scope range. We didn't catch him till he started up. Too late, then.'

I began to yawn.

'We'll get you inside now.'

I managed to uncase my ankle knife.

'Try it and you'll be minus a thumb.'

'You need rest.'

'Then bring me a couple more blankets. I'm staying.'

I fell back and closed my eyes.

Someone was shaking me. Gloom and cold. Spotlights bled yellow on the deck. I was in a jury-rigged bunk, bulked against the center blister. Swaddled in wool, I still shivered.

'It's been eleven hours. You're not going to see anything now.'

I tasted blood.

'Drink this.'

Water. I had a remark but I couldn't mouth it.

'Don't ask me how I feel,' I croaked. 'I know that comes next, but don't ask me. Okay?'

'Okay. Want to go below now?'

'No. Just get me my jacket.'

'Right here.'

'What's he doing?'

'Nothing. He's deep, he's doped but he's staying down.'

'How long since last time he showed?'

'Two hours, about.'

'Jean?'

'She won't let anyone in the Slider. Listen, Mike says to come on in. He's right behind you in the blister.'

I sat up and turned around. Mike was watching. He gestured; I gestured back.

I swung my feet over the edge and took a couple of deep breaths. Pains in my stomach. I got to my feet and made it into the blister.

'Howza gut?' queried Mike.

I checked the scope. No Ikky. Too deep.

'You buying?'

'Yeah, coffee.'

'Not coffee.'

'You're ill. Also, coffee is all that's allowed in here.'

'Coffee is a brownish liquid that burns your stomach. You have some in the bottom drawer.'

'No cups. You'll have to use a glass.'

'Tough.'

He poured.

'You do that well. Been practicing for that job?'

'What job?'

'The one I offered you—'

A blot on the scope!

'Rising, ma'am! Rising!' he yelled into the box.

'Thanks, Mike. I've got it in here,' she crackled.

'Jean!'

'Shut up! She's busy!'

'Was that Carl?'

'Yeah,' I called. 'Talk later,' and I cut it.

Why did I do that?

'Why did you do that?'

I didn't know.

'I don't know.'

Damned echoes! I got up and walked outside.

Nothing. Nothing.

Something?

Tensquare actually rocked! He must have turned when he saw the hull and started downward again. White water to my left, and boiling. An endless spaghetti of cable roared hotly into the belly of the deep.

I stood awhile, then turned and went back inside.

Two hours sick. Four, and better.

'The dope's getting to him.'

'Yeah.'

'What about Miss Luharich?'

'What about her?'

'She must be half dead.'

'Probably.'

'What are you going to do about it?'

'She signed the contract for this. She knew what might happen. It did.'

'I think you could land him.'

'So do I.'

'So does she.'

'Then let her ask me.'

Ikky was drifting lethargically, at thirty fathoms.

I took another walk and happened to pass behind the Slider. She wasn't looking my way.

'Carl, come in here!'

Eyes of Picasso, that's what, and a conspiracy to make me Slide...

'Is that an order?'

'Yes – No! Please.'

I dashed inside and monitored. He was rising.

'Push or pull?'

I slammed the 'wind' and he came like a kitten.

'Make up your own mind now.'

He balked at ten fathoms.

'Play him?'

'No!'

She wound him upwards – five fathoms, four . . .

She hit the extensors at two, and the caught him. Then the graffles.

Cries without and a heat of lightning of flashbulbs.

The crew saw Ikky.

He began to struggle. She kept the cables tight, raised the graffles.

Up.

Another two feet and the graffles began pulsing.

Screams and fast footfalls.

Giant beanstalk in the wind, his neck, waving. The green hills of his shoulders grew.

'He's big, Carl!' she cried.

And he grew, and grew, and grew uneasy . . .

*'Now!'*

He looked down.

He looked down, as the god of our most ancient ancestors might have looked down. Fear, shame, and mocking laughter rang in my head. Her head, too?

'Now!'

She looked up at the nascent earthquake.

'I can't!'

It was going to be so damnably simple this time, now the rabbit had died. I reached out.

I stopped.

'Push it yourself.'

'I can't. You do it. Land him, Carl!'

'No. If I do, you'll wonder for the rest of your life whether you could have. You'll throw away your soul finding out. I know you will, because we're alike, and I did it that way. Find out now!'

She stared.

I gripped her shoulders.

'Could be that's me out there,' I offered. 'I am a green sea

422

serpent, a hateful, monstrous beast, and out to destroy you. I am answerable to no one. Push the Inject.'

Her hand moved to the button, jerked back.

'Now!'

She pushed it.

I lowered her still form to the floor and finished things up with Ikky.

It was a good seven hours before I awakened to the steady, sea-chewing grind of Tensquare's blades.

'You're sick,' commented Mike.

'How's Jean?'

'The same.'

'Where's the beast?'

'Here.'

'Good.' I rolled over. '... Didn't get away this time.'

So that's the way it was. No one is born a baitman, I don't think, but the rings of Saturn sing epithalamium the sea-beast's dower.

# The Great Slow Kings

Drax and Dran sat in the great Throne Hall of Glan, discussing life. Monarchs by virtue of superior intellect and physique – and the fact that they were the last two survivors of the race of Glan – theirs was a divided rule over the planet and their one subject, Zindrome, the palace robot.

Drax had been musing for the past four centuries (theirs was a sluggish sort) over the possibility of life on other planets in the galaxy.

Accordingly, 'Dran,' said he, addressing the other (who was becoming mildly curious as to his thoughts), 'Dran, I've been thinking: There may be life on other planets in the galaxy.'

Dran considered his reply to this, as the world wheeled several times about its sun.

'True,' he finally agreed, 'there may.'

After several months, Drax shot back, 'If there is, we ought to find out.'

'Why?' asked Dran with equal promptness, which caused the other to suspect that he, too, had been thinking along these lines.

So he measured his next statement out cautiously, first testing each word within the plated retort of his reptilian skull.

'Our kingdom is rather underpopulated at present,' he observed. 'It would be good to have many subjects once more.'

Dran regarded him askance, then slowly turned his head. He closed one eye and half-closed the other, taking full stock of his co-ruler, whose appearance, as he suspected, was unchanged since the last time he had looked.

'That, also, is true,' he noted. 'What do you suggest we do?'

This time Drax turned, reappraising him, eye to eye.

'I think we ought to find out if there is life on other planets in the galaxy.'

'Hmm.'

Two quick roundings of the seasons went unnoticed, then, 'Let me think about it,' he said, and turned away.

After what he deemed a polite period of time, Drax coughed.

'Have you thought sufficiently?'

'No.'

Drax struggled to focus his eyes on the near-subliminal streak of bluish light which traversed, re-traversed and re-re-traversed the Hall as he waited.

'Zindrome!' he finally called out.

The robot slowed his movements to a statue-like immobility to accommodate his master. A feather duster protruded from his right limb.

'You called, great Lord of Glan?'

'Yes, Zindrome, worthy subject. Those old spaceships which we constructed in happier days, and never got around to using. Are any of them still capable of operation?'

'I'll check, great Lord.'

He seemed to change position slightly.

'There are three hundred eighty-two,' he announced, 'of which four are in functioning condition, great Lord. I've checked all the operating circuits.'

'Drax,' warned Dran, 'you are arrogating unauthorized powers to yourself once more. You should have conferred with me before issuing that order.'

'I apologize,' stated the other. 'I simply wanted to expedite matters, should your decision be that we conduct a survey.'

'You have anticipated my decision correctly,' nodded Dran, 'but your eagerness seems to bespeak a hidden purpose.'

'No purpose but the good of the realm,' smiled the other.

'That may be, but the last time you spoke of "the good of the realm" the civil strife which ensued cost us our other robot.'

'I have learned my lesson and profited thereby. I shall be more judicious in the future.'

'I hope so. Now, about this expedition – which part of the galaxy do you intend to investigate first?'

A tension-filled pause ensued.

'I had assumed,' murmured Drax, 'that you would conduct the expedition. Being the more mature monarch, yours should be a more adequate decision as to whether or not a particular species is worthy of our enlightened rule.'

'Yes, but your youth tends to make you more active than I. The journey should be more expeditiously conducted by you.' He emphasized the word 'expeditiously.'

'We could both go, in separate ships,' offered Drax. 'That would be truly expeditious—'

Their heated debating was cut short by a metallic cough-equivalent.

'Masters,' suggested Zindrome, 'the half-life of radioactive materials being as ephemeral as it is, I regret to report that only one spaceship is now in operational condition.'

'That settles it, Dran. *You* go. It will require a steadier *rrand* to manage an unpowered ship.'

'And leave you to foment civil strife and usurp unfranchised powers? No, you go!'

'I suppose we could *both* go,' sighed Drax.

'Fine! Leave the kingdom leaderless! *That* is the kind of muddleheaded thinking which brought about our present political embarrassment.'

'Masters,' said Zindrome, 'if *someone* doesn't go soon the ship will be useless.'

They both studied their servant, approving the rapid chain of logic forged by his simple statement.

'Very well,' they smiled in unison, '*you* go.'

Zindrome bowed quite obsequiously and departed from the Great Hall of Glan.

'Perhaps we should authorize Zindrome to construct fac-similes of himself,' stated Dran, tentatively. 'If we had more subjects we could accomplish more.'

'Are you forgetting our most recent agreement?' asked Drax. 'A superfluity of robots tended to stimulate factionalism last time – and certain people grew ambitious . . .' He let his voice trail off over the years, for emphasis.

'I am not certain as to whether your last allusion contains a hidden accusation,' began the other carefully. 'If so, permit me to caution you concerning rashness – and to remind you who it was who engineered the Mono-Robot Protection Pact.'

'Do you believe things will be different in the case of a multitude of organic subjects?' inquired the other.

'Definitely,' said Dran. 'There is a certain irrational element in the rationale of the organic being, making it less amendable to direct orders than a machine would be. Our robots, at least, were faithful when we ordered them to destroy one another. Irresponsible organic subjects either do it without being told, which is boorish, or refuse to do it when you order them, which is insubordination.'

'True,' smiled Drax, unearthing a gem he had preserved for millennia against this occasion. 'Concerning organic life the only statement which can be made with certainty is that life is uncertain.'

'Hmm.' Dran narrowed his eyes to slits. 'Let me ponder that a moment. Like much of your thinking it seems to smack of a concealed sophistry.'

'It contains none, I assure you. It is the fruit of much meditation.'

'Hmm.'

Dran's pondering was cut short, by the arrival of Zindrome who clutched two brownish blurs beneath his metal arms.

'Back already, Zindrome? What have you there? Slow them down so we can see them.'

'They are under sedation at present, great Masters. It is the movements caused by their breathing which produce the unpleasant vibration pattern on your retinas. To subject them to more narcosis could prove deleterious.'

'Nevertheless,' maintained Dran, 'we must appraise our new

subjects carefully, which requires that we see them. Slow them down some more.'

'You gave that order without—' began Drax, but was distracted by the sudden appearance of two hairy bipeds.

'Warm-blooded?' he asked.

'Yes, Lord.'

'That bespeaks a very brief life-span.'

'True,' offered Dran, 'but that kind tends to reproduce quite rapidly.'

'That observation tends to be correct,' nodded Drax. 'Tell me, Zindrome, do they represent the sexes necessary for reproduction?'

'Yes, Master. There are two sexes among these anthropoids, so I brought one of each.'

'That was very wise. Where did you find them?'

'Several billion light years from here.'

'Turn these two loose outside and go fetch us some more.'

The creatures vanished. Zindrome appeared not to have moved.

'Have you the fuel necessary for another such journey?'

'Yes, my Lord. More of it has evolved recently.'

'Excellent.'

The robot departed.

'What sort of governmental setup should we inaugurate this time?' asked Drax.

'Let us review the arguments for the various types.'

'A good idea.'

In the midst of their discussion Zindrome returned and stood waiting to be recognized.

'What is it, Zindrome? Did you forget something?'

'No, great Lords. When I returned to the world from which I obtained the samples I discovered that the race had progressed to the point where it developed fission processes, engaged in an atomic war and annihilated itself.'

'That was extremely inconsiderate – typical, however, I should say, of warm-blooded instability.'

Zindrome continued to shift.

'Have you something else to report?'

'Yes, great Masters. The two specimens I released have multiplied and are now spread over the entire planet of Glan.'

'We should have been advised!'

'Yes, great Lords, but I was absent and—'

'They themselves should have reported this action!'

'Masters, I am afraid they are unaware of your existence.'

'How could that have happened?' asked Dran.

'We are presently buried beneath several thousand layers of alluvial rock. The geological shifts—'

'You have your orders to maintain the place and clean the grounds,' glowered Dran. 'Have you been frittering away your time again?'

'No, great Lords! It all occurred during my absence. I shall attend to it immediately.'

'First,' ordered Drax, 'tell us what else our subjects have been up to, that they saw fit to conceal from us.'

'Recently,' observed the robot, 'they have discovered how to forge and temper metals. Upon landing, I observed that they had developed many ingenious instruments of a cutting variety. Unfortunately they were using them to cut one another.'

'Do you mean,' roared Dran, 'that there is strife in the kingdom?'

'Uh, yes my Lord.'

'I will not brook unauthorized violence among my subjects!'

'*Our* subjects,' added Drax, with a meaningful glare.

'*Our* subjects,' amended Dran. 'We must take immediate action.'

'Agreed.'

'Agreed.'

'I shall issue orders forbidding their engagement in activities leading to bloodshed.'

'I presume that you mean a joint proclamation,' state Drax.

'Of course. I was not slighting you, I was simply shaken by the civil emergency. We shall draft an official proclamation. Let Zindrome fetch us writing instruments.'

'Zindrome fetch—'

'I have them here, my Lords.'

'Now, let me see. How shall we phrase it . . . ?'

'Perhaps I should clean the palace while your Excellencies—'

'No! Wait right here! This will be very brief and to the point.'

'Mm. "We hereby proclaim . . ." '

'Don't forget our titles.'

'True. We, the imperial monarchs of Glan, herebeneath undersigned, do hereby . . .'

A feeble pause of gamma rays passed unnoticed by the two rulers. The faithful Zindrome diagnosed its nature, however, and tried unsuccessfully to obtain his monarchs' attention. Finally, he dismissed the project with a stoical gesture typical of his kind. He waited.

'There!' they agreed flourishing the document. 'Now you can tell us what you have been trying to say, Zindrome. But make it brief, you must deliver this soon.'

'It is already too late, great Lords. This race, also, progressed into civilized states, developed nuclear energy and eradicated itself while you were writing.'

'Barbarous!'

'Warm-blooded irresponsibility!'

'May I go clean up now, great Masters?'

'Soon, Zindrome, soon. First, though, I move that we file the proclamation in the Archives for future use, in the event of similar occurrences.'

Dran nodded.

'I agree. *We* so order.'

The robot accepted the crumbling proclamation and vanished from sight.

'You know,' Drax mused, 'there must be lots of radioactive material lying about now . . .'

'There probably is.'

'It could be used to fuel a ship for another expedition.'

'Perhaps.'

'This time we could instruct Zindrome to bring back

430

something with a longer lifespan and more deliberate habits – somewhat nearer our own.'

'That would have its dangers. But perhaps we could junk the Mono-Robot Protection Pact and order Zindrome to manufacture extras of himself. Under strict supervision.'

'That would have its dangers too.'

At any rate, I should have to ponder your suggestion carefully.'

'And I yours.'

'It's been a busy day,' nodded Dran. 'Let's sleep on it.'

'A good idea.'

Sounds of saurian snoring emerged from the great Throne Hall of Glan.

# The Keys to December

Born of man and woman, in accordance with Catform Y7 requirements, Coldworld Class (modified per Alyonal), 3.2-E, G.M.I. option, Jarry Dark was not suited for existence anywhere in the universe which had guaranteed him a niche. This was either a blessing or a curse, depending on how you looked at it.

So look at it however you would, here is the story:

It is likely that his parents could have afforded the temperature control unit, but not much more than that. (Jarry required a temperature of at least -50 C to be comfortable.)

It is unlikely that his parents could have provided for the air pressure control and gas mixture equipment required to maintain his life.

Nothing could be done in the way of 3.2-E grav-simulation, so daily medication and physiotherapy were required. It is unlikely that his parents could have provided for this.

The much-maligned option took care of him, however. It safe-guarded his health. It provided for his education. It assured his economic welfare and physical well-being.

It might be argued that Jarry Dark would not have been a homeless Coldworld Catform (modified per Alyonal) had it not been for General Mining, Incorporated, which had held the option. But then it must be borne in mind that no one could have foreseen the nova which destroyed Alyonal.

When his parents had presented themselves at the Public Health Planned Parenthood Center and requested advice and medication pending offspring, they had been informed as to the available worlds and the bodyform requirements for them. They had selected Alyonal, which had recently been purchased by General Mining for purposes of mineral exploitation. Wisely, they had elected the option; that is to say, they had signed a contract on behalf of their anticipated offspring, who would be eminently qualified to inhabit that world, agreeing that he would work as an employee of General Mining until he achieved his majority, at which time he would be free to depart and seek employment wherever he might choose (though his choices would admittedly be limited). In return for this guarantee, General Mining agreed to assure his health, education and continuing welfare for so long as he remained in their employ.

When Alyonal caught fire and went away, those Coldworld Catforms covered by the option who were scattered about the crowded galaxy were, by virtue of the agreement, wards of General Mining.

This is why Jarry grew up in a hermetically sealed room containing temperature and atmosphere controls, and why he received a first-class closed circuit education, along with his physiotherapy and medicine. This is also why Jarry bore some resemblance to a large gray ocelot without a tail, had webbing between his fingers and could not go outside to watch the traffic unless he wore a pressurized refrigeration suit and took extra medication.

All over the swarming galaxy, people took the advice of Public Health Planned Parenthood Centers, and many others had chosen as had Jarry's parents. Twenty-eight thousand, five hundred sixty-six of them, to be exact. In any group of over twenty-eight thousand five hundred sixty, there are bound to be a few talented individuals. Jarry was one of them. He had a knack for making money. Most of his General Mining pension check was invested in well-chosen stocks of a speculative nature. (In fact, after a time he came to own considerable stock in General Mining.)

When the man from the Galactic Civil Liberties Union

had come around, expressing concern over the pre-birth contracts involved in the option and explaining that the Alyonal Catforms would make a good test case (especially since Jarry's parents lived within jurisdiction of the 877th Circuit, where they would be assured favorable courtroom atmosphere), Jarry's parents had demurred, for fear of jeopardizing the General Mining pension. Later on, Jarry himself dismissed the notion also. A favorable decision could not make him an E-world Normform, and what else mattered? He was not vindictive. Also, he owned considerable stock in G.M. by then.

He loafed in his methane tank and purred, which meant that he was thinking. He operated his cryo-computer as he purred and thought. He was computing the total net worth of all the Catforms in the recently organized December Club.

He stopped purring and considered a sub-total, stretched, shook his head slowly. Then he returned to his calculations.

When he had finished, he dictated a message into his speech-tube, to Sanza Barati, President of December and his betrothed:

'Dearest Sanza – the funds available, as I have suspected, leave much to be desired. All the more reason to begin immediately. Kindly submit the proposal to the business committee, outline my qualifications and seek immediate endorsement. I've finished drafting the general statement to the membership. (Copy attached.) From these figures, it will take me between five and ten years, if at least eighty percent of the membership backs me. So push hard, beloved. I'd like to meet you someday, in a place where the sky is purple. Yours, always, Jarry Dark, Treasurer. P.S. I'm pleased you were pleased with the ring.'

Two years later, Jarry had doubled the net worth of December, Incorporated.

A year and a half after that, he had doubled it again.

When he received the following letter from Sanza, he leapt onto his trampoline, bounded into the air, landed upon his feet at the opposite end of his quarters, returned to his viewer and replayed it:

Dear Jarry,

Attached are specifications and prices for five more worlds. The research staff likes the last one. So do I. What do you think? Alyonal II? If so, how about the price? When could we afford that much? The staff also says that a hundred Worldchange units could alter it to what we want in 5-6 centuries. Will forward costs of this machinery shortly.

Come live with me and be my love, in a place where there are no walls . . .

Sanza


'One year,' he replied, 'and I'll buy you a world! Hurry up with the costs of the machinery and transport . . .' When the figures arrived Jarry wept icy tears. One hundred machines, capable of altering the environment of a world, plus twenty-eight thousand coldsleep bunkers, plus transportation costs for the machinery and his people, plus . . . Too high! He did a rapid calculation.

He spoke into the speech-tube:

'. . . Fifteen additional years is too long to wait, Pussycat. Have them figure the time-span if we were to purchase only twenty Worldchange units. Love and kisses, Jarry.'

During the days which followed, he stalked above his chamber, erect at first, then on all fours as his mood deepened.

'Approximately three thousand years,' came the reply. 'May your coat be ever shiny – Sanza.'

'Let's put it to a vote, Greeneyes,' he said.


Quick, a world in 300 words or less! Picture this . . .

One land mass, really, containing three black and brackish looking seas; gray plains and yellow plains and skies the color of dry sand; shallow forests with trees like mushrooms which have been swabbed with iodine; no mountains, just hills brown, yellow, white, lavender; green birds with wings like parachutes, bills like sickles, feathers like oak leaves, an inside-out umbrella behind; six very distant moons, like spots before

435

the eyes in daytime, snowflakes at night, drops of blood at dusk and dawn; grass like mustard in the moister valleys; mists like white fire on windless mornings, albino serpents when the air's astir; radiating chasms, like fractures in frosted windowpanes; hidden caverns, like chains of dark bubbles; seventeen known dangerous predators, ranging from one to six meters in length, excessively furred and fanged; sudden hailstorms, like hurled hammerheads from a clear sky; an icecap like a blue beret at either flattened pole; nervous bipeds a meter and a half in height, short on cerebrum, which wander the shallow forests and prey upon the giant caterpillar's larva, as well as the giant caterpillar, the green bird, the blind burrower, and the offal-eating murkbeast; seventeen mighty rivers; clouds like pregnant purple cows, which quickly cross the land to lie-in beyond the visible east; stands of windblasted stones like frozen music; nights like soot, to obscure the lesser stars; valleys which flow like the torsos of women or instruments of music; perpetual frost in places of shadow; sounds in the morning like the cracking of ice, the trembling of tin, the snapping of steel strands . . .

They knew they would turn it into heaven.

The vanguard arrived, decked out in refrigeration suits, installed ten Worldchange units in either hemisphere, began setting up cold-sleep bunkers in several of the larger caverns.

Then came the members of December down from the sand-colored sky.

They came and they saw, decided it was almost heaven, then entered their caverns and slept. Over twenty-eight thousand Coldworld Catforms (modified per Alyonal) came into their own world to sleep for a season in silence the sleep of ice and of stone, to inherit the new Alyonal. There is no dreaming in that sleep. But had there been, their dreams might have been as the thoughts of those yet awake.

'It is bitter, Sanza.'

'Yes, but only for a time—'

'. . . To have each other and our own world, and still to go forth like divers at the bottom of the sea. To have to crawl when you want to leap...'

'It is only for a short time, Jarry, as the sense will reckon it.'

'But it is really three thousand years! An ice age will come to pass as we doze. Our former worlds will change so that we would not know them were we to go back for a visit – and none will remember us.'

'Visit what? Our former cells? Let the rest of the worlds go by! Let us be forgotten in the lands of our birth! We are a people apart and we have found our home. What else matters?'

'True... It will be but a few years, and we shall stand our tours of wakefulness and watching together.'

'When is the first?'

'Two and a half centuries from now – three months of wakefulness.'

'What will it be like then?'

'I don't know. Less warm...'

'Then let us return and sleep. Tomorrow will be a better day.'

'Yes.'

'Oh! See the green bird! It drifts like a dream...'

When they awakened that first time, they stayed within the Worldchange installation at the place called Deadland. The world was already colder and the edges of the sky were tinted with pink. The metal walls of the great installation were black and rimed with frost. The atmosphere was still lethal and the temperature far too high. They remained within their special chambers for most of the time, venturing outside mainly to make necessary tests and to inspect the structure of their home.

Deadland... Rocks and sand. No trees, no marks of life at all.

The time of terrible winds was still upon the land, as the world fought back against the fields of the machines. At night, great clouds of real estate smoothed and sculpted the stands of stone, and when the winds departed the desert would shimmer as if fresh-painted and the stones would stand like flames within the morning and its singing. After the sun came up into

437

the sky and hung there for a time, the winds would begin again and a dun-colored fog would curtain the day. When the morning winds departed, Jarry and Sanza would stare out across the Deadland through the east window of the installation, for that was their favorite – the one on the third floor – where the stone that looked like a gnarly Normform waved to them, and they would lie upon the green couch they had moved up from the first floor, and would sometimes make love as they listened for the winds to rise again, or Sanza would sing and Jarry would write in the log or read back through it, the scribblings of friends and unknowns through the centuries, and they would purr often but never laugh, because they did not know how.

One morning, as they watched, they saw one of the biped creatures of the iodine forests moving across the land. It fell several times, picked itself up, fell once more, lay still.

'What is it doing this far from its home?' asked Sanza.

'Dying,' said Jarry. 'Let's go outside.'

They crossed a catwalk, descended to the first floor, donned their protective suits and departed the installation.

The creature had risen to its feet and was staggering once again. It was covered with a reddish down, had dark eyes and a long, wide nose, lacked a true forehead. It had four brief digits, clawed, upon each hand and foot.

When it saw them emerge from the Worldchange unit, it stopped and stared at them. Then it fell.

They moved to its side and studied it where it lay.

It continued to stare at them, its dark eyes wide, as it lay there shivering.

'It will die if we leave it here,' said Sanza.

'. . . And it will die if we take it inside,' said Jarry.

It raised a forelimb toward them, let it fall again. Its eyes narrowed, then closed.

Jarry reached out and touched it with the toe of his boot. There was no response.

'It's dead,' he said.

'What will we do?'

'Leave it here. The sands will cover it.'

438

They returned to the installation, and Jarry entered the event in the log.

During their last month of duty, Sanza asked him, 'Will everything die here but us? The green birds and the big eaters of flesh? The funny little trees and the hairy caterpillar?'

'I hope not,' said Jarry. 'I've been reading back through the biologists' notes. I think life might adapt. Once it gets a start anywhere, it'll do anything it can to keep going. It's probably better for the creatures of this planet we could afford only twenty Worldchangers. That way they have three millennia to grow more hair and learn to breathe our air and drink our water. With a hundred units we might have wiped them out and had to import coldworld creatures or breed them. This way, the ones who live here might be able to make it.'

'It's funny,' she said, 'but the thought just occurred to me that we're doing here what was done to us. They made us for Alyonal, and a nova took it away. These creatures came to life in this place, and we're taking it away. We're turning all of life on this planet into what we were on our former worlds – misfits.'

'The difference, however, is that we are taking our time,' said Jarry, 'and giving them a chance to get used to the new conditions.'

'Still, I feel that all that – outside there' – she gestured toward the window – 'is what this world is becoming: one big Deadland.'

'Deadland was here before we came. We haven't created any new deserts.'

'All the animals are moving south. The trees are dying. When they get as far south as they can go and still the temperature drops, and the air continues to harm their lungs – then it will be all over for them.'

'By then they might have adapted. The trees are spreading, are developing thicker barks. Life will make it.'

'I wonder . . .'

'Would you prefer to sleep until it's all over?'

'No; I want to be by your side, always.'

439

'Then you must reconcile yourself to the fact that something is always hurt by any change. If you do this, you will not be hurt yourself.'

Then they listened for the winds to rise.

Three days later, in the still of sundown, between the winds of day and the winds of night, she called him to the window. He climbed to the third floor and moved to her side. Her breasts were rose in the sundown light and the places beneath them silver and dark. The fur of her shoulders and haunches was like an aura of smoke. Her face was expressionless and her wide, green eyes were not turned toward him.

He looked out.

The first big flakes were falling, blue, through the pink light. They drifted past the stone and gnarly Normform; some stuck in the thick quartz windowpane; they fell upon the desert and lay there like blossoms of cyanide; they swirled as more of them came down and were caught by the first faint puffs of the terrible winds. Dark clouds had mustered overhead and from them, now, great cables and nets of blue descended. Now the flakes flashed past the window like butterflies, and the outline of Deadland flickered on and off. The pink vanished and there was only blue, blue and darkening blue, as the first great sigh of evening came into their ears and the billows suddenly moved sidewise rather than downwards, becoming indigo as they raced by.

'The machine is never silent,' Jarry wrote. 'Sometimes I fancy I can hear voices in its constant humming, its occasional growling, its crackles of power. I am alone here at the Deadland station. Five centuries have passed since our arrival. I thought it better to let Sanza sleep out this tour of duty, lest the prospect be too bleak. (It is.) She will doubtless be angry. As I lay half-awake this morning, I thought I heard my parents' voices in the next room. No words. Just the sounds of their voices as I used to hear them over my old intercom. They must be dead by now, despite all geriatrics. I wonder if they thought of me much after I left? I couldn't even shake my father's

440

hand without the gauntlet, or kiss my mother goodbye. It is strange, the feeling, to be this alone, with only the throb of the machinery about me as it rearranges the molecules of the atmosphere, refrigerates the world, here in the middle of the blue place. Deadland. This, despite the fact that I grew up in a steel cave. I call the other nineteen stations every afternoon. I am afraid I am becoming something of a nuisance. I won't call them tomorrow, or perhaps the next day.

'I went outside without my refrig-pack this morning, for a few moments. It is still deadly hot. I gulped a mouthful of air and choked. Our day is still far off. But I can notice the difference from the last time I tried it, two and a half hundred years ago. I wonder what it will be like when we have finished? —And I, an economist! What will my function be in our new Alyonal? Whatever, so long as Sanza is happy...

'The Worldchanger stutters and groans. All the land is blue for so far as I can see. The stones still stand, but their shapes are changed from what they were. The sky is entirely pink now, and it becomes almost maroon in the morning and the evening. I guess it's really a wine-color, but I've never seen wine, so I can't say for certain. The trees have not died. They've grown hardier. Their barks are thicker, their leaves darker and larger. They grow much taller now, I've been told. There are no trees in Deadland.

'The caterpillars still live. They seem much larger, I understand, but it is actually because they have become woollier than they used to be. It seems that most of the animals have heavier pelts these days. Some apparently have taken to hibernating. A strange thing: Station Seven reported that they had thought the bipeds were growing heavier coats. There seem to be quite a few of them in that area, and they often see them off in the distance. They looked to be shaggier. Closer observation, however, revealed that some of them were either carrying or were wrapped in the skins of dead animals! Could it be that they are more intelligent than we have given them credit for? This hardly seems possible, since they were tested quite thoroughly by the Bio Team before we set the machines in operation. Yes, it is very strange.

'The winds are still severe. Occasionally, they darken the sky with ash. There has been considerable vulcanism southwest of here. Station Four was relocated because of this. I hear Sanza singing now, within the sounds of the machine. I will let her be awakened the next time. Things should be more settled by then. No, that is not true. It is selfishness. I want her here beside me. I feel as if I were the only living thing in the whole world. The voices on the radio are ghosts. The clock ticks loudly and the silences between the ticks are filled with the humming of the machine, which is a kind of silence, too, because it is constant. Sometimes I think it is not there; I listen for it, I strain my ears, and I do not know whether there is a humming or not. I check the indicators then, and they assure me that the machine is functioning. Or perhaps there is something wrong with the indicators. But they seem to be all right. No. It is me. And the blue of Deadland is a kind of visual silence. In the morning even the rocks are covered with blue frost. Is it beautiful or ugly? There is no response within me. It is a part of the great silence, that's all. Perhaps I shall become a mystic. Perhaps I shall develop occult powers or achieve something bright and liberating as I sit here at the center of the great silence. Perhaps I shall see visions. Already I hear voices. Are there ghosts in Deadland? No, there was never anything here to be ghosted. Except perhaps for the little biped. Why did it cross Deadland, I wonder? Why did it head for the center of destruction rather than away, as its fellows did? I shall never know. Unless perhaps I have a vision. I think it is time to suit up and take a walk. The polar icecaps are heavier. The glaciation has begun. Soon, soon things will be better. Soon the silence will end, I hope. I wonder, though, whether silence is not the true state of affairs in the universe, our little noises serving only to accentuate it, like a speck of black on a field of blue. Everything was once silence and will be so again – is now, perhaps. Will I ever hear real sounds, or only sounds out of the silence? Sanza is singing again. I wish I could wake her up now, to walk with me, out there. It is beginning to snow.'

*

442

Jarry awakened again on the eve of the millennium.

Sanza smiled and took his hand in hers and stoked it, as he explained why he had let her sleep, as he apologized.

'Of course I'm not angry,' she said, 'considering I did the same thing to you last cycle.'

Jarry stared up at her and felt the understanding begin.

'I'll not do it again,' she said, 'and I know you couldn't. The aloneness is almost unbearable.'

'Yes,' he replied.

'They warmed us both alive last time. I came around first and told them to put you back to sleep. I was angry then, when I found out what you had done. But I got over it quickly, so often did I wish you were there.'

'We will stay together,' said Jarry.

'Yes, always.'

They took a flier from the cavern of sleep to the World-change installation at Deadland, where they relieved the other attendants and moved the new couch up to the third floor.

The air of Deadland, while sultry, could now be breathed for short periods of time, though a headache invariably followed such experiments. The heat was still oppressive. The rock, once like an old Normform waving, had lost its distinctive outline. The winds were no longer so severe.

On the fourth day, they found some animal tracks which seemed to belong to one of the larger predators. This cheered Sanza, but another, later occurrence produced only puzzlement.

One morning they went forth to walk in Deadland.

Less than a hundred paces from the installation, they came upon three of the giant caterpillars, dead. They were stiff, as though dried out rather than frozen, and they were surrounded by rows of markings within the snow. The footprints which led to the scene and away from it were rough of outline, obscure.

'What does it mean?' she asked.

'I don't know, but I think we had better photograph this,' said Jarry.

443

They did. When Jarry spoke to Station Eleven that afternoon, he learned that similar occurrences had occasionally been noted by attendants of other installations. These were not too frequent, however.

'I don't understand,' said Sanza.

'I don't want to,' said Jarry.

It did not happen again during their tour of duty. Jarry entered it into the log and wrote a report. Then they abandoned themselves to lovemaking, monitoring, and occasionally nights of drunkenness. Two hundred years previously, a biochemist had devoted his tour of duty to experimenting with compounds which would produce the same reactions in Catforms as the legendary whiskey did in Normforms. He had been successful, had spent four weeks on a colossal binge, neglected his duty and been relieved of it, was then retired to his coldbunk for the balance of the Wait. His basically simple formula had circulated, however, and Jarry and Sanza found a well-stocked bar in the storeroom and a hand-written manual explaining its use and a variety of drinks which might be compounded. The author of the document had expressed the hope that each tour of attendance might result in the discovery of a new mixture, so that when he returned for his next cycle the manual would have grown to a size proportionate to his desire. Jarry and Sanza worked at it conscientiously, and satisfied the request with a Snowflower Punch which warmed their bellies and made their purring turn into giggles, so that they discovered laughter also. They celebrated the millennium with an entire bowl of it, and Sanza insisted on calling all the other installations and giving them the formula, right then, on the graveyard watch, so that everyone could share in their joy. It is quite possible that everyone did, for the recipe was well-received. And always, even after that bowl was but a memory, they kept the laughter. Thus are the first simple lines of tradition sometimes sketched.

\*

'The green birds are dying,' said Sanza, putting aside a report she had been reading.

'Oh?' said Jarry.

'Apparently they've done all the adapting they're able to,' she told him.

'Pity,' said Jarry.

'It seems less than a year since we came here. Actually, it's a thousand.'

'Time flies,' said Jarry.

'I'm afraid,' she said.

'Of what?'

'I don't know. Just afraid.'

'Why?'

'Living the way we've been living, I guess. Leaving little pieces of ourselves in different centuries. Just a few months ago, as my memory works, this place was a desert. Now it's an ice field. Chasms open and close. Canyons appear and disappear. Rivers dry up and new ones spring forth. Everything seems so very transitory. Things look solid, but I'm getting afraid to touch things now. They might go away. They might turn into smoke, and my hand will keep on reaching through the smoke and touch – something... God, maybe. Or worse yet, maybe not. No one really knows what it will be like here when we've finished. We're traveling toward an unknown land and it's too late to go back. We're moving through a dream, heading toward an idea... Sometimes I miss my cell... and all the little machines that took care of me there. Maybe I can't adapt. Maybe I'm like the green bird...'

'No, Sanza. You're not. We're real. No matter what happens out there, we will last. Everything is changing because we want it to change. We're stronger than the world, and we'll squeeze it and paint it and poke holes in it until we've made it exactly the way we want it. Then we'll take it and cover it with cities and children. You want to see God? Go look in the mirror. God has pointed ears and green eyes. He is covered with soft gray fur. When He raises His hand there is webbing between His fingers.'

445

'It is good that you are strong, Jarry.'

'Let's get out the power sled and go for a ride.'

'All right.'

Up and down, that day, they drove through Deadland, where the dark stones stood like clouds in another sky.

It was twelve and a half hundred years.

Now they could breathe without respirators, for a short time.

Now they could bear the temperature, for a short time.

Now all the green birds were dead.

Now a strange and troubling thing began.

The bipeds came by night, made markings on the snow, left dead animals in the midst of them. This happened now with much more frequency than it had in the past. They came long distances to do it, many of them with fur which was not their own upon their shoulders.

Jarry searched through the history files for all the reports on the creatures.

'This one speaks of lights in the forest,' he said. 'Station Seven.'

'What . . . ?'

'Fire,' he said. 'What if they've discovered fire?'

'Then they're not really beasts!'

'But they were!'

'They wear clothing now. They make some sort of sacrifice to our machines. They're not beasts any longer.'

'How could it have happened?'

'How do you think? *We* did it. Perhaps they would have remained stupid – animals – if we had not come along and forced them to get smart in order to go on living. We've accelerated their evolution. They had to adapt or die, and they adapted.'

'D'you think it would have happened if we hadn't come along?' he asked.

'Maybe – some day. Maybe not, too.'

Jarry moved to the window, stared out across Deadland.

'I have to find out,' he said. 'If they are intelligent, if they are – human, like us,' he said, then laughed, 'then we must consider their ways.'

'What do you propose?'

'Locate some of the creatures. See whether we can communicate with them.'

'Hasn't it been tried?'

'Yes.'

'What were the results?'

'Mixed. Some claim they have considerable understanding. Others place them far below the threshold where humanity begins.'

'We may be doing a terrible thing,' she said. 'Creating men, then destroying them. Once, when I was feeling low, you told me that we were the gods of this world, that ours was the power to shape and to break. Ours *is* the power to shape and break, but I don't feel especially divine. What can we do? They have come this far, but do you think they can bear the change that will take us the rest of the way? What if they are like the green birds? What if they've adapted as fast and as far as they can and it is not sufficient? What would a god do?'

'Whatever he wished,' said Jarry.

That day, they cruised over Deadland in the flier, but the only signs of life they saw were each other. They continued to search in the days that followed, but they did not meet with success.

Under the purple of morning, however, two weeks later, it happened.

'They've been here,' said Sanza.

Jarry moved to the front of the installation and stared out.

The snow was broken in several places, inscribed with the lines he had seen before, about the form of a small, dead beast.

'They can't have gone very far,' he said.

'No.'

'We'll search in the sled.' Now over the snow and out, across the land called Dead they went, Sanza driving and Jarry peering at the lines of footmarks in the blue.

They cruised through the occurring morning, hinting of fire and violet, and the wind went past them like a river, and all about them there came sounds like the cracking of ice, the trembling of tin, the snapping of steel strands. The bluefrosted stones stood like frozen music, and the long shadow of their sled, black as ink, raced on ahead of them. A shower of hailstones drumming upon the roof of their vehicle like a sudden visitation of demon dancers, as suddenly was gone. Deadland sloped downward, slanted up again.

Jarry placed his hand upon Sanza's shoulder.

'Ahead!' She nodded, began to brake the sled. They had it at bay. They were using clubs and long poles which looked to have fire-hardened points. They threw stones. They threw pieces of ice. Then they backed away and it killed them as they went. The Catforms had called it a bear because it was big and shaggy and could rise up onto its hind legs . . . This one was about three and a half meters in length, was covered with bluish fur and had a thin, hairless snout like the business end of a pair of pliers. Five of the little creatures lay still in the snow. Each time that it swung a paw and connected, another one fell. Jarry removed the pistol from its compartment and checked the charge.

'Cruise by slowly,' he told her. 'I'm going to try to burn it about the head.'

His first shot missed, scoring the boulder at its back. His second singed the fur of its neck. He leapt down from the sled then, as they came abreast of the beast, thumbed the power control up to maximum, and fired the entire charge into its breast, point-blank.

The bear stiffened, swayed, fell, a gaping wound upon it, front to back.

Jarry turned and regarded the little creatures. They stared up at him.

'Hello,' he said. 'My name is Jarry. I dub thee Redforms—'

He was knocked from his feet by a blow from behind.

He rolled across the snow, lights dancing before his eyes, his left arm and shoulder afire with pain.

A second bear had emerged from the forest of stone.

He drew his long hunting knife with his right hand and climbed back to his feet.

As the creature lunged, he moved with the catspeed of his kind, thrusting upward, burying his knife to the hilt in its throat.

A shudder ran through it, but it cuffed him and he fell once again, the blade torn from his grasp.

The Redforms threw more stones, rushed toward it with their pointed sticks.

Then there was a thud and a crunching sound, and it rose up into the air and came down on top of him.

He awakened.

He lay on his back, hurting, and everything he looked at seemed to be pulsing, as if about to explode.

How much time had passed, he did not know.

Either he or the bear had been moved.

The little creatures crouched, waiting.

Some watched the bear. Some watched him.

Some watched the broken sled . . .

The broken sled . . .

He struggled to his feet.

The Redforms drew back.

He crossed to the sled and looked inside.

He knew she was dead when he saw the angle of her neck. But he did all the things a person does to be sure, anyway, before he would let himself believe it.

She had delivered the deathblow, crashing the sled into the creature, breaking its back. It had broken the sled. Herself, also.

He leaned against the wreckage, composed his first prayer, then removed her body.

The Redforms watched.

He lifted her in his arms and began walking, back toward the installation, across Deadland.

The Redforms continued to watch as he went, except for the one with the strangely high brow-ridge, who studied instead the knife that protruded from the shaggy and steaming throat of the beast.

*

Jarry asked the awakened executives of December: 'What should we do?'

'She is the first of our race to die on this world,' said Yan Turl, Vice President.

'There is no tradition,' said Selda Kein, Secretary. 'Shall we establish one?'

'I don't know,' said Jarry. 'I don't know what is right to do.'

'Burial or cremation seem to be the main choices. Which would you prefer?'

'I don't – No, not the ground. Give her back to me. Give me a large flier ... I'll burn her.'

'Then let us construct a chapel.'

'No. It is a thing I must do in my own way. I'd rather do it alone.'

'As you wish. Draw what equipment you will need, and be about it.'

'Please send someone else to keep the Deadland installation. I wish to sleep again when I have finished this thing – until the next cycle.'

'Very well, Jarry. We are sorry.'

'Yes – we are.'

Jarry nodded, gestured, turned, departed.

Thus are the heavier lines of life sometimes drawn.


At the southeastern edge of Deadland there was a blue mountain. It stood to slightly over three thousand meters in height. When approached from the northwest, it gave the appearance of being a frozen wave in a sea too vast to imagine. Purple clouds rent themselves upon its peak. No living thing was to be found on its slopes. It had no name, save that which Jarry Dark gave it.

He anchored the flier.

He carried her body to the highest point to which a body might be carried.

He placed her there, dressed in her finest garments, a wide

450

scarf concealing the angle of her neck, a dark veil covering her emptied features.

He was about to try a prayer when the hail began to fall. Like thrown rocks, the chunks of blue ice came down upon him, upon her.

'God damn you!' he cried and he raced back to the flier.

He climbed into the air, circled.

Her garments were flapping in the wind. The hail was a blue, beaded curtain that separated them from all but these final caresses: fire aflow from ice to ice, from clay aflow immortally through guns.

He squeezed the trigger and a doorway into the sun opened in the side of the mountain that had been nameless. She vanished within it, and he widened the doorway until he had lowered the mountain.

Then he climbed upward into the cloud, attacking the storm until his guns were empty.

He circled then above the molten mesa, there at the south-eastern edge of Deadland.

He circled above the first pyre this world had seen.

Then he departed, to sleep for a season in silence the sleep of ice and stone, to inherit the Alyonal. There is no dreaming in that sleep.

Fifteen centuries. Almost half the Wait. Two hundred words or less... Picture—

...Nineteen mighty rivers flowing, but the black seas rippling violet now.

...No shallow iodine-colored forests. Mighty shag-barked barrel trees instead, orange and lime and black and tall across the land.

...Great ranges of mountains in the place of hills brown, yellow, white, lavender. Black corkscrews of smoke unwinding from smoldering cones.

...Flowers, whose roots explore the soil twenty meters beneath their mustard petals, unfolded amidst the blue frost and the stones.

. . . Blind burrowers burrowing deeper; offal-eating murk-beasts now showing formidable incisors and great rows of ridged molars; giant caterpillars growing smaller but looking larger because of increasing coats.

. . . The contours of valleys still like the torsos of women, flowing and rolling, or perhaps like instruments of music.

. . . Gone much windblasted stone, but ever the frost.

. . . Sounds in the morning as always, harsh, brittle, metallic.

They were sure that they were halfway to heaven.

Picture that.

The Deadland log told him as much as he really needed to know. But he read back through the old reports, too.

Then he mixed himself a drink and stared out the third floor window.

'. . . Will die,' he said, then finished his drink, outfitted himself, and abandoned his post.

It was three days before he found a camp.

He landed the flier at a distance and approached on foot. He was far to the south of Deadland, where the air was warmer and caused him to feel constantly short of breath.

They were wearing animal skins – skins which had been cut for a better fit and greater protection, skins which were tied about them. He counted sixteen lean-to arrangements and three campfires. He flinched as he regarded the fires, but he continued to advance.

When they saw him, all their little noises stopped, a brief cry went up, and there was silence.

He entered the camp.

The creatures stood unmoving about him. He heard some bustling within the large lean-to at the end of the clearing.

He walked about the camp.

A slab of dried meat hung from the center of a tripod of poles.

Several long spears stood before each dwelling place. He advanced and studied one. A stone which had been flaked into a leaf-shaped spearhead was affixed to its end.

452

There was the outline of a cat carved upon a block of wood...

He heard a footfall and turned.

One of the Redforms moved slowly toward him. It appeared older than the others. Its shoulders sloped; as it opened its mouth to make a series of popping noises, he saw that some of its teeth were missing; its hair was grizzled and thin. It bore something in its hands, but Jarry's attention was drawn to the hands themselves.

Each hand bore an opposing digit.

He looked about him quickly, studying the hands of the others. All of them seemed to have thumbs. He studied their appearance more closely.

They now had foreheads.

He returned his attention to the old Redform.

It placed something at his feet, and then it backed away from him.

He looked down.

A chunk of dried meat and a piece of fruit lay upon a broad leaf.

He picked up the meat, closed his eyes, bit off a piece, chewed and swallowed. He wrapped the rest in the leaf and placed it in the side pocket of his pack.

He extended his hand and the Redform drew back.

He lowered his hand, unrolled the blanket he had carried with him and spread it upon the ground. He seated himself, pointed to the Redform, then indicated a position across from him at the other end of the blanket.

The creature hesitated, then advanced and seated itself.

'We are going to learn to talk with one another,' he said slowly. Then he placed his hand upon his breast and said, 'Jarry.'

Jarry stood before the reawakened executives of December.

'They are intelligent,' he told them. 'It's all in my report.'

'So?' asked Yan Turl.

'I don't think they will be able to adapt. They have come

453

very far, very rapidly. But I don't think they can go much further. I don't think they can make it all the way.'

'Are you a biologist, an ecologist, a chemist?'

'No.'

'Then on what do you base your opinion?'

'I observed them at close range for six weeks.'

'Then it's only a feeling you have . . . ?'

'You know there are no experts on a thing like this. It's never happened before.'

'Granting their intelligence – granting even that what you have said concerning their adaptability is correct – what do you suggest we do about it?'

'Slow down the change. Give them a better chance. If they can't make it the rest of the way, then stop short of our goal. It's already livable here. We can adapt the rest of the way.'

'Slow it down? How much?'

'Supposing we took another seven or eight thousand years?'

'Impossible!'

'Entirely!'

'Too much!'

'Why?'

'Because everyone stands a three-month watch every two hundred fifty years. That's one year of personal time for every thousand. You're asking for too much of everyone's time.'

'But the life of an entire race may be at stake!'

'You do not know that for certain.'

'No, I don't. But do you feel it is something to take a chance with?'

'Do you want to put it to an executive vote?'

'No – I can see that I'll lose. I want to put it before the entire membership.'

'Impossible. They're all asleep.'

'Then wake them up.'

'That would be quite a project.'

'Don't you think the fate of a race is worth the effort? Especially since we're the ones who forced intelligence upon

454

them? We're the ones who made them evolve, cursed them with intellect.'

'Enough! They were right at the threshold. They might have become intelligent had we *not* come along.'

'But you can't say for certain! You don't really know! And it doesn't really matter how it happened. They're here and we're here, and they think we're gods – maybe because we do nothing for them but make them miserable. We have some responsibility to an intelligent race, though. At least to the extent of not murdering it.'

'Perhaps we could do a long-range study...'

'They could be dead by then. I formally move, in my capacity as Treasurer, that we awaken the full membership and put the matter to a vote.'

'I don't hear any second to your motion.'

'Selda?' he said.

She looked away.

'Tarebell? Clond? Bondici?'

There was silence in the cavern that was high and wide about him.

'All right. I can see when I'm beaten. We will be our own serpents when we come into our Eden. I'm going now, back to Deadland, to finish my tour of duty.'

'You don't have to. In fact, it might be better if you sleep the whole thing out...'

'No. If it's going to be this way, the guilt will be mine also. I want to watch, to share it fully.'

'So be it,' said Turl.

Two weeks later, when Installation Nineteen tried to raise the Deadland Station on the radio, there was no response.

After a time, a flier was dispatched.

The Deadland Station was a shapeless lump of melted metal.

Jarry Dark was nowhere to be found.

Later than afternoon, Installation Eight went dead.

A flier was immediately dispatched.

Installation Eight no longer existed. Its attendants were found several miles away, walking. They told how Jarry Dark had forced them from the station at gunpoint. Then he had burnt it to the ground, with the fire-cannons mounted upon his flier.

At about the time they were telling this story, Installation Six became silent.

The order went out: MAINTAIN CONTINUOUS RADIO CONTACT WITH TWO OTHER STATIOINS AT ALL TIMES.

The other order went out: GO ARMED AT ALL TIMES. TAKE ANY VISITOR PRISONER.

Jarry waited. At the bottom of a chasm, parked beneath a shelf of rock, Jarry waited. An opened bottle stood upon the control board of his flier. Next to it was a small case of white metal.

Jarry took a long, last drink from the bottle as he waited for the broadcast he knew would come.

When it did, he stretched out on the seat and took a nap.

When he awakened, the light of day was waning.

The broadcast was still going on...

'...Jarry. They will be awakened and a referendum will be held. Come back to the main cavern. This is Yan Turl. Please do not destroy any more installations. This action is not necessary. We agree with your proposal that a vote be held. Please contact us immediately. We are waiting for your reply, Jarry...'

He tossed the empty bottle through the window and raised the flier out of the purple shadow into the air and up.

When he descended upon the landing stage within the main cavern, of course they were waiting for him. A dozen rifles were trained upon him as he stepped down from the flier.

'Remove your weapons, Jarry,' came the voice of Yan Turl.

'I'm not wearing any weapons,' said Jarry. 'Neither is my flier,' he added; and this was true, for the fire-cannons no longer rested within their mountings.

Yan Turl approached, looked up at him.

'Then you may step down.'

456

'Thank you, but I like it right where I am.'

'You are a prisoner.'

'What do you intend to do with me?'

'Put you back to sleep until the end of the Wait. Come down here!'

'No. And don't try shooting – or using a stun charge or gas, either. If you do, we're all of us dead the second it hits.'

'What do you mean?' asked Turl, gesturing gently to the riflemen.

'My flier,' said Jarry, 'is a bomb, and I'm holding the fuse in my right hand.' He raised the white metal box. 'So long as I keep the lever on the side of this box depressed, we live. If my grip relaxes, even for an instant, the explosion which ensues will doubtless destroy this entire cavern.'

'I think you're bluffing.'

'You know how you can find out for certain.'

'You'll die too, Jarry.'

'At the moment, I don't really care. Don't try burning my hand off, either, to destroy the fuse,' he cautioned, 'because it doesn't really matter. Even if you should succeed, it will cost you at least two installations.'

'Why is that?'

'What do you think I did with the fire-cannons? I taught the Redforms how to use them. At the moment, these weapons are manned by Redforms and aimed at two installations. If I do not personally visit my gunners by dawn, they will open fire. After destroying their objectives, they will move on and try for two more.'

'You trusted those beasts with laser projectors?'

'That is correct. Now, will you begin awakening the others for the voting?'

Turl crouched, as if to spring at him, appeared to think better of it, relaxed.

'Why did you do it, Jarry?' he asked. 'What are they to you that you would make your own people suffer for them?'

'Since you do not feel as I feel,' said Jarry, 'my reasons would mean nothing to you. After all, they are only based upon my

457

feelings, which are different than your own – for mine are based upon sorrow and loneliness. Try this one, though: I am their god. My form is to be found in their every camp. I am the Slayer of Bears from the Desert of the Dead. They have told my story for two and a half centuries, and I have been changed by it. I am powerful and wise and good, so far as they are concerned. In this capacity, I owe them some consideration. If I do not give them their lives, who will there be to honor me in snow and chant my story around the fires and cut for me the best portions of the woolly caterpillar? None, Turl. And these things are all that my life is worth now. Awaken the others. You have no choice.'

'Very well,' said Turl. 'And if their decision should go against you?'

'Then I'll retire, and you can be god,' said Jarry.

Now every day when the sun goes down out of the purple sky, Jarry Dark watches it in its passing, for he shall sleep no more the sleep of ice and of stone, wherein there is no dreaming. He has elected to live out the span of his days in a tiny instant of the Wait, never to look upon the New Alyonal of his people. Every morning, at the new Deadland Installation, he is awakened by sounds like the cracking of ice, the trembling of tin, the snapping of steel strands, before they come to him with their offerings, singing and making marks upon the snow. They praise him and he smiles upon them. Sometimes he coughs.

Born of man and woman, in accordance with Catform Y7 requirements, Coldworld Class, Jarry Dark was not suited for existence anywhere in the universe which had guaranteed him a niche. This was either a blessing or a curse, depending on how you looked at it. So look at it however you would, that was the story. Thus does life repay those who would serve her fully.

# The Last Defender of Camelot

The three muggers who stopped him that October night in San Francisco did not anticipate much resistance from the old man, despite his size. He was well-dressed, and that was sufficient.

The first approached him with his hand extended. The other two hung back a few paces.

'Just give me your wallet and your watch,' the mugger said. 'You'll save yourself a lot of trouble.'

The old man's grip shifted on his walking stick. His shoulders straightened. His shock of white hair tossed as he turned his head to regard the other.

'Why don't you come and take them?'

The mugger began another step but he never completed it. The stick was almost invisible in the speed of its swinging. It struck him on the left temple and he fell.

Without pausing, the old man caught the stick by its middle with his left hand, advanced and drove it into the belly of the next nearest man. Then, with an upward hook as the man doubled, he caught him in the softness beneath the jaw, behind the chin, with its point. As the man fell, he clubbed him with its butt on the back of the neck.

The third man had reached out and caught the old man's upper arm by then. Dropping the stick, the old man seized the mugger's shirtfront with his left hand, his belt with his right, raised him from the ground until he held him at arm's length above his head and slammed him against the side of the building to his right, releasing him as he did so.

He adjusted his apparel, ran a hand through his hair and

retrieved his walking stick. For a moment he regarded the three fallen forms, then shrugged and continued on his way.

There were sounds of traffic from somewhere off to his left. He turned right at the next corner. The moon appeared above tall buildings as he walked. The smell of the ocean was on the air. It had rained earlier and the pavement still shone beneath streetlamps. He moved slowly, pausing occasionally to examine the contents of darkened shop windows.

After perhaps ten minutes, he came upon a side street showing more activity than any of the others he had passed. There was a drugstore, still open, on the corner, a diner farther up the block, and several well-lighted storefronts. A number of people were walking along the far side of the street. A boy coasted by on a bicycle. He turned there, his pale eyes regarding everything he passed.

Halfway up the block, he came to a dirty window on which was painted the word READINGS. Beneath it were displayed the outline of a hand and a scattering of playing cards. As he passed the open door, he glanced inside. A brightly garbed woman, her hair bound back in a green kerchief, sat smoking at the rear of the room. She smiled as their eyes met and crooked an index finger toward herself. He smiled back and turned away, but . . .

He looked at her again. What was it? He glanced at his watch.

Turning, he entered the shop and moved to stand before her. She rose. She was small, barely over five feet in height.

'Your eyes,' he remarked, 'are green. Most gypsies I know have dark eyes.'

She shrugged.

'You take what you get in life. Have you a problem?'

'Give me a moment and I'll think of one,' he said. 'I just came in here because you remind me of someone and it bothers me – I can't think who.'

'Come into the back,' she said, 'and sit down. We'll talk.'

He nodded and followed her into a small room to the rear. A threadbare oriental rug covered the floor near the small table at which they seated themselves. Zodiacal prints and faded psychedelic posters of a semireligious nature covered the walls. A crystal ball stood on a small stand in the far corner beside a vase of cut flowers. A dark, long-haired cat slept on a sofa to the right of it. A door to another room stood slightly ajar beyond the sofa. The only illumination came from a cheap lamp on the table before him and from a small candle in a plaster base atop the shawl-covered coffee table.

He leaned forward and studied her face, then shook his head and leaned back.

She flicked an ash onto the floor.

'Your problem?' she suggested.

He sighed.

'Oh, I don't really have a problem anyone can help me with. Look, I think I made a mistake coming in here. I'll pay you for your trouble, though, just as if you'd given me a reading. How much is it?'

He began to reach for his wallet, but she raised her hand.

'Is it that you do not believe in such things?' she asked, her eyes scrutinizing his face.

'No, quite the contrary,' he replied. 'I am willing to believe in magic, divination and all manner of spells and sendings, angelic and demonic. But—'

'But not from someone in a dump like this?'

He smiled.

'No offense,' he said.

A whistling sound filled the air. It seemed to come from the next room back.

'That's all right,' she said, 'but my water is boiling. I'd forgotten it was on. Have some tea with me? I do wash the cups. No charge. Things are slow.'

'All right.'

She rose and departed.

He glanced at the door to the front but eased himself back into his chair, resting his large, blue-veined hands on its padded arms. He sniffed then, nostrils flaring, and cocked his head as at some half-familiar aroma.

After a time, she returned with a tray, set it on the coffee table. The cat stirred, raised her head, blinked at it, stretched, closed her eyes again.

'Cream and sugar?'

'Please. One lump.'

She placed two cups on the table before him.

'Take either one,' she said.

He smiled and drew the one on his left toward him. She placed an ashtray in the middle of the table and returned to her own seat, moving the other cup to her place.

'That wasn't necessary,' he said, placing his hands on the table.

She shrugged.

'You don't know me. Why should you trust me? Probably got a lot of money on you.'

He looked at her face again. She bad apparently removed some of the heavier makeup while in the back. room. The jawline, the brow ... He looked away. He took a sip of tea.

'Good tea. Not instant,' he said. 'Thanks.'

'So you believe in all sorts of magic,' she asked, sipping her own.

'Some,' he said.

'Any special reason why?'

'Some of it works.'

'For example?'

He gestured aimlessly with his left hand.

'I've traveled a lot. I've seen some strange things.'

'And you have no problems?'

He chuckled.

'Still determined to give me a reading? All right. I'll tell you a little about myself and what I want right now, and you can tell me whether I'll get it. Okay?'

'I'm listening.'

'I am a buyer for a large gallery in the East. I am something of an authority on ancient work in precious metals. I am in town to attend an auction of such items from the estate of a private collector. I will go to inspect the pieces tomorrow.

462

Naturally, I hope to find something good. What do you think my chances are?'

'Give me your hands.'

He extended them, palms upward. She leaned forward and regarded them. She looked back up at him immediately.

'Your wrists have more rascettes than I can count.'

'Yours seem to have quite a few, also.'

She met his eyes for only a moment and returned her attention to his hands. He noted that she had paled beneath what remained of her makeup, and her breathing was now irregular.

'No,' she finally said, drawing back, 'you are not going to find here what you are looking for.'

Her hand trembled slightly as she raised her teacup. He frowned.

'I asked only in jest,' he said. 'Nothing to get upset about. I doubted I would find what I am really looking for, anyway.'

She shook her head.

'Tell me your name.'

'I've lost my accent,' he said, 'but I'm French. The name is DuLac.'

She stared into his eyes and began to blink rapidly.

'No . . .' she said. 'No.'

'I'm afraid so. What's yours?'

'Madam LeFay,' she said. 'I just repainted that sign. It's still drying.'

He began to laugh, but it froze in his throat

'Now – I know – who – you remind me of . . .'

'You reminded me of someone, also. Now I, too, know.'

Her eyes brimmed, her mascara ran.

'It couldn't be,' he said. 'Not here . . . Not in a place like this . . .'

'You dear man,' she said softly, and she raised his right hand to her lips. She seemed to choke for a moment, then said, 'I had thought that I was the last, and yourself buried at Joyous Gard. I never dreamed . . .' Then, 'This?' gesturing about the room. 'Only because it amuses me, helps to pass the time. The waiting—'

She stopped. She lowered his hand.

'Tell me about it,' she said.

'The waiting?' he said. 'For what do you wait?'

'Peace,' she said. 'I am here by the power of my arts, through all the long years. But you – How did you manage it?'

'I—' He took another drink of tea. He looked about the room. 'I do not know how to begin,' he said. 'I survived the final battles, saw the kingdom sundered, could do nothing – and at last departed England. I wandered, taking service at many courts, and after a time under many names, as I saw that I was not aging – or aging very, very slowly. I was in India, China – I fought in the Crusades. I've been everywhere. I've spoken with magicians and mystics – most of them charlatans, a few with the power, none so great as Merlin – and what had come to be my own belief was confirmed by one of them, a man more than half charlatan, yet . . .' He paused and finished his tea. 'Are you certain you want to hear all this?' he asked.

'I want to bear it. Let me bring more tea first, though.'

She returned with the tea. She lit a cigarette and leaned back.

'Go on.'

'I decided that it was – my sin,' he said, 'with . . . the Queen.'

'I don't understand.'

'I betrayed my Liege, who was also my friend, in the one thing which must have hurt him most. The love I felt was stronger than loyalty or friendship – and even today, to this day, it still is. I cannot repent, and so I cannot be forgiven. Those were strange and magical times. We lived in a land destined to become myth. Powers walked the realm in those days, forces which are now gone from the earth. How or why, I cannot say. But you know that it is true. I am somehow of a piece with those gone things, and the laws that rule my existence are not normal laws of the natural world. I believe that I cannot die; that it has fallen my lot, as punishment, to wander the world till I have completed the Quest. I believe I will only know rest the day I find the Holy Grail. Giuseppe Balsamo, before he became known as Cagliostro, somehow saw this and said it to me just as I had thought it, though I never said a word of it to him. And so I have traveled the world, searching. I go no more as knight, or soldier, but as an appraiser. I have been in nearly every museum on Earth, viewed all the great private collections. So far, it has eluded me.'

'You *are* getting a little old for battle.'

He snorted.

'I have never lost,' he stated flatly. 'Down ten centuries, I have never lost a personal contest. It is true that I have aged, yet whenever I am threatened all of my former strength returns to me. But, look where I may, fight where I may, it has never served me to discover that which I must find. I feel I am unforgiven and must wander like the Eternal Jew until the end of the world.'

She lowered her head.

'. . . And you say I will not find it tomorrow?'

'You will never find it,' she said softly.

'You saw that in my hand?'

She shook her head.

'Your story is fascinating and your theory novel,' she began, 'but Cagliostro was a total charlatan. Something must have betrayed your thoughts, and he made a shrewd guess. But he was wrong. I say that you will never find it, not because you are unworthy or unforgiven. No, never that. A more loyal subject than yourself never drew breath. Don't you know that Arthur forgave you? It was an arranged marriage. The same thing happened constantly elsewhere, as you must know. You gave her something he could not. There was only tenderness there. He understood. The only forgiveness you require is that which has been withheld all these long years – your own. No, it is not a doom that has been laid upon you. It is your own feelings which led you to assume an impossible quest, something tantamount to total unforgiveness. But you have suffered all these centuries upon the wrong trail.'

When she raised her eyes, she saw that his were hard, like ice or gemstones. But she met his gaze and continued: 'There is not now, was not then, and probably never was, a Holy Grail.'

'I saw it,' he said, 'that day it passed through the Hall of the Table. We all saw it.'

'You thought you saw it,' she corrected him. 'I hate to shatter an illusion that has withstood all the other tests of time, but I fear I must. The kingdom, as you recall, was at that time in turmoil. The knights were growing restless and falling away from the fellowship. A year – six months, even – and all would have collapsed, all Arthur had striven so hard to put together. He knew that the longer Camelot stood, the longer its name would endure, the stronger its ideals would become. So he made a decision, a purely political one. Something was needed to hold things together. He called upon Merlin, already half-mad, yet still shrewd enough to see what was needed and able to provide it. The Quest was born. Merlin's powers created the illusion you saw that day. It was a lie, yes. A glorious lie, though. And it served for years after to bind you all in brotherhood, in the name of justice and love. It entered literature, it promoted nobility and the higher ends of culture. It served its purpose. But it was – never – really – there. You have been chasing a ghost. I am sorry Launcelot, but I have absolutely no reason to lie to you. I know magic when I see it. I saw it then. That is how it happened.'

For a long while he was silent. Then he laughed.

'You have an answer for everything,' he said. 'I could almost believe you, if you could but answer me one thing more – Why am I here? For what reason? By what power? How is it I have been preserved for half the Christian era while other men grow old and die in a handful of years? Can you tell me now what Cagliostro could not?'

'Yes,' she said, 'I believe that I can.'

He rose to his feet and began to pace. The cat, alarmed, sprang from the sofa and ran into the back room. He stooped and snatched up his walking stick. He started for the door.

'I suppose it was worth waiting a thousand years to see you afraid,' she said.

He halted.

'That is unfair,' he replied.

'I know. But now you will come back and sit down,' she said.

466

He was smiling once more as he turned and returned.

'Tell me,' he said. 'How do you see it?'

'Yours was the last enchantment of Merlin, that is how I see it.'

'Merlin? Me? Why?'

'Gossip had it the old goat took Nimue into the woods and she had to use one of his own spells on him in self-defense – a spell which caused him to sleep forever in some lost place. If it was the spell that I believe it was, then at least part of the rumor was incorrect. There was no known counterspell, but the effects of the enchantment would have caused him to sleep not forever but for a millennium or so, and then to awaken. My guess now is that his last conscious act before he dropped off was to lay this enchantment upon you, so that you would be on hand when he returned.'

'I suppose it might be possible, but why would he want me or need me?'

'If I were journeying into a strange time, I would want an ally once I reached it. And if I had a choice, I would want it to be the greatest champion of the day.'

'Merlin...' he mused. 'I suppose that it could be as you say. Excuse me, but a long life has just been shaken up, from beginning to end. If this is true...'

'I am sure that it is.'

'If this is true... A millennium, you say?'

'More or less.'

'Well, it is almost that time now.'

'I know. I do not believe that our meeting tonight was a matter of chance. You are destined to meet him upon his awakening, which should be soon. Something has ordained that you meet me first, however, to be warned.'

'Warned? Warned of what?'

'He is mad, Launcelot. Many of us felt a great relief at his passing. If the realm had not been sundered finally by strife it would probably have been broken by his hand, anyway.'

'That I find difficult to believe. He was always a strange man – for who can fully understand a sorcerer? – and in his later years he did seem at least partly daft. But he never struck me as evil.'

'Nor was he. His was the most dangerous morality of all. He was a misguided idealist. In a more primitive time and place and with a willing tool like Arthur, he was able to create a legend. Today, in an age of monstrous weapons, with the right leader as his catspaw, he could unleash something totally devastating. He would see a wrong and force his man to try righting it. He would do it in the name of the same high ideal he always served, but he would not appreciate the results until it was too late. How could he – even if he were sane? He has no conception of modern international relations.'

'What is to be done? What is my part in all of this?'

'I believe you should go back, to England, to be present at his awakening, to find out exactly what he wants, to try to reason with him.'

'I don't know . . . How would I find him?'

'You found me. When the time is right, you will be in the proper place. I am certain of that. It was meant to be, probably even a part of his spell. Seek him. But do not trust him.'

'I don't know, Morgana.' He looked at the wall, unseeing. 'I don't know.'

'You have waited this long and you draw back now from finally finding out?'

'You are right – in that much, at least.' He folded his hands, raised them and rested his chin upon them. 'What I would do if he really returned, I do not know. Try to reason with him, yes – Have you any other advice?'

'Just that you be there.'

'You've looked at my hand. You have the power. What did you see?'

She turned away.

'It is uncertain,' she said.

That night he dreamed, as he sometimes did, of times long gone. They sat about the great Table, as they had on that day, Gawaine was there and Percival. Galahad . . . He winced. This day was different from other days. There was a certain tension in the air, a before-the-storm feeling, an electrical thing . . . Merlin stood at the far end of the room, hands in the sleeves of his long robe, hair and beard snowy and unkempt, pale eyes staring – at what, none could be certain . . .

After some timeless time, a reddish glow appeared near the door. All eyes moved toward it. It grew brighter and advanced slowly into the room – a formless apparition of light. There were sweet odors and some few soft strains of music. Gradually, a form began to take shape at its center, resolving itself into the likeness of a chalice . . .

He felt himself rising, moving slowly, following it in its course through the great chamber, advancing upon it, soundlessly and deliberately, as if moving underwater . . .

. . . Reaching for it.

His hand entered the circle of light, moved toward its center, neared the now blazing cup and passed through . . .

Immediately, the light faded. The outline of the chalice wavered, and it collapsed in upon itself, fading, fading, gone . . .

There came a sound, rolling, echoing about the hall. Laughter.

He turned and regarded the others. They sat about the table, watching him, laughing. Even Merlin managed a dry chuckle.

Suddenly, his great blade was in his hand, and he raised it as he strode toward the Table. The knights nearest him drew back as he brought the weapon crashing down.

The Table split in half and fell. The room shook.

The quaking continued. Stones were dislodged from the walls. A roof beam fell. He raised his arm.

The entire castle began to come apart, falling about him and still the laughter continued.

He awoke damp with perspiration and lay still for a long while. In the morning, he bought a ticket for London.

Two of the three elemental sounds of the world were suddenly with him as he walked that evening, stick in hand. For a dozen days, he had hiked about Cornwall, finding no clues to that

469

which he sought. He had allowed himself two more before giving up and departing.

Now the wind and the rain were upon him, and he increased his pace. The fresh-lit stars were smothered by a mass of cloud and wisps of fog grew like ghostly fungi on either hand. He moved among trees, paused, continued on.

'Shouldn't have stayed out this late,' he muttered, and after several more pauses, '*Nel mezzo del cammin di nostra vita mi ritrovai per una selva oscura, che la diritta via era smarrita,*' then he chuckled, halting beneath a tree.

The rain was not heavy. It was more a fine mist now. A bright patch in the lower heavens showed where the moon hung veiled.

He wiped his face, turned up his collar. He studied the position of the moon. After a time, he struck off to his right. There was a faint rumble of thunder in the distance.

The fog continued to grow about him as he went. Soggy leaves made squishing noises beneath his boots. An animal of indeterminate size bolted from a clump of shrubbery beside a cluster of rocks and tore off through the darkness.

Five minutes . . . ten . . . He cursed softly. The rainfall had increased in intensity. Was that the same rock?

He turned in a complete circle. All directions were equally uninviting. Selecting one at random, he commenced walking once again.

Then, in the distance, he discerned a spark, a glow, a wavering light. It vanished and reappeared periodically, as though partly blocked, the line of sight a function of his movements. He headed toward it. After perhaps half a minute, it was gone again from sight, but he continued on in what he thought to be its direction. There came another roll of thunder, louder this time.

When it seemed that it might have been illusion or some short-lived natural phenomenon, something else occurred in that same direction. There was a movement, a shadow-within-shadow shuffling at the foot of a great tree. He slowed his pace, approaching the spot cautiously.

There!

A figure detached itself from a pool of darkness ahead and to the left. Manlike, it moved with a slow and heavy tread, creaking sounds emerging from the forest floor beneath it. A vagrant moonbeam touched it for a moment, and it appeared yellow and metallically slick beneath moisture.

He halted. It seemed that he had just regarded a knight in full armor in his path. How long since he had beheld such a sight? He shook his head and stared.

The figure had also halted. It raised its right arm in a beckoning gesture, then turned and began to walk away. He hesitated for only a moment, then followed.

It turned off to the left and pursued a treacherous path, rocky, slippery, heading slightly downward. He actually used his stick now, to assure his footing, as he tracked its deliberate progress. He gained on it, to the point where he could clearly hear the metallic scraping sounds of its passage.

Then it was gone, swallowed by a greater darkness.

He advanced to the place where he had last beheld it. He stood in the lee of a great mass of stone. He reached out and probed it with his stick.

He tapped steadily along its nearest surface, and then the stick moved past it. He followed.

There was an opening, a crevice. He had to turn sidewise to pass within it, but as he did the full glow of the light he had seen came into sight for several seconds.

The passage curved and widened, leading him back and down. Several times, he paused and listened, but there were no sounds other than his own breathing.

He withdrew his handkerchief and dried his face and hands carefully. He brushed moisture from his coat, turned down his collar. He scuffed the mud and leaves from his boots. He adjusted his apparel. Then he strode forward, rounding a final corner, into a chamber lit by a small oil lamp suspended by three delicate chains from some point in the darkness overhead. The yellow knight stood unmoving beside the far wall. On a fiber mat atop a stony pedestal directly beneath the lamp lay an old man in tattered garments. His bearded face was half-masked by shadows.

He moved to the old man's side. He saw then that those ancient dark eyes were open.

'Merlin . . . ?' he whispered.

There came a faint hissing sound, a soft croak. Realizing the source, he leaned nearer.

'Elixir . . . in earthern rock . . . on ledge . . . in back,' came the gravelly whisper.

He turned and sought the ledge, the container.

'Do you know where it is?' he asked the yellow figure.

It neither stirred nor replied, but stood like a display piece. He turned away from it then and sought further. After a time, he located it. It was more a niche than a ledge, blending in with the wall, cloaked with shadow. He ran his fingertips over the container's contours, raised it gently. Something liquid stirred within it. He wiped its lip on his sleeve after he had returned to the lighted area. The wind whistled past the entranceway and he thought he felt the faint vibration of thunder.

Sliding one hand beneath his shoulders, he raised the ancient form. Merlin's eyes still seemed unfocussed. He moistened Merlin's lips with the liquid. The old man licked them, and after several moments opened his mouth. He administered a sip, then another, and another . . .

Merlin signalled for him to lower him, and he did. He glanced again at the yellow armor, but it had remained motionless the entire while. He looked back at the sorceror and saw that a new light had come into his eyes and be was studying him, smiling faintly.

'Feel better?'

Merlin nodded. A minute passed, and a touch of color appeared upon his cheeks. He elbowed himself into a sitting position and took the container into his hands. He raised it and drank deeply.

He sat still for several minutes after that. His thin hands, which had appeared waxy in the flamelight, grew darker, fuller. His shoulders straightened. He placed the crock on the bed beside him and stretched his arms. His joints creaked the first time he did it, but not the second. He swung his legs over the edge of the bed and rose slowly to his feet. He was a full head shorter than Launcelot.

'It is done,' he said, staring back into the shadows. 'Much has happened, of course...'

'Much has happened,' Launcelot replied.

'You have lived through it all. Tell me, is the world a better place or is it worse than it was in those days?'

'Better in some ways, worse in others. It is different.'

'How is it better?'

'There are many ways of making life easier, and the sum total of human knowledge has increased vastly.'

'How has it worsened?'

'There are many more people in the world. Consequently, there are many more people suffering from poverty, disease, ignorance. The world itself has suffered great depredation, in the way of pollution and other assaults on the integrity of nature.'

'Wars?'

'There is always someone fighting, somewhere.'

'They need help.'

'Maybe. Maybe not.'

Merlin turned and looked into his eyes.

'What do you mean?'

'People haven't changed. They are as rational – and irrational – as they were in the old days. They are as moral and law-abiding – and not – as ever. Many new things have been learned, many new situations evolved, but I do not believe that the nature of man has altered significantly in the time you've slept. Nothing you do is going to change that. You may be able to alter a few features of the times, but would it really be proper to meddle? Everything is so interdependent today that even you would not be able to predict all the consequences of any actions you take. You might do more harm than good; and whatever you do, man's nature will remain the same.'

473

'This isn't like you, Lance. You were never much given to philosophizing in the old days.'

'I've had a long time to think about it.'

'And I've had a long time to dream about it. War is your craft, Lance. Stay with that.'

'I gave it up a long time ago.'

'Then what are you now?'

'An appraiser.'

Merlin turned away, took another drink. He seemed to radiate a fierce energy when he turned again.

'And your oath? To right wrongs, to punish the wicked...?'

'The longer I lived the more difficult it became to determine what was a wrong and who was wicked. Make it clear to me again and I may go back into business.'

'Galahad would never have addressed me so.'

'Galahad was young, naive, trusting. Speak not to me of my son.'

'Launcelot! Launcelot!' He placed a hand on his arm. 'Why all this bitterness for an old friend who has done nothing for a thousand years?'

'I wished to make my position clear immediately. I feared you might contemplate some irreversible action which could alter the world balance of power fatally. I want you to know that I will not be party to it.'

'Admit that you do not know what I might do, what I can do.'

'Freely. That is why I fear you. What *do* you intend to do?'

'Nothing, at first I wish merely to look about me, to see for myself some of these changes of which you have spoken. Then I will consider which wrongs need righting, who needs punishment, and who to choose as my champions. I will show you these things, and then you can go back into business, as you say.'

Launcelot sighed.

'The burden of proof is on the moralist. Your judgment is no longer sufficient for me.'

'Dear me,' the other replied, 'it is sad to have waited this long for an encounter of this sort, to find you have lost your faith in me. My powers are beginning to return already, Lance. Do you not feel magic in the air?'

'I feel something I have not felt in a long while.'

'The sleep of ages was a restorative – an aid, actually. In a while, Lance, I am going to be stronger than I ever was before. And you doubt that I will be able to turn back the clock?'

'I doubt you can do it in a fashion to benefit anybody. Look, Merlin, I'm sorry. I do not like it that things have come to this either. But I have lived too long, seen too much, know too much of how the world works now to trust any one man's opinion concerning its salvation. Let it go. You are a mysterious, revered legend. I do not know what you really are. But forgo exercising your powers in any sort of crusade. Do something else this time around. Become a physician and fight pain. Take up painting. Be a professor of history, an antiquarian. Hell, be a social critic and point out what evils you see for people to correct themselves.'

'Do you really believe I could be satisfied with any of those things?'

'Men find satisfaction in many things. It depends on the man, not on the things. I'm just saying that you should avoid using your powers in any attempt to effect social changes as we once did, by violence.'

'Whatever changes have been wrought, time's greatest irony lies in its having transformed you into a pacifist.'

'You are wrong.'

'Admit it! You have finally come to fear the clash of arms! An appraiser! What kind of knight are you?'

'One who finds himself in the wrong time and the wrong place, Merlin.'

The sorcerer shrugged and turned away.

'Let it be, then. It is good that you have chosen to tell me all these things immediately. Thank you for that, anyway. A moment—'

Merlin walked to the rear of the cave, returned in moments attired in fresh garments. The effect was startling. His entire

475

appearance was more kempt and cleanly. His hair and beard now appeared gray rather than white. His step was sure and steady. He held a staff in his right hand but did not lean upon it.

'Come walk with me,' he said.

'It is a bad night.'

'It is not the same night you left without. It is not even the same place.'

As he passed the suit of yellow armor, he snapped his fingers near its visor. With a single creak, the figure moved and turned to follow him.

'Who is that?' Merlin smiled.

'No one,' he replied, and he reached back and raised the visor. The helmet was empty. 'It is enchanted, animated by a spirit,' he said. 'A trifle clumsy, though, which is why I did not trust it to administer my draught. A perfect servant, however, unlike some. Incredibly strong and swift. Even in your prime you could not have beaten it. I fear nothing when it walks with me. Come, there is something I would have you see.'

'Very well.'

Launcelot followed Merlin and the hollow knight from the cave. The rain had stopped, and it was very still. They stood on an incredibly moonlit plain where mists drifted and grasses sparkled. Shadowy shapes stood in the distance.

'Excuse me,' Launcelot said. 'I left my walking stick inside.'

He turned and re-entered the cave.

'Yes, fetch it, old man,' Merlin replied. 'Your strength is already on the wane.'

When Launcelot returned, he leaned upon the stick and squinted across the plain.

'This way,' Merlin said, 'to where your questions will be answered. I will try not to move too quickly and tire you.'

'Tire me?'

The sorcerer chuckled and began walking across the plain. Launcelot followed.

'Do you not feel a trifle weary?' he asked.

'Yes, as a matter of fact, I do. Do you know what is the matter with me?'

'Of course. I have withdrawn the enchantment which has protected you all these years. What you feel now are the first tentative touches of your true age. It will take some time to catch up with you, against your body's natural resistance, but it is beginning its advance.'

'Why are you doing this to me?'

'Because I believed you when you said you were not a pacifist. And you spoke with sufficient vehemence for me to realize that you might even oppose me. I could not permit that, for I knew that your old strength was still there for you to call upon. Even a sorcerer might fear that, so I did what had to be done. By my power was it maintained; without it, it now drains away. It would have been good for us to work together once again, but I saw that that could not be.'

Launcelot stumbled, caught himself, limped on. The hollow knight walked at Merlin's right hand.

'You say that your ends are noble,' Launcelot said, 'but I do not believe you. Perhaps in the old days they were. But more than the times have changed. You are different. Do you not feel it yourself?'

Merlin drew a deep breath and exhaled vapor.

'Perhaps it is my heritage,' he said. Then, 'I jest. Of course, I have changed. Everyone does. You yourself are a perfect example. What you consider a turn for the worse in me is but the tip of an irreducible conflict which has grown up between us in the course of our changes. I still hold with the true ideals of Camelot.'

Launcelot's shoulders were bent forward now and his breathing had deepened. The shapes loomed larger before them.

'Why, I know this place,' he gasped. 'Yet, I do not know it. Stonehenge does not stand so today. Even in Arthur's time it lacked this perfection. How did we get here? What has happened?'

He paused to rest, and Merlin halted to accommodate him.

477

'This night we have walked between the worlds,' the sorcerer said. 'This is a piece of the land of Faerie and that is the true Stonehenge, a holy place. I have stretched the bounds of the worlds to bring it here. Were I unkind I could send you back with it and strand you there forever. But it is better that you know a sort of peace. Come!'

Launcelot staggered along behind him, heading for the great circle of stones. The faintest of breezes came out of the west, stirring the mists.

'What do you mean – know a sort of peace?'

'The complete restoration of my powers and their increase will require a sacrifice in this place.'

'Then you planned this for me all along!'

'No. It was not to have been you, Lance. Anyone would have served, though you will serve superbly well. It need not have been so, had you elected to assist me. You could still change your mind.'

'Would you want someone who did that at your side?'

'You have a point there.'

'Then why ask – save as a petty cruelty?'

'It is just that, for you have annoyed me.'

Launcelot halted again when they came to the circle's periphery. He regarded the massive stands of stone.

'If you will not enter willingly,' Merlin stated, 'my servant will be happy to assist you.'

Launcelot spat, straightened a little and glared.

'Think you I fear an empty suit of armor, juggled by some Hell-born wight? Even now, Merlin, without the benefit of wizardly succor, I could take that thing apart.'

The sorcerer laughed.

'It is good that you at least recall the boasts of knighthood when all else has left you. I've half a mind to give you the opportunity, for the manner of your passing here is not important. Only the preliminaries are essential.'

'But you're afraid to risk your servant?'

'Think you so, old man? I doubt you could even bear the

weight of a suit of armor, let alone lift a lance. But if you are willing to try, so be it!'

He rapped the butt of his staff three times upon the ground.

'Enter,' he said then. 'You will find all that you need within. And I am glad you have made this choice. You were insufferable, you know. Just once, I longed to see you beaten, knocked down to the level of lesser mortals. I only wish the Queen could be here, to witness her champion's final engagement.'

'So do I,' said Launcelot, and he walked past the monolith and entered the circle.

A black stallion waited, its reins held down beneath a rock. Pieces of armor, a lance, a blade and a shield leaned against the side of the dolmen. Across the circle's diameter, a white stallion awaited the advance of the hollow knight.

'I am sorry I could not arrange for a page or a squire to assist you,' Merlin, said, coming around the other side of the monolith. 'I'll be glad to help you myself, though.'

'I can manage,' Launcelot replied.

'My champion is accoutered in exactly the same fashion,' Merlin said, 'and I have not given him any edge over you in weapons.'

'I never liked your puns either.'

Launcelot made friends with the horse, then removed a small strand of red from his wallet and tied it about the butt of the lance. He leaned his stick against the dolmen stone and began to don the armor. Merlin, whose hair and beard were now almost black, moved off several paces and began drawing a diagram in the dirt with the end of his staff.

'You used to favor a white charger,' he commented, 'but I thought it appropriate to equip you with one of another color, since you have abandoned the ideals of the Table Round, betraying the memory of Camelot.'

'On the contrary,' Launcelot replied, glancing overhead at the passage of a sudden roll of thunder. 'Any horse in a storm, and I am Camelot's last defender.'

Merlin continued to elaborate upon the pattern he was drawing as Launcelot slowly equipped himself. The small wind continued to blow, stirring the mist. There came a flash of lightning, startling the horse. Launcelot calmed it.

Merlin stared at him for a moment and rubbed his eyes. Launcelot donned his helmet.

'For a moment,' Merlin said, 'you looked somehow different...'

'Really? Magical withdrawal, do you think?' he asked, and he kicked the stone from the reins and mounted the stallion.

Merlin stepped back from the now-completed diagram, shaking his head, as the mounted man leaned over and grasped the lance.

'You still seem to move with some strength,' he said.

'Really?'

Launcelot raised the lance and couched it. Before taking up the shield he had hung at the saddle's side, he opened his visor and turned and regarded Merlin.

'Your champion appears to be ready,' he said. 'So am I.'

Seen in another flash of light, it was an unlined face that looked down at Merlin, clear-eyed, wisps of pale gold hair fringing the forehead.

'What magic have the years taught you?' Merlin asked.

'Not magic,' Launcelot replied. 'Caution. I anticipated you. So, when I returned to the cave for my stick, I drank the rest of your elixir.'

He lowered the visor and turned away.

'You walked like an old man...'

'I'd a lot of practice. Signal your champion.'

Merlin laughed.

'Good! It is better this way,' he decided, 'to see you go down in full strength! You still cannot hope to win against a spirit!'

Launcelot raised the shield and leaned forward.

'Then what are you waiting for?'

'Nothing!' Merlin said. Then he shouted, 'Kill him, Raxas!'

A light rain began as they pounded across the field; and staring ahead, Launcelot realized that flames were flickering behind his opponent's visor. At the last possible moment, he shifted the point of his lance into line with the hollow knight's blazing helm. There came more lightning and thunder.

His shield deflected the other's lance while his went on to strike the approaching head. It flew from the hollow knight's shoulders and bounced, smouldering, on the ground.

He continued on to the other end of the field and turned. When he had, he saw that the hollow knight, now headless, was doing the same. And beyond him, he saw two standing figures, where moments before there had been but one.

Morgan Le Fay, clad in a white robe, red hair unbound and blowing in the wind, faced Merlin from across his pattern. It seemed they were speaking, but he could not hear the words. Then she began to raise her hands, and they glowed like cold fire. Merlin's staff was also gleaming, and he shifted it before him. Then he saw no more, for the hollow knight was ready for the second charge.

He couched his lance, raised the shield, leaned forward and gave his mount the signal. His arm felt like a bar of iron, his strength like an endless current of electricity as he raced down the field. The rain was falling more heavily now and the lightning began a constant flickering. A steady rolling of thunder smothered the sound of the hoofbeats, and the wind whistled past his helm as he approached the other warrior, his lance centered on his shield.

They came together with an enormous crash. Both knights reeled and the hollow one fell, his shield and breastplate pierced by a broken lance. His left arm came away as he struck the earth; the lancepoint snapped and the shield fell beside him. But he began to rise almost immediately, his right hand drawing his long sword.

Launcelot dismounted, discarding his shield, drawing his own great blade. He moved to meet his headless foe. The other struck first and he parried it, a mighty shock running down his arms. He swung a blow of his own. It was parried.

They swaggered swords across the field, till finally Launcelot saw his opening and landed his heaviest blow. The hollow knight toppled into the mud, his breastplate cloven almost to the point where the spear's shaft protruded. At that moment, Morgan Le Fay screamed.

Launcelot turned and saw that she had fallen across the pattern Merlin had drawn. The sorcerer, now bathed in a bluish light, raised his staff and moved forward. Launcelot took a step toward them and felt a great pain in his left side.

Even as he turned toward the half-risen hollow knight who was drawing his blade back for another blow, Launcelot reversed his double-handed grip upon his own weapon and raised it high, point downward.

He hurled himself upon the other, and his blade pierced the cuirass entirely as he bore him back down, nailing him to the earth. A shriek arose from beneath him, echoing within the armor, and a gout of fire emerged from the neck hole, sped upward and away, dwindled in the rain, flickered out moments later.

Launcelot pushed himself into a kneeling position. Slowly then, he rose to his feet and turned toward the two figures who again faced one another. Both were now standing within the muddied geometries of power, both were now bathed in the bluish light. Launcelot took a step toward them, then another.

'Merlin!' he called out, continuing to advance upon them. 'I've done what I said I would! Now I'm coming to kill you!'

Morgan Le Fay turned toward him, eyes wide.

'No!' she cried. 'Depart the circle! Hurry! I am holding him here! His power wanes! In moments, this place will be no more. Go!'

Launcelot hesitated but a moment, then turned and walked as rapidly as he was able toward the circle's perimeter. The sky seemed to boil as he passed among the monoliths.

He advanced another dozen paces, then had to pause to rest. He looked back to the place of battle, to the place where the two figures still stood locked in sorcerous embrace. Then the scene was imprinted upon his brain as the skies opened and a sheet of fire fell upon the far end of the circle.

Dazzled, he raised his hand to shield his eyes. When he lowered it, he saw the stones falling, soundless, many of them fading from sight. The rain began to slow immediately. Sorceror and sorceress had vanished along with much of the structure of the still-fading place. The horses were nowhere to be seen. He looked about him and saw a good-sized stone. He headed for it and seated himself. He unfastened his breastplate and removed it, dropping it to the ground. His side throbbed and he held it tightly. He doubled forward and rested his face on his left hand.

The rains continued to slow and finally ceased. The wind died. The mists returned.

He breathed deeply and thought back upon the conflict. This, this was the thing for which he had remained after all the others, the thing for which he had waited, for so long. It was over now, and he could rest.

There was a gap in his consciousness. He was brought to awareness again by a light. A steady glow passed between his fingers, pierced his eyelids. He dropped his hand and raised his head, opening his eyes.

It passed slowly before him in a halo of white light. He removed his sticky fingers from his side and rose to his feet to follow it. Solid, glowing, glorious and pure, not at all like the image in the chamber, it led him on out across the moonlit plain, from dimness to brightness to dimness, until the mists enfolded him as he reached at last to embrace it.

HERE ENDETH THE BOOK OF LAUNCELOT,
LAST OF THE NOBLE KNIGHTS OF THE
ROUND TABLE, AND HIS ADVENTURES
WITH RAXAS, THE HOLLOW KNIGHT,
AND MERLIN AND MORGAN LE FAY,
LAST OF THE WISE FOLK OF CAMELOT,
IN HIS QUEST FOR THE SANGREAL.

*QUO FAS ET GLORIA DUCUNT.*

**Roger Zelazny (1937–1995)** was born in Euclid, Ohio in 1937. He had a life-long love of the written word: in high school he was the editor of the school newspaper and joined the Creative Writing Club; he graduated from Western Reserve University in 1959 with a B.A. in English; he then went on to study a Master's degree at Columbia University, New York, specialising in Elizabethan and Jacobean drama. He wrote science fiction alongside working for the U.S. Social Security Administration before finally becoming a full-time writer in 1969. He was an active member of the Baltimore Science Fiction Society while he lived there, and also of SAGA – The Swordsmen and Sorcerers' Guild of America.

During his career he won various awards, including six Hugos, three Nebulas, two Locus awards, two Seiun awards, two Balrog awards and a Prix Tour-Apollo award. He wrote a swathe of novels, novelettes, short stories, poems and plays, and is credited as the inspiration for many authors that followed. He died at the age of 58, and he was posthumously inducted into the Science Fiction Hall of Fame in 2010.

# ACKNOWLEDGEMENTS

'A Rose for Ecclesiates' was first published in *The Magazine of Fantasy and Science Fiction*, November 1963.

'The Doors of His Face, the Lamps of His Mouth' was first published in *The Magazine of Fantasy and Science Fiction*, March 1965.

'Divine Madness' was first published in *New Worlds SF*, October 1966.

'For a Breath I Tarry' was first published in *New Worlds SF* in March 1966.

'The Great Slow Kings' was first published in *Worlds of Tomorrow*, December 1963.

'He Who Shapes' was first published in *Amazing Stories*, January and February 1965.

'Permafrost' was first published in *Omni*, April 1986.

'Corrida' was first published in *Anubis #3*, 1968.

'Last Defender of Camelot' was first published in *Asimov's SF Adventure Magazine*, Summer 1979.

'The Keys to December' was first published in *New Worlds*, August 1966.

'LOKI 7281' was first published in *R-A-M Random Access Messages of the Computer Age* (Hayden Pub., ed. Thomas F. Monteleone), 1984.

'Damnation Alley' was first published by G.P. Putnam's and Sons, 1969.

'Home is the Hangman' was first published in *Analogue Science Fiction/Science Fact*, November 1975.